Penguin Books
The Greenlander

Mark Adlard was born and brought up near Hartlepool,
and still lives in that area. He was for a time a senior
executive of a large steel and engineering group, but is
now a full-time writer. *The Greenlander* is the first volume
of an ambitious series. His other works include *Interface*,
Volteface and *Multiface*.

Mark Adlard

The Greenlander

Penguin Books

Penguin Books Ltd, Harmondsworth,
Middlesex, England
Penguin Books, 625 Madison Avenue,
New York, New York 10022, U.S.A.
Penguin Books Australia Ltd, Ringwood,
Victoria, Australia
Penguin Books Canada Ltd, 2801 John Street,
Markham, Ontario, Canada L3R 1B4
Penguin Books (N.Z.) Ltd, 182–190 Wairau Road,
Auckland 10, New Zealand

First published in Great Britain by Hamish Hamilton 1978
Published in Penguin Books 1980

Set, printed and bound in Great Britain by
Cox & Wyman Ltd, Reading
Set in Intertype Plantin

For Vanessa
when she is a big girl

One

It will be four years after the return of the William Scoresby
Senior *when Captain Stapleton first sees the Northumbrian
engineman. A group of the town's leading citizens – Mr
Winspear, Mr Foster, Mr Agar, Mr Milburn and a few others –
form a reception committee in the Angel Hotel on the quayside.*

*Captain Stapleton feels slightly out of place amongst these
strictly commercial interests, and he stands back a little to observe
their distinguished visitor. After some reflection he decides that
the engineman is in his middle fifties. His white hair, suggesting
advanced years and mental toil, is contradicted by the ruddy
cheeks of someone who is used to walking for miles in the open
air. He is tall and burly besides, a good man to have on your side
in a tug-of-war brawl. His clothes are good, of a cloth and cut
that somehow look too expensive for the wearer, and the front of
his shirt is as rumpled as if he's been wrestling in it. The hands
aren't white enough for those of a gentleman, and the shape of
the nails suggest that the fingers had once been accustomed to
much heavier toil than holding a pen.*

But Captain Stapleton's attention returns to the face.

*There is the simplicity that he'd observed four years ago in the
face of his Second Mate on the* William Scoresby Senior, *as plain
to see as a nose. Once again it is the simplicity of a man who is
possessed by a single purpose.*

*In the engineman's face, this singleness of purpose is combined
with a self-confidence so total, so consuming, so vibrant that the
air seems to quiver with it. Here is a man, it is clear, who has
absolute faith in himself and in everything he is doing and
intends to do. In the unswerving gaze of the clear, grey eyes, and
in the unwavering lines around the straight mouth, are indications that emotions less admirable and almost as powerful are
being subordinated to the main drive.*

7

There is pride, huge and overbearing, bringing with it a measureless contempt for anyone who might dare to challenge, and a quick jealousy of anyone who might appear to gain a temporary advantage. There is ignorance of the kind that is due to lack of leisure and opportunity early in life. This is compensated for, perhaps over-compensated for, by intelligence and shrewdness and the will to win at any cost to himself or others.

It is the face of a man who knows he is right all the time, and who will never admit it even if he is proved wrong. The obstinate engraving on his forehead shows that this personality is cast in iron. It will endure as long as the flesh that bears its heavy imprint.

An unusual man, Captain Stapleton decides, and in some ways a frightening one.

Mr Winspear and a select handful of the town's citizens approach the visitor and speak to him with every token of respect. The engineman turns his proud head, and the domineering grey eyes look directly into their questioning faces. His reply is in an accent so thick that the townsmen feel obliged to approach a little closer to their uncompromising guest. Mr Winspear repeats the question.

Captain Stapleton looks away. It troubles him to see the simple faith of Mr Dryden, his Second Mate, remembered from that conversation four years ago while they rode at anchor in Bressay Sound, transformed into something he can't understand.

I

It had been long after his usual time when Arthur Storm's father returned from the sail loft. His mam adopted the tone which was habitual with her on such occasions.

'Mr Winspear's been requiring more of tha services than usual, has he?' she asked. 'Or did thee fall in wi' old friends? Some important news perhaps, that could be related only in t' Seven Stars or Jolly Butchers?'

'Nay, missus,' he said, and winked at Arthur. 'It's me that kept Mr Winspear waiting after hours.'

'Been giving him some advice, I suppose.'

Mr Storm pretended not to have noticed the familiar tone. 'Aye, tho could say that,' he said. The more he turned the idea over, the more his wife's phrase seemed to fit the case. 'Aye, tho could put it that way. Been giving him some advice, that's what I've been doing.'

It was clear to Arthur that his father was very pleased about something; and it was equally clear that he didn't want to tell them all about it at once. They had to wait while Mr Storm related how Mr Winspear had taken seven sixty-fourth shares in the new ship from Fishburn and Brodrick. So naturally the other owners would have to sit up and listen when Mr Winspear waved his shiny black stick and said which sail loft would provide the canvas. That was only right and proper. They couldn't do better in any case than come to Mr Winspear for their canvas. Nobody could do better. Even the Hull owners were after them for canvas. Best sail loft in the land was Mr Winspear's.

'I can testify that to any man,' added Mr Storm.

Mr Storm had been pacing around the small room and now he came to a halt before a wooden stand placed near the door. It contained an ornamental walking stick that had been in Mrs Storm's family for generations. It had been carved by her great-grandfather while his ship was beset in the days of the Spitzbergen fishery. The stick was made of narwhal tusk and much too heavy for use. Mr Storm lifted it a few inches in the wooden stand.

'It's not just the canvas,' he continued. 'Seeing as Mr Winspear has seven sixty-fourths of the new ship, the other owners will have to sit up and listen if he mentions a particular lad that he'd like to put in as an apprentice.' Mr Storm dropped the walking stick. The wooden base of the stand received the scrimshawed ivory with a hard, unaccommodating sound.

Arthur sat perfectly still and looked at his father without breathing. His mam was rearranging the boxes and tins, the tallow candles set in scallop shells, and the usual clutter of things that were always threatening to overflow the mantelpiece. Her hands pretended to be busy while she listened.

'So naturally Mr Winspear stayed behind to listen when I told him I knew of a bright lad that would make a good apprentice.' Mr Storm raised the stick higher, but it still came down with a dead sound that fell short of the effect he wanted to achieve. 'A very bright lad, and a good one too, whose fayther is willing and able to do what is necessary to arrange indentures.'

Arthur felt the hot blood rush into his face.

Mrs Storm swept a couple of the tallow candles to the floor as she swung round and threw her arms up to Arthur's neck. 'The brightest lad there is,' she said. 'The brightest and best lad in t' whole world.'

Arthur, held tight in his mam's embrace, could feel her shaking.

'Thinking of our Edward,' said Mr Storm in a low voice.

And from that day, or not long after, the stock in the big iron pot standing on its hob continued to richen. Into it went marrowbones and giblets, occasional scraps of poultry and even rare trimmings of lean meat. His mam put everything in with the quiet smile of someone scraping up every penny and investing it in a secret gold mine. Next to the iron pot broth was simmering in a deep saucepan, sending out an aroma that thickened the air until simply to breathe became a pleasure.

'It'll be a bit before tho sees a dinner like this,' his mam laughed as she brought the saucepan to the table, and ladled out the broth.

'Aye,' his father agreed, sitting down and winking at him. 'And it's a bit *since* I saw its like, an' all.'

Mrs Storm paused in the act of ladling, and raised the wooden spoon as if to correct her husband's misplaced humour with a blow to the head.

'Not since our Edward went,' said his father, by way of some slight modification.

It was the finest broth ever created, Arthur decided, as he dunked his bread. The stock from the pot had been transformed to unimaginable glory by the addition of scrag-end of mutton, pearl barley, diced turnip, celery, carrot and onion, all seasoned with peppercorns and other things that only his mam could have put a name to.

'Tho'llt come to no harm with Captain Stapleton,' his father said. 'And in any case, it's a vast of difference to what it was in t' old days. When I was a lad the only folk who went to t' fishery were madmen and second sons of bankrupt farmers.'

'They do say,' said Mrs Storm, sitting down at the table but making no move to serve herself, 'that a lot of men went that were disappointed in love.'

Her husband sucked noisily at his spoon. 'I've included them,' he said, 'in t' madmen.'

'That'll do,' she said sharply. 'That'll do.'

Arthur had never been so excited and happy. He could scarcely credit his good fortune. Every youth dreamed of going to the fishery. It was the high road – in fact it was the only road – to fame and fortune. The Captain on the quarter deck was a prince of the realm, and to serve him as an apprentice was the privilege of only a fortunate few.

'No, no, mam, no!'

His mother had brought the saucepan to the table and was again ladling broth into his bowl. 'What's the matter wi' thee?'

He put his hand on her arm to restrain her, but she ignored the protest and refilled his bowl to the very top.

'Get it down,' she ordered. 'It's got to last thee a long time.'

'Nay,' he said, 'tho shouldn't have done it. I'll be able to eat naught else.'

'Eh! What's that?' His mam placed her head on one side and then on the other, in an attempt to show astonishment. 'What makes tha think there's aught else for thee?'

Arthur restrained a smile at her antics and spooned the new helping of broth. Did his mam think he didn't notice anything? She'd soaked and boiled the split peas hours ago, and later in the forenoon she'd mashed them with butter, pepper and salt. Then she'd added a beaten egg and a couple of pinches of sugar before returning everything to the bag in which it was now boiling.

'I'll see if we've got aught else for the lad,' she said, rising from her chair and disappearing into the tiny scullery.

Mr Storm, apparently summoned by the scraping of a chair that was being repositioned, also retired. Arthur knew, with absolute certainty, that his father must be lifting down the York ham which had been suspended from its hook with such secrecy the previous night. After more scraping and some heavy breathing his father reappeared, looking incredibly mysterious and pleased with himself.

His mam came back carrying thin, pink textured slices on a plate.

'What's this? What's this?' demanded his father, pretending to be astounded beyond all measure.

She transferred the slices to a pan of hot fat next to the fire where they spat like cats in a hay loft. The smell immediately banished the sense of fullness from Arthur's stomach and could have convinced him that he hadn't eaten for days.

'York ham!' his father announced, and if he'd had a trumpet he would most assuredly have blown it. 'I chose it myself at the Tolbooth.'

The moment Arthur raised the last spoonful of broth his mam removed the bowl and promptly replaced it with a hot plate bearing the fried ham. Before he lifted his knife and fork his father had taken the cloth bag from the boiling water and tipped out the pease pudding.

'There tho are!' his father said, with the air of a conjuror who had performed his last but most eye-catching trick. 'How's that?'

Arthur cut a piece of ham and half-covered it with a bit of pease pudding. The light pink of the meat and the dark yellow of the pudding set each other off like colours contrived for a picture. Flesh and vegetable rejoiced in each other's presence. He raised the fork and all the little nerves along his tongue, round his mouth, down his throat and in the linings of his stomach joined together in a silent hymn.

Mr Storm extracted a clay pipe from amongst the jumbled articles on the mantelpiece, and retired to his rocking chair on the left of the fireplace. He scraped inside the bowl of the pipe with his knife, using as much care as if he were intent on producing a piece of scrimshaw to rival the narwhal walking stick in its wooden stand. Mrs Storm had meanwhile seated herself in the tall chair with the interlaced whalebone back, and drawn up the wobbly, three-legged stool that carried her work box.

This work box was amongst the earliest of Arthur's memories. It had pictures around its sides. First there was a ship, shallow-draught and three-masted with graceful, sweeping lines. She was a caravel, lateen-rigged, the kind of ship in which the first men had rounded the Cape of Storms and seen the Southern Cross. For as far back as Arthur could remember those triangular sails,

ABOUT THE AUTHOR

Freelance writer Ben Counter is one of the Black
Library's most popular SF authors. An Ancient
History graduate and avid miniature painter, he
lives near Portsmouth, England.

WARHAMMER
40,000

WOLF'S HONOUR

A SPACE WOLF NOVEL BY LEE LIGHTNER

'Ragnar is back in action with another
storming adventure.'
– Enigma

suspended from their sloping yards, had been filled by winds of promise and mystery.

The next picture was of an island lapped by the lazy waves of a placid sea. It was crowned by dark trees whose downward curving arms threw black shadows on to the yellow sand. It was easy to imagine the branches waving towards the weary mariners, inviting them to leave their ship and linger for a while in their languorous shades.

On the next side there was another picture of the same caravel, with her pointed sails swelling under a following wind.

Round the corner, on the last side of the box, was some kind of house or temple. It stood upon columns and had a high pitched roof. The front contained a rectangular opening which was presumably a door, but so narrow that a man would have difficulty in entering even if he turned sideways. Perhaps there was a more comfortable door at the back. Above this central opening were windows, square and black, revealing nothing of what might be inside. Above these windows was a verandah, and above that a single round window in the pointed apex of the gable wall. All the square windows were opaque and impenetrable, and all of them equally uncommunicative. The gable window was also black: but this circular window, by its singularity and exalted position, seemed to conceal something more important and more extraordinary than the row of square windows below it.

And so you returned to the beginning. The ship reappeared and sailed on again to the same dreaming island and to the same temple of many windows.

Mr Storm put his knife away and stood up to take some tobacco from a jar on the mantelpiece. His crooked finger, as rigid and specific as if it had been designed solely for that purpose, moved rhythmically up and down until the tobacco was wadded into the bowl. He lit a taper from the fire, applied it judiciously, and made two or three exploratory puffs. He settled back in his chair, secure in the knowledge that everything was exactly as it should be.

Arthur ate more slowly. He'd already eaten more than he needed but it would be unthinkable to leave anything on his plate.

He listened to the clicking of his mother's needles, stitching an audible pattern in the air as unvarying and predictable as the purl and plain of her stocking stitch. He listened to the intermittent noises made by his father's lips on the clay pipe stem, which sounded exactly like small trout rising in the Esk and taking flies on summer afternoons. It seemed impossible that these moments shouldn't last for ever.

2

The *William Scoresby Senior*, of 400 tons admeasurement, was spanking new and the pride of the town.

She was built of slow-growing oak from the Helmsley forests and she was doubled with an additional layer of planks. The stem and stern were fortified outside with plates of puddled iron, and buttressed within by a complex and massive system of oak beams and stanchions. The hold beams were placed low so as to offer extra resistance against squeezing, and also to provide sufficient space between decks for stowing the boats during heavy storms. The large and roomy hold carried three tiers of casks.

The only evident item of economy was in the providing of the casks. They had been well-scrubbed, but even the most untutored nose could have certified that most of them had been stuffed with the yellow fat of previous kills.

Those with an eye for such things could recognize the *William Scoresby Senior* immediately as being from Fishburn and Brodrick's yard on the west side of the river. Her ancestry could be traced in every lineament, from her keel up to her trucks, from her flying jib to the gilded windows that looked aft from the cabin. The bluff bows and square stern were descended from the cat-built colliers that plied between the Tyne and the Thames, and which had been reborn to greater fame when Captain Cook had taken the *Endeavour, Resolution* and *Adventure* to the South Seas. The broad beam and extra strength were inherited from that other *Resolution* sold to Peterhead the previous year, and from the *Esk* that had been lost on her return from the fishery four years ago.

And now, as the *William Scoresby Senior* waited at her moorings in the inner harbour, there wasn't a man in the whole town who didn't take some pride in her.

Even Mr Clarkson, who had kept to his house for years, turned out to look at her. He was an almost legendary figure, already an experienced Greenlander when he served under Captain Scoresby Senior on the *Henrietta*, named after one of the Cholmley girls; he'd been with both the Scoresbys when they sailed the *Resolution* nearer to the Pole than anyone before or since; and he'd been one of those who helped Captain Scoresby Junior to save the *Esk* when she lost a long piece of her keel.

The pressure of people was insistent on all sides. They pushed more roughly and called more loudly. There was a sense of impending change, of something being about to happen. Above them the seagulls wheeled against the clear blue sky, keening and lamenting like cats.

A slight scuffle parted the crowd and released a man whose serious, almost grim features contrasted with the lively faces around him. Under his left arm he clutched a stack of pamphlets, of which he had a sample in his right hand that he waved above his head.

'It's Mr Hugill again,' said Harry Hodgson, who worked in a boiling house on the west side.

This information was received with laughter, groans or mere indifference. Mr Hugill was doing his best to interest people in his pamphlets but most of them had heard it all before. Besides, they were too concerned with seeing fathers, husbands, brothers and sons safely aboard the ships, and with saying their last farewells for another season. But there was something so earnest in Mr Hugill's manner, and so strident in his voice, that he captured attention here and there for a moment.

'It's time to wake up!' he shouted, waving the pamphlet in his hand. 'If we opened our eyes and used them for seeing we'd find that it's time to stop looking at the sea. It's time to look inland.'

A young man with the russet cheeks of a coble fisherman, in a much mended gansey, was tempted to lead him on.

'What'll we find there, John?'

'Who knows?' demanded Mr Hugill.

The laughter that greeted this rhetorical question infuriated

Mr Hugill. He waved the sample pamphlet furiously above his head. It could almost have been a flag of distress.

'We might find coal or iron,' he shouted.

Harry Hodgson decided that this was the moment to elicit the final absurdity. 'And then what'll we do, John?'

'Build a railway.'

Laughter washed in from all sides and the tormentors returned their attention to the business of the day. John Hugill and the railway were forgotten again.

3

Mr Storm was preoccupied with a broken lobster creel; then he examined a shrimp net so worn that its mesh wouldn't have retained a medium-sized codfish for more than a second; now he kicked importantly at a pile of abandoned rope; next he put his hands on his knees and talked to a collie dog that wagged its bushy tail and seemed to have as little to do as himself. Mrs Storm, incapable of such dissimulation, stood quietly with her head inclined and her features hidden by the cowl of her flowered Staithes bonnet.

Arthur was desperate to be away. His father's bustling to and fro didn't fool him for a moment; and his mother's fixed smile filled him with a kind of pain. How he wished the time were an hour from now, when he would have escaped from the suffocation of it all! From now onwards his place was with the rough Greenlanders who were milling about on the quay, smelling of beer, swearing and joking.

'Where's tha fayther?' Mrs Storm said. 'How is it he's never where he's wanted?'

Mr Storm squeezed his way into view. He was returning from an exhaustive survey of the foot-delved steps in one of the ghauts, the appearance of which hadn't changed one jot in living memory.

'There tho art,' she said. 'This is no time to be gallivanting about.'

'Nay missus, I was just – '

'I'd better be getting aboard,' Arthur interrupted, aware of his rudeness and relishing it for some reason. 'I can't stand on t' quay all day.'

His father, recalled by these remarks to what was actually happening, suddenly became very serious and held out his hand. A firm clasp and nothing said, although he smiled and his lips moved around some silent words. Arthur was grateful to him. He took his mam's hands, wondered if he could take leave of her without doing anything else, then out of pity gave her a swift kiss on the cheek.

To his horror she immediately burst into tears.

'It's our Edward,' Mr Storm explained to Arthur and to anyone else who cared to listen. 'She's thinking of our Edward.'

'Tha stockings,' she sobbed, 'tho've got plenty of stockings. Change them during the day if need be, two or three pair at a time. There's no need to scant thyself with stockings. And don't forget the gansey that tha grandma's knit is big enough to pull ower everything.'

'It's our Edward,' Mr Storm repeated to a small but sympathetic audience, before turning to comfort his wife. 'Don't think about Edward,' he advised her, with unbelievable lack of tact, 'at least our Arthur's going to come home again.'

Arthur would have turned and run away if he could. In despair, not knowing what to do, he kissed her again. Her tears came out in a flood.

'By the time our Arthur gets back,' said Mr Storm, vaguely aware of his oversight, and struggling like a negligent lock-keeper to reclose the sluice-gates, 'I'll bet we have a letter from our Edward.'

'Tha flannel drawers,' his mam wailed, attracting a larger group of bystanders. 'Tho've got two pairs of best flannel drawers, and flannel shirts an' all besides the striped cotton, and as for gloves and mittens I don't know anybody who — '

'Don't come any further,' Arthur pleaded. 'I must get along now. Don't follow me!'

He pushed his way through the surrounding crowd and hurried towards the ships. So anxious was he to be aboard, or at any rate to escape, that he barged at full tilt into a girl who stepped directly into his path. She coloured and so did he.

'Ann! I'm sorry. I didn't see you until I . . .'

She looked put out but curiously pleased at the same time. 'I wouldn't like to be on t' same ship as you, Arthur Storm. I'd be frightened of getting knocked out into t' watter.'

'No, I wouldn't,' he protested. 'I mean you wouldn't. You wouldn't get knocked overboard, I mean. Not by me, anyway.'

Ann Paylor smiled at him, and he looked at her regular, white teeth in astonishment. He must have seen her smile before, but somehow he'd never noticed her teeth. She was shy, he thought, perhaps even a little nervous, looking this way and that as if uncertain what to do. When she moved her head to one side a little more he noticed a blue ribbon in her hair.

'Have you come to see someone off?' he asked.

'No. Nobody in particular.'

'I see. You just . . .'

'I just think Sailing Day is exciting, that's all. Don't you?'

'Of course I do. Everybody does.'

She tossed her head and the blue ribbon sparkled in her fair hair. 'I just like to see the ships leave, the same as everyone else. There's naught wrong with that, is there? Most folks come out on Sailing Day, whether they're seeing off somebody in particular or not. At least I think they do, but perhaps you'll tell me I'm wrong.'

'No, no, no,' he said.

'What? I'm wrong, am I?'

'No, no. I mean you're right, absolutely right.'

Ann Paylor tossed her head with the same gesture as before. The blue ribbon was very long, and it glinted brightly when its smooth folds caught the morning sun. It was loosely tied in a bow at the back of her head.

'I like your ribbon, Ann.'

'What ribbon?'

'The blue one in your hair.'

'Aw, that.'

She blushed again and lowered her face, so that he couldn't see anything but the top of her head and the large bow behind it. Now that it was presented to him in this way he saw that the bow would slip off quite easily. The short time remaining, the prospect of the long voyage ahead, and the emotions that the sight of her long hair quickened in him, all combined to give him more courage than he thought he had.

'Ann ... Do you think I can have your ribbon?'

She raised her head. Her eyes, previously as clear as the sky, were now deepening to the colour of the sea. Her face turned crimson.

'Arthur Storm! If you think I put this ribbon in my hair just so that you could snatch it off, then you're very much mistaken.'

He snatched. The bow untied at the first pull, almost as if it had been designed for that purpose, and the entire shining length came away in his fingers. He turned and ran with it.

She caught up with him at the ship's side but made no attempt to retrieve her property.

'I'll think of you,' he said. 'Will you promise to think of me?'

'Take care, Arthur.'

'Will you think of me?'

'I will, I will, but take care, Arthur.'

So elated was he by her reaction that he wanted to leap above the main chainplate, with its clustered deadeyes and their reeved lanyards, and jump directly into the shrouds.

As soon as he crossed the bulwark he bounded to the ratlines and climbed swiftly to the main top. This was already higher than he'd ever been in his life and he was tempted to take the easy way and crawl up through the lubber's hole. But pride and a desire to appear well in the eyes of Ann Paylor sent him up over the futtock shrouds. I must go higher, he thought, I must show her how grateful I am and how proud she has made me and I must make her proud as well.

He climbed the centre ratlines, past the mainmast cap and up to the topmost trestletree. The wind blew much more freshly up here. How quiet it was! Hoping he might see Ann's upturned face amongst the hundreds of people on the quayside, he looked down.

A few feet under the soles of his shoes was the topsail yard, with its braces running from each end to the mizzen trestletree somewhere behind him. The tarred rope of the mizzen stay, far below, ran downwards and forwards to the main top. The paired mainmast backstays strained away to his left and right on their long way down to the bulwarks. And far below everything else were the people on the quayside. It shocked him to discover how small they were.

Perhaps if Ann waved he might be able to identify her. He swayed and gripped the ropes more tightly. How terrible it would be, he thought, how ridiculous, if I fell and killed myself before we'd even left the inner harbour! But I must go higher. I must go as high as I can.

He ascended into the upper ratlines and his fingers touched the horns of the crosstree. The wind whistled in the double strands of the topgallant braces. He tried not to look down as he took the ribbon from his pocket. The empty air belonged to him and the silver-grey gulls that glided above his head. A variety of handkerchiefs and scarves were already attached to the top yard lift, but he knotted Ann Paylor's ribbon above them all. The wind gusted in his trousers and under his jacket, and the long blue streamer unrolled and crackled over his shoulder.

Slowly, carefully, trembling now but not looking down, he descended the shrouds back to the deck. As he was stepping down from the larboard pinrail a large hand pushed him roughly between the shoulder blades.

'Out of the way, boy! This is no place for bairns. If you want to play you should have stayed at home with your toys.'

Arthur staggered and clenched his fists in fury. The man had already turned his back to climb the mainmast but there wasn't any mistaking Mr Nellis. That spiky red hair and those huge shoulders were usually to be seen whenever there was a fight outside the public houses in Brewster Lane. Arthur was a big lad, but there weren't many men who would be prepared to exchange blows with Mr Nellis. Besides, he was the ship's Specksioneer and therefore senior officer after the Second Mate.

Mr Nellis had some odd garment knotted around his thick neck, and it was soon obvious that he was rolling drunk. His upward progress was a triumph of habitual skill over temporary incapacity. The breeze plucked at the garment around his neck, unfolding it little by little until it was revealed as a bedraggled pair of women's pantaloons trimmed with gaudy lace. This display was greeted with drunken cheers from the deck and a volley of good-natured but coarse inquiries from the loafers on the quayside.

Mr Beaufort, the First Mate, strutted out on to the quarter deck and the proceedings assumed a more dignified air. He was wearing an immaculate velvet jacket, and his sealskin cap was set at a jaunty angle so as to reveal the dark curls on his brow. He issued an order. They loosed the topsails, and there was a mighty cheer from both deck and quayside as they ran the anchor up. The *William Scoresby Senior* moved slowly towards the draw-bridge that separated the inner and outer harbours.

Arthur moved over to the larboard side to look for Ann. There wasn't a sign of her but he saw his parents.

His parents! He waved frantically. He'd forgotten them!

It was as if they'd ceased to exist for a while and had popped back into life only this very second. It stupefied him to realize that he hadn't once thought of them since he barged into Ann Paylor and saw her blue eyes and the blue ribbon in her hair. They must have watched every inch of his unskilled progress up the topgallant mast to the royal yard. What must their thoughts and fears have been? And his own thoughts had been only of the girl, and his only fear that he wouldn't appear well in her eyes.

His father was waving mechanically, maintaining a set smile on his face, hoping that he would be seen by his son wherever he was in the crowded waist of the ship. His mam's sharper eyes darted here and there until she picked him out. He saw the sudden light in her face as she directed his father's gaze in the right direction. They both waved to him madly.

A hand closed upon his heart, squeezing it with iron fingers until the blood pumped into his head with a hurtful violence. How could he have forgotten them? It was unbelievable!

He saw the fireside, the big iron stock pot, the jumbled mantelpiece, the narwhal walking stick, his father filling his clay pipe with crooked fingers, his mam sitting in the chair with the whalebone back, and the caravel sailing on for ever to the mysterious island and the temple with black windows. He waved at them desperately, desperately.

The hinged leaves of the draw bridge lifted. The *William Scoresby Senior* passed between the stone piers with her anchors catted. The *William and Ann* and the *Phoenix* followed her into the outer harbour.

The windows and wooden balconies of the houses all along Staithside from the bridge were full of cheering, waving people. The buildings themselves hung out over the water on piles driven into the river bed, as if to shorten the distance between the departing ships and the mothers, wives and sweethearts who leaned even further forward to throw their kisses and call their prayers.

Then he saw Ann Paylor at the top of a curved flight of steps which led down to the outer harbour. She must have run all the way round from the inner harbour through Haggersgate, and she paused for breath as she looked out at the *William Scoresby Senior*.

He jumped and waved until she waved back to show that she'd seen him. He pointed upwards to remind her of where the blue ribbon was, and saw her raise her hand over her eyes as if she were having difficulty in seeing it. He looked up at the topgallant mast. Alas! The ribbon was almost indistinguishable; but behind the main royal a pair of bedraggled pantaloons, trimmed with gaudy lace, kicked their shameless legs in the wind.

When Arthur lowered his gaze he saw that she was skipping down the steps, and on the road to the pier she ran to come abeam. The ground was uneven and groups of waving people were in the way. He watched her feet moving under her long skirt and he watched the wind blowing her loosened hair. By the time she reached the start of the west pier the ship had left her well behind.

The *William Scoresby Senior*, with her topsails sheeted home and her anchors fished, escaped from the embracing piers and entered the north sea.

4

Captain Stapleton came up on to the quarter deck and moved aft to look back over the taff rail at the town that had made him. A town? More like a city-state in ancient Greece or Renaissance

Italy. It was as self-sufficient as Athens, as independent as imperial Venice.

He looked at the white houses. His eyes were puckered as if looking to windward. Now that he was old the distended muscles wouldn't relax and the flesh around his eyes was puffy all the time.

The white houses along this strip of coastal cliffs reminded him of nesting kittiwakes. The scattered villages, like the bird colonies, shared an ancient and common heritage. Above their red roofs the moors began and rolled inland through miles of desolation, interrupted only by heaps of stones where primitive men had buried their dead, and by isolated farms where the second sons were dreaming of life at sea. Below the pale faces of the houses rolled the dark, cold water that had brought the Angles, and then St Hilda, and then the Vikings.

In spring the daffodils marched along the dales and bottoms and the high tides smashed their big waves against the cliffs. Summer brought more flowers, pink, red and blue, that the whalers never saw, and the bright sun created miniature rainbows in the spray above the broken water. In autumn bushy heather straggled over the moors and the flowers turned their pale, crinkled mouths away from the salt winds blowing from the sea. Each night in winter the blind hunter climbed out of the ocean, with his sword and belt glittering wet, and he looked enormous despite the wide expanse of sky he had to grope in.

The revolving seasons, with their preordained flowers and changing aspects of the sea, provided the frame within which a pattern of life had developed. Life like mine, Captain Stapleton thought.

A distant clatter followed by a cry attracted his attention. He turned and came forward to the quarter deck steps, where the wind fluffed the white hair over his ears.

'Mr Beaufort!'

The First Mate hurried aft to the foot of the steps. 'Captain Stapleton?'

'What was that noise?'

'Man fallen down the forward hatch, sir.'

'Who is it?'

'Peter Gill, sir. Mr Nellis's line-manager.'

'Drunk?'

'Yes, sir. But no more than usual considering what day it is.'

Captain Stapleton's features showed a quiet resignation. 'Have you sufficient sober men to send aloft?'

'Certainly, sir!'

'Then I'd like to see those royals unfurled.'

'Sir.'

The First Mate turned to hurry away but he called him back.

'One other thing, Mr Beaufort. I shouldn't like to be without a Specksioneer when we reach the fish. So I don't want to see Mr Nellis in the shrouds again before tomorrow.'

Mr Beaufort didn't permit himself a smile. 'No need for him, Captain Stapleton.'

'Very well, Mr Beaufort. The ship is yours.'

'Thank you, sir.'

Captain Stapleton returned to the taff rail and looked back at the town under the cliff. Not only each season but each month, each week had its customary expectations, rituals and pleasures. Every Saturday people from the surrounding countryside brought their produce to the market place in front of the Tolbooth. The girls giggled over their private jokes as they walked along the banks of the Esk in their simple dresses and their drooping, linsey-woolsey petticoats. Their mothers and the old women wore black felt hats, and shawls over their shoulders which they pinned below the throat and confined at the waist with their apron strings. Sometimes the farmers themselves came into the town and sometimes they had travelled over the moors from as far away as the Marishes, or Pickering, or Ryedale, or even the Vale of York. Ostensibly they were heading for the market with their butter and eggs; but often they stopped short and knocked on a door in Church Street, or turned aside into Grape Lane or Baxtergate. It soon appeared that the main purpose of the butter and eggs was to cover the sovereigns in the bottoms of their baskets: the real object of their journey was to buy a share in one of the whaling ships being built by Fishburn and Brodrick on the west, or by somebody renting Henry and George Barrick's yard on the east, or indeed by any of the well-known families who built the world's best ships on both sides of the river.

The next day everyone came in from the outlying villages, the men in their best and darkest jackets despite the journey and the women in their Staithes bonnets. They toiled up the Church Stairs, with the flattened resting places for coffin bearers, to the top of the east cliff. They pathed through the graveyard and into the parish church of St Mary. Their families had used the same seats for generations in the box pews that bore the names of their homes: Uggle Barnby, Hawsker cum Stainsacre, Aislaby, Ruswarp, Newholm cum Dunsley. Under cover of the tall-backed pews the villagers relaxed and munched the provisions they had brought from home, while everyone waited for the Cholmleys. And then the Cholmleys, having mounted from outside by their private stairs, suddenly appeared in.

Many ceremonies were those proper to religious festivals and provided a good excuse for eating. When Captain Stapleton thought about it he was as sure many of the festivals didn't appear in the church calendar of Holy-Days or table of Moveable Feasts.

On Collop Monday they banqueted on chunks of stewed meat and streaky bacon. The next day, Shrove Tuesday, they made sure they used up all their eggs in pancakes fried in fat put aside from the previous day. By this time they were so well fortified that on Ash Wednesday, the first day of Lent, little virtue was required to begin the fast. *Tid, Mid, Misere, Carling, Palm and Pace Egg Day.*

Mothering Sunday was the fourth Sunday in Lent, when they remembered the feeding of the five thousand and broke the fast by giving Simnel cakes stuffed with currants. The fifth was Care Sunday when they ate carlings fried in oil; the sixth was Palm Sunday when the men attached sprigs of goat-willow to their coats. Then on Easter Day, which gave all the days their meaning and on which they depended, the children received their pace eggs which had been given every colour imaginable by boiling with onion skins, rug clippings and bits of coloured cloth.

How many of these children knew what they were commemorating as they rolled their eggs across the yards and down the ghauts? It was a re-enactment of the stone being rolled away from the mouth of the sepulchre outside Jerusalem. It didn't matter now. But they would think about what it meant when they were older and had children of their own rolling and jarping eggs on Easter Day.

Other events had less connection with the religious calendar. In November, on Martinmas, farm labourers congregated in Church Street as they had done for centuries in hope of their yearly hire. Those who had some special skill took care to advertise it: waggoners carried whipcord around their necks, and shepherds displayed tufts of wool in their hats. The farmers came to look them over, feel their muscles, make them walk up and down, and ask them questions; while the farmers' wives looked on and worried about how much the strongest men would eat.

The labourers who were engaged received a *fest* penny to seal the bargain. Those who weren't successful went to the next hiring at Egton, or Castleton, or Guisborough, and if necessary going south of the moorlands as far as Helmsley. Meanwhile those who'd been successful spent their fest pennies and more in the Black Bull Inn nearby, whence they dribbled on to the Seven Stars and the Jolly Butchers in Brewster Lane.

Just like the Lerwick boatmen, reflected Captain Stapleton. We shall see them doing the same thing in a few days' time when we hand them their bounty money. Fest penny and bounty money. It means the same thing to them. Nothing changes.

With the approach of Christmas people's thoughts returned to feasting. First of the good things was gingerbread, consumed in vast quantities on Christmas Eve. For this the baker had kneaded his dough, slowly working in the black treacle, adding brown sugar, cinnamon, caraway and coriander as well as ground ginger, and sometimes sultanas, currants and candied peel. On Plough Monday, the first Monday after Twelfth Night, the farm labourers came back and dragged ploughs around the streets in a procession, pretending to be oxen. With the money they were given for this traditional entertainment they once more retired to the inns in the Market Place and Brewster Lane, and with normal luck were roaring drunk for the second time in three months.

To every thing there is a season, and a time to every purpose under the heaven. Captain Stapleton recalled the words of Ecclesiastes as he looked back at the receding harbour. The two

piers lay upon the water like encircling arms. On the piers un-
identifiable figures still waved at the *William and Ann* and the
Phoenix. Beyond them the masts and rigging of a hundred more
ships clustered together in a dense, leafless forest. Tomorrow,
when the festivities of Sailing Day were over, both sides of the
river would resound again with the clang of caulking jerries following the trails of the deck rimers, and the smell of pitch would
be added to the other smells that never left the harbour.

The houses on the east side, with their pantiles rich red against
the blue sky, seemed to climb on each other's shoulders up the
cliff to win a better view to seaward. On top of the cliff, surrounded by its graveyard, the parish church of St Mary tried to
squat out of the north east wind. Beyond that was the Abbey of
St Hilda with its central tower black against the clear sky.

Vanity of vanities, said the writer of Ecclesiastes, *vanity of
vanities; all is vanity*. The north sides of the choir and the nave,
and the north transept of the ruined Abbey, looked out upon the
sea. The bodies of King Edwin, first of the Christian kings, of
King Oswy and his Queen, of princes, princesses and saints of
the royal Northumbrian blood, of the first poet of all England
and of holy men and women without number, had long since
rotted in the wet earth when those walls were new and cast their
first shadows on their graves. *What profit hath a man of all his
labour which he taketh under the sun?*

St Hilda's central tower, raised like a portent against the sky,
had watched the departure of a hundred whaling fleets. From
this distance it wasn't difficult to imagine that the tower hadn't
been raised by men. Those ancient stones were a natural out-
growth of the cliff and would withstand the assault of storms and
salt winds until the end of time. *All is vanity and vexation of
spirit*, Captain Stapleton remembered. *In much wisdom is much
grief, and he that increases his knowledge increases his sorrow.
Men are beasts, they have all one breath, destined to the same
end, all are of the dust and all turn to dust again.*

The wise and sad man who wrote Ecclesiastes had seen that
there is a season for everything and a time for every purpose. He
saw something else. *The thing that hath been, it is that which
shall be; and that which is done is that which shall be done; and
there is no new thing under the sun.* That was the real wisdom

of Ecclesiastes. *That which hath been is now; and that which is to be hath already been; and God requireth that which is past.*

Perhaps that was it. Perhaps that's why these villages on this isolated coast continued to remember our ceremonies and rituals, our traditional ways of doing things. These shared customs bind us together into a community which is larger and richer than our individual selves. We know that our fathers who are dust did these things before us, and we know that our sons will do these things when we ourselves are turned again to dust.

This is a special kind of wisdom that we have won for ourselves over the ages.

Captain Stapleton rested his hands on the taff rail and watched the backs of the waves as they followed each other towards the shore, rising and falling, breaking and expiring, being sucked back into the body of the sea. Perhaps these recurring activities, these customary words, gestures and foods, are appearances only; and their repetition, generation after generation, helps us to understand something in the human spirit that continues for ever. If this is so then we must preserve our way of life. It would be a terrible thing for us, for everyone, if anything happened to change it.

And there were some festivals that they didn't share with the neighbouring villages at all.

Of these the most important, beyond any possible dispute, was Sailing Day. It had the same place in the secular life of the community that Easter Day had in the church calendar, and the two days frequently came close together in early April.

Sailing Day was the one time in every year when all the endeavours of the town, no matter how scattered and even antagonistic they might normally appear to be, came together and made their separate contributions to a common goal that they all recognized to be good. The shipwrights from the yards on the east and west sides of the rivers, the caulkers and coopers and carpenters, the Quaker owners in Bagdale and the bankers in Grape Lane, the workmen from the sail lofts and the rope walks, the foundry men from Baxtergate, the shop keepers from Church Street and the chandlers from Sandgate, all of them saw something of their enterprise and labour during the previous year when the fleet was ready to sail. And not a mother, nor a wife, nor a sister, nor a daughter but had someone she loved on one of the ships.

Ports to the north and south of this particular strip of coast also sent fleets to the northern fishery – especially Peterhead, Aberdeen, Dundee and Hull – and they had their own Sailing Days. But this small town had some ceremonies that couldn't have been found anywhere else.

There was, for example, the planting of the Penny Hedge or Horngarth. This took place on the eve of Ascension Day, and so no matter how soon the Paschal moon might fall the ceremony was always well after Sailing Day. Captain Stapleton consequently hadn't seen the Horngarth for many years, but he remembered it clearly from the days before his apprenticeship.

A select procession carrying stakes and branches came down Church Street along the riverside and past the Seamen's Hospital. At the Town End they halted, chose their ground, and a number of the men hammered the stakes into the damp sand of the foreshore. Once this work was under way the others began to cut and shape the branches to make interlacing cross pieces so that the structure would form a compact hedge. When the job was finished a bailiff appeared, blew lustily on a horn, and shouted at the top of his voice: 'Out upon you! Out upon you!'

The procession reformed and went back along Church Street. The tide, coming up the estuary in the opposite direction, soon covered the hedge and hid it from view. But when the tide went out the hedge continued to stand firm.

The hedge always survived the ebb and flow for a couple of days. It had to withstand the three tides specified by the Hermit of Eskdale who, three hundred years earlier, had sheltered a wounded boar in his cell. The beast was being hunted by the lords of Sneaton and Fylingdales. They lost trace of their quarry, and being heated by the chase they made alternative sport with the old hermit. The Abbot arrived on the scene and sentenced the hot-heads to death. The dying hermit interceded, begging mercy for his murderers, and the Abbot spared them on one condition: every year on Ascension Eve they and their descendants had to construct a fence down to the river with a penny knife; and if this hedge failed to withstand three tides their lands would be forfeit to the Abbey.

Captain Stapleton smiled. I shall see the Horngarth again soon, he thought, after all these years. There isn't long to go now. Perhaps they will ask me to join the procession and help to hammer the stakes.

The west pier was now little more than a black smudge on the water, partly obscured by the unfurled canvas of the *William and Ann* and the *Phoenix*. Captain Stapleton turned on his heel and came back to the head of the quarter deck steps. The Second Mate immediately came aft from the waist of the ship.

'Mr Dryden.'

'Captain Stapleton, sir.'

'Has Peter Gill hurt himself?'

'Nothing serious, sir.'

Mr Dryden was about to leave but the Captain detained him.

'Ask Mr Beaufort if he intends to look for eggs on Kettle Ness.'

'Sir?'

'Tell him I want to be further out to sea.'

'Yes, sir.'

Captain Stapleton went back to his position at the rail. There was something else that he'd missed during his annual absences at the fishery: something more exciting than the ceremony of the Horngarth. Captain Jeffries of the *Horn* of Dundee had once told him that he always managed to take a few salmon before Sailing Day. But they spawned earlier up there, and the fish were in the Tay weeks before they entered the Esk.

Ah yes! Captain Stapleton remembered how the news of the first sighting ran through the town. Before the tide turned he and the other boys joined the old men and together they leaned over the pier to watch for the flashing of silver flanks. Sometimes the fish came so close to the surface, and the water ran so clear, that they could see the big red and black spots. The old men with their quiet skills and the young boys in their eagerness knew that their separate lives had overlapped, like pieces of cloth that against all expectation made a complete garment.

The boys followed the old men down to the cobles and they pleaded, almost with tears, to be allowed in the boats. The fishing ground was beyond the harbour where the migrating fish pushed their noses from the salt of the north sea and smelled the fresh, sparkling water brought down by the moorland becks. It was here that the boats dropped their weighted jazz nets, working together in pairs. Captain Stapleton's fingers, bitten by the arctic frosts of over fifty visits to the northern fishery, tightly clenched the taff rail as he remembered the heavy kicking in the net as the cobles came together and they hauled in.

How beautiful they were! How graceful and strong! You could see how they'd been fattening themselves in the depths of the sea, ready for the Lenten journey up the river into Cleveland.

The first salmon he took home was small but it appeared enormous to him. As he carried it along Flowergate he kept turning it this way and that, so that he could show off its bright eyes and clear red gills to the passers-by. He laid it on the table with the happiness of a hunter. He was more proud of that salmon than he was of his first whale.

'He's a real good 'un, he is,' approved his father. 'Just look at his little head and his little tail, and then look at the breadth of his shoulders. Another few years on him and a pair of arms and he'd pull an oar with the best of them.'

'Come by, fayther,' his mam said, 'and let's be doing.'

Captain Stapleton stared at the distant red pantiles, tumbled higgledy piggledy under the cliff, at the flat roof of the parish church and at the black ruin of St Hilda's beyond. He wasn't seeing them.

His mam's recipe for cooking salmon was the simplest and the best. She scaled, emptied and washed it with the greatest nicety, but quickly so that the white curds between the flakes of flesh didn't have time to melt. Now she put fresh water into a fish-kettle and stirred in plenty of salt. A couple of minutes boiling, then she laid the fish on the strainer and poached it gently until her eye told her that this was the moment.

'Just look at him!' his father said, as she lifted out the strainer and rested it across the pan. 'Just tho look at him! There's no lass can keep the colour and set the curd like our mam.'

'Come by, come by,' his mam said, pleased and pretending not to be. 'Make thyself useful.'

His father carved, serving slices alternately from the thick end and the thin. They all knew that the thin end was the creamiest. The curdy flesh made the buttered potatoes taste like some newly discovered vegetable.

The *William Scoresby Senior* rounded Kettle Ness well ahead of the *William and Ann* and the *Phoenix*. Captain Stapleton continued to stare over the taff rail, unaware that the headland had now cut off the view.

5

A brig from the Tyne had unloaded its coal on to the jetty at Sandsend. Men were shovelling it from there to the beach, ready for burning under the leaden pans containing alum liquor.

All along this part of the coast, as far up as Saltburn, gangs with iron bars were mining the blue-grey shale from the cliffs. At Kettle Ness, Boulby and Loftus, the smouldering pyramids of bluish shale were almost a hundred feet high; and the thick smoke curled into the sky above the sandstone buildings of the alum houses and steeping pits. The bleak, industrial landscape was broken only at Runswick, where flowered gardens overhung the red roofs of houses down below; and again at Staithes, where gulls mewed and keened around the fish quay.

Arthur Storm had often seen hessian sacks of alum crystals waiting for shipment not far away from his home in Ellerby Lane. They had to add human urine to make the solid alum crystals appear from the liquor. Mr Nellis, the Specksioneer of the *William Scoresby Senior*, kept a barrel outside his front door for that specific purpose. Despite the protests of his neighbours he steadfastly replenished this vessel with urine produced by himself and – so it was said – a couple of his more cooperative lady friends. Mr Nellis boasted that the price he obtained from the alum works enabled him to drink half as much beer again as men with more private habits.

The alum industry had existed for centuries. Exports of alum had made the town important a hundred years before it sent a ship to the northern fishery. This corner of Cleveland was England's only source of a material that was used for tanning leather and dyeing textiles, as well as providing medication for a multitude of ills where its efficacy was less open to proof.

Arthur watched the men trundling their barrows laden with quarried rock. A few of them stopped and waved, and he waved in return. Are they envious of me? Probably not. For generations son had followed father in those little village communities, and mining shale for the alum houses was the only way of life they could imagine. How fortunate I am! How much better to seek a livelihood from the big fish, than to scratch about on those bare cliffs in the north-east winds.

A cluster of wave-washed scars were followed by a river estuary. He looked at the wide, empty mouth, with sand banks running away on each side. There wasn't a sign of life anywhere apart from hundreds of seals and thousands of sea birds paddling in the shallow waters. Occasionally the birds took wing and blew away over the mud flats like smoke, and then abruptly changed direction and came back to where they'd started from. Why they kept taking flight and changing their minds in mid air he couldn't imagine: they were as unmolested as he supposed wild creatures must have been at the dawn of the world. The peaceful river with its dozing seals and wading birds, its sandy wastes and grassy banks, seemed to have been freshly created and to be awaiting some supervening event.

'The River Tees,' said a voice next to him.

The man beside him had the sinewy, rather thin frame that often developed in men who went to the fishery year after year. He was wearing a gansey, cable stitched up to the oxters but plain above, showing that the upper parts had been re-knitted at least once and probably many more times.

'Jim Richardson,' the man said. 'Line-manager in Mr Dryden's boat.'

Arthur nodded respectfully. Line-managers were senior men, ranking after the boat-steerers when there was a lowering.

'The River Tees,' Arthur repeated. 'It makes a change to what's gone before.'

The contrast was abrupt and complete. The coastline from Sandsend to Loftus, with its succession of alum factories, belonged to the world of men and labour and artificial dirt. It would have been difficult, Arthur thought, to find anywhere else on earth with such a long and almost unbroken line of chimneys pumping their thick smoke into the air. But here, at the mouth of the Tees, all was peace and the beauty of undisturbed nature. This gentle estuary and its neighbouring coast were remote from any kind of business enterprise or economic endeavour. Here there wasn't anything that could testify to the reshaping hand of man. The river was asleep between its sandy banks in a dream of seals and sea birds.

'Aye, it looks peaceful,' Jim said, 'but there's things up that river that folk don't know about.'

Arthur didn't wish to appear entirely ignorant of affairs outside his own town. 'I've heard of an old crossing place where the monks from Whitby used to go over on their way up to Durham. It's got a name, I think.' He pondered for a moment. 'Middleburg or Middlesburg.'

'Pooh! Middleburg or whatever you want to call it! Nothing but a handful of sheep and a few owld folk.' He dismissed the virtually nonexistent place with a contemptuous wave of his hand, as if he were sweeping a troublesome fly from somewhere near the end of his nose. 'It's further up the river I'm thinking of, round about Stockton way.'

Arthur was determined to be credited with knowing something useful. 'There's ships built at Stockton and Yarm.'

'Aye, aye,' conceded the Greenlander, in the tone of a man agreeing that the world was round. 'But I mean something entirely new.'

'There's no new thing under the sun.'

'So you think to quote the Preacher against me?'

Arthur felt his cheeks redden. 'I thought it was an old proverb.'

'And it is. The Preacher is full of old proverbs. *Is there any thing whereof it may be said, See, this is new? It hath been already of old time.* But I'm telling you now that all that old wisdom is going to be overturned.'

'Why?'

'Because of what's happening up yon river.'

Arthur would have liked to draw on the line-manager's experiences at sea and to hear what he thought of the prospects for the new season. 'Like some new kind of ship or sailing rig?'

Jim Richardson fended off a huge swarm of imaginary flies with two flailing hands.

'Like what then?' asked Arthur.

'Like a railroad.'

Arthur laughed, thinking immediately of Mr Hugill and his pamphlets.

'It's nothing to laugh at. D'you know what a railroad is?'

'I've heard talk by men who've served on colliers. It's a method of fixing wooden rails to the ground so that the coal wagons run on them instead of the road. They say the horses can pull more than twice as much.'

Jim Richardson grunted with the deep relish of someone who knew he was about to shatter another man's assumptions. 'Well I'll tell you something you don't know about a new railroad to Stockton. It's made of iron. And not only that. The horses on this new railroad are made of iron an' all.' He observed Arthur's expression of astonishment for several seconds with evident gratification. 'They're a kind of engine on wheels that runs with steam from a boiler.'

Jim reached inside his shirt as if he were about to produce some conclusive proof of his own veracity. But any revelation of this sort was blocked by the sudden appearance of Mr Beaufort, who strode down towards the main hatch and shouted an order. Jim Richardson leaped away to help in unfurling the courses.

Arthur stayed where he was at the ship's side. North of the river mouth and its mud flats were salt marshes; and then miles of sand, as pure and bright as a bar of beaten gold, running back to wind-blown dunes and sparse grassland. It was a desolate and strangely remote scene, where nothing moved except huge flocks of tiny birds running this way and that above the moving water line.

After half a dozen miles the sand dunes were followed by a village, with the white fronts of fishermen's cottages looking out towards sandstone rocks and cobles with flat transoms pulled up on to the beach. After another couple of miles there was a headland with a harbour, and a walled town with an old grey church. That must be where St Hilda had received the king's daughter. Arthur didn't believe in the legends of the bowing birds and of the snakes turned into stone, nor that the Lady Hilda sometimes appeared in her shroud within a high window of the Abbey choir. But he knew that King Oswy, grateful for avenging Edwin and Oswald, had given his daughter to Hilda. That must have been a thousand years before the first alum factories.

A new sense of time, a new feeling for all the years that had passed and of all the people who had lived and suffered, made Arthur's heart leap. I am part of this strange stream of life, he thought, and so is Ann Paylor; and it seemed a marvellous thing.

A steep-sided dene carried its beck down to the shore. Then came limestone arches and gaping mouths in a cliff face. A collier brig, her squat hull rolling in the swell, laboured by to seaward. Two more colliers toiled in her wake, their bluff bows like dirty clenched fists pushing the sea aside.

Jim Richardson, his spell of duty over, rejoined Arthur at the ship's side. 'Good life,' he said, 'being an apprentice.'

'Better than being in one of those,' Arthur replied, nodding towards the colliers.

'That was how Captain Cook learned most of what he knew.'

'A terrible life for all that. If they've time to look over they must think we're gentlefolk up from t' south to look at the scenery.'

The waves continued to roll away on to empty sands. From time to time a wave larger than its predecessors dashed itself against the rough cliffs that lay beyond, and which formed a continuous grey wall except for the occasional intrusion of the steep-sided denes.

'While we're outward bound,' Jim said, 'we've more leisure than any crews afloat. There's so many of us that we can share the work out and laze around. Like officers on an East Indiaman.' He spat into the sea. It was a simple gesture and yet it conveyed a number of meanings: on the one hand it confirmed his satisfaction with his present idleness; yet on the other it expressed contempt for ignorant colliers who might draw incorrect conclusions – and also for officers on East Indiamen to whom such idleness was presumably habitual. 'But wait till we're up beyond Cape Farewell,' he added. 'We'll all be wishing we had twice as many men with two hands on each arm.'

The colliers were becoming more numerous. The *William Scoresby Senior* put out to sea so as to be clear of them. By the time she was approaching the Wear the distant coal fleet resembled a swarm of dark bees laden with honey from darker flowers.

'Look at them all,' Jim said, indicating the crowded river. 'And that's nothing to what there'll be up at the Tyne.'

'I can't help feeling sorry for folk in London,' said Arthur. 'It's not their fault they've no coal of their own, and yet I suppose they feel the cold just like ordinary people.'

'Feel the cold! They don't have cold weather down there!'

Arthur, who had scarcely forgotten his astonishment at the idea of iron horses, raised his eyebrows in renewed amazement.

'It's true, I tell you, and I should know because I lived in London.' Jim reached inside his shirt front again but this time he pulled out the talisman he was looking for. It was a jet cross, suspended from his neck by a cord, which he displayed in the palm of his hand as if it were a pearl beyond price. 'I swear by this crucifix that everything I tell you is true. I had lodgings in Mile End, and of a Sunday I used to walk down towards Wapping, almost into t' docks, to say my devotions in Saint Thomas Shadwell. There were lots of seamen there, every Sunday, and lots of our lads in t' graveyard on a more permanent basis. I met an old man who knew Captain Cook when he was in t' congregation in t' self-same church. And I can tell you this,' Jim concluded, with heavy emphasis, 'it was never what you'd call cold.'

He returned the cross within his shirt. A sloop of the previous century, freighted to her waterline with coal, laboured by and her black-faced crew gave them a cheer. The southbound colliers became even thicker between the *William Scoresby Senior* and the coast, and she stood further off again so as to avoid the traffic in and out of the Tyne. The bluff, black hulks of the colliers faded away to larboard.

Once again the natural coastline asserted itself, more wild and rugged than before. Long, dark waves crawled up on to wide, silver sands. Tall crags, some of which could have been fortresses, reared their broken heads against the grey sky.

'How forgotten everything looks,' Arthur said.

'What d' you mean by that?'

Arthur continued to gaze at the receding coast line with something like awe. As the *William Scoresby Senior* kept going seaward the shore became even more forlorn and yet a kind of enchantment hung over it.

'I mean,' he said, 'everything looks as if it's been left behind by people who died a long time ago, or by people who went away and never came back. I can't help feeling as if I'm the first person to look at those rocks for hundreds of years. I mean ... everything looks as if nobody knows it's there ... I can't explain it.'

Jim Richardson humphed. 'We see it every year on t' way to the fishery.'

'Yes. But who else sees it? Who else?'

Jim thought for a moment, and then his face lightened and softened in an extraordinary way. 'I'll tell you of somebody else who knows about it, and he one of the greatest men in t' land.'

'Who?' He made a guess. 'King George?'

'Nay, nay. I don't suppose King George would even recognize it as part of his kingdom.'

'Who then?'

Jim Richardson waved towards the shore and declaimed in a loud and artificial voice:

> 'And now the vessel skirts the strand
> Of mountainous Northumberland.
> Towns, towers, and halls, successive rise,
> And catch the nuns' delighted eyes.'

Arthur gaped at him. 'A rhyme!'

In appearance Jim Richardson was a typical Greenlander, lean and sinewy, with the muscular arms of a boatman, and the level eyes of a man who was used to looking upon space; but typical Greenlanders couldn't even read. And yet Jim now went on to explain that he'd been quoting from a long poem – a *poem* – by a famous Scottish writer.

'Tell me about it, 'Arthur asked him.

Jim told him how Marmion wooed Constance de Beverley, and how for love of him she fled from her convent and travelled with his men disguised as a horse-boy; and how he then met Clare, who was an heiress to rich lands and very pretty besides. Marmion broke his promises to Constance, and the wretched girl was tried for her sins against the evil and sentenced on Holy Island.

38

The *William Scoresby Senior* had remained well out to sea in order to avoid the Farne Islands, and beyond them Holy Island was indistinguishable. Arthur looked towards the area where Jim said it was as he listened to the rest of the story.

The Abbess of Whitby sailed up this coast to listen to the case, and she confirmed the terrible punishment. Arthur could picture the scene with dreadful clarity. He saw the penitential vault, airless, cold and dark; and he saw Constance de Beverley in her page's doublet, blindfolded, being led to the narrow niche in the wall. It quickened his sense of the horror of it all to reflect that he, in this ship, had followed the same route as the implacable Abbess.

The pictures moved about in his mind as if they were alive. How is it that these imaginary events can have such power over me? Why should Holy Island, which I haven't even seen, be a name that is suddenly full of mystery and sadness? Is it simply because a poet invented a story about an unhappy girl who was walled up there?

Perhaps it's because I'm thinking about Ann Paylor. Yes, that's it, he told himself. But how different my own case is! It would be impossible for me to forget her as Marmion did, no matter how rich or beautiful another girl might be.

6

His first meeting with Ann Paylor had taken place under circumstances that he would never forget; although he had thought little enough about her as an individual person either then or for some time afterwards.

It was late March or early April, the season of spring tides. He had left home very early, crossed the river by the drawbridge and mounted the empty west cliff. Vague, orange streaks showed where the sun was struggling to rise in a muffler of grey clouds. The air was cold and sharp in his lungs as he climbed to the top.

Below him the beach was invisible. The mist covered it as lightly as some rare and lightly textured fabric. He stood until his chest rose and fell with a slower rhythm. The silvery sheet below him became transparent in places as if it were being stretched. A soft breeze ruffled it, pulled it into holes and folded it back at the corners. Slowly, gently, the salt wind was going about the first job of the day and unwrapping the beach.

He walked along the west cliff, came to a narrow cleft he knew well and began to descend. The tide was already far down and the sea was as silent as if it had been painted. Between the waves and the cliffs the beach was as flat and empty as a meadow, with only the humped backs of the rocks to interrupt the yellow pastures.

The sun's brow appeared, red and bright as blood, but its face was still swathed in clouds. At the very limits of hearing the sea became audible as each long, dark wave rolled forward and slowly broke up into sparkling darts of silver. The murmur of those myriad drops of water, separating and reforming into innumerable waves, reached his ears as a low humming.

A few paces from the foot of the cliff he reached the high tide mark. The retreating sea had flagged the furthest reach of its advance by leaving hostages of drift wood, sea weed, shells and pebbles. He found a large whelk, fully formed and perfect, which held within its convolutions not the murmur of the sea but the sound of the wind blowing across the moors: a deep note of sorrow that he tried to forget by thinking of the fireside at home in Ellerby Lane, and of his grandma's cheerful parlour in The Bolts at Bay Town.

Below the high tide mark the ebb and flow of the retreating sea had given a rippled surface to the sand. The beach itself had the appearance of a sheet of water made choppy by the wind lippers, and this uneven, ribbed area turned his feet this way and that as he walked.

The first rocks were pink and low-lying, seeming almost to float in shallow, isolated pools where the water was as still as glass. He didn't think of them as real rocks at all. They were only stones, the familiar and homely sights of every day, which might have drifted along to this fierce coast in the wake of some gentle current.

He always wanted to ignore the small pink rocks and their placid pools; and as always he had to force himself to work conscientiously round them all. Some day his patience might be rewarded, unexpectedly. It would be like finding a big salmon lost in a beck. But it made him feel ridiculous to plodge in these lagoons, so shallow and still that the water wasn't even properly cold; and to peer under the smooth rocks, and look into such obvious holes that showed their smallest contents directly to the sky.

Why am I doing this? I know there isn't anything here. There never was and there never will be. Yet I've done this every time and I'll do it next time. Otherwise I'll be tormented for the rest of the day by the thought that I've missed something. I'd have to come back and look to make sure. It's like having a plate of ham and our mam's pease pudding and not being able to leave it until I've finished every scrap. And it's something more than that. It's because I want to be certain about everything.

Arthur splashed out of the last of the shallow pools and left the pink rocks behind. His feelings were a mixture of disappointment at his lack of success, and relief that he could now get on with the real business. I was wrong, he thought, as he looked at the massive black rocks ahead. It hasn't got anything to do with wanting to be certain that I haven't missed anything. No, I fool around the pink rocks and their childish pools, because the delay increases the excitement of what is to come.

He reached the first of the dark rocks. They appeared only when the tide was low, and they were completely different from the small, smooth things he'd left behind.

It wasn't merely that these rocks were another colour or so much larger or less rounded. These were the rough and massive remnants of a more primitive world. They were so deeply rooted that their visible crags and scars might be the sea-washed tips of mountains buried in the sand during some upheaval countless aeons ago. These rocks were old and venerable, life-long neighbours of this ancient sea. Their wave-worn heads, instead of being pink and bald, were overgrown with dank moss and tangled weeds; and they smelled of tides that had flowed and neaped in some distant time when the moon first pulled at the waters of the world.

He stopped at the first uptilted rock and looked underneath.

The lower half of his vision was filled by a miniature lagoon of perfectly clear water, and its sandy floor was scattered with

41

coloured pebbles. The upper half was an arching, green roof, encrusted with shells as bright as stars.

The watery horizon was broken by a curved, pale rim as if a pocket moon were about to rise and illuminate this marine world with its reflected light. It was very quiet in there apart from the intermittent tinkle of water dropping from the suspended shells and disturbing the coloured patterns on the floor. The pocket moon had regular indentations around its edge like his mam's thumb marks circling the crust of an apple pie. It was going to be a good morning.

He reached inside with his iron hook. At the first touch the pale rim sank in a puff of sand, and a string of bubbles broke the surface. The end of the hook caught in the satisfying way he knew so well, and a dark red hump appeared for a moment before the iron pulled free. Now the sand had been well stirred up and it was impossible to see anything in the pool. But it didn't matter.

A pair of tiny eyes rested on top of the water like shiny black beads. He passed the iron beneath them. A large pink claw broke the surface and waved a pair of black tipped pincers at his face.

He raked it clear without any more fuss: a cock crab of rather more than medium size, the best kind there was. The claws would be packed tight to their furthermost corners with firm, white flesh. He took a long piece of string from his pocket, and knotted one end round the joint of one of the big claws.

It was certainly going to be a good morning. The sky and the sea, the climbing sun on his neck and the salt breeze in his nose, everything told him so as he continued to move further out.

The rocks became larger, darker, more thickly matted with moss and weeds. There was something about them that proclaimed they belonged to the water and not to the land. When he bent down to look into their secret places there was a more pungent smell, a sharper sense of penetration into some darker mystery. The water level under these rocks, and in the crevices and pools, was no longer constant but rose and fell according to impulses travelling from the deep sea. I mustn't waste time, he thought. I must keep moving if I want to get round them all before the tide turns.

He proceeded methodically from rock to rock. In less than an hour he had over twenty crabs knotted to the line and not one of them under five inches across the back. It was one of his best mornings ever and he could scarcely wait to return home with his cargo. He would soon have finished now.

A cry ahead of him divided the morning air.

At first he thought it must be one of the birds that were soaring overhead. The harsh cry of a peewit gull, maybe, or the yelping of a sea mew. While he stood still, trying to recall the sound exactly, a small seed of misgiving somewhere in the lining of his stomach shot out little tendrils of apprehension. He waited. A long time passed. He listened to the growling of the waves ahead and the wailing of the gulls above. Slowly the tendrils started to wither and die. He was about to move when the cry was repeated.

There wasn't any doubt this time. The cry split the air like a sharp knife.

The mingling of pain and fear made his scalp tingle. He quickly identified the nearest high rock and climbed its slippery back with reckless speed. On top of it he balanced, his hook in one hand and his string of captive crabs in the other. The rocks surrounded him on all sides like stranded sea creatures.

There was a fainter cry, a sound of despair.

It had come from a cluster of big rocks some way ahead. His eyes traced the savage outline of bent backs and dark openings, the tangles of blackened weeds and bladder wrack on the wet sand. And then he saw her.

He slithered down from his observation post. It was quicker to splash around through the chains of pools than to climb up and down the treacherous slime of the intervening rocks.

The small figure was lying on its side with its back to the sea and facing one of the largest rocks. Arthur stared at a pair of bare feet. They were very small and bright pink from walking over shells and sharp pebbles in the cold water. Above the white ankles smooth legs astonished him with their nakedness, which extended as far as a pair of calico drawers.

He bent down and touched her lightly on the shoulder. She jerked with surprise and twisted her head round to look at him. But she remained lying on her side.

'What's the matter with you? Are you badly?'

The face on which he looked was as pale as sea foam, and the eyes were open so wide that the entire circle of each blue iris was visible. Her lips were parted but she said nothing.

'Have you broken a leg or something?'

He looked at her in a kind of disbelief. If she'd told him that she was a mermaid waiting for the return of the tide he wouldn't have been surprised.

But she only cried.

He saw that she was lying so awkwardly on her side, with her face towards the rock, because her left arm was thrust into a horizontal cleft. He stooped, held her slender shoulders and pulled gently. A cry of pain stopped him.

'Is your hand fast?'

She nodded.

'Can't you work it about so as to make it loose?'

'No,' she sobbed, and he had to bend down to hear what she was saying. 'It hurts too much.'

He eased her light body away from the side of the rock, altering the angle of her arm and trying to cause as little pain as he could. In the space created he was able to kneel on the sand and look into the aperture where her arm was trapped. As he lowered his head a rivulet traced its way around the rock, wetting his knees and the hem of the girl's dress.

'What's holding it so fast?'

'I div'n't know.'

The tears coursed down her white cheeks. He laid the side of his face against the sand and peered into the cleft. The floor was littered with empty shells and a handful of dead starfish pointed at each other with stiffened legs. From the roof clusters of mussels hung down like stalactites.

Water hit him in the face and made him gasp for breath. This time it wasn't a mere rivulet but a small wave that covered his feet up to the ankles and wetted the curling ends of the long hair that trailed over the girl's shoulders. He watched the water drain away slowly, slowly, through channels in the rock, while his heart laboured like a pump in a leaking hull.

The tide had turned.

He quickly lowered his head again. Her forearm and the dim outline of part of her hand were visible. But what was holding her? He stared into the dark depths, his forehead pressing against

44

the black moss on the stone until it hurt, and blinked his eyes.

Then he saw it. Or rather he saw sufficient to know what it was and to guess its size. He'd never imagined that dog crabs could grow so huge.

Another wave felt its blind way round the rock, soaking the girl's hair and clouting him in the face again. He wiped his eyes on the back of his hand and moved the hook forward. The water had reached the opening and the area was so flooded that he couldn't see the outline of the girl's small hand. He advanced the hook parallel to her arm and waited for the water to drain.

The water sucked out of the hole and he reached further forward. The crab was partly obscured by a formation in the rock which joined the floor and roof like a supporting pillar. He passed the hook over the part of the back which was visible until he felt the point engage securely in the crab's rear.

He pulled. It didn't move. He pulled with all his strength, screwing his eyes tight with the intensity of his effort. Nothing happened.

A wave groped its way round the rock, swifter and deeper than its predecessor, and slapped him across the eyes. He dropped the hook and heard the girl scream and then start to cough. The wave foamed and bubbled around them, hissed over the hairy rock and began to drain away. He scrabbled frantically in the swirling sand, oblivious of the choking girl and the sting of salt in his eyes.

He touched the iron with his finger tips, lost it again, thought he'd found the wooden handle but discovered it was a stone. He selected the main channel of ebbing water and used his arm as a kind of weir. It was a full minute before the hook knocked against his fingers.

When the armoured form of the crab reappeared above the falling water line he lunged at it without delay. The points of the hanging mussels ripped the skin of his forearm. The hook caught and slipped. He forced himself to work more patiently. The hook found a lodging somewhere behind the spiky back, and he pulled until the sweat came out on his forehead and ran down to mingle with the salt in his eyes.

The creature had wedged itself in some way against the rock.

The next wave came, higher and more turbulent than any

before. The girl coughed and gurgled and then stopped her noises completely.

Despair gave Arthur an added strength. The hook slipped. No! There had been a movement! And the hook still held.

The girl's head was almost completely submerged, and her fair hair fanned out upon the surface of the water like the bleached flower of a giant sea anemone. He tugged again and the resistance gave way so suddenly that for a moment he feared the end had broken off his hook. The girl's arm came out of the opening, and she was trying to stand up when the next wave arrived and knocked her over.

He scooped her up with one of his arms under her back and the other under her legs and turned to face the shore. The expanse of water between him and the beach surprised and frightened him.

Stumbling and slipping, sometimes changing course to avoid the treacherous slopes of rocks and shelving pools, he made his way towards the dry sand. The tide had turned fully and was running strongly. He kept his eyes ahead of his feet, looking for hazards in the moving water and trying to ignore the writhing, spidery thing that was embracing her left hand with its multijointed legs. The sea rose above his knees; once he stepped into an unexpected hollow that brought the water above his waist, and he feared the next wave or its undertow would lift him from his feet.

He laid her on the sand. Water came out of the sides of her mouth, and her previously curly hair was wrapped round her head like string. The dog crab, by its remaining claw, was attached to the middle finger of her left hand just above the knuckle. As well as a claw a portion of its shell was missing. Some part of its interior anatomy was revealed, but this exposure of its vital machinery to the air had no effect upon its tenacity.

Arthur held the long, clamped claw in one hand and took the body in the other. The underside was a shiny, repellent orange, and the upper shell was almost black, armed with spikes as tough as knife blades and studded with small, white shells. Holding the claw steady, he twisted the body round and round. The eight purple legs released the small hand and waved unavailingly in the air. After a couple more complete turns of the body there was a stretching of sinews and the cracking of a joint: the legs flexed and probed the air in a frenzy. Round and round he twisted until there was a loud click. A clear fluid ran out of the new hole in the side of the shell where the second claw had been attached.

He threw the defenceless body as far as he could. The legs knotted tightly underneath the orange belly, and it plopped into the advancing sea like a ball.

The isolated claw continued to nip the girl's finger. He found a stick that he could insert between the pincers, but the stick broke. He searched for a flat pebble that he could use as a lever, but the girl cried more loudly and he came back to her.

'Do you think you can walk?'

She shook her head. The experience had robbed her of her ability to do anything. The next wave didn't break until it was within a dozen yards of them, and it drenched them afresh.

He carried her across the white sand, up the cloven ascent, down from the west cliff and over the drawbridge. Her left arm hung loosely, waving this way and that. The purple claw, with its orange pincers, continued to crush the finger that was now as purple as itself.

Arthur carried her to her home in Henrietta Street up on the east cliff. After a hasty explanation to her horrified parents he ran to the doctor's, and then returned to his own home in Ellerby Lane. He had scarcely finished his meal when there was a knock on the door.

'It's Mr Paylor from Henrietta Street,' announced his father.

A pleasant, fresh-faced man came into the room. He had clear, blue eyes like his daughter. Mrs Storm pounced at the table and first by speed, then by stealth, removed every trace of the meal to the scullery while the men talked. Mr Paylor said that the doctor had been forced to use a special kind of little saw to cut through the crab's pincers. He then went on to say how grateful he was to Arthur, but his blue eyes filled with tears and he had to content himself with shaking Arthur by the hand.

'Anyway,' said Mrs Storm, full of sympathy but desperately anxious to look on the bright side, 'the main thing is that the lass is all right.'

'Oh, aye, she's all right,' Mr Paylor agreed. 'She'll lose her middle finger but she's all right.'

Then Mr Paylor and Mr Storm settled down to a pipe of

tobacco and the more usual kind of talk. Mr Paylor was a boat-steerer with the *Aimwell*, although Arthur wasn't reminded of that until some years later.

What Arthur didn't forget was the way that severed limb continued to obey the last wish of its drowned brain. He used to think of it as being like a mindless but well trained soldier, who continued to fight although his leader had gone; but when he grew older he thought that perhaps he'd discovered some bitter truth about the world.

7

The Second Mate spoke to Arthur in a friendly way a couple of days after clearing port. 'You one of the new apprentices?'

'Yes, Mr Dryden.'

The Second Mate smiled, apparently out of simple pleasure at being identified so readily. This prompt recognition shouldn't have caused him any surprise because he was a memorable man, besides being a senior officer. It wasn't simply his tallness, which he seemed anxious to minimize by walking with a stoop and by bending his head when he was talking or being spoken to; nor was it the rather mournful moustaches that drooped contradictorily on each side of his smiling mouth. It was rather that there was something youthful, almost childishly innocent about him, which appeared slightly ridiculous in such a large and powerful man.

'What's your name?'

Arthur told him.

'Storm. That's a Bay Town name.'

Arthur said that his father had come from Bay Town, and that his grandparents still lived in The Bolts.

'I know the place,' Mr Dryden said. 'Half-way down Bay Bank just before you come to t' beck. You go through an archway into a little alley.'

'That's right, Mr Dryden. They say it's the way Bay folk used to run to get away from the Press Gang and Excisemen.'

The *William Scoresby Senior* was sailing on a bowline with the sailtacks hauled close and the canvas was shivering as she luffed up. The Second Mate looked at the braces and clew lines with a critical eye, and satisfied himself that nothing else could be done to bring her closer to the wind. With a suddenly relaxed air he turned to Arthur.

'D'you know how to span a harpoon?'

'No, Mr Dryden. But I'd like to find out.'

'Come on, lad. It's about time you did.'

He led the way down below to the 'tween decks where the boats were stored, and crossed over to a boat on the larboard quarter in which a couple of men were working. With that diffidence which never left him, and yet with a proprietory air, he rapped on the smooth, carvel-built side with his rough knuckles.

'My boat,' he said.

A head popped up over the gunwale.

'Don't let us disturb you, Jim,' said Mr Dryden. 'We're not coming in yet for a bit.'

'Aye, aye, sir.'

Numerous tools, bits of equipment, boxes, tubs and pieces of rope were lying about. Mr Dryden cleared an area with his foot, squatted on his hunkers and fished out a harpoon from the debris under the boat.

'There it is,' he said, holding it before him with a kind of admiration and balancing it on his hand. 'Men have been using this for over two hundred years, and we still can't think of any way of improving on it.'

Arthur looked at the familiar shape. The words of the Second Mate, and the respectful way he was holding the harpoon, made his words seem mysterious and somehow important.

'I never pick one up without thinking of the tons of North Riding oak we use to make our ships, and the endless trouble we undergo to fortify them against the ice. And how we recruit all these men and take provisions aboard to feed them for six months. And how we have trained officers to plot out courses and read magnetic compasses and recognize stars millions of miles away.' He held the harpoon higher, then lowered and raised it, measuring its weight in his big hand. 'But if we can't make this piece of iron stick in t' fish's back the whole enterprise goes for naught.'

He lowered the harpoon on to a wooden block, clamped it under his foot and picked up a file. He began to file away at the point and at the edges of the barbs.

'This end is called the mouth because it bites the fish,' he continued. As he filed he commented on the different parts as he reached them. 'When the harpoon enters the fat it's held in it, with a bit of luck, by these two withers. If it gets pulled out, not all the way but so as to be held by one wither only, then this other little wither, inside here, helps to keep it fast. If it doesn't hold fast then your fish is as loose as if you'd never struck him.'

Mr Dryden put the file aside and rotated the mouth of the harpoon so as to examine its freshly sharpened edges. He blew on it, wiped it, and squinted at it as if he were a watchmaker examining some mechanism so delicate as to be virtually invisible.

'The whole of our undertaking,' he said, 'Mr Foster and Mr Winspear and the other owners, the bankers in Church Street, the men in the yards and sail lofts and rope walks, and all the men in this ship, and all their wives and families, they all have to feed through this iron mouth.'

He picked up the file and rasped at the edge of one of the barbs that fell imperceptibly short of perfection. Arthur watched intently. He was filled with an expanded sense of the way things were connected to each other. The canvas rippling above his head – canvas that his father had helped to stitch in Mr Winspear's sail loft – depended for its final usefulness upon this iron point.

Mr Dryden, still on his hunkers, examined the cutting edges with the leathery ball of his thumb. Somewhat reluctantly, he put the file aside for the last time. He looked up at Arthur and the drooping moustaches diverged as he grinned.

'And yet there's another part that's even more important,' he said.

'More important than the harpoon?'

Mr Dryden settled back on his heels. 'Than the mouth.'

He picked up a mallet, but instead of using it for any more usual purpose he began to twist the shank of the harpoon round the wooden shaft in a tight spiral. He proceeded slowly, with a kind of self-indulgence, so as to prolong the satisfaction he so obviously took in what he was doing.

'When you've got the mouth fast into t' fish, and he starts to sound or run or breach, the shank gets twisted and bent every which way. If it snaps you've lost your fish and some expensive line besides. I've seen harpoons twice as old as I am, still fast in an owld fish's fat, and pulled into knots and figures of eight like they'd been nobbut bits of string.'

He unwound the shank, slowly and deliberately, relishing every moment, as if it were some delicious morsel he was about to eat.

'This shows it's good iron. Now I know it won't snap no matter which way the fish turns and swims.' He placed the curly shank on the deck and started to straighten it with expert blows of the mallet. 'It's made of stubs, owld horse shoe nails that've been formed into rods and welded together. They make the best and toughest iron.' The shank had by now almost resumed its original straightness. He removed it to the block of wood and tapped it more gently, almost affectionately, with the mallet. 'Marvellous stuff, is iron. I sometimes think they'll make everything out of it.'

'What! Even ships?'

Mr Dryden smiled so widely that the sides of his moustache lifted high enough to reveal his eye teeth. 'No, no,' he laughed. 'You'll never beat Bilsdale oak for a ship's planks.' He shook his head to show the hopelessness of any alternatives. 'But iron is marvellous stuff for all that.'

He gave the shank a few more superfluous taps with the mallet. It was, if anything, straighter than it had been before he wrapped it round the shaft.

A distant voice sang: 'Mr Dryden!' A nearer voice echoed it more loudly: 'Mr Dryden!'

The first call came from Captain Stapleton on the quarter deck. It was relayed by Mr Beaufort who shouted down the main hatch.

'We'll start spanning after we've completed our crew at Lerwick,' said Mr Dryden over his shoulder as he moved towards the stairs.

'Mr Dryden! A word if you please!'

The Second Mate was already at the top of the companionway.

8

Arthur was standing near the mizzen fife rail wondering whether Constance de Beverley had fair hair and blue eyes. Jim Richardson came along to replace a belaying pin.

'When I had lodgings in Mile End,' Jim said, harking back to his London days, 'I shipped on a merchantman built at Green's Blackwall Yard.' He slid the pin into a hole in the rail. 'By lad! She was a tremendous ship, with more canvas on her mainmast than we have on all our yards added together and stored in the line room besides. And she had a moonraker o' top.'

Jim Richardson looked up at the topgallants and royals of the *William Scoresby Senior* as if to aid his imagination in remembering how much taller that other ship really was. Arthur waited expectantly. It was a strange and wonderful world that Jim had known.

'The Captain was so grand and proud he could hardly walk, and he used to pretend he couldn't tell the difference between one collier and another. He was a real London gent, he was. We came out of India Dock into Limehouse Reach and when we were abeam the entrance to Greenland Dock he clapped a big silk handkerchief to his nose. And then he was sick down his waistcoat. It was the prettiest thing you ever saw, braided with pink flowers and silvery leaves. A very well-bred stomach, had the Captain. Three bottles of vintage port at a sitting didn't trouble his stomach at all.'

Arthur defended the unknown Captain. 'At least he knew where the Greenland Dock was.'

'In those days, when London looked after itself a bit more than it does now, you could smell blubber houses all along the river from the Tower to Greenwich Hospital. I don't like Mr Nellis's language and I don't approve of his way of doing things. But I had to agree when he said that a drunken man with a cold in his nose and his head jammed up a pig's arse could have walked straight to Greenland Dock from Dover without inquiring the way of anybody.' Jim nodded his head judiciously. 'It was a smelly place,' he added.

'It must be a big responsibility,' Arthur said, 'being Captain of an East Indiaman.'

'You're right, there.' Jim made his backside comfortable against the fife rail so as to indulge in the pleasures of memory with added luxury. 'We came back from China with sugar and all the spices you could put a name to, and waited in t' Downs for the tide into London. The Captain, who'd had more thirteen-gun salutes and guards of honour than you've had hot dinners, was wining and dining the Revenue officers in his cabin, while his contraband was being safely stowed into the luggers . . .'

Something in Arthur's face must have shown that he found these last details incredible. Jim reached inside his shirt front and would have pulled out the jet cross suspended there, but Arthur nodded his head energetically to show that he'd thought better of it and accepted every word.

'Then those Deal luggers,' continued Jim, 'made off and told the nearest French privateer of the fat prize that was waiting for them. We just to say got off with the tide.'

Arthur was so dumbfounded by this additional piece of news that he found it quite impossible to compose his features into any show of ready belief. Jim undoubtedly would have reproduced his jet cross, in order to testify to the truth of every word he uttered, but Mr Beaufort appeared from nowhere beside the after hatch and bawled another order. Jim leaped as if the fife rail had bitten a piece out of his hindquarters, and hurried forward to clew up the foresail. Other duties supervened, and Arthur didn't see the line-manager again until they returned to their berth for the night.

Jim sat on the lower bunk and pulled off his stockings. 'Any family history in t' fishery?' he asked.

'On our mam's side,' Arthur said, wishing he could produce the narwhal walking stick from its stand next to the door in Ellerby Lane. 'On our mam's side they went to Spitzbergen in the old days.'

Jim was trying to wiggle his bare toes. 'I'm pleased to hear it. It's much better if it's in your blood.' The attempt to wiggle his toes seemed to give him much pleasure, although there was little movement to illustrate it. Several toes were missing entirely and the remainder were without their ends. 'Look here.' He dipped inside his shirt and withdrew the cross. 'This was made from a piece of jet that my great-great-grandfayther picked up on t' beach under the west cliff. He wore it, and my great-grand-fayther, and my grandfayther, and my fayther, and they all died at home despite going every year to the fishery. All except my grandfayther.'

'What happened to him?'

'He was killed by what every man fears. A fish's tail came down on t' boat. And d' you know why?' Jim held the cross in the palm of his hand, in a way that showed he was used to holding it there. 'They found this crucifix in his sea chest afterwards with his other things. If he'd been wearing it that fish's tail wouldn't have touched him.' He pushed the cross back inside his shirt.

'Any other family?'

'I've an older brother, Edward.'

'What's he do?'

'He always wanted to go to the fishery. But about the time he was old enough the *Aimwell* was lost at Greenland. The next year was the last time the *Valiant* and *James* were sent to the fishery, and the *Volunteer* was sold to Hull.'

'Wonderful old ship, the *Volunteer*,' Jim said. 'I was a green-man under Captain Dawson in 1811 when she killed twenty-three fish. And she was over fifty year old even then.'

'Then the year after that the *Lively* was lost at Greenland and the *Esk* – '

Jim did his imitation of a man bothered by flies, but his expression showed that this time they were a species that carried a painful sting. 'She was off Redcar and in sight of home. I went to hear young Scoresby preach the sermon in St Mary's.'

'Anyway,' resumed Arthur, 'the prospects of work in the fishery seemed very bad at that time. There weren't any new ships being laid down for it, and even Fishburn and Brodrick weren't doing anything. We thought – at least Edward and our dad did – that it would be best if he went somewhere else. Our mam nearly went mad.' He shook his head at the memory of it. 'But once our Edward had made his mind up to go, he thought he might as well make a proper job of it and he went to America.'

Jim Richardson took this news very gravely indeed. 'America, you say! Now I can tell you about America, no man better.' He made himself comfortable against the wooden post at the end of the bunk, to indicate that he was prepared to devote the time to this matter which its importance merited. 'When I had lodgings in Mile End and used to go down to Wapping, I often came across Yankee whalers in the pubs around Tower Hill. A rare mixture they are, I can tell you. You can't even imagine it, because you're part of a crew that all come from the same town, all speaking the same kind of language, all sharing the same patch of sea and sky, all from t' same side of moors. We're a kind of community, if you know what I mean. But the crew of a Yankee whaler comes from all over. Portugee Mates from the Cape Verde Islands, mainly. And then the rest – Indians from the prairies, Kanakas from the South Seas, longshoremen that are black, brown, red and yellow as well as white all crammed together in a fo'c's'le stinking of rye whisky and molasses. No, you can't imagine it.'

'Our Edward always got on well with different people.'

Jim guffawed. 'It'll be a stiff test for him, for all that.'

'What were they like to talk to?'

'Swaggering bastards! They talked about naught but how many times they'd had their legs over the lasses in Wapping and Poplar and how big the fishes are in t' southern fishery. You know they catch the sperm whales or cachalots or whatever you want to call them. Some folk call them pot fish because of the pot of spermaceti they carry around in their heads. But mind you, if we took care to cut the fat properly, and boiled it up quick instead of bringing it home, I reckon the oil of our Greenland fish would be just as good. Maybe better.'

'But it must have been interesting to listen to them?'

'Naw, naw. They were full of tall tales that go round the fo'c's'les in all the American whalers. There was a story about a fish that gnashed its teeth and attacked a ship – what was she called? The *Essex*? – and stove her bows in so that she sank. And there was a whole collection of stories about a big fish that was white all ower, either from old age or some trick o' nature. They'd even given the fish a name – Mocha Dick, I remember – and they said he was so fierce he chased ships' boats back to the davits.

They said somebody ought to write a book about him. I told them it would have to be a Yankee because nobody else would be a big enough liar.'

Jim laughed at the memory of this verbal masterstroke, and Arthur joined in as duty required.

'All their stories,' Jim continued, 'were to let you know what a vicious monster their pot fish is, and how brave the Yankees must be to go into t' same sea with him. And they all said what nice, kindly animals our Greenland fishes are, what with having whalebone instead of teeth an' all.'

'Perhaps there's something in what they say.'

Jim did a spirited imitation of the man sweeping flies away. 'You listen to me. Those pot fish, teeth or no teeth, are so timid that when they see the boats coming they shit ambergris. The Yankee whalers find it floating everywhere after a lowering. And if those Yankees heard a Greenland fish bring its tail down two miles away, they'd jump straight out of their boats. Then you'd find a lot of stuff floating about that's twice as smelly as ambergris but a damn sight less valuable.'

'They build good ships over there,' Arthur said, discovering in himself a wish to find something good in the old colony, if only for his brother's sake. 'That's one of the things our dad was always telling our Edward when he was trying to decide what to do.'

'What made him say that?'

'Think of the old *Truelove* of Hull. Our dad told us all about her. She was a privateer against British shipping. Then she was captured and used for general cargoes. Then she worked the wine trade and was chased by the French during the war with Napoleon. But before any of that she was built in America as a merchant. In America! think of that! And yet now she's strengthened for the ice and everyone says she's the luckiest ship in t' fishery. My dad says everyone in Hull wants to sail on her.'

Jim swatted another invisible fly with contemptuous ease. 'Luck! Don't talk to me of lucky ships.' He pulled the jet cross out again and held it in the palm of his hand. 'I don't care what ship I'm on as long as this hangs round my neck. My grandfayther didn't know it but I do. And this is where it stays, day and night. I don't have any need of luck, as long as I don't take this off.'

Having delivered himself of this sentiment with deep feeling, Jim hauled himself up to the top bunk with the conviction that he'd scouted any claims the Yankees might have to be builders of ships.

9

Any apprentice from Whitby, or from the dockland areas of King's Lynn, Hull, Shields, Newcastle, Dundee, Aberdeen or Peterhead, knew that all ships bound for the northern fishery put in at the Orkneys or the Shetlands to make up their crews. And an apprentice with anything about him would know the reason.

A ship fitted out for the fishery was entitled to a bounty, and could import the produce of its catch under favourable terms, provided it had conformed with a number of regulations set down by Acts of Parliament. A licence to proceed to the fishery in the expectation of enjoying these benefits was granted by the Commissioners of His Majesty's Customs, but only after they'd visited the ship before it left port and satisfied themselves that all the legal requirements had been met.

One of the most important of these requirements was that the number and classifications of the men making up the crew must be of a certain standard. For example, a ship of three hundred tons burthen and upward, such as the *William Scoresby Senior*, had to carry six harpooners, six boat-steerers, six line-managers, ten sea-men, six green-men and six apprentices, to give a total of forty-two men including the master and surgeon.

Harpooners, boat-steerers and line-managers employed in the fishery couldn't be impressed for service in warships; and more limited protection was given to sea-men or common mariners employed in the same fishery. They carried certificates at all times to protect themselves from the press gang, whether they were going to or returning from the fishery, or were employed in some quite different business outside the season.

This isn't to say that such certificates were always respected by the press gangs and naval officers. Unhappy incidents occurred, frequently violent and tragic ones, and sometimes Greenlanders were taken from their returning ships within sight of their waiting and weeping families.

For these and other reasons it was often difficult, particularly during the wars against France, to make up the full complement of men at the clearing port. Consequently a legal privilege was offered under which ships bound for the northern fishery could put in at certain Scottish ports to make up their crews, provided they didn't take on more than three men for every fifty tons' burthen.

After the defeat of Napoleon and the return of peace it would in most cases have again been possible to take up the full legal complement of men in the clearing ports. It was decided, however, that it would be unjust suddenly to withdraw opportunities for employment from men in outlying and neglected parts of the kingdom who'd given their services when they were needed. The hardy, hungry youths of Shetland and Orkney had made it possible to continue the fishery during the French wars, and so it was decided by the authorities that these good men should be rewarded and kept in their employment when the wars were over.

The legal privilege was therefore extended so that ships could make up their crews just as they had during the war. This extension of the law met with less resistance than it otherwise might have done from the ship owners, and others who had a financial interest in their operation, because the hardy and hungry youths of the northern islands could be hired for lower wages than the youths at home.

The news this season was that most ships were putting into Stromness in Orkney and then going directly to Davis Strait. But the *William Scoresby Senior*, followed by the *Lady Clifford* of Hull, was going in to make up her crew at Lerwick in Shetland and then sail for the Greenland Sea.

Arthur Storm had heard Lerwick mentioned many times. Indeed it was referred to as often as any neighbouring village or the market towns on the other side of the moors. When he was a child he used to hear the name by accident, or so it seemed, and always in lowered tones when there was mixed company. When he was older, and especially when he met youths older than himself who swapped stories in the Seven Stars and the Jolly Butchers in Brewster Lane, he discovered that the mere mention of the town was sufficient to cause laughter and references to obscure jokes and anecdotes.

Lerwick was a part of the life of every man who'd been to the fishery, or at least of all the older men. Some of the younger men had been only to the newer fishery in Davis Strait, for which the crews were usually completed in Orkney. They tried to talk about Stromness in the same way that the more experienced had always talked of Lerwick. But even these latecomers knew all about Lerwick by hearsay, and they had to admit (if only to themselves) that Stromness had only a reflected or upstart glory – if glory were the proper word to use. Lerwick was a shared experience which caused knowing smiles or frowns of disapproval wherever men talked together about the northern fishery. The name itself, *Lerwick*, made Arthur's heart beat faster.

The harbour was alive with small boats, many of which made for the *William Scoresby Senior* and accosted her before she'd dropped her anchors. The nearest boatmen held up their wares, extolling the virtues of their fish and eggs which they offered to barter for salt beef and pork. Mr Beaufort appeared on the quarter deck wearing a white frilled shirt, and told them sharply to take their custom elsewhere. Most of the boats pulled away towards the *Lady Clifford* which now appeared at the harbour mouth, or returned to other ships already at anchor. A few of the islanders remained, waving their goods and shouting.

Mr Nellis, the Specksioneer, went to the ship's side and bellowed at them with his tremendous voice. 'Is that all you've got for us? Stinking fish and rotten eggs? It's fresh meat I'm interested in.'

One of the islanders rested on his oar and waved towards the town. 'Ye'll have tae gae ashore if it's red meat ye're after. It's in the usual place.'

The other men in the boat laughed.

'And the fresh meat that he's talking about,' said Jim Richardson, 'stinks more than any fish.'

The islander who'd shouted the advice to Mr Nellis was now backing it up with a one-man pantomime. Its obscenity and vigour were no doubt intended to illustrate the Specksioneer's probable course of action as soon as he was ashore. The men in the other boats joined in the laughter. They all seemed to be familiar with Mr Nellis's habits.

The *William Scoresby Senior* hove to in Bressay Sound and immediately there was much to be done.

Mr Beaufort sent men aloft to remove the streamers and souvenirs from the yards and rigging, and had to intervene when jealousy over the possession of a keepsake was about to lead to fighting. The blue ribbon that Arthur had tied with such tenderness to the top yard lift had blown away, and he watched with a sense of defeat while Mr Nellis recovered the bedraggled pantaloons trimmed with cheap lace.

The lodberries, or landing stages at the south end of the harbour, were crowded by crofters' sons from all the islands between Unst and Fair Isle. For them this was the only possible escape from a crushing poverty made worse by tithes and rack-renting landlords. For some it was their first time away from their home island. They gawped at the big ships and craned their necks to look up at the topgallants and royal sails.

Mr Beaufort had himself rowed ashore in one of the ship's boats, and the crowd made way for him with elaborate displays of respect. They followed him to the Custom House, deference and eagerness waging a hurtful battle inside each hungry man, and the strongest were signed on. Mr Beaufort paid over the bounties which bound them to serve on the *William Scoresby Senior* and told them when they had to be aboard. Those of the chosen few who lived nearby went home to tell their families, receive congratulations and collect their sea chests. The rest of the lucky ones, who'd brought their chests with them or at least a bag containing their belongings, went directly to the nearest public houses. Here their sole intent was to drink themselves into such a state of oblivion, that the only items still floating in their brains would be the name of the ship and the time they had to present themselves on deck.

Arthur was in a gang under the instructions of Mr Dryden, told off to trim the ship and complete its ballast by filling the empty casks with water. Many of the casks had been used in previous seasons, and the fresh water revived the stench of the long-dead whales. The labour was heavy, and he was glad when the time came for retiring to his berth.

The following morning Arthur learned that he was one of a party that had been given leave to go ashore.

'Are you going?' asked Jim Richardson.

'Of course I am.'

'Do you know what it'll be like?'

The question irritated him. 'That's why I'm going. To find out.'

Jim looked as if he were about to say more. But he thought better of it and went away to find Mr Dryden. There was a purposeful air about him when he returned.

'I'm going with you,' he said.

The shore party, laughing and joking like boys let out of school, filled two of the ship's boats. In the morning light the town was a sober, dignified place. The stone houses had their backs to the waterside, as if to show they didn't want to be disturbed by anything arriving from that quarter. Fort Charlotte, away to their left, nodded over the dreaming streets and the still water in the harbour with a sleepy vigilance. Dark hills enclosed a sombre, silent scene in which the voices of the Greenlanders sounded like sparrows chirruping in a cathedral.

They hadn't been ashore more than a couple of minutes before Arthur's first impression of the town began to change.

In Commercial Street they met a party from the *Lady Clifford*, still drunk from the preceding night and with their clothes only half on. They were singing tunelessly and mournfully as they made their circuitous way back to the quayside. The opposing parties greeted each other, the one fresh and anticipatory, the other weary and sated.

'Now you Hull whoremasters,' shouted Mr Nellis. 'Have you left us any fish?'

A seaman with a droll, handsome face, who seemed to be acquainted with Mr Nellis, swayed forward to make himself the spokesman for the *Lady Clifford*. 'There's a few still to be flensed. But they've all got big holes in their tails.'

'All the better, James. No need to cut new ones before you reeve them.'

'That's true,' the seaman replied doubtfully. 'But the one I was fast to had been hauled too far and too often by too many for there to be any sport in it.'

'Are they still floating,' asked Mr Nellis, 'or have you let them sink?'

'When we left them they were on their backs.'

'With their bellies up?'

'Just ask for Blackie,' advised James, the man with the droll face. 'She'll work her way through your muster list, examine all credentials, and certify every man that's fit for the fishery. And once she – '

'Blackie!' yelled Mr Nellis in a near paroxysm. 'Blackie! Is she still swimming in these waters?'

'As strongly as she ever did,' the seaman called over his shoulder as he lurched away. 'When she fans her tail you'd best back oars and stern hard, in case she splits you with one of her flukes.'

Mr Nellis roared with laughter. 'Not me, James. I'm carvel-built and soon repaired for another lowering.'

The two parties had by now passed each other. The men from the *Lady Clifford* staggered down to the lodberries and those from the *William Scoresby Senior* advanced with even higher spirits.

'James Tickelpenny,' said Mr Nellis, ruminating. 'What a lad he is. Ran off and married a gentleman's daughter from Louth. But still goes to the fishery every year for the sake of a day in Lerwick.'

One of the green-men came up beside him. 'You know this Blackie, Mr Nellis?'

'Know her! I've seen her every season since I was a lad, except for the years when we went to Davis Strait. If I had a penny for every time I've had my hook into her cant-piece, I'd be living in one of those big houses in Bagdale with all the steps.'

'Does she let you keep it in, Mr Nellis?' asked another of the green-men, with a sly grin.

'You've only got to touch her with the tip of your iron and she takes it all in right up to the end of the shank. You can twist any way you want but she keeps you fast by the withers. Then when she sounds she takes all the lines out of your boat, and out of as many other boats as are able to follow.'

'She sounds like a good runner, Mr Nellis.'

'That she is! God bless her! And at the end she goes into her flurry and dies like a good 'un.'

The shore party from the *William Scoresby Senior* continued up the narrow street with loud whoops of laughter. Greenlanders from an Aberdeen ship and local girls were dancing round the Market Cross, and some of the men were inclined to linger. Mr Nellis urged them forward with assurances of better and more certain pleasures. They passed rows of dilapidated, stone-built houses. Sometimes a door was wrenched open from within and a man came out to shake his fist at them; and sometimes a window was thrown up and a woman screeched imprecations. The Greenlanders responded with invitations to come out and fight and volleys of abuse.

An old woman with long grey hair came out into the road and screamed. 'Leave our lasses alone, ye filthy English pigs!'

'Don't be jealous, grandma,' Mr Nellis bellowed, holding his forearm erect and balling his fist into a phallic knob. 'You got your share in t' days of Spitzbergen.'

This exchange drew delighted laughter from the shore party. The Specksioneer took them under a dark archway, across a small yard and along an alley with high, stone walls. They came to a door with well-worn steps and a knocker that was much too large for it.

Mr Nellis ignored the knocker, kicked open the door and led the way inside. The rest followed him into a long, dark corridor, but Arthur's attention was caught by the knocker and he paused for a few seconds on the threshold.

The knocker was made of cast iron, and presented a realistic picture of that moment in the fishery which honest men said struck fear into even the bravest heart. It showed a fish's tail, pointing at the sky with extended flukes, at the moment of its greatest elevation just before it started to come down. Iron letters encircled the iron picture with the traditional maxim: *A Dead Fish or a Stove Boat*.

'There's no need to bother with that,' Jim Richardson said. 'This is a door that's always open.'

They followed the others along the dim corridor into a low room at the end of it.

63

10

Captain Stapleton, as had been his custom for many years, gave his instructions directly instead of through his officers when it came to the building of the crow's nest. He personally supervised the carpenter, nodding his large, grey head, as he examined the wooden laths, and he helped to fix the canvas cover himself. Only after rolling it about, banging the sides and sitting in it for several minutes with his telescope, did he give permission for the structure to be taken away. It was now ready for lifting to its place at the masthead above the main crosstree.

And with the ballast completed, the fresh water tanks filled and the Shetlanders selected, Captain Stapleton could relax with his senior officers for the last time before they sailed for the Greenland Sea. There were three of them with him in the cabin: Mr Beaufort, the First Mate; Mr Dryden, the Second Mate; and young Mr McCabe, the Surgeon. Mr Nellis, the Specksioneer, had asked leave to go with a shore party as he always did. He'd be useless for twenty-four hours after his return. But that was the way it was, and Mr Nellis knew his trade.

The stove had made the cabin warm and partly for this reason, partly in readiness for pipes being brought out, the window was open wide. The dirty dishes had been taken away by the steward. On the table were a polished wooden bowl of pippins, a board of white and crumbly Wensleydale, and tulip-shaped glasses. Mr Beaufort, lounging in his chair with his velvet jacket unbuttoned, was so amazed by what the Second Mate had said that he was sitting transfixed with his hand on the neck of the decanter.

It was Mr Beaufort himself who had caused the post-prandial conversation to take a slightly contentious turn. He'd just spilled some port down the front of the new shirt that he'd had made in York, and doubtless this had affected his temper.

'We're hoping to catch some size fish, Mr McCabe,' he said, dabbing irritably at the white silk shirt with his napkin. 'But I don't suppose you'll worry much about that so long as you get home with some good stories.'

Mr McCabe turned slightly red and tried to protest, but the First Mate continued with his observations.

'Yes, Mr McCabe. I can see you now with a nice, comfortable practice in Scarborough or Harrogate. And young ladies stepping from their carriages and pulling t' bell and begging you to look down their little pink throats, just so as to be touched by a man who used to catch fish that weighed seventy tons – no, a thousand tons apiece.'

The puckered flesh encroached upon Captain Stapleton's eyes as he smiled. Old William Scoresby, when he was in command of the *Henrietta* and earning £2,000 per annum for her Pickering owners, had been the first to bring in medical students from Edinburgh as full-time surgeons. Some of the traditional officers were still unable to overcome their suspicion that the young men came for a bit of adventure before they settled down to a humdrum existence.

'I assure you, gentlemen,' said Mr McCabe, pushing his spectacles up on his nose and by now very red, 'I am as anxious as yourselves for the success of this voyage.' He turned somewhat timidly to Captain Stapleton. 'I do promise you, sir, that you can include me with your other officers in that respect.'

'Thank you, Mr McCabe, I'm sure I can. And yet I think that perhaps we all have our own slightly different reasons for going to the fishery.' Captain Stapleton's white beard pointed interrogatively around the table, like a wandering needle in a compass, until it settled upon his Second Mate. 'What do you say, Mr Dryden? Tell us why you go to the fishery.'

The Second Mate had cut one of the apples into four exactly equal portions. As he replied he removed the core segments with precise movements of his knife.

'My view of the matter is a simple one, Captain Stapleton. When God sent our first parents out of the garden, where all things grew and prospered of their own accord, he told them that they and their children would have to work for their bread in future. That's the way it is with all of us, and for my part I'm glad of it. Neither of the Scoresbys fished on a Sunday, but with God's help they made up for it during the rest of the week. When I'm working I know that I'm fulfilling my purpose. The better I do my work the closer I come to fulfilling that purpose completely. It's not a matter of faith only, but of common experience that's available to every man. If I do my job in t' fishery as well as

I possibly can, then I'm a happy man and I know I'm happy. If I skimped it, or did it less well than I knew I could, then I'd not be fulfilling my purpose and I'd be wretched. The only other thing I can add is that I'm grateful to be in a job that lets me fulfil that purpose so completely.'

Mr Dryden popped one of the meticulously prepared apple segments into his mouth, and his long moustaches diverged and subsided slightly as he chewed it. Mr Beaufort, who'd been intending to pour himself another glass of port, had paused with his hand on the neck of the decanter and was staring at Mr Dryden as if he couldn't believe his ears.

'Do you hope we come home full?' he asked, and his voice was high and querulous.

'Of course I do. But if we come home clean, and we've done our job properly, we shouldn't grieve.'

Captain Stapleton looked from one Mate to the other. 'Not your sentiments, Mr Beaufort?'

'I can't think of anything less like them.' Mr Beaufort recovered from his stupefaction sufficiently to pour himself another drink. 'When God put our parents out of the garden – if you want to think of it that way – it was a punishment. To have to earn your bread by the sweat of your brow is a curse and not a blessing. All men prefer leisure to work. Ordinary common sense tells you that. The only reason we work in t' fishery is so that we can have money in our pockets when we're not there. When I see a size fish the only thing I'm concerned about is the guinea I'll get for killing him. And I'm sure Mr Nellis would say the same if he was here. Except, of course,' he added, taking a snuff box carved from walrus ivory out of his waistcoat pocket, 'that he gets half a guinea.'

'So you'd say that good work isn't good in itself,' Captain Stapleton said, 'but only as a means to something good.'

Mr Beaufort thumbed snuff into his right nostril. 'Work is never good. If you could convince me, Captain, that shoddy work and idleness would catch more fish, I'd never span another harpoon.'

Captain Stapleton nodded appreciatively. This turn in the conversation seemed to delight him. He took the decanter and without even looking at it pushed it on its wide, flat base towards

Mr McCabe. The Surgeon was poking at crumbs of cheese on his plate, and examining them on the ends of his fingers.

'Perhaps, Mr McCabe, you're not yet of an age when you'll have developed any views on these matters?'

The Surgeon hastily wiped his finger ends in his napkin and looked up. His eyes were timid but intent behind the spectacles. 'Indeed I have, Captain Stapleton.'

'Let's hear them, Mr McCabe.'

'It's my belief, sir,' he said, with great diffidence, but speaking with more force as he warmed to his theme, 'that the abiding passion of all men is a desire to understand things. At its lowest it's a simple curiosity about how things work and at its highest it's the intellectual craving of philosophy. I'm sure it's also true, as Mr Beaufort has implied, that men are lazy by nature. How fortunate, therefore, that necessity obliges us to work, because by working we lay hold upon some small part of the mystery of things. It doesn't matter what work a man does. It doesn't matter how menial it is. Even a man who has to break stones all day has a key to one of the many doors that lead to knowledge. I'm thankful I have the job I have, like Mr Dryden, because it helps me to understand the greatest mystery of all.'

Mr McCabe had an uneasy sensation that he shouldn't have revealed his ideas so frankly, and tried to cover his embarrassment by sipping from his empty glass.

Mr Beaufort turned on him again. 'So you think acquiring knowledge for its own sake has some special merit? I tell you it's naught but self-indulgence. I was a boy on the *Esk* when it was commanded by Captain Scoresby Junior, and I saw some of his experiments with ice lenses and water pressures and magnetism and the insides of animals . . .' Mr Beaufort waved his snuff box in the air to show that there were dozens of other equally abstruse subjects that he could add to the list if required. 'I dare say he wrote learned papers that stood him well with grand folk in London – and even in Edinburgh, the Athens of the North as some wag called it.' He snorted with laughter and savoured the joke for a moment. 'It's my conviction that if William Scoresby Junior had so much spare time while he was afloat he should have been trying to discover how to come across a run of fish.'

Mr McCabe might have responded; but he'd poured himself a

little more port and gulping it quickly had brought on a fit of coughing. His plight worsened when Mr Dryden lit his pipe, because the thick smoke had to make its way around his head on its way to the open window. He coughed until his spectacles slid half-way down his nose.

'You can say what you like about the Scoresbys,' Mr Dryden said, puffing contentedly and quite unaware of the distress he was causing. 'They were the most successful whaling family of them all. And I'm not forgetting about the Sadlers of Hull nor the Grays of Peterhead.'

Mr Beaufort replenished his glass. 'The Grays are still fishing,' he said, not wishing to concede the point entirely.

The flat-bottomed decanter arrived once more at the head of the table. Captain Stapleton was oblivious of its renewed presence.

'We all go to t' fishery for different reasons,' he said, 'and for different reasons we all think the necessity of going is good for us. And yet perhaps the necessity is good in another way that we don't think of.' He looked round the table and their faces regarded him. 'If men weren't obliged to work they wouldn't live in a new Garden of Eden. On the contrary, it's my belief that we would live in a state of barbarism and chaos. It's the necessity of work that makes us see that we're dependent on each other. It's the outward sign of something inside us, and the necessity of working should teach us all this great truth. We need each other because we need to work, but we might grow to see that we need each other anyway. Work is perhaps only a device for making us act as if we were more civilized than we really are. It makes us assume a grace that we haven't yet deserved.'

Captain Stapleton became aware of the decanter. He gazed at it for some seconds, apparently without comprehension, and then passed it on.

'I'm sure,' he continued, 'that your average Greenlander enjoys doing a good job like Mr Dryden, and he looks forward to his six pennies a fish as Mr Beaufort says. And I know that the fishery gives most of our men the best view they'll ever have of the mystery of this world, such as Mr McCabe approves of. But more than all that, the fishery teaches us to stop living as individuals in a herd and to become members of a true community.'

The cabin had remained warm despite the open window. Faint sounds of revelry, laced by the melody of a violin, reached them from the town across the still waters of Bressay Sound. The clear, white light from the suspended lamp illuminated the faces of the men in the cabin: Captain Stapleton, with his wrinkled eye-lids, looked at each man in turn; Mr Beaufort, his glass full once more and his eyes half closed, roused himself to take some more snuff; Mr McCabe, excited and a little nervous at what lay ahead, polished his spectacles and cut himself an experimental piece of cheese; and Mr Dryden – his face expressed the simple faith of a man driven by a single purpose. Captain Stapleton would recall that expression four years from now and remember it with pain.

II

The smell struck Arthur across the face like an open hand.

'What is it?' he gasped.

Jim Richardson screwed up his face. 'You keep close to me.'

The room was fairly large although it was low; yet it seemed smaller than it really was because of the crowd already in it, which was now further compressed by the influx from the *William Scoresby Senior*. In one corner a peat fire was smouldering on the mud floor. Its thick, blue fumes lay under the low ceiling like swathes of fog, and drifted slowly towards the cracks around the ill-fitting door.

At the other end of the room a woman was sitting on a table with her legs crossed. She was wearing a hessian skirt, that looked as if it could have been made from one of the sacks the alum factories used to dispatch their products for shipment. A short black pipe was stuck in her mouth, and she was sucking at it with evident enjoyment.

'What's the smell?' asked Arthur.

Jim was sarcastic. 'Which smell?'

The smell that had struck Arthur when he first entered the room was everywhere. It lay in the joints between the stones in the walls and the cracks in the wooden roof like a ghastly, invisible cement. He could feel it clouding his eyeballs, coating his teeth and tongue, furring the insides of his nose and ears and crusting each individual hair on his head. We shall all smell differently when we leave this room, and the smell will stay with us for ever.

And yet Jim was right to ask which smell he meant, because he realized that there was a mixture of them, some more pungent than others.

The walls and ceiling were blackened by the peat fire, and his throat and lungs had filled with its acrid smoke. But there was something more dreadful overlying it. His eyes prickled and watered. He coughed, inhaled again more sharply, and coughed with increased violence. The woman sitting on the table looked at him across the smoke-filled room.

'Puir wee boy!' she said, taking the black pipe out of her mouth. 'Gie him something tae wash his throat.'

Mr Nellis must have been pushing his way through the crowd, because it was now that he burst into view next to the table on which the woman was sitting.

'Blackie!' he said, his voice thick, leaning forward and putting his hand on her fleshy thigh. 'My own Blackie, that I never stop thinking about.'

She pushed his hand away. 'So ye're back again, Nellie? Dunnerin' brass and clatterin' cymbal.'

'Blackie! We had to make up crews at Stromness last year and the year before. I was missing you all the time.'

'As impudent as a gannet and twice as greedy.'

'Only for my favourite fish, Blackie! Only because it's so long since I've seen you.'

'Like the gannets of Herma Ness,' she continued. 'Noisiest on the nest.'

'Blackie!'

She returned the pipe to her mouth, sucked until her cheeks hollowed, and blew a cloud of tobacco smoke into his face.

An old woman, with skin as yellow and wrinkled as ancient parchment, put a glass in Arthur's hand. He raised it against the uncertain light of a lamp that hung from the low ceiling. A muddy liquid was visible inside.

'Whisky,' she wheezed at him. 'The best whisky in the islands.'

He gave her some money, was overwhelmed with confusion when she cawed for more and hurriedly gave her twice as much as she'd demanded. The whisky smelled of peat. That meant little enough in a room where everything seemed to be flavoured by the smoke from the peat fire. He sipped the liquor carefully. It was rough and fiery, and rasped his throat. He coughed again and his eyes watered afresh.

Mr Nellis had managed to ingratiate a portion of his ample backside on to the table beside the woman. She continued to sit with her legs crossed, sucking at the short, black pipe, and from time to time blowing smoke into the Specksioneer's face. This behaviour appeared to increase Mr Nellis's ardour. He snuffed up every exhalation, returned his hand to her thigh, and finding that this time he wasn't repulsed he pushed it under her petticoats.

'Do you still want to know what the smell is?' asked Jim Richardson.

'Yes, but there's so many of them.'

'I'll tell you the name of the main one. It's the smell of corruption.'

The woman sitting on the table was laughing, and she pushed her greasy, black hair away from her sweating face. Her eyes were very large and very bright, glowing like lamps in the dark alcoves below her forehead. Sometimes she laughed with the pipe clenched between her teeth; and sometimes her hilarity reached such a peak that she had to remove the pipe from her mouth, and then she threw back her head and shouted her glee at the begrimed ceiling.

Arthur looked up, too, as if he expected to discover the source of her amusement. He saw the suspended lamp, which contained a sickly flame that threw its flickering light across the ceiling, the walls and the ranks of white faces. And now he realized that the lamp was where the smell came from. Not all the smells, but the smell that had hit him when he first entered the room.

The room was filled with the smells of whisky and tobacco, of peat and clay, of men and women, of damp stones and rotten wood, which wrestled with each other for a minor predominance. But the smell from the lamp was the clear victor and would remain so for as long as its sickly flame was alight. It was the stench of *kreng*, bits of whale's flesh, floating in dregs of oil that anyone else would have thrown away even if it had been filtered. It was the smell of putrefaction and death. It was the smell of corruption, although he guessed that Jim Richardson had meant something else when he used the word.

Arthur lowered his gaze. The woman's big, dark eyes were shining like beacons in her shadowed face; like harbour lights, he thought, when they are first glimpsed by a ship coming home through a low-lying fog. She knocked Mr Nellis's exploring hands away from the folds of her crumpled petticoat and prepared to stand up on the table. There were groans of pleasure from those nearby when she bent her legs and they had a glimpse of parts that had been hidden by her hessian skirt. When she was upright Mr Nellis kept a hand on her ankle in the pretence that this was needed to steady her. She was of less than average height, and her slight plumpness gave to her rounded form an appearance of overflowing health and vitality. When she spoke her voice had a hard edge to it that showed she was used to command. The voice contrasted oddly with the softness of her figure.

'Fair guid day tae ye all from the *Lady Clifford*,' she announced.

Mr Nellis interrupted and pulled at her leg until she bent down to listen to him.

'From the *William Scoresby*,' she amended. 'I hope ye enjoy yeurselves and that we'll see ye again next year. If ye don't find what ye're leuking for it's yeur ain fault. Awa noo! Let's hae some music and let's hae some mair drinks!'

A skinny old man, previously invisible in a murky corner, came out into the yellow light from the lamp and tucked a fiddle under his chin. At the first stroke of his bow men and youths rushed forward to help Blackie from the table. But Mr Nellis was there before them and he lifted her clear and lowered her to the floor.

'Come on, Blackie!' he yelled, throwing his brawny arms round her. 'Now I'm fast and won't be shaken off.'

The fiddler was playing a wild and lilting melody. Under the stress of the music he wagged his head from side to side and the grey skin of his old face became suffused with blood. This redness brought to life a livid scar which traced its jagged course from the corner of one eye to the side of his working mouth. Mr Nellis, with Blackie in his arms, careened about the room and knocked people aside with every step.

'Where's your jack?' one of the boatmen called. 'Show your jack if you're fast.'

'My jack is up, sailor. Even if you can't see it, she can feel it.'

Mr Nellis continued to dance her around the floor in his own fashion. His big face was shiny with happiness and his red hair was plastered to his head with sweat.

'My lance is ready,' he bawled. 'Give me a few minutes, lads. A few thrusts at her vital parts and I'll put her in her flurry.'

With a sudden twist she freed herself from his arms and skipped to the other side of the room. Someone held out a drink for her which she took and swallowed at a gulp.

'The fish is loose!' yelled a boatman.

Others took up the cry. 'A loose fish! A loose fish! A loose fish!'

Her eyes sparkled with mischief and amusement as she scanned the men who almost encircled her. She seized on one of the green-men and pulled him to a clear space on the floor. The shouting became louder.

'Watch out for flukes, sailor!'

'She's got the biggest tail in t' fishery.'

'Mind you're not underneath when she fans it!'

She whirled her new partner away to the sound of the music. The melody of the fiddle was everywhere, in the wooden roof, the stone walls and the clay floor. The men clapped, stamped and shouted. Mr Nellis staggered after the dancing couple, but other people had started to dance and the room was packed too tightly for pursuit.

All the women, whatever their age or appearance, quickly found partners and joined the scrimmage on the crowded floor. The slowly drifting smoke from the peat fire lay across the room in streamers, and tailed around the gyrating couples like some insubstantial kind of clothing. The wailing of the fiddle grew louder and more abandoned.

Arthur looked at the scene with bloodshot eyes. The cavorting figures, the raucous voices, the swirling smoke, the smells and the strangeness of the music all combined to overwhelm him with a sense of unreality.

'Wad ye like some mair whisky, sir?'

Nobody had called him *sir* before and he blushed scarlet. The woman was already filling his glass, and would have topped it up to the brim if he hadn't snatched it away from her jug. Some of the liquor went on the floor.

'What are ye doing?' she demanded, and it horrified him to see the temper in her face.

'I'll pay for what's spilled,' he said.

She stated the price. If he'd been anywhere else he would have argued, but in his haste to have done with her he dropped an additional coin on the floor. He bent down and actually had the coin in his fingers when her foot descended on his hand, and pressed it painfully to the ground with the heel of her shoe.

'I wis the first tae see it,' she said, 'but ye wadna expect a lady tae bend doon and pick it up. Wad ye, sir?'

He tried to remove his hand, but she pressed upon it more tightly.

'Ye wadna expect it of a lady, wad ye, sir? Not a southern gentleman like ye, sir?'

He shook his head.

She raised her foot slowly. 'I put ye on yeur honour as a gentleman,' she said.

He took the coin in his bruised fingers, straightened up and gave her the money. She snatched it, gave him a mocking curtsy and was lost in the crowd.

'She robbed you twice in less than a minute,' Jim said, 'but she's no worse than any of t' others in this place.'

Arthur sipped his drink. 'But they're so poor. The start of the season must be the only bright spot in t' year for the folk who live in these parts.'

'That doesn't mean they're not thieves and worse.'

Arthur swallowed another mouthful and discovered that the whisky no longer burned his throat. Use was making it smoother. What had previously been the stink of peat was now a pleasant aroma. A profound feeling of contentment began to emanate from somewhere in his stomach. What if these people were thieves? They couldn't help it. He liked them.

Blackie was still with her partner in the middle of the floor. Largely as a result of her own exertions in swinging him round and round with herself at the centre, the couple had cleared an empty space for themselves. She swung him faster and faster, pirouetting on the tips of her toes. The sailor was circling so rapidly that he was tripping over his own feet.

'Use your rudder!'

'Furl courses and reef topsails!'

'His yards are jammed.'

'All you can do is pray, sailor.'

Faster, even faster they went, and after a couple more turns she gave him a tremendous spin and let go. Everybody had stood still to watch, laughing, clapping and shouting advice. He turned like a top for a while, sagged at the knees, straightened up again, floundered two or three steps and finally toppled sideways into the appreciative audience.

'She's the worst of them all,' Jim said. 'Her name is a byword in every half deck from Deptford to Peterhead.'

'A bit coarse,' Arthur said, and was surprised to discover how far away his voice sounded. It was almost as if he were listening to somebody else. 'A bit free,' the voice continued, 'but I can't see anything downright bad with her.'

Jim spat between his feet. 'They say that when the last ship has made up her crew she goes to bed and sleeps till the first ship comes back from t' fishery. And when they've all come and gone away back home she goes to bed again and sleeps till the start of the next season.'

'I can well believe it,' Arthur said, nodding gravely. 'Otherwise where'd she get her energy from?'

He nodded again, as if to agree with himself. In all his life he'd never said anything half so wise or witty. He continued to nod, but now in the direction of Blackie, who seemed intent on confirming the accuracy of his remarks.

Free of her partner and resisting all others, she began to dance on her own.

She was swaying slowly to a melancholy tune from the fiddle, holding one hand above her head while the fingers of the other hand straddled her prominent hip. The light from the whale oil lamp gained an extra lustre when it was reflected from her dark eyes. She threw back her head and her loose hair lifted like a raven's wings and beat the layers of peat smoke that floated beneath the grimy ceiling. Arthur looked at her sloe eyes, her arched brows and the full, disdainful curve of her mouth.

'She looks like a gipsy,' he said.

Jim agreed. 'You've only got to look at the light in those eyes to know that they don't belong in t' head of a lass from these islands.'

'Where do they come from then?'

'From between the legs of some lusty Spaniard who swam ashore nearly two hundred years since.'

Arthur didn't follow the argument.

'When the armada galleons were trying to get round the top,' Jim explained, 'and got blown on to the rocks. I'll bet you my share of every fish we catch that's where she gets her hot blood from.'

The fiddler assaulted the air with a more lively melody and she began to turn round, working her large hips up and down with exaggerated movements. The men cheered and clapped. She turned more quickly and her hessian skirt and petticoat lifted sufficiently to give an occasional view of her legs below the knee. The sailors stamped with excitement and shouted encouragement. She kicked her shoes off and the men scrambled after them, pushing and wrestling, in the hope that they might be able to make some claim upon her when the performance was over.

'She shaves her legs while the first ship is dropping its anchors,' Jim said. 'Then by the back end of the year she's as hairy as a bear again.'

Arthur stared at her in a kind of wonder. The shouting, stamping and clapping of the men became inaudible to him. The suspended lamp, the blackened ceiling and the rough stone walls disappeared. He was aware only of the large, glowing eyes, the waving strands of long hair, the bare feet and dark legs, the gleam of her teeth when she yelled some obscenity at her audience. This woman belonged to another part of the world; another island perhaps, where the skies were an unclouded blue and an untroubled sea rolled its green waves on to the yellow sands. He was adrift in some exotic ship and a wind laden with the scents of spices and fruit filled his sails.

The ill-fitting door opened and cold air unsettled the bands of smoke which then drifted and thinned out beneath the peat-stained roof. Two women came in, probably no more than girls but looking much older than their years. Their eyes were tired, but somehow still inquisitive. They'd been speaking together in Gaelic as they opened the door, but they stopped as soon as they were in the room and able to study its human contents.

Blackie had started to gyrate more quickly, turning one way and then the other. Each time she changed direction her rough skirt lifted a little higher than before. The fiddle strings responded in a plaintive ecstasy. She unwrapped her shawl and threw it away across the heads of the nearest onlookers. There was another scramble for possession. Now the shape of her breasts could be guessed through her blouse as she jigged up and down. The circle of spectators tightened around her.

One of the two women who'd just entered the room spoke. 'Another shipload, but the same auld faces.'

'I can see a fresh one,' her friend said, and put her hand on Arthur's arm. 'What ship are ye from?'

He told her.

'Ah – ah,' she nodded. 'That's a new name.'

She had a thin, white face, and a faded flower in her hair. Each time she spoke he could smell the whisky on her breath, despite the thickness of the surrounding air. She put her arm round his waist.

'Do ye want tae dance?' she asked.

She stretched and raised her face for him to kiss her. He discovered at this closer distance that there were wet sores on her face, inexpertly covered with a white powder.

'No,' he said.

He'd never had a young woman's arm round him in his life. It made him uncomfortable but he wasn't sure what he could do about it.

'He'd rather watch Blackie making a fool of herself,' the other girl said.

'Would you? Would you rather leuk at Blackie? There's mair

fish in the sea than that, and those that know say that it isna the ones with the thickest blubber that makes the best oil.'

Arthur pretended not to be watching.

'Dinna bother with him,' the other girl said. 'He's big but he's only a boy. Leuk at his face. It's got less hair on it than the cheeks of my arse.'

Jim intervened, in the spirit of a man who is prepared to ally himself with the devil provided the cause is a good one. 'Only a boy,' he confirmed. 'Leave him be. Can't you see he's had more to drink than is good for him?'

Arthur swung round to protest at the injustice of this last remark, and in so doing almost fell over. The woman withdrew her arm from his waist and Jim took hold of him by the shoulders.

'Stay close by me, Arthur.'

Both the young women laughed harshly, and yet with a kind of acceptance. They moved away to find company elsewhere.

The old fiddler had quickened his tempo and Blackie was moving ever more quickly. Her back kept arching like a yew bow being strung and then snapping straight again. The fiddle sobbed and wept in delirium. The sailors crowded more closely upon her. Her movements became frantic, as if it were desperately important for her to complete some ritual while there was still sufficient floor space. At each spasm her shoulders shook, her head jerked backwards and her black hair streamed behind her as if it had been caught by a gust of wind.

A woman escorted by a seaman came out of the crowd; although it would be more accurate to say that the seaman was merely doing his best to walk beside her, and would have fallen several times had she not clutched him tightly. Just before they reached the door he gave way at the knees and sprawled full length despite the efforts of the woman to keep him on the move. His face was swollen and distorted by drink, but Arthur recognized the dark bristles of his hair.

The woman beseeched their help. 'Gae us a hand before he falls asleep completely.'

Arthur took a step forward but Jim restrained him.

'It's Mr Nellis's line-manager,' Arthur said.

'Peter Gill.' Jim pronounced the name contemptuously. 'He'll come to less harm if he lies where he is.'

She swore ferociously at them both and raised her voice to attract wider attention. 'Gae me a hand, lads. Just tae the bottom of the stairs and I'll trouble ye nae mair.'

A couple of men left the crowd, lifted the unconscious line-manager and carried him out into the corridor. The woman followed at their heels.

The fiddle was shrieking and wailing with an even greater urgency and Blackie was responding with an even greater violence. Her face was running with sweat and it seemed impossible that she could continue at this rate for more than another minute. But just when it appeared that her dance had reached its climax the strings began to screech at a higher pitch and her body obeyed with redoubled frenzy. The long hair no longer flapped above her head but was stuck to her brow. The sailors were by now crowding her so closely that she hadn't room to turn.

The fiddle died. The dance was over. The woman laughed. Arthur couldn't see what was happening because of the people round her.

More women and young girls squeezed into the room from the corridor and quickly found partners. The fiddler, after wetting his whistle, started up again with a slow tune that seemed to speak of forsaken homelands over the sea. The dancing recommenced, although it was more difficult than ever to move about on the overcrowded floor. Somebody refilled Arthur's glass and he drank it off. He didn't cough at all. The glass was refilled immediately and the same person, or perhaps it was somebody else, took money out of his pocket.

'Let's be getting back to t' boats,' Jim said.

'I like it here.'

Jim tried to take the glass out of his hand.

'My drink,' Arthur said. 'Leave it alone.'

Jim took him by the point of the elbow and used it to steer him towards the door. Arthur knocked his hand away.

'I can take care of myself,' he said. 'It's the first time in my life I've been further than Runswick, and I'm a free man. I'm not having anyone telling me what to do.'

He collided with a drunken boatman from one of the Dundee

ships, who promptly gripped Arthur by the front of his shirt and said he had to fight him. Jim again intervened. In no time at all the Dundee man was shaking Jim by the hand and wouldn't let go, said he was a 'forthochtlie chiel', insisted that he knew he was a good man the minute he saw him, promised to be his friend for always and asked to be shown the way back to the lodberries at the south end of the harbour. Jim, more than a little exasperated, had to walk out to the street with this new and unwelcome companion.

Arthur wandered a few steps with his glass in his hand.

The cavorting figures flickered across the floor like shadows in a fire. They were clutching at each other and falling against each other in some unintelligible rite: impelled by an invisible force to move, to hop and jump up and down, to embrace each other ever more tightly. The fiddle sounded like the voice of some strange species of animal, now wailing with deprivation and despair, now shrieking with ecstasy. The livid scar on the old man's cheek shone under the lamp as he plied his bow, testifying to some deep and temporarily forgotten pain.

And everywhere, in every fissure of the blackened ceiling, in every niche of the grimy walls, in every crease and fold of the clothing on the sweating bodies of the dancers and the drinkers, the stench of the dead and dismembered whale crawled like a breath of the plague.

Where am I? What am I doing? Where am I going?

'I said why aren't ye dancing?' asked a soft Shetland voice with a hard edge in it.

Blackie was even shorter than he'd thought she was. He must have been looking straight over her head when she first asked the question. That head was tilted backwards so as to look directly up into his face, and her dark eyes were sparkling in the smoky light of the suspended lamp. How was it possible for the juice of a dead fish to shine with so much life? How could her eyes be so dark and so bright at the same time?

'I don't know how to,' he replied.

She smiled. Her teeth were strong and regular. 'I'll show ye how to.'

There was a new stillness around him, almost a silence. He became vaguely aware of expectant faces, some laughing and some sneering. He didn't feel her hands under his belt until they had crept back, as soft and sinuous as ferrets, to rest behind his hips. She pressed herself to him and he could sense every contour of her body from her toes and bare feet, her knees and plump thighs up to her belly, from her wide hips up to the rounded chin which she rested on his chest to look up at him.

New sensations leapfrogged along the nerves in his body. It wasn't simply that she was pressing herself hard against him, so that he was made more aware of her flesh as well as his own. It was more as if her body were sending out signals, hundreds and hundreds of them, which his own body was able to interpret. He could sense the thickness and texture of every article of clothing she was wearing.

She pushed him around amongst the other dancers. As they moved he could feel the alternating roundness of her breasts against his lower ribs. The grey blotches of men's faces floated past. People shouted things to him and made signs. He looked down at the smoky eyes and white teeth.

'Is this your first trip tae the fishery?'

He nodded down at her.

'Are ye a green-man?'

'No. Apprentice.'

She pulled a face, as if to beg his pardon and admit that she should have known better. Green-men were merely men who'd never been to the fishery before. First-year apprentices hadn't, either, but they had better prospects.

He was soon very dizzy. His feet didn't belong to him and set off in different directions at the same time. He trod on her bare toes and kicked her ankles. She seemed prepared to tolerate this, but he started crashing into other people and fights were again being mentioned.

'Come on, bonny lad,' she said. 'Ye'd best serve the next part of your apprenticeship in another place.'

And now it was his turn to stagger towards the ill-fitting door; and to fall down; and to be helped to his feet by rough but friendly hands; and to have advice shouted at him.

'Back oars when she fans her tail!'

'Mind your stem when she goes into her flurry!'

And someone was trying to tell him a story about a boat that was pulled down by a sounding fish and never seen again. The story had lots of circumstantial details that the men around him thought were very important and also very funny, but he could make neither head nor tail of it.

'Be careful,' Blackie said, guiding him gently.

He found the first stair with the tip of his shoe, mounted and found the next one. There were people lying about on the stairs. Some of them were groaning and some of them had been sick. She took his hand.

'Easy does it,' she said.

It seemed a long time before they reached the top of the stairs. She opened a door, looked in, laughed and closed it again. Still holding him tightly by the hand she led the way to the next room and pulled him inside after her. He made his way unsteadily towards a low bed and sat down on the lumpy mattress.

'Lie doon,' she told him.

He obeyed and felt the bed prickle his back. From below he heard the sound of the fiddle, muffled by the intervening floor boards and very far away. Against the insides of his eyelids the couples danced, Greenlanders and Shetland girls, falling against each other and holding each other tighter and tighter.

Blackie sat on the side of the bed and began to undo the cloth buttons on his shirt.

'What a pretty shirt,' she said.

'Our mam made it.'

'Nice,' she said, and her nimble fingers pursued their course.

The door was kicked open and slammed against the bed. Blackie jumped to her feet but Arthur scarcely stirred. Jim Richardson stood inside the room.

'You whoer!' he shouted at her. 'Don't you realize he's only a bairn?'

She stood up to him without flinching, with her hands on her broad hips and an impudent smile on her face. 'He's an apprentice,' she said, 'and there's nothing I enjoy mair than apprentices. If there was sufficient of them I'd have one for supper every nicht that the guid God sends me.'

'You're a blasphemer as well as a whoer!'

Jim tried to push her aside but she clutched his arm and pulled him away. Arthur watched the struggle without being able to take much interest in it. They were shouting at each other at the tops of their voices. Blackie was biting, scratching and kicking like a demented thing. Jim didn't know how to deal with her, and was concentrating on trying to keep her at arm's length without actually hurting her.

Now another figure burst into the room and paused for only a moment to weigh up the situation.

'No fighting, Nellie!' she screamed.

The burly Specksioneer pushed her out of the way, strode across to the bed, dragged Arthur out through the door and hurled him across the landing. Arthur hit the handrail. Half a dozen banisters cracked and gave way. For a mindless second he was in space, and then his fall was cushioned by some of the bodies on the stairs.

'I'll tell you one of my principles,' bawled Mr Nellis from the gap in the shattered balustrade. 'I never let a boy do a man's work.'

The Specksioneer stamped back into the room. A loud reproach from Blackie was cut off by the slamming of the door. Jim Richardson's feet descended the stairs.

12

On their way back they met a party from a Peterhead whaler hurrying up from the quay, who made ribald jokes about Arthur's pooped appearance. By the time Arthur reached the boat he knew he'd never felt so ill. Wherever he sat and wherever he lay, his head continued to spin and he had to keep changing his position.

'No bones broken, anyway,' Jim said.

A sensation of nausea squeezed Arthur's stomach and he leaned over the gunwale. He vomited again and again until his stomach tugged at its moorings like a coble in an ebb tide and he gasped for breath. Then he sat in the bottom of the boat with his back against a thwart and wiped his eyes and mouth with his sleeve. It was much better with his stomach empty.

'We'll have to wait for some of the others before we take the boat,' Jim said, sitting on the next thwart.

'That's all right. I'll spend the time thinking.'

'What about?'

What he was actually thinking about was the money he'd wasted. The money in his pocket had come from a cloth bag that his mam had made him tie round his neck, and the money in the bag had come out of his father's meagre earnings in Mr Winspear's sail loft. No, no, he must think about something else.

'I'll think about what it must have been like to be a great man like Marmion, with more horses and servants than even the Cholmleys have.'

Jim was pleased to find his poem recalled so readily, but tried not to show it. 'If you take better care of yourself you'll have a pleasure that Marmion never dreamed of. Nor the Cholmleys, nor Lord Mulgrave neither.'

Arthur looked up. 'What can that be?'

'To be pulled through the sea by a big fish.'

Arthur smiled and made himself comfortable against the thwart. He listened to the waters of Bressay Sound lapping against the carvel-built sides, and thought about Marmion and how he'd betrayed Constance de Beverley.

As soon as he thought of Constance de Beverley she appeared in his mind with the face of Ann Paylor, looking at him with eyes as fresh and blue as a summer sky. He thought of the deep, dank vault where the unhappy Constance had been walled up. Slowly, the imaginary crypt was transformed into something he recognized. It was the interior of the church on the east cliff, and he remembered a dim, dark day when he kneeled there.

The aisles, nave and chancel of St Mary's had stood for seven centuries on ground which contained the bones of kings and queens who ruled the old kingdom long before it was ruled from London. They said that the first poet in all England was buried here. People had worshipped in this spot in the days of Saxons, Normans, Danes and Anglians. The candles at the five altars were made from the cleanest oil the whales could yield, and they had been maintained for generations by the endowments of the poorer folk. Oil that had kept whales warm in the bays of Spitzbergen provided a constant light, by which the chanting priests could read their missals and sing masses and dirges financed by bequests from people of the grander sort.

Arthur Storm's young voice was submerged under the volume of sound that broke against the ancient walls:

> Eternal Father, strong to save,
> Whose arm hath bound the restless wave,
> Who bidd'st the mighty ocean deep
> Its own appointed limits keep:

The voices rose, slow and massive like the swell on a heavy sea, and fell back only to climb higher than before. Again they fell to a lower pitch, where they gathered their strength to rise once more, ponderously climbing wave upon wave.

But then came the refrain:

> O hear us when we cry to Thee
> For those in peril on the sea.

The voices climbed from unplumbed depths, mounting in thunderous stages until they reached a new peak which threatened to overwhelm everything; but then the wave broke, a ribbon of white spume appeared upon its crest, and as it toppled over the monstrous swell subsided.

And yet the ocean returned with unabated energy:

> O Christ, whose voice the waters heard
> And hushed their raging at Thy word . . .

Arthur looked at the large blue stone in the middle of the chancel floor that marked the family vault of the Cholmleys; and he pictured the headstones outside, illegible and eroded by the salt winds that blew in from the sea. What difference now between the beautiful Lady Catherine lying in the vault below, and the brittle bones of some old fisherwoman whose very name had disappeared from her sandstone tablet?

> O hear us when we cry to Thee
> For those in peril on the sea.

His voice rose with the refrain, like a cork floating on the back of a wave. The timbers of the roof shook under the impact of the swelling voices.

Ships' carpenters had built the new roof over two hundred years ago, making it low and flat to avoid the full rigour of the north-east wind. The Yorkshire oak that had provided the hold beams of the first ships supplied the timbers for the rafters; the adzes that had squared the carlines under those early decks shaped the purlins beneath the roof; the same stock of iron bolts that secured the chess-trees for the mainsail clews was used to fasten the roof joists at their intersections; and the berths in a 'tween deck spawned the galleries packed together below the ceiling. Shipwrights from the neighbouring yards had carved the ornate Cholmley pew and placed it on its twisted columns. The men who built that roof were the ancestors of those who would build the double-planked and fortified ships for the northern fishery.

> O Holy Spirit, who didst brood
> Upon the waters dark and rude ⸳ ⸳ ⸳

On every side the hymn rolled like a mighty sea. Arthur looked up at the roof as he sang. The sky lights and side windows made it easy to imagine that he was on the half deck of an ancient ship built by Jarvis Coates on the west side in the place where Fishburn and Brodrick now had their yard.

Another smooth mound formed on the flat, grey field of sound. It rolled forward slowly and disappeared. But it returned and kept growing until it was as big as a hill. This time it subsided more slowly. The sea became almost flat, undulating gently and disturbed only by windlippers. The growling of the organ was full of menace, and the deep reverberation of the men's voices showed that they weren't deluded by this apparent calm. They knew that the sea was hiding its real strength, accumulating extra powers from hidden depths, and sure enough it gathered itself into another mound and another hill; it grew into a black cliff, then a mountain, then a furious volcano with white lava overflowing from its head. It rushed forward with a roar.

The refrain came like an incantation:

> O hear us when we cry to Thee
> For those in peril on the sea⸳

The magic seemed to work. The wave broke and its energy

dispersed. It passed and faded away. The sweetness of women's voices shone like silver bubbles in its harmless wake.

The three-decker pulpit straddled the top of the central walkway like a bridge, rearing up on iron legs that were attached to the pews on left and right. The Reverend Francis Southern was an old man, and the congregation had almost finished the last verse by the time he'd climbed to the second tier. Here he paused to recover his breath and leaned forward with his soft hands on the wooden rail. The whale oil candles in the brass chandelier made his bald head glisten with white fire.

The refrain sounded for the last time:

> Thus evermore shall rise to Thee
> Glad hymns of praise from land and sea.

And everyone knew that the magic hadn't worked.

The people sat down with a noise that might have been made by the wings of a huge bird. Only when they were seated was it possible to see how full the church was. Men and women sat elbow to elbow in all the box pews, and even the seats reserved for the inland villages were packed tight up to their doors. Row after row of faces upstairs showed that the galleries had been crammed to their utmost capacity.

The last feet stopped shuffling. In the stillness the sound of the organ pipes lingered somewhere under the stone floor, and then even that phantom noise died away. The silence was interrupted only by the slow tread of the Reverend Francis Southern as he continued up to the third deck. At the top he turned and leaned with his shaky old hands on the lectern. He was almost as high as the gallery of the Cholmley Pew, which stood in front of the chancel arch and bestrode the central walkway like a second and grander bridge.

The Reverend Francis Southern began to speak. Arthur knew that people from the other end of the country, or at least those who'd been properly educated, all spoke in that strange way. But the Reverend Francis Southern was the only such person he'd ever so much as seen, and he still couldn't grow used to his voice. Instead of actually coming out with what he wanted to say, and speaking roundly and openly, the Reverend Francis Southern sneaked up on words, and chewed them, and let them slither sideways from his mouth. Arthur tried to listen but soon wearied of the slurred 'r's and the miaowing vowels.

His attention wandered to his father's grave face, tilted to look up at the third deck of the pulpit; and beyond to his mam in her best Staithes bonnet, almost hidden by his father's erect form, who had her head bowed and was dabbing at her nose with a rarely seen cambric handkerchief. His attention drifted further, to the wooden tablets on the walls with their biblical inscriptions, to the rows of heads in the galleries upstairs, and then back to the glistening head at the top of the three-decker pulpit.

What if the iron props gave way? What if the Reverend Francis Southern was thrown into the congregation and broke his neck?

He would go straight to Heaven. There couldn't be any doubt about it because he was a servant in God's church. If people were really so concerned about going to Heaven, why didn't they all try to become bishops and vicars and things like that? Then they'd have nothing to worry about. His mam was certain to go to Heaven. She was so good. Everybody said that. But what about his father? He was a good man, a very good man, but he sometimes went to the Seven Stars and the Jolly Butchers in Brewster Lane. Wouldn't that count against him? Wouldn't it have been safer if he'd become a preacher instead of working in Mr Winspear's sail loft?

A ripple of increased attention ran through the congregation like a cat's paw on slack water. Even people from the outlying villages – from Uggle Barnby, Hawsker, Stainsacre and the rest – stopped eating and sat up properly in the tall-backed pews.

His father's face became even more steadfastly directed to the third deck of the pulpit; his mam raised her head and stopped dabbing at her nose with the cambric handkerchief. The rows of heads in the galleries all moved forward slightly as if they were all being moved by the same lever.

The Reverend Francis Southern, conscious that two thousand pairs of eyes were following his every gesture, turned to left and right upon his elevated perch so as to encompass all the galleries; and, aware that an equal number of ears were intent on sucking in his every word, he raised his voice to reach even those who were sitting on the floor inside the porch: his words bounced against the ancient Yorkshire oak of the rafters and purlins and echoed against the skylights and carpentry of the old shipwrights.

Arthur looked up and tried to imagine that he was on the half deck of a ship that Jarvis Coates had built. Alas! Those unsounded 'r's and mewling vowels had destroyed the illusion. And the people were waiting, waiting, waiting for the message.

The Reverend Francis Southern asked for a particular blessing upon those who that day were grieving over the news lately arrived from Shields. He begged that these poor people should be given extra strength to bear their loss and special grace to understand that God's love embraced all things.

'They that go dahn to the sea in ships: and occupah theyah business in gwate watahs; these men see the works orv the Lord: and his wondahs in the deep.' He bowed his head, and the whale oil candles in the chandelier gave it a nimbus like the head of a saint in an illuminated psalter. 'And God enduahs for evah and evah. World withaht end. Ahhhmen.'

It was over. The Reverend Francis Southern commenced his slow and stately descent from the topmost deck.

Arthur Storm sat back and surreptitiously stretched the muscles in his arms and across his shoulders. He was longing to stand up and feel his weight on his legs, but to his despair his parents slid forward on to their hassocks again. After some moments of irritation he reluctantly did the same, and asked God to bless everyone who was made unhappy by the news from Shields. How could his parents, with their old legs, bear to kneel for so long? Why did his own young joints ache as if he had arthritis?

He looked sideways. His parents couldn't have been more immobile if they'd been cleats bolted to a ship's deck, and a quick glance showed that most of the congregation were similarly transfixed. So he said the Lord's Prayer to himself, slowly sounding all the phrases in his mind and saying some of them two and three times, so as to be sure it would be time to stand up before he reached the end. Was everyone else made of wood? Were they going to stay here all day? But there! His father raised his hands to the back of the pew in front and cleared his throat in a conclusive kind of way. His father sat up and Arthur followed. Aw, the relief!

His mam was still kneeling on her hassock, hands clasped and eyes tightly closed. What could she be praying about for so long? The news from Shields didn't affect anybody connected with their family, nor even anybody in Ellerby Lane, he was sure of that. His father had to clear his throat a couple of times with even greater finality before she stirred herself. Then she sat back, screwed the cambric handkerchief into a small ball and blinked her eyes.

At a movement from his father, guessed at rather than seen, they all three rose together and filed into the crowded walkway. Most of the congregation was standing up. There was much opening of doors from the box pews and much exchanging of grave courtesies.

The organ squealed. Arthur sensed a feeling of relief all around him. People were glad of the noise. It made it easier to look round, to smile, to shake hands and to talk of other things.

'A good bellows, Mr Storm.'

The gentleman was in a tailored coat and carried an ebony walking stick in his gloved hand.

'Aye, it is that, Mr Winspear,' said his father. 'It blows like a back ender.'

'I was observing that we have a good bellows to feed the wind-box of our new organ, Mrs Storm.'

She smiled and inclined her Staithes bonnet.

The rich harmony rose to the flat roof, then plunged deep down so that the big, metal pipes seemed to be playing under the worn stones of the nave. Just like the sea. Just like a black wave climbing with white streaks along its back, and the bitter wind blowing the spray off its crest.

He saw a face so white that it could have been composed of wind-blown spray. Her head was still lowered in prayer and the curve of her white flesh above the cheek bone was as soft as sand untouched by the tide. The features were hidden by the pale fingers of her hands, and he lingered in the hope of seeing them.

As if to satisfy his desire she raised her head and stared at the cross on the altar. Her lips moved and she pressed her hands palm to palm like a praying child.

The eyes were light blue, but looked darker under the sorrowing brow like pools of sea water under the shadow of a rock. They were wet and sore, and after only a few seconds the paper-white eyelids closed to solace them with darkness. Only then did he notice that one of her fingers was missing above the knuckle.

'Come by!' his mother ordered.

He followed his parents out of the porch where the gentleman with the ebony walking stick was waiting for them and spoke again.

'It's a bad day for us all, Mrs Storm.'

'It's a very sad day for some, Mr Winspear.'

Arthur had noticed before that men often liked an excuse to speak to his mother. But Mr Winspear, instead of smiling at her as they usually did, was inclined to be irritable.

'I say it's a bad day for us all. It's been a bad season. A very bad season. And this news about the *Aimwell* puts the cap on it.'

'It's bad, it's bad,' Mr Storm said, nervously. 'But it's sadder for some folk than for others.'

Mr Winspear lowered his chin into his white linen and rested his gloved hands on the knob of his walking stick. 'If things go on like this, Mr Storm, we'll end up making sails for nobody but Hull. And what that might mean I can only leave to your imagination.'

Mr Winspear excused himself with a sharp bow to Mrs Storm, and turned away to enter into conversation with Mr Agar who happened to issue from the church at that very moment. He ran one of the banks in Church Street, and was looking terribly afflicted and important. Mr Agar was being followed by Mr Milburn, who owned the rope-walk beyond Town End. They were joined almost immediately by Mr Foster, who was one of the Quaker ship owners and kept his hat on in church.

Arthur followed his parents away from the porch and on to the path that led through the graveyard. His mother was walking erect, as she always did; but his father seemed to have crumpled up. Perhaps, following upon Mr Winspear's suggestion, all his energy had drained away into his imagination.

The news from Shields had thrown the whole town into mourning. Arthur had felt a natural sympathy for those who'd refused to despair and kept hoping for good news as the weeks passed. Now they knew that their prayers hadn't been answered. Familiar faces would no longer be seen at their accustomed places on the quays or in the ghauts or by the Tolbooth; and there would be black dresses that for years to come would identify the widows of men lost on the *Aimwell*. Arthur had felt sorry for them all, but only in an abstract kind of way. None of them lived in Ellerby Lane.

A white face and a pair of blue eyes had changed all that.

He followed his parents down the long flight of stone stairs, with the level resting places for coffin bearers, that descended the east cliff alongside the Donkey Road. The air was sharp with the mixed smells of sea weed, wet rocks, tarred ropes and rigging, fresh fish and a dozen other things besides. He looked down on the clustered pantiles of the town. The evening light had dimmed the bright red roofs to orange, and soon the lamp lighter would be igniting the whale oil gas jets along Church Street. To the left of the lowered draw-bridge was the upper harbour with its forest of masts and spars. To the right was the outer harbour, where the Esk made its imperceptible progress between the piers to the open sea.

It was very quiet. For the past hour the parading gulls must have had the narrow streets to themselves. The caulking hammers were silent in the yards on both sides of the river, and the multifarious business of making ships was waiting for tomorrow.

Everything looked different. Everything had changed because of a white face and pale hands that concealed a pair of blue eyes with shadows in them.

Until now death had been something that happened to other people. It was a remote thing that hadn't anything to do with his own life. Ann Paylor's grief was personal in a way he'd never imagined it. She'd lost her father, who was a boat-steerer on the *Aimwell*. He remembered the fresh-faced, pleasant man, who had knocked at the door in Ellerby Lane and shaken his hand and smoked a pipe with his father. And in the deep pools of his daughter's eyes he'd experienced a sorrow that was suddenly close to him.

As they approached the bottom of the stone stairway a big man with long, uncombed hair, caught up with them. He pushed past while he spoke, but then turned and stood on the next step so that they were virtually obliged to stop.

'A bad day for us all,' he said.

'Aye, aye, aye, it is that,' said Mr Storm.

'For all of us,' he said. 'For me and you and all of us.'

It was Harry Hodgson, who worked in the boiling house on the other side. Mrs Storm climbed backwards a step and tried to put herself to windward of him.

'It's a poor enough little fleet we're left with,' he continued. 'It's not what you'd call a fleet, any road. When I wasn't much more than a boy we used to fit out four times as many ships every season. You'll remember that? And they were always well fished an' all.'

Mr Storm, sensitive to his wife's antagonism, moved slightly to the left in the hope of recommencing their downward movement. 'I'm sure Mr Brodrick will be building again,' he said uncertainly.

'That's the trouble.' Harry put a red hand on his shoulder that smelled of dead fish and glue and charnel houses. 'Fishburn and Brodrick don't build ships to keep poor folk like us in work. Aw, no. They build ships because grander folk with money to spare, like Mr Foster or Mr Winspear, order them and undertake to pay for them.'

'They'll order another one,' said Mr Storm unhappily, trying to assume a tone of voice that would indicate he really couldn't say any more on the matter.

Harry banged him on the shoulder to emphasize what he was saying. 'Why should they? Too many owners have lost their money in the last few years. Quakers never throw good money after bad, and them as know their business copy them. I reckon this last season has made them wonder whether their money is in t' right place, and the loss of the *Aimwell* must have convinced them that it isn't. I can't see anyone being in a hurry to put up a share in another ship.' A final bang on the shoulder, heavier than the others. 'Can you?'

Mrs Storm entered the conversation for the first time. 'May God forgive you, Harry Hodgson, for even thinking about such things, when other people have lost their loved ones.'

Harry Hodgson stared at her in amazement, quite unable to grasp for a moment what she'd said. Then he tried to laugh and appear amused. He touched his forehead, swung one leg off the step in an embarrassed sort of manner and went on his way. The smell of blubber slowly dispersed.

'And God forgive me,' Mrs Storm said, 'for presuming to set myself up in judgement over others.'

'Hush, missus, hush!' said her husband roughly, very pleased with her for having routed Harry Hodgson more effectively than he could have done. 'I was just going to tell him that if he had naught to boil next season he could boil his head.'

He resumed his downward course more cheerfully.

'Come by!' ordered his wife in an urgent whisper.

Mr Storm looked over his shoulder and promptly moved to one side. He slightly inclined his head towards the couple who were about to move past.

Ann Paylor's hand was tucked inside her mother's arm, which she clenched as frantically as if she were in danger of drowning. Her head was bowed but Arthur could see the pale face and the curve of her sand-soft cheeks, wet and shining. Her small feet wavered above each step, uncertain whether there was anything there.

'Don't stare!' his mother hissed.

Mrs Paylor's shawl was blowing in the fresh wind, and as the couple passed it flapped over their bent heads like the wing of some large, menacing bird. The girl's left hand came out of its hiding place, seized the end of the wayward shawl and tucked it back in at her mother's waist. The small hand drew Arthur's eyes. Yes, it was the middle finger that was missing above the knuckle. Why did people have to be hurt like that?

'Do you hear me?' his mother demanded.

At the bottom of the steps the sorrowing couple turned away towards Henrietta Street. They were so locked in each other's arms that it was impossible to tell which one was supporting the other.

Arthur continued to stare despite the nudges in his ribs. The nudges became more violent.

'Arthur! Arthur!' Jim said.

The nudges were followed by a hard kick.

'Get hold of an oar,' Mr Nellis roared at him, 'if you don't want to swim back to t' ship.'

13

A piercing sensation inside Arthur Storm's head turned out to be the ship's whistle. He discovered that in addition to a splitting head he had severely bruised ribs. Mr Nellis, red-eyed from drink and lack of sleep, nevertheless came down into the 'tween decks and kicked the sluggards out of their beds.

On deck everything was chaos. James Tickelpenny, the man with the droll face whom they'd met the previous evening, came up to Mr Nellis and inquired in a thick voice what he was doing aboard the *Lady Clifford*. Mr Nellis was a profoundly worried man for a few seconds. He looked about him with bleary eyes, identified the deck furniture without too much difficulty, and roared for Peter Gill. After an unequal struggle they succeeded in throwing James Tickelpenny overboard, and the men crowded to the side and gave him a cheer as he swam to his own ship.

Order slowly prevailed on the *William Scoresby Senior*. The green-men found their places. The ship's pipes stopped blowing. A solitary voice sang a few words. Other voices joined in. The crew of the *Lady Clifford* struck up with another song, and the crews of the other ships added other songs again, and the accents of Hull, Whitby, the Tyne, Dundee, Aberdeen and Peterhead mingled together in the sharp morning air. While the anchors were being catted and the canvas was being spread their voices rebounded from the surrounding hills until the entire harbour was filled with song. The crofters' families came down to the sides of the quays and waved good-bye.

As soon as Unst was behind them Arthur snatched the first opportunity of speaking to the Second Mate.

'You said we could start spanning, Mr Dryden. You said we could start after we'd completed our crew at Lerwick.'

The Second Mate led the way down to the 'tween decks. Something about the dispersion of his moustaches showed that he was pleased by this insistence. They were becoming friends, despite the difference in age and rank.

'Hand me that piece of rope, Arthur.'

Nearby, amidst several bits of tackle, was a thick piece of rope several yards long. Arthur handed it over.

'Best white hemp,' Mr Dryden said, and held it in his hands with a kind of respect, almost of reverence, so that what had appeared as no more than a length of stout rope now took on the aspect of something quite remarkable. 'Best that money can buy. It's got to be, because it'll have to take a greater strain than any rope in t' world. It's called the foreganger. When I've spanned this one you can try your hand on t' next.'

Mr Dryden's large, but surprisingly nimble fingers, untwisted the strands of hemp at one end of the foreganger. He worked with a kind of restrained passion, a total absorption in the job.

He showed Arthur how to splice the strands tightly round the shank of the harpoon. The shank was thickened at the end further from the mouth, and it was obvious that this would prevent the eye of the splice from sliding off. This thickened end contained a cup into which Mr Dryden fitted a wooden stock as tall as himself. Slowly and carefully he fitted the foreganger to it.

He looked up at Arthur with the spanned harpoon across his knees. The angle of his moustaches and the expression in his eyes somehow confirmed that the weapon was now completely assembled.

'And has it really been the same,' asked Arthur, thinking back to one of Mr Dryden's early comments, 'has it been the same for over two hundred years?'

'Some things don't change.'

Mr Dryden lowered the spanned-in harpoon and placed it under the lee of the neighbouring boat. He took a piece of oiled canvas and wrapped it round the sharpened point as tenderly as if he were tucking a baby into its cot.

'It's almost the same weapon,' he said, 'as the Basques brought up here in the earliest days of the fishery. Then the Dutch improved it like they did everything else.'

'The Dutch?'

'Of course. They were our masters in everything. A lot of the special words we use are theirs.'

Arthur was rather shocked by this ready acceptance of foreign supremacy, even although it was in the past. 'They can't teach us anything now, can they? We're on top now, aren't we?'

'Aye, we are an' all!' Mr Dryden laughed. 'We're on top of everybody now and no mistake.'

96

They continued to span harpoons in the 'tween decks duri[ng] subsequent days whenever there was an opportunity. The hours of tuition were almost entirely silent. Arthur watched an[d] waited for each task to be given to him. Sometimes he elicited [a] grunt of approval; and sometimes the work was taken out of his hands so that he could watch more closely and try again.

Arthur discovered that a spirit of dedication was being born inside himself. He experienced the first stirrings of an ambition to be almost as good at everything as the Second Mate. To have wished to be as good would be presumptuous; and to have wished to be better, by however small a margin, would be unthinkable.

As the days went by and the weather grew colder, Arthur began to wonder whether these various tasks had some purpose other than the spanning of harpoons. What this other purpose might be he couldn't guess. It was altogether too deep and inscrutable for him even to imagine. Perhaps he and Mr Dryden were working together in a silent pursuit of some kind of perfection of which these perfectly spanned harpoons were no more than an emblem; perhaps these harpoons could be used to penetrate something more intangible than black skin.

The day came when the last of the spare harpoons had been assembled and wrapped in oiled canvas. Mr Dryden stood up, stretched his long legs, elongated his back until the vertebrae crackled in his spine and then resumed his habitual stoop.

'Would you like to see a reminder of the great days of the Dutch?'

'Yes, sir.'

Anything that interested Mr Dryden was of interest to him. He followed him up the companionway to the main deck and across to the larboard side. Mr Dryden rested his big hands on the bulwark and looked to the westward.

An island rose precipitously from the sea. Its high cliffs had cracked open, and the rocky clefts contained frozen torrents and cataracts that glowed with a green light. The dead land was covered with a blanket of clouds as thick as itself. Above the clouds, as startling as a giant's hand, a solitary mountain raised its white crest.

'Jan Mayen Island,' Mr Dryden said, bending down a little

from his own great height. 'A hundred years ago its shore was crowded with men. Dutchmen.'

Arthur stared at the bare rock.

'It was a Dutch boiling station. They didn't take the pieces home in those days. They were there with their coppers, their tents, their cooperages and their warehouses. It must have been as busy as a hive at that time.'

The volcanic mountain, so stark and unchanging, reminded Arthur of St Hilda's central tower on the east cliff at home. It was as if countless aeons of solitude had given it some special dignity and strength. The mountain's white head seemed to be looking down on the clouds that encircled its waist. For a brief moment men had come to its feet, their boiling station had spluttered and prospered, and then they'd all disappeared like bubbles in a river. The mountain still stood there as if these things had never been; as if this island had never had any purpose other than to serve as its pedestal.

'In those days,' Mr Dryden said, 'the Dutch must have thought they were lords of the fishery to the end of time.'

Arthur continued to stare at the desolate rock. His earlier jubilance at thinking how the British had swept the Dutch out of the whaling grounds had somehow lost its savour. For the first time there crept upon him an intimation of the meaning of change.

'Let's back to work,' said Mr Dryden. 'It's cold up here today.'

Arthur followed the lanky Second Mate back down to the boats. Jim Richardson swung his legs over a gunwale and dropped to the deck.

'This 'un 's ready for you, Mr Dryden.'

'Thank you, Jim.'

Jim Richardson and a couple of other men moved across to empty and clean another boat on the other side of the 'tween deck. Mr Dryden squatted on his heels in the lee of the vacated boat and took up the end of a piece of rope. He threw the end of another piece to Arthur.

'Now we've reached the line,' he said. 'Two and a quarter inches in circumference like the foreganger, but much longer.'

He picked up a marlin spike and began to untwist the strands at the end of the rope. A nod to Arthur showed that he should act similarly.

98

'Each of these lines is a hundred and twenty fathoms long, and we have six in each boat. That gives us seven hundred and twenty fathoms to fish with. Most times a fish won't sound any further than that.'

'What if it does?'

At times Mr Dryden's concentration reached such a pitch, as now, that he became totally unaware of everything except what he was actually doing. He didn't reply.

When the ends of the two ropes were unravelled, Mr Dryden's large, capable hands began to weave them together. His mind was completely occupied by the making of a perfect splice. Arthur regarded him silently. The very hairs of his long moustache expressed a deep, inner contentment.

'What if the fish goes further down than 720 fathoms?' Arthur resumed.

'Mmm?'

'What if you run out of line?'

'You make sure you don't.'

'How, Mr Dryden?'

'Mmm?'

'How do you make sure you don't run out of line?'

'Wait and see.'

When the six lines had been joined together in one continuous length Mr Dryden spliced an eye into one end; and then he spliced the foreganger to the other end so that the harpoon now had 720 fathoms of line behind it.

'Now we come to the most important part in the whole of the fitting out of the boats. If we don't get it right it'll be worse than if we'd not done anything at all.' Mr Dryden swung his long legs into the boat that Jim Richardson and his men had left for them. 'Give me the foreganger, Arthur.'

He handed up the spanned-in harpoon and climbed in after. Mr Dryden laid the harpoon on the floor of the boat and together they pulled in the whole length of spliced line.

Mr Dryden began to coil the line in a tub, laying each loop with meticulous care exactly upon the top of the preceding one. The line snaked from his guiding hands with such precision that it seemed impossible for it to lay anywhere other than where he wanted it. But then, although Arthur couldn't discern the tiniest irregularity in what had been done, Mr Dryden suddenly shook the line out of its coils and started the work again.

Arthur watched without speaking, almost without breathing, so evident was Mr Dryden's concentration on what he was doing. He was a long time about it, but finally the line was coiled to his satisfaction and he straightened up.

'Look at the man in t' next boat,' he said in a low voice, 'and tell me what you think of him.'

In the next boat along on the same side of the 'tween deck was a man with a long, white face, and black hair as stiff as the whalebone bristles of a cleaning brush. Arthur had been glad to avoid him up to now because of the permanent expression of ill-temper that moulded his features. This man, also, was coiling line.

'What do you think of him?' repeated Mr Dryden.

'It's Peter Gill.'

'That's right. The line-manager in Mr Nellis's boat.' Mr Dryden moved on and was about to start coiling the next section of line into the second tub. But he looked up again before continuing and nodded towards the other boat. 'Observe the way he goes to work and tell me honestly what you think.'

Arthur, puzzled by the question, stared at Peter Gill. Despite his spindly frame and smaller size, the other man didn't have the grace of the hulking Second Mate. There was besides a list-lessness, an absence of tension, almost a lack of direction in the movements of his arm.

'What d' you think?' asked Mr Dryden, without taking his eyes off the tub.

'He doesn't work as smoothly as you do.'

The long moustaches moved up and down around an invisible grimace. Mr Dryden was both embarrassed and irritated by the answer. Arthur watched the big hands as they continued to coil the next section. They never faltered. They moved in a ritual like hands sowing corn in the bottoms of the Cleveland dales. Then he looked across at Peter Gill. The other man was jerky and his movements were without rhythm.

Peter Gill finished his coiling, hoisted a leg over the gunwale and dropped to the deck. There he overbalanced for a moment, and supported himself on one hand before straightening up and slouching away.

Mr Dryden hadn't looked up. He continued, as patient and painstaking as ever, until the two main sections of line had been coiled to his unreserved satisfaction and lay in their two tubs. Arthur was certain he'd never seen anything so neatly and beautifully done.

'Come ower here,' Mr Dryden said, and stepped into the stern.

About six fathoms of line remained loose. This was the end with the eye splice. Mr Dryden coiled it separately and placed it in a compartment at the stern.

'This is what we call the stray-end,' he said, dropping the eye.

But Arthur had the impression he'd been called aft to hear something else not directly connected with the job in hand. Mr Dryden was shaking his head as if to deny the unspoken thought. Then he stooped and spoke with great earnestness.

'Did you see him leave the boat?'

'What? Who? Peter Gill. Yes, I did.'

Mr Dryden tried to speak more casually. 'Did you notice anything fremd about him? Anything at all?'

'No. I don't think so.'

'He didn't do anything that made him seem . . .' Mr Dryden searched miserably for the words he wanted '. . . made him seem strange?'

'Well, he's a bit clumsy, isn't he, if that's what you mean? But I think he hurt his leg when he fell down the forward hatch on Sailing Day.'

Mr Dryden sucked in a great lungful of air, and was suddenly as tightlipped as if his moustaches had been used to wire his jaws together. He made his way round Arthur and went into the bow to position the harpoon. The mouth, in its oiled canvas shield, he placed on the stem. The stock he rested upon a support designed for it – 'this is called the *mik*,' he said – and coiled the foreganger beneath it with his habitual care.

'I always coil my own lines,' he said, drawing himself as upright as he ever did. His normally pleasant face was set in sombre lines, and his moustaches drooped mournfully around the sides of his mouth. 'It's a job I'd never leave to anyone. Not only my own life, but the lives of all the men in my boat depend on these lines being coiled without the faintest kink or quirk to make them snag.' He had another thought. 'Of course,' he added quickly,

'I'm not criticizing the way other folk go about things. There's good officers who leave the entire fitting of their boats in the charge of their boat-steerers or line-managers. There's nothing further from my mind than to criticize Mr Nellis's practice,' he went on, unhappily. 'All I'm saying is that I wouldn't leave the coiling of my lines to my line-manager. Not that I don't trust Jim Richardson. He's a better line-manager than Peter Gill. It's just that I coil my own lines because I . . .'

Mr Dryden discovered that he was going round and round on the same capstan without raising anything of interest. With a dark flush he turned himself to an inventory of the boat's tackle. He roughly instructed Arthur to identify each piece of equipment when he named it.

'Spare harpoon, properly covered . . . three lances on each side resting on t' thwarts . . . a jack to show when we're fast . . piggin, that's the wooden bailer for keeping the bollard wet . . . tail knife, grapnel, boat hooks, mallet, snow shovel . . . winch in working order, Jim Richardson 'll have seen to that . . . spare tholes and grommets . . . axe within reach here . . . oars in their proper places . . . a good man is Jim Richardson, one of the best . . .'

They left the boat and walked towards the steps of the companion. Mr Dryden, not wanting to terminate this opportunity for private conversation, turned aside and led the way back to the boat. At the pointed stem he halted, trailed his fingers up and down on the gunwale, and after much wagging of his head and clearing of his throat managed to come out with it.

'I don't want to speak ill of any man, particularly where there's naught but appearances to go on. God knows we all have our follies and I'm aware of mine.' In his agitation Mr Dryden walked round to the other side of the boat and Arthur had to follow him. 'Look here,' he said, despairingly, 'would you say, or wouldn't you say, that Peter Gill was drunk?'

Arthur stopped dead. Mr Dryden continued to stalk forwards, with his shoulders hunched up and his neck drawn in like a heron. Finding himself alone he turned round and came back for a reply.

'*Drunk*! But I thought that was impossible. I thought Captain Stapleton was most strict about who had the key.'

'Aye. That he is, that he is,' agreed Mr Dryden, and his

moustaches wagged remorsefully. 'What can I be thinking of? God forgive me for mentioning such a thing. Aye, it's impossible, as you say.'

He took a few more paces about the deck, but returned and placed his large hands on Arthur's shoulders. He gripped them hard and stooped low.

'Listen, lad! We'll never refer to this talk again.'

'Not if you don't want to.'

'But you must promise me one thing.'

'Yes, Mr Dryden.'

'Do you swear it?'

'Yes, sir.'

He looked into the Second Mate's face, and saw that his level eyes were boring into his own with a painful seriousness. The lips were slightly withdrawn to reveal his teeth set hard together. So tense and rigid was he that it seemed the limp arms of his moustache were about to stiffen.

'What do you want me to promise?' Arthur asked, expecting it would be a simple request to forget the suggestion that Peter Gill might have been drunk.

'Promise me that if you ever find out that Peter Gill is able by some means to get his hands on liquor, above what Captain Stapleton might authorize from time to time, that you'll waste not a moment but come straight away and tell me.'

'I promise, Mr Dryden.'

The powerful fingers squeezed the muscle fillets above his shoulders. 'You'll come straight away, no matter what you're doing. Swear it, lad.'

'I swear it, Mr Dryden.'

A final squeeze to show the ordeal was over. He was released.

'You're in t' Captain's Watch, aren't you?' asked Mr Dryden in a completely different tone of voice. 'Well, I've charge of that watch and I'll remind you that we're all due for eight hours' rest.'

'I'm not tired yet.'

'You take my advice and make sure you use your eight hours for as long as we're on t' quarter watch. When we get amongst fish and go on to the half watch you'll get only four hours at a time, and with any luck they'll be interrupted. So get a long sleep while you can.'

'Yes, Mr Dryden.'

They went forward to the companionway. Here they separated and Arthur went further forward again to the crew's quarters. Jim Richardson was already asleep in the upper bunk, and despite his denial of being tired Arthur was soon asleep himself.

He dreamed he was alone on Jan Mayen Island. He walked for miles over the black sand until his feet were bruised and swollen; he climbed the volcanic rocks in order that he might better survey the desolate landscape. There wasn't any life anywhere of any kind: not an animal, not a bird, not an insect, not even a sprig of vegetation. I am alone, he thought, I am more alone than any man ever was.

Then in his dream he remembered the Dutch boiling station and the huge bustle and activity that would have surrounded him a hundred years ago. It couldn't have all disappeared without a trace. He overturned rocks and dug amidst the loose stones, searching for something, anything, that could testify to those past endeavours. Anything would do – pieces of whalebone, bits of iron, shards of copper, sawn wood – anything that showed the intervention of men. There was nothing.

The upper reaches of the mountain were invisible, hidden by cloud. But he knew that it rose above him like a huge admonitory finger; and he knew that even if he could climb its precipitous face and gaze out from that greater elevation he would still see nothing that moved, nothing at all.

The feeling of loneliness was so intense that it awakened him. He discovered that he was now thinking about St Hilda's central tower on the east cliff, and with that thought he went quickly back to sleep.

14

The *William Scoresby Senior* was closehauled and beating to windward with the wind on her starboard quarter. Mr Beaufort, his sealskin cap pushed back on his curly head, shouted instructions to the men aloft. The yards were moved to bring the bows right ahead to wind with all sails aback. The ship remained in stays until she was made to fall off. Mr Beaufort went forward and lounged against the knightheads while the *William Scoresby Senior*, with her tacks and sheets adjusted, went ahead with the wind on her other quarter.

Captain Stapleton came up on to the quarter deck. His head looked even larger and more square-shaped against the sky. The grey hair was sparse on top, but more abundant at the sides where it fluffed out over his ears like feathers in a gull's wings. His beard was pure white, shaped and rounded like a blubber-spade.

The Captain looked up into the running rigging with its stressed pattern of braces pulling at the ends of the yards. He was more familiar with them than the lines on the palms of his hands, together with the multitude of lifts, ties, truss pendants, halyards, guys, jear falls and travellers. It might have been thought that he was trying to determine a better setting and trim for his ship. But he made not the slightest attempt to intervene in Mr Beaufort's management, and he appeared to be concerned with some more abstract problem of even greater complexity and magnitude.

This air of abstraction caused Captain Stapleton to be known in some circles as an 'odd one'. Arthur Storm, seeing him so contemplative on the quarter deck, was conscious of the Captain as a man set apart by something more than his station. He asked Jim Richardson what the Captain might be thinking about. Jim said he might be worrying about how many fish there were left in the Greenland Sea. Arthur was convinced that he was thinking about less immediate things.

Captain Stapleton was acknowledged by everyone to be a hard working and practical commander. His record in the northern fishery was a good one: several times he'd returned full and scarcely ever had he come back clean. Many hundreds of tons of bone and thousands of tons of oil had been brought back in ships under his command. He did everything that the most conscientious captain could possibly do, delegating to his officers only what was necessary or customary, and ensuring to the limits of his very great ability that each voyage was a commercial success.

Yet there was something puzzling in his dedication to his duties. Arthur Storm couldn't have said what it was, but he was aware of a difference when he compared the Captain with the Second Mate.

Mr Dryden had a singleness of purpose in everything he did. The actual job of undertaking a piece of work, and of doing it as well as it could possibly be done, occupied him entirely. This whole-hearted devotion to the matter in hand gave to the Second Mate a solidity that Arthur could understand.

Captain Stapleton gave the impression of being somehow detached from his command of the ship and the arrangement of its affairs. Perhaps he issued his orders and carried out his functions by instinct, or else long experience and increase in knowledge had made his decisions almost mechanical. He appeared to do his work by employing only some superficial part of his brain and personality, while his best abilities were engaged elsewhere for some unknown purpose.

And the Captain's puckered eyes, although keen and true, seemed to register the external world with a kind of accurate disbelief. It was as if his eyes, in their painstaking unconcern, were hiding their real activity and were looking inwards upon some mystery less readily accessible to mere sense.

15

Arthur Storm lay in his berth and looked up at the lamp. It swung gently with the movement of the ship, and made black shadows come and go among the oak beams and the bunks in the 'tween decks. He listened to the sea washing against the double-layered bows, then falling away into silence before it returned with a soft, rippling smack.

'Jim,' he said, quietly.

The top bunk creaked. Jim Richardson's head appeared over the side, with the jet cross dangling from his neck.

'I thought you might be asleep, Jim.'

'You were nearly right. Stay of the same mind for another minute and I'll not contradict you.' The head was about to disappear but bobbed back. 'Unless I'm disturbed, of course.'

Arthur grunted. 'I'll never get used to the half watch. You

can't expect someone to keep going to sleep for only four hours at a stretch. And during daylight, an' all.'

'I used to think the same,' said Jim, 'before I'd pulled an oar in a Greenland boat. Then I found I could sleep the full four hours at any time of the day or night, lying down or standing up, whenever anybody would let me. And with your permission I'm going to make a start now.'

The head withdrew.

'Jim?'

There was an artificial snore from the top bunk.

'Jim, I'm truly sorry to trouble you, I truly am, but there's something important I want to ask you.'

The other bunk wheezed and Jim's face, its habitual good nature under some strain, looked down at him. 'What is it, lad? You're not just checking to see whether I'm asleep?'

'I was wondering, Jim, if I could take your oar.'

Jim sounded too sleepy to understand. 'My oar?'

'Yes. What about me taking your place in t' boat?'

Surprise brought Jim fully awake. 'What do you want to do that for?'

'Because I want to see my first fish. I want to be in one of the boats so I can see what happens. I want to see a strike.'

'You'd have your back to t' fish and you'd see naught.'

'But I want to be in t' boat and –'

'You'll be in t' boat soon enough when you're out of your apprenticeship. Then you'll find that rowing after a sixty-foot fish that's out for a swim is the worst kind of torture that men ever devised for themselves.'

'That isn't what you said after we'd been ashore at Lerwick.'

Jim didn't try to answer that point. 'You'll have to wait.'

'But my indentures are for three years! I don't want to wait that long before I find out what I'm here for.'

Jim adopted the reasonable tone of the man who knows he is right but is nevertheless determined to be patient. 'What would Mr Dryden think when he saw you in his boat? What would you say to him? *Aw Mr Dryden*, you'd say, *I felt like stretching my back for a bit*. And what would I say to him when he sent for me? *Aw, Mr Dryden*, I'd say, *my rheumatiz is badly so I thought I'd spend the afternoon in bed and take care of myself*.'

'I'm sure Mr Dryden wouldn't mind for just once.'

But Jim was taken up with the idea of these imaginary conversations. '*Good day to you, Mr Fenby*, you'd say.'

'Who's Mr Fenby?'

'He's the boat-steerer that sits facing me. *Good day to you, Mr Fenby*, you'd say. *I hope you're keeping well, Mr Fenby*, you'd say. *I thought it might be a nice change for you to look at me instead of Jim Richardson. What with having had to stare at him for the last several seasons an' all.*'

'Just once,' Arthur said, 'that's all I ask.' He talked more quickly, fearing that if he didn't make any impression now he never would. 'I don't mean that I want to take your place at every drop. Only once. Only one drop and I'll be satisfied. Let me take your oar when Mr Dryden's boat is lowered. Then no matter if we don't get near to a fish, no matter if we don't even *see* a fish, I won't ask again.'

But Jim continued in the same tone of voice, exactly as if he hadn't heard a word. 'And if one of the boats catches a fish and we bring it back, what's Mr Nellis going to say? What'll he think when he doesn't see you all clean and fresh with the other apprentices? What if he decides to have the new apprentices in t' mallemauk boat? *Aw, Mr Nellis*, you'll say, *Aw, Mr Nellis, I thought I'd have an outing in t' whale boat and get some fresh air.*'

The thick Shetland voice of Rasmie Hughson issued from the tumbled sheets of the next bunk along. 'Wad ye mind putting the wrappers back on yeur tongues. If they wag any mair I shall no be able tae wag me oar when the time comes.'

'You're right, Rasmie,' answered Jim immediately. 'Good night to you.'

Arthur drew in his head like a bruised snail. He was embarrassed to think that his pleading should have been listened to by others and that he should have put Jim in the wrong. So he bit his tongue, but remained just as determined to pull an oar in one of the boats if the opportunity offered.

From now onwards Captain Stapleton was spending most of his waking hours, and perhaps a few of his sleeping ones, at the main topgallant head. His barrel-shaped crow's nest was of the kind that William Scoresby Senior had introduced to the fishery. Thither he took his provisions and his speaking trumpet, and thence he swept the horizon with his glass in a continuous endeavour to find fish and avoid ice.

Six boats were ready for immediate service. Four of them were suspended from davits by the sides of the ship, and the crews for two of these boats were always standing by. No matter what the time of day, two fully manned boats could be in the water in less than a minute of sighting.

The neighbouring sea was still free from ice. The sky was clear, the air fresh and sharp. Officers and men were restless. The watch on deck fidgeted about, waiting to hear the call from above. The watch below found it difficult to sleep.

It was a bright, sunny forenoon when the first call came from the crow's nest. Mr Dryden's watch was on deck and Arthur, his heart bounding, ran to the ship's side. Men were scrambling into the boats as if their lives depended on it. But Captain Stapleton's restraining voice sounded again from the speaking trumpet.

'Avast, Mr Dryden! Avast! Keep your boats where they are!'

The *William Scoresby Senior* turned a couple of points into the wind but Arthur couldn't see anything. Mr Dryden spoke quietly to the two crews who were waiting impatiently for the drop. Captain Stapleton remained silent for a full ten minutes of further sailing. The men in the boats occupied the time laughing and making jokes to each other.

'Lower away!' came cheerfully from the trumpet.

The two boats hit the water simultaneously and a few seconds later Arthur saw the fish. He then saw that there were two fish, a mother and her calf, playing together and still completely unaware of the ship's arrival. Captain Stapleton ordered the courses to be brailed up, and the main topsail to be backed so as to lay the ship to.

At about twenty boat lengths the big fish saw the danger. She immediately pushed her calf under the surface and placed herself where she would be between it and the boats when her youngster came up again. The calf, presumably thinking this was a continuation of the game, banged her with its nose-end and tried to circle her rump. With a clout from her tail that would have stove a boat, she turned its head and gave the calf a mighty nudge to start it swimming away. The calf dived, managed to wriggle under its frantic mother, and came up within ten paces of the first boat whence Mr Dryden harpooned it with a smooth, perfectly executed throw.

The big fish was desperate. She swam to and fro alongside her stricken calf, and so unmindful of her own welfare that Mr Dryden was able to push the harpoon in without even letting go of it. A couple of seconds later he and the harpooner of the second boat were lancing her vitals.

The usual procedure would have been for the fast boat to raise a jack in order to indicate a strike, and for the ship to respond with a jack at her mizzen-peak. But all the action was taking place in such a confined area, and was clearly to be of such short duration, that the normal formalities could be dispensed with.

The fish sounded, but only for a few fathoms and she had to come up to blow almost straight away. The twin spouts were streaked with crimson and the men gave a hearty cheer. She went into her flurry and churned the water as white as milk. Her frenzy ended, she rolled on to her back and displayed her enormous belly to the sky.

The officers in the boats prepared the fish for bringing alongside. Mr Dryden put two holes in the tail, passed a rope through them and lashed it to his boat's bow. Mr Fenby, his boat-steerer, was meanwhile retrieving the short length of line with a grapnel and he cut it at the foreganger splice. Mr Caspol, the harpooner from the second boat, went on to the fish where he cut the fins and reeved them together across its belly. The calf was still alive, but it was determined not to leave its mother's side and so it was a simple matter to lance and secure it in a similar manner.

Mr Beaufort brought along the watch below without unnecessary haste, and all the boats formed a line to take the fish in tow. The men were still fresh, and before long they had the big fish by the larboard side, with its head towards the stern and its tail opposite the fore chains. The rump-rope and nose-tackle were attached, the right hand fin was lashed towards the gunwale, and the cant-purchase was hooked into the fat of the neck. The calf would probably not produce so much as a ton of oil, but it was brought round to the starboard side and secured there until it could be dealt with.

After the windlass had been used to raise the body of the big fish a few inches out of the water, Captain Stapleton sent for his First Mate. Mr Beaufort returned from the quarter deck with a broad smile and announced there would be hot stew with potatoes for everyone before they started flensing. This news was greeted with less enthusiasm than it might have been because the men had been hoping for a dram. Arthur was disappointed because he'd never tasted rum and he was looking forward to the experience.

The Specksioneer, the harpooners and the men who would be helping to flay the fish, took their food ahead of the rest of the crew and hurried to change their clothes. Arthur sought out Jim Richardson.

'A good start to t' season,' Jim said, almost jumping for joy. 'The Captain knew what he was doing when he decided to give the Greenland Sea another try. One and a half fish and done naught but row a couple of lengths.'

Arthur tried to keep the disappointment out of his voice. 'It all looked so easy, Jim. I mean the fish was almost asking you to bring her alongside.'

'That's where we see the hand of God in all things,' Jim said, suddenly very serious despite his joy. 'The maker of all things has given the instinct of motherhood and childlike affection even to these great beasts, so that the capture of one makes it easier to take the other. Aye, Arthur lad, it's Almighty God we have to thank for the beauty of this world and its convenience to man. That's what God meant in Moses' first book when He said He would let men have dominion over the fish of the sea.'

They went across to the larboard side where the air was already thick with circling birds. The two mallemauk boats, manned by second and third year apprentices, were standing by. Arthur envied them their place near the centre of activity. Mr Nellis went down on to the fish, followed by Mr Dryden and Mr Caspol, the other harpooner.

During flensing the Specksioneer assumed command in accordance with the most ancient customs of the fishery. The First and Second Mates, who were his superior officers at all other times, now dwindled into ordinary harpooners and were, theoretically at least, expected to do his bidding. Even a ship's

Master wouldn't do anything to diminish his Specksioneer's authority while a fish was alongside.

And so Mr Nellis stood on the fish, with his legs somewhat apart and his iron spurs securely lodged in the skin of its belly. You could tell from his stance and the set of his red head that he was king.

The birds, far from being intimidated by these arrivals, became more daring. Many of them were fulmars, or 'mollies' as most of the men called them, gliding with stiff, straight wings. A group of these birds had joined the ship shortly after leaving Lerwick, and they'd picked up every scrap of meat and offal thrown overboard since that day. It had been a meagre enough diet for them on the way up here; but in their silent watchfulness they had seemed to know that their long journey would be rewarded with something much more substantial if only they would be patient. And now here it was.

There were flocks of gulls as well. Arthur recognized the kittiwakes with their graceful, black-tipped wings, and there were others so pure and pearly white they could have been mistaken for doves. Hovering above them all were a number of gulls with a wing span almost as long as a man, and Jim Richardson told him that those lordly creatures had been named *Burgomasters* by the Dutch many years ago.

'Knives!' called Mr Nellis.

The apprentices immediately supplied him with long-handled knives from their armoury on the mallemauk boats. Mr Nellis inspected these instruments before handing them to the other two men on the fish. The two men, under his supervision, proceeded to cut oblong strips from the exposed belly.

'Spades!' called Mr Nellis.

He smacked one of the apprentices over the head for proffering the wrong article, and almost knocked him out of the boat. Arthur's envy of the other youths abruptly diminished. Mr Nellis found the kind of spades he wanted and handed them on. The two men plied the spades to detach the slips from the underlying flesh and bone; and they fastened straps and tackle to the end of the slips as soon as the fat could be lifted.

'Next spades!' bawled Mr Nellis.

The frightened apprentices offered their wares with some diffidence.

Men on deck, under the direction of Mr Beaufort, jumped to the two capstans. One man raised his voice, and after the first two or three familiar words the rest joined in a shanty that had been sung in the northern fishery for over a hundred years:

> It was eighteen hundred and thirty-oh
> On march the seventeenth day
> We weighed our anchor to our bow
> And for Greenland bore away brave boys
> And for Greenland bore away.

The capstans hauled on the tackle and tore off the remainder of the slips. The men on the fish helped the oblong pieces on their way with thrusts from the second set of spades. The two slips came off one after the other in lumps weighing about a ton each. They were swung up on to the deck where Mr Beaufort supervised the cutting up into more convenient pieces. Mr Dryden and Mr Caspol began to loosen the next two slips.

The birds had been circling nearer and nearer during these operations, and now the sight and smell of the yellow flesh under the black skin was driving them crazy. Hundreds more birds appeared, as if from nowhere, and the sky was overcast with their crowded wings.

The fulmars flaked down like snow until there must have been over a thousand of them swimming around the carcase. Scores of them landed on the fish itself and kept climbing back on as quickly as Mr Nellis kicked them off. The kittiwakes landed on the water and dived for pieces of fat which dropped when the slips were ripped away. The ivory gulls fluttered about overhead, darting down whenever they saw a titbit that they could take on the wing. And when any of these different kinds of birds captured a particularly attractive morsel one of the burgomasters would be sure to descend, with a lordly spread of silvery-grey wings, and take away the selected piece of meat as if it were a feudal right fixed from time immemorial.

When the belly had been flayed and the right fin removed, the men on deck used the windlass to haul on the cant-purchase and cant the fish through ninety degrees on to its right side. As Arthur watched the fat again being flayed off, it made him think of a Portuguese orange that his father had brought back from the Tolbooth as a curiosity, and of how he had peeled the tough rind away with his thumb.

The left fin was removed, and after another canting Mr Nellis took away the lip to expose the whalebone on one side of the head. The exterior of the head was adorned with patches of rough, white skin that was studded with barnacles. The largest patch was on top of the head near the blow holes, and it was not unlike a fine lady's lace bonnet.

'Hand spikes!' shouted Mr Nellis. 'Bone knives and bone spades!'

Something new in the apprentices' manner drew Arthur's attention. It was more than a nervousness of Mr Nellis as they leaned out of the mallemauk boats to hand over the tools. When the instruments had been transferred they no longer jostled and joked among themselves. On the contrary, they sat quietly in the middle of the thwarts as if they were afraid to rock the boat.

Jim Richardson, temporarily released from the levers of a capstan, pointed to a gap that had appeared in the floating array of fulmars. 'I pity anyone who falls in now.'

'They'd have nothing to worry about,' said Mr Beaufort, exuding friendliness to everybody after this early strike. 'I've never known them attack a man, greedy though they be.'

'You're right, Mr Beaufort, I'm sure of it,' Jim agreed. 'But I'd hate to be the exception that proves the rule.'

Another man came over to the ship's side whom Arthur had seen only once or twice before, but there wasn't any mistaking him because he was the only man on the ship who wore spectacles. In addition to that, his timid manner and clothes set him apart from the other officers. He was young, clean-shaven, with restless, inquiring eyes.

'Could I inquire what it is you're all looking at?' asked Mr McCabe politely.

Mr Beaufort pointed to the bare patch of sea amidst the floating fulmars, that had started to boil like water behind the top gates of a filling lock. 'Look there! Now that we've canted her over the sharks have come along to feed on t' kreng.'

'Greenland sharks?'

'Aye. Stupidest animals in t' Arctic. But they're big ones by the looks on t' faces of those boys.'

The educated, Edinburgh accent of the ship's surgeon couldn't conceal his excitement. His eyes shone behind his spectacles. 'Do you think I could catch one, Mr Beaufort?'

'There's nothing easier. Getting it up into t' ship is the only problem.'

'Do you think some of your men would be prepared to help me?'

The First Mate showed his teeth in a comradely grin. This strike had made the good humour ooze out of him and he was everybody's friend. 'I dare say they will if I tell them they have to. But you'll have to wait until we've finished flensing. Your sharks won't go away before then, I can promise you. In the meantime you could be baiting the biggest hook you can find with a piece of fat. Throw it over when we cut the calf loose on t' other side, and don't hold on to the line too hard.'

Arthur, who had listened to this conversation between his superiors with the greatest interest, looked at the deserted patch of water. Ripples were radiating round a number of pointed snouts. His pulse quickened joyfully at the thought of what he was going to see.

The fish was canted for the third and last time. The blubber was flayed from its right side, the rest of the whalebone was lifted out of its mouth and the cant-piece and rump fat were stripped away with a massive hook. The huge kreng was cast off to become a prey to the demented birds and the voracious sharks.

The Specksioneer, the harpooners and the mallemauk boats transferred themselves to starboard to deal with the calf. The sharks had ripped away the outer black skin, and were feeding side by side on the calf's white flesh like a row of puppies sucking at their dam. Hundreds upon hundreds of fulmars drifted up and down, too gorged to fly. What with fish and birds the carcase was almost flensed already, and it took less than half an hour to transfer what was left up to the deck.

The small kreng was cut loose and Mr McCabe threw a big iron hook after it, heavily baited with a succulent piece of fat. The line tightened immediately and became as stiff and straight as a backstay. Mr McCabe pulled but he couldn't have made less impression if he'd caught his hook under the keel.

'Oh, Mr Beaufort!' he called. 'Oh, Mr Beaufort! I think I've got a bite!'

The men who'd just finished working the nearer of the capstans started to snigger, but they shut up when Mr Beaufort waved them all across to help the surgeon. The shark was firmly hooked but didn't show the slightest sign of being worried about the situation. The gang of men hauled on the line as if they were in a tug of war. The shark came to the side of the ship and looked up at his captors with bright green eyes.

Mr Beaufort came across and had a look. 'Get a bight under his chest and another under his rump. You'll never get him up otherwise.'

Jim Richardson hurried away and came back with some ropes. The men kept a tight line, holding the shark's head up as if it were a spirited horse, and with some finesse and much patience they managed to loop two lengths of rope underneath the body. At the first lift the heavy bulk slithered out of the constraining sling and re-entered the water with a tremendous slap. The fish could easily have evaded capture the second time also, merely by exerting itself a little, but instead it lay passively in the supporting ropes and was hauled up to the bulwarks; nor did it react in the slightest when Peter Gill chopped the spike of his pick-haak into its side, so as to provide extra leverage for pulling the shark in over the side. It behaved like a living dead thing.

The shark was rather more than the length of two men and lay sullenly on the deck in a growing pool of water. Arthur's gaze was drawn repeatedly to its eyes which had emerald green pupils surrounded by blue, and things like worms growing out of them. When he managed to pull his own eyes away from this particular attraction the general shape reminded him of a dog fish that his father had once brought back from the fish quay. It hadn't tasted very good, and his mam said it was a stupid thing to bother with, but the skin had made a marvellous shagreen cloth that his mam still used.

The fish was so still that if it hadn't been for the brilliant eyes you would have said it was dead. But suddenly it opened its mouth very wide. The stupefied men stared at row after row of pointed teeth. Just as suddenly the mouth closed and the rows of teeth meshed together with a harsh, rasping noise.

The men overcame their surprise and whooped with a kind of delighted appreciation at the performance. A rough game developed in which they pushed one another towards the menacing snout. Mr Beaufort had gone down to the half deck to arrange for the disposal of the blubber in the flens-gut. Mr Dryden and Mr Nellis hadn't yet returned. Mr McCabe was entirely engrossed in poking at the spiracles on the shark's neck, and in any case he made no attempt to exert any authority. In the absence of their senior officers the men played their game with increasing exuberance and there were some violent scuffles.

After a particularly rough encounter Jim Richardson backed out of the scrimmage with his hand raised to his throat. His eyes were distraught. A second later Peter Gill held up a shiny black cross on a broken cord.

'Look at the pretty thing I've found,' he shouted. 'What am I bid for this pretty thing?'

'It's mine,' Jim said, relief flooding his face and pulling it into a wide grin as he came forward with his hand extended.

But Peter Gill could see the start of a new game. He threw the cross over Jim's head into the ready hands of another man who waited until Jim had almost reached him and then, after feinting with one hand, used the other to throw the trinket back to Gill. Laughing and shouting, rejoicing in their freedom, more men joined in the game.

Pain, like a big hand, squeezed Arthur's heart. Jim was skipping from one tormentor to the next, always just too late to snatch his property. He had a fixed smile on his face, and was doing his best to make it appear that he was sharing in the fun. But Arthur could read the anguish in his eyes and it made him wretched.

Peter Gill had just caught the flying object again when the shark opened its mouth for the second time. Without hesitation, seemingly as a continuation of the gesture with which he'd caught it, Gill threw the cross neatly into the yawning cavity. Everyone stood still. The oppressive silence was broken when the fish closed its mouth with the clash of a spring-loaded iron trap and Peter Gill broke into laughter.

'Eat anything, sharks will,' he shrieked, and doubled up with the force of his amusement.

Jim remained perfectly still, one foot forward and arms half raised, as rigid as a chess-tree.

The expression on Jim's face set fire to something in Arthur's body. It burned in every nerve and set his legs in rapid motion. It threw him on to the cackling line-manager whose shoulders he gripped with aching fingers. He was still shaking him, inarticulate with rage, when he became aware that the legs of the men surrounding them had backed away. He looked up and reluctantly released his hold.

Mr Nellis had returned to the main deck and his expression was frightening. Arthur stood up smartly. Peter Gill arose more slowly, and stood awkwardly to show he'd been hurt.

'What's this?' Mr Nellis shouted, his face going almost as red as his beard. 'What are you doing?'

Peter Gill reassured him. 'Just a game, Mr Nellis. Just a harmless game with a stupid toy until this lad tried to turn it into a brawl.'

Mr Nellis turned to Arthur. There was malice and satisfaction in his eyes. 'What do you say, boy?'

'It was something more than a toy,' said Arthur, looking directly into the Specksioneer's fierce face but noticing that Mr Dryden had also come up on deck. 'It was something that – '

'I saw you assault one of your shipmates,' Mr Nellis bawled. 'A senior man, my line-manager. There's no room for people like you on a whaler. If we can't live as a community we soon stop living at all. We end up dead. When I tell Captain Stapleton what I've seen I reckon that without any urging from me he'll put an end to your apprenticeship.'

Arthur felt ill. Of more importance than his own shame would be the disappointment of his parents. He looked at Mr Nellis's big hands. It would be much better to receive a good braying and then let the matter be forgotten.

'Why did you start a fight? Had you any good reason?'

The question was put with a show of temper by Mr Dryden. Arthur, switching his eyes to the Second Mate, gained the impression that he'd adopted this manner in order to support Mr Nellis. After all, he couldn't afford to appear partial in an affair that involved his own line-manager as well as the Specksioneer's.

'It was something more than a toy,' Arthur repeated. 'It was something I happen to know is very important to Jim Richardson.'

Jim had remained in the same rigid position, with an expression of disbelief frozen on his face. It must have been clear that he had something to do with the quarrel.

'And Mr Gill threw it into the shark's mouth,' he added.

Mr Nellis waved his hands to dismiss this point of view, but Mr Dryden spoke again and it was in a milder tone.

'Nothing's lost, Jim. We're not going to throw the fish away, at any rate not until we've had his liver out. There'll be a barrel of good oil in there, and we can ... Yes, that's a good idea, Mr McCabe.'

The surgeon, more sensitive than the typical Greenlander, had perhaps guessed at the depth of Jim's distress. He had slipped away at the crisis and was now returning with his saw. Mr Beaufort also, having seen to matters in the flens-gut, returned to the main deck. He quickly informed himself about the situation and took command.

'I want six men sitting on the fish's back,' he said. 'Sharp now, because we've got other things to do.'

Half a dozen men came forward, glad of this further diversion from the labour and filth of making-off, and sat astride the shark like men going for a ride. The fish lay quietly on its belly, showing no signs of life except for the brightness of the green discs in its eyes, and the occasional movement of the five spiracles on each side of its neck. It didn't flinch when Mr McCabe made the first, tentative pass with his saw some inches behind where he judged the head to be, nor when he proceeded to saw away with long, careful strokes.

The blade sounded as if it were going through a wet, soggy log. The shark remained immobile and its green eyes continued to shine with the full brightness of life. The men on its back realized they were superfluous and grinned foolishly. There would have been more horse play if it hadn't been for the presence of the officers.

When Mr McCabe had accomplished about half his task the mouth opened a fraction of an inch. It was sufficient to show only the gleam of the first row of teeth, but with every subsequent stroke the jaws opened wider by a similar amount. It was as if Mr McCabe, instead of using a saw, were operating a ratchet that was geared to the shark's jaw bones. Backwards and forwards went the saw, wider and wider opened the jaws, more and more rows of teeth came into view. And then, like a jewelled brooch displayed on a velvet cushion, the jet cross was revealed on a pad of thick, grey flesh.

Soon the mouth was stretched so wide that from the front nothing else of the shark was visible. Surely it wouldn't open any wider? But as Mr McCabe completed the final strokes the jaws strained another fraction until it seemed inevitable that the bones at the sides of its head must spring apart.

The head came away from the body. The blade of the saw was smeared red. Mr McCabe took off his spectacles and wiped the lenses. Jim Richardson came out of his trance and moved forwards.

'No!' Mr Dryden shouted.

But Jim was already putting out his hand. Again there was the sound of spikes in an iron trap being clashed together.

Only then did the shark's eyes begin to lose their lustre.

16

The *William Scoresby Senior* remained hove to with her courses clewed up. Captain Stapleton sent Mr Dryden and Mr McCabe down below with the mutilated man; and then, no doubt expecting and certainly hoping to strike another fish soon, lost no more time before giving instructions for making-off.

Mr Caspol, the harpooner from Mr Dryden's second boat, supervised the placing of the speck-trough so that the square hole in its bottom was directly over the main hatch way. The experienced men were taking up their places without waiting for instructions: the krengers, who would cut away the deleterious matter in the blubber; the other harpooners, who would then slice off the black skin; and the boat-steerers, who would chop up what was left and put it in the speck-trough.

Arthur watched them. The image of Jim Richardson, staring at the end of his arm before the pain hit him, wouldn't go away from his mind.

Mr Beaufort had gone down to break out the hold. He stayed to see the ground tier of casks uncovered and left directions for the ballast water to be pumped out. A stench of decay, the pungent memory of fishes killed in the previous season, followed him up the companionway. Arthur, catching a first whiff of it, remembered the wild melody of the fiddle and the feel of Blackie's wide hip bones when she pressed against him as they danced.

On his return to the upper deck Mr Beaufort detailed some of the green-men to assist the harpooners. He showed them how to lift a piece of blubber with a pick-haak and place it on a closh ready for skinning. After a while Mr Caspol took over the responsibility of supervising the men with the pick-haaks. Arthur would have liked a job assisting Mr Caspol, or any of the other harpooners for that matter except Mr Nellis.

'Nothing to do, eh?' demanded Mr Beaufort, suddenly coming up behind him. 'I'd better find you something before you pick a fight with somebody.'

'Yes, Mr Beaufort.'

He followed the First Mate down the companionway to the half deck. The stench was worse here, irritating his nose and making his eyes water. The smell of corruption and decay was everywhere. Again he recalled the suspended whale-oil lamp with its smell of kreng; and again he heard the plaintive moaning of the fiddle and felt Blackie's plump thighs against his legs.

For a moment he feared that Mr Beaufort was going to put him down in the hold, where the smell must have been like a foretaste of death itself. It was a relief when instead he led him across to a vertical, canvas tube that seemed to join together the roof and the floor of the half deck.

'Do you know what this is?'

'It looks like a pipe, Mr Beaufort.'

'It's called the lull. The top end goes through the hatch and is fixed to the hole in t' bottom of the speck-trough, and the lower end reaches down to the tubs in t' hold. Your job is to work these nippers.' Mr Beaufort pointed to two sticks placed around the pipe which were hinged together at one end and free at the other.

He showed how bringing the free ends of the sticks together closed the pipe, and how separating them opened it. 'The line-managers are in t' hold and you take your instructions from them. Do you understand?'

Arthur had a warm feeling of happiness.

'Do you understand?' he asked, more sharply.

'Yes, Mr Beaufort.'

The warm feeling spread inside him. The line-managers were in the hold! He forgot about the fiddle music and the shape of Blackie pressing hard against him. The line-managers were in the hold! He thought of Peter Gill down there in that terrible stink and it made him happy.

Mr Beaufort reached the stairs up to the main deck but turned round and came back again.

'Another thing,' he said, wrinkling his brow and almost smiling. 'I'm not saying there's anything treacherous in Peter Gill, but if he finds out that it's you working the lull he'll perhaps try to be a bit awkward. Now I want you to remember that a line-manager is an officer. That being the case, I don't want to hear any remarks from you on his behaviour.'

'No, Mr Beaufort.'

'I won't listen to any criticism of Peter Gill from you. It wouldn't be acceptable. Do you understand?'

'Yes, sir.'

Mr Beaufort went away. Arthur waited. He wanted the action to start so that he could think of Peter Gill working down there in that choking gas. He didn't want to think about Blackie dancing. He wanted to think about Peter Gill sweating it out in the hold.

An instruction came up from below. 'Let lob! Hey there! Let lob!'

It was Peter Gill. Arthur stepped up to the lull and opened the nippers. The lower end of the lull was accommodated in the half deck by a hole of somewhat greater diameter than its own, and through the gap Arthur could see a portion of Gill's back as he put his tub in position. The nauseous smell of the emptied casks came up from the hold, and the chopped blubber slithered down the tube to meet it. How could they breathe down there and still live?

'Nip! Nip the lull, you blockhead!'

Arthur closed the sticks and the flow of blubber stopped. There was a pause while Peter Gill dragged his tub away to the casks and one of the other line-managers put his tub into position.

'Let lob!'

Arthur opened the nippers and rejoiced afresh that Peter Gill was one of the men breathing the ghastly vapours in the hold. Each time Gill came to the bottom of the lull and shouted his instructions up to the half deck Arthur took a shameless delight in imagining his suffering. He didn't think about Blackie at all but he couldn't help thinking about Jim. Imagining Peter Gill down there helped to blur the memory of Jim. But not much. He would have liked to shout some insult down through the gap while Peter Gill stood with his tub at the bottom, and probably would have done so if it hadn't been for the clear warning left by Mr Beaufort.

Heavy feet clattered on the stairway. Arthur looked up and saw the shaggy red head and broad shoulders of Mr Nellis. With a quick instinct for his own well-being Arthur moved away up the half deck and risked leaving the lull unattended for a while. Mr Nellis came over to the lull and shouted down into the hold.

'Peter Gill.'

Some movement below. 'Yes, Mr Nellis.'

'Mr Beaufort wants you to check the fitting out of the boat that Mr Dryden used today.'

A short silence. 'There was hardly any line run out.'

'The line tubs were upset when the boat was lifted so the entire line needs recoiling.'

Another silence.

'Are you there, Gill? What are you doing?'

'I was thinking that Mr Dryden always coils his own lines, Mr Nellis.'

'I know that!' Mr Nellis roared, and Arthur saw him clench a big fist and shake it at the aperture around the lull. 'I've known that for years. But he's with the surgeon helping to deal with the man who normally ought to coil them but who can't in any case because of the game you played with him. You haven't forgotten about that already, have you?' Mr Nellis's temper got the better of him and he hammered at the lull with his fist, battering the chunks of blubber that had accumulated above the nippers. 'Get yourself up here and see to that boat. If the Captain sees a fish and those boats aren't fitted out you'll have another fight on your hands. And it'll be a real fight this time, not a childish wrestling match with a boy apprentice that you should have brayed any road. I'll make you a promise. If that boat isn't ready for dropping I'll kick your arse until it looks like blubber left in t' cask from the previous season.'

Mr Nellis was stamping away when he glimpsed Arthur on the other side of a stanchion.

'You!' he shouted. 'Stand by these nippers!'

Arthur came slowly forward. As soon as Mr Nellis recognized him Arthur could tell from the change in his expression that his earlier instinct for keeping out of sight had been well founded.

The Specksioneer's face was working in a fearsome way. Perhaps he'd taken an instant dislike to Arthur when he shouldered him aside at the bottom of the ratlines on Sailing Day; undoubtedly the way Blackie had danced with Arthur and taken him upstairs had left a painful wound; and the Mate had intervened when he thought he'd found good cause to make Arthur suffer. Perhaps there were other emotions flowing in Mr Nellis, and for some reason Arthur provided the best conduit for leading them away.

Arthur turned his head just before the massive fist reached his chin, and then the other fist swung into his ribs and sent him skittering across the planks of the half deck.

'Oh, dearie me,' Mr Nellis said. 'Our young apprentice has fallen down the companionway. You'll have to take better care in future, won't you?'

The Specksioneer whistled as he climbed the stairs. Arthur lay for a little while before turning over on to his front and bending a knee ready for standing up. A foot was placed on his shoulder. The leg straightened abruptly and put him on his back again. He looked up into the face of Peter Gill.

The line-manager's normally white face had a good deal of colour in it. His nose was inflamed and his eyelids so swollen that they almost overwhelmed the blood-shot slits between them. His face was so pitifully changed that Arthur couldn't help thinking that Peter Gill must be glad of the additional work, because it had taken him out of the hold before the making-off was finished.

'It's the sneaking apprentice again.' Peter Gill kicked him in the stomach and in the groin. 'Just fallen down the stairs like Mr Nellis said.'

Arthur rolled away from him and stood up painfully. Peter Gill came after him and thrust his face close. His blood-shot eyes were full of water. The stench he brought with him was appalling, but there was a sweet smell mixed with it that Arthur hadn't come across before.

'You touch me again, young 'un, and you'll not get off so lightly.'

Arthur would have loved to punch the dark, bristly head. But he was mindful of what Mr Beaufort had said, so he did nothing and remained silent. If he let this develop into a fight his career in the fishery would be over almost before it started.

One of the other line-managers was shouting up from below. He limped across to the lull and opened the nippers. Peter Gill followed. He ignored him. Peter Gill didn't want to be ignored.

'In future you keep your cake-hole well caulked. Do you hear me?'

Arthur remained silent.

Peter Gill thrust his face close again and seized the front of Arthur's shirt. The sweet, nauseating smell returned.

'D' you hear me?'

'I hear you, Mr Gill.'

'Don't forget then.'

The line-manager gave him a violent push and lurched away to check the fitting of the boats and the coiling of the lines.

Hours of standing at the lull and the fumes from the hold made Arthur glad when he could retire to his berth. He was very tired. Even so he was dreading the prospect of seeing Jim Richardson, and when he reached his bunk he was tremendously relieved to find that Jim was asleep, or at least unconscious.

Rasmie Hughson, the big Shetlander in the next bunk, was waggling his little finger about in his ear to clean it; but he desisted long enough to tell Arthur something of the trouble Mr Dryden had in holding Jim down. Mr McCabe had come in with a piece of iron heated until it was red in the cook's fire and seared the ragged end.

Arthur lay gratefully on his bed and waited for sleep to rush up and cover him like an incoming tide. But sleep flowed up and ebbed away. He kept seeing the severed shark's head and Jim's arm with the hand missing. Sometimes this picture faded and in its place he saw the severed claw of a dog crab holding on like grim death, as the saying so appropriately was, to a small white hand. And he saw the small hand, with the middle finger missing above the knuckle, take hold of her mother's shawl that was blowing in the wind. Why can't we all remain as we are? What is this terrible thing that insists on changing us, destroying us, and that we can't resist?

Sleep swept up to him and receded again. What was it, Something important, his brain insisted, something he had to understand. Sleep washed up to him but like a more successful Canute he willed it to keep its distance for a few seconds longer.

'Rasmie?'

'What is it, laddie?'

'What's that smell? A kind of sweet, sickly smell?'

The Shetlander laughed. 'That wis Mr McCabe again. Mr Dryden held Jim doon, as I told ye, and Mr McCabe poured rum intae his throat until he wis sick but they still kept pouring it in. A terrible waste. And he still went crazy when they poot the iron on.'

'Rum? It's rum?'

'Ye wad think the Captain cuid hae given us all a wee dram tae help wae the making-off, wadn't ye?'

The tide of sleep rolled in and almost engulfed Arthur's last waking thoughts. So that was the smell of rum, was it? It was the same sickly, sweet smell that Peter Gill brought up from the hold with him. The importance of this discovery kept him awake for a few moments longer. He'd have to tell Mr Dryden. Mr Beaufort had told him he wouldn't listen to any criticism of Peter Gill. Wouldn't be acceptable, was what he said. And Peter Gill had told him to caulk his cake-hole. And Mr Nellis would want to kill him for causing trouble for his line-manager again.

But I'll have to tell Mr Dryden. I promised, I absolutely promised after we'd spanned the harpoons. Peter Gill is drinking rum in secret! That was why he wasn't walking properly. I'll have to tell Mr Dryden. Have to.

And then the tide came right up.

17

'A fall! A fall! A fall!'

It seemed to Arthur that he'd no sooner fallen asleep before he was awakened by a frantic stamping on the deck above his head. The men up there were shouting at the tops of their voices.

'A fall! A fall! A fall!'

The call had been known to him for years, as it was to every youth who listened to stories about the fishery. It meant that one of the boats had struck a fish and relayed the fact back to the ship by raising a jack. The ship was responding by sending a jack up to her mizzen-peak to show that she was dispatching immediate assistance. The present racket was to tell the watch below that it was needed. Actually to hear the call, accompanied by the stamping, was so much more alarming than the mere telling of it that Arthur didn't realize at first what was happening. Then he saw men leaping out of their beds and seizing their bundles of clothes.

The uproar penetrated Jim Richardson's rum-drenched mind and his head appeared over the side of the top bunk. 'The cross,' he whispered. 'My great-great-granfayther's cross. No harm, they said. No harm if you had faith in it.' He started to cry. 'Not if you had faith. They all told me.'

Jim couldn't go! Of course!

Arthur's tiredness dropped from him and he jumped out of bed. Cursing the lack of foresight that had prevented him from tying his clothes in a secure bundle, he snatched up the various pieces from where he'd dropped them and dashed to the stairs.

'They all told me,' Jim wailed. 'I believed it because they all told me.'

Despite his haste, Arthur was one of the last out of the companion. He almost fell on to the deck and was soon jostling other men who, wearing nothing but their night clothes, were all scrambling into the boats. He laughed happily. It would have been easy to imagine that the ship was sinking and that these desperate men, each with his small bundle of treasured possessions, were intent on escaping while any boats remained.

Arthur climbed into the larboard quarter boat with his clothing tightly held in both arms and took the line-manager's place at the after oar. He was shaking with cold even before he sat down. The other oarsmen had already untied their bundles and were desperately trying to finish putting their clothes on before the boat was lowered.

'Who told you to get into Mr Dryden's boat?' asked the boat-steerer, who was sitting facing him.

Arthur picked up his shirt. 'I thought he mightn't have had time to name a replacement for Jim Richardson.'

'You thought that, did you?' Mr Fenby seemed to consider that an extraordinary thought to have. As if to explore a little further Arthur's peculiar modes of thinking he asked him another question. 'What do you think that is? Look, standing there!'

Arthur's head came out of his shirt and he saw one of the green-men standing forlornly beside a davit with his clothes under his arm. He was looking very bewildered, uncertain whether to come aboard or not.

'Too late!' shouted Mr Fenby, waving the man away. 'Go back to bed.'

Arthur was reaching for his trousers when the sheaves whirred in their blocks. He only had time to seize his oar before the boat hit the water.

'Pull!' exploded Mr Dryden's voice from the other end of the boat. 'Pull! Give way! Bend your backs!'

The boat, double-ended and carvel-built of steamed oak, leaped forward like a startled fish when the six oars cut the water. Arthur, although prepared for it, was amazed and slightly awed by the urgency. It was a kind of panic. Each man was pulling his oar as if determined to squander his entire life's stock of energy and die of exhaustion within the next five minutes.

'Pull!' shouted Mr Dryden from the bow, and it was incredible that he should be pulling his oar along with the rest of them, and yet have sufficient breath left over for so much as a whisper. 'Pull! What's the matter with you?'

At some sign invisible to Arthur the boat-steerer took over the job of exhortation. After the frenzied start they had settled down to a cracking pace, and Mr Dryden presumably wanted to save what breath he could for the additional jobs he might soon have to undertake.

'Pull!' yelled Mr Fenby almost in Arthur's face, plying his long steering oar. The nature of his function permitted him to scull without submitting to the general discipline of the other six men, and he could indulge himself with longer sentences than the Second Mate. 'Pull! Sweat that Lerwick whisky out of your bellies! Pull! Get the smell of peat out of your lungs. Pull! If you've got boils now's the time to burst them! Pull! Make those Shetland bugs wish they'd stayed at home!'

Arthur was no longer shivering. The rhythmic pulling of the oar and the quickened beating of his heart soon pumped warmth into his sweating body. The six oars dipped together, pulled together and came back together in perfect unison, like the legs of some enormous insect running on the water. The six oars were six limbs of flesh and blood, moving harmoniously under the control of a central mind. The oars, the boat, the men and their separate personalities, were all parts of this new being.

How could that tubby, stubby whaling ship, maternal figure though she was, have given birth to such a limber creature? This graceful child must be a changeling; or else the ancient viking blood, temporarily lost sight of in the bluff bows and broad beam of the parent, was now reasserting itself.

The boat was a bird, light-boned and long-winged, a thing of air and not of water. It was skimming over the black waves of this arctic sea like a swallow over a village pond.

Arthur's spirit flew with it. I am no longer an individual person with a will of my own. I've become something else, something greater and more powerful than myself. No, that's wrong. I am still myself, with all my memories, private thoughts and particular ways of doing things. In fact I am more myself than ever I was because I've never been more alive, more alert, more aware of this extraordinary thing that is myself. And I've never been so happy. Even this fatigue that is making my legs numb, this aching in my fingers where they curl round the oar, this return of coldness to my feet, all these different kinds of pain are different kinds of joy to me. But this change has happened because at the same time I've become part of something else. It's something that contains Mr Dryden in the bows and the boat-steerer opposite me, and the other boatmen, and the oars in their rope grommets, and the boat itself and the men on the west side who cut and steamed the wood, and the cold sea and the big black fish that are swimming in it. We are all different and yet we are all parts of the same thing.

Mr Dryden resumed command of the boat. At his word they ceased their labours and sat still with the six oars out of the water. The sweat dried on Arthur's naked legs and within a few seconds he was shivering. Each boatman was responsible for observing the restricted area of water at which his oar pointed. Mr Dryden and the boat-steerer, at opposite ends of the boat, kept twisting round so as to scan the entire area.

It was very quiet. The boat drifted slowly round until Arthur could see the other three boats. From noting what was happening now it was easy to reconstruct the preceding events.

Mr Beaufort, in the first boat, had struck the fish and raised his jack. Mr Nellis, in the second boat, had been called upon to give assistance and had attached his lines to those of the fast boat. The fish, wherever it was, must be a big one and it was still sounding. Captain Stapleton must have decided to lower his third and fourth boats without delay.

Mr Dryden's task was to estimate where the fish would rise and to place his boat there before it did so. He was trying to answer the question by observing the direction and speed with which the lines were being taken out of Mr Beaufort's boat, and by guessing at the depth and distance the fish could have travelled. He arrived at a conclusion and signalled to Mr Fenby, who quietly deployed his long oar until the boat was in a position that accorded with the Second Mate's wishes.

If Mr Dryden's computations were to prove perfectly accurate then the fish would come up directly under the boat. But the area of sea in which the fish might rise, and the large margin of error in even the best estimate, meant that the odds against such an occurrence made it one of the least worrying hazards in the fishery.

The fourth boat, a five-oared boat, had followed them with all possible speed. It was placed between Mr Nellis and Mr Dryden. The men in all four boats were silent. They waited with their oars horizontal to the surface of the water, and their muscles tensed to begin rowing at the first syllable of command.

The fish continued to sound. It had by now drawn all the lines out of the fast boat, where Mr Beaufort stood casually in the bow with a lance in his hand. The fish was taking the lines out of the second boat at such a rate that Mr Nellis cast two turns round the bollard in the front to retard it. The friction of rope on wood sent up a cloud of smoke that almost screened the Specksioneer from view. Peter Gill, his line-manager, snatched up the piggin, filled it with water and doused the smouldering bollard. The angle of the line to the water became more oblique, but the fish was sounding with undiminished vigour. Peter Gill continued to wet the bollard and he kept disappearing in a mixture of steam and smoke.

The second boat raised an oar vertically.

'Pull!' erupted Mr Dryden.

Six oars hit the water simultaneously and they got away so fast that the bow came well up. But the fourth boat had started with equal promptness and it was a good deal nearer to begin with.

'Put up oars,' Mr Dryden said. 'We'll leave it to Mr Caspol. Those who need to can finish getting dressed, but be quick about it.'

This short burst of activity had pumped the warm blood back into Arthur's hands and feet, and he wouldn't have minded rowing hard for another hour. The possibility of again sitting still with elevated oars, while the air numbed his half-naked body, had filled him with dread. But this was better than anything. He fell to his knees to recover his trousers from the bottom of the boat.

'Careful how you sit down again,' Mr Fenby cautioned him. 'If you catch it under your leg it'll crack off like an icicle.'

The other boatmen laughed.

'Quiet, my lads,' said Mr Dryden.

Arthur dragged the crumpled trousers over his shivering legs, and by the time he'd pulled down his second flannel shirt the other men had put on their pea jackets. As he reached for the gansey his grandma had knitted he saw Mr Nellis's boat point a second oar upwards; and by the time he'd pulled it down over his head the boat had raised a third oar, and a fourth one followed.

A vertical oar was the universally accepted signal that a boat needed assistance, and these additional oars meant that their requirement for more line must have become desperate. The fourth boat hadn't covered much more than half the intervening distance.

Mr Nellis grabbed the piggin from Peter Gill and took over the job of pouring water on the bollard. He stood in the bow, a huge, dimly seen figure labouring amid the smoke. The fast boat was in serious trouble. The strain on the line had pulled the black sheer strakes at the bow down to sea level and they were shipping water. Everyone except the Specksioneer crowded into the stern which, despite their combined weight, stayed clear of the surface.

'The fish has made fools of them,' said an old boatman behind Arthur. 'They should have put their oars up long ago.'

Arthur finished buttoning his jacket. At last he was completely dressed and could give all his attention to what was happening. The men in the assisting boat were straining every muscle in their attempt to close the gap and join their lines in time. The fish was still diving at the same speed. The men who'd crowded into the stern of the fast boat were beginning to show signs of panic.

'Too late,' said Mr Dryden. 'He'll have to cut the line.'

Mr Nellis abandoned his work with the piggin. But instead of taking the axe from its cupboard he retreated from the dipping bows and made his way towards the stern. A small flame popped up on the over-heated bollard. Mr Nellis appeared to be busy with the end of the line, and his boatmen made way for him to approach the ring at the stern.

'No, no, no,' Mr Dryden said, in pained disapproval.

The assisting boat was only a few lengths away when Mr Nellis and all his men leaped into the water. The men in Mr Dryden's boat groaned in sympathy. Within the same second the stem of the fast boat disappeared. The stern pointed straight up at the sky and then it followed.

'He's given the boat to t' fish!' exclaimed a voice behind Arthur. 'I wonder what the Captain will say about that.'

'I wonder what Mr Foster would say,' added another.

Mr Fenby pulled at the rim of his woollen headgear until a charitable eye might have conceded that it bore some vague resemblance to a Quaker hat. 'Why didst thou give one of my boats to a fish?' he inquired in a solemn voice. 'Didst thou not know that fishes can swim and have no need of boats?'

The third boat arrived amongst the floundering men who all found hand-holds on the gunwales. They were helped out of the freezing water without delay. Mr Beaufort's boat came alongside and took off half the passengers so that the load was equally shared. Both the overloaded boats turned and headed for the ship so as to avoid permanent injury to the wetted men. The ship had been brought to the wind with her main topsail hove aback to await their return. The two remaining boats had been dropped some time before, but they were still a long way off.

'Nobody will have any complaints,' Mr Dryden said, 'provided we find the boat and it's still fast.'

'And provided those lads don't take any harm,' said the old boatman behind Arthur.

There was a murmur of agreement.

'Quiet please,' Mr Dryden said.

He had readjusted his estimate of the fish's whereabouts and made a signal. The boat-steerer sculled them to the new position. There they waited, oars parallel with the surface of the sea.

When Mr Nellis became certain that he would run out of line before assistance arrived, the usual course would have been for him to cut the rope. Instead of doing that he'd fastened the end of the line to the iron ring. The fish was as loose as if the rope had been cut, but the extra impediment of the waterlogged boat was bound to tire it more quickly than a harpoon and a mere few hundredweight of line. If the fish were lost then Mr Nellis had made a bad decision. But what rankled with the men in Mr Dryden's boat was the way Mr Nellis had been prepared to give his boatmen a ducking despite the cold.

'Just because Nellie has a skin as thick as a fish,' said Mr Fenby in a low voice, 'and a brain to match, he thinks he –'

'*Pull!*'

The six oars cut the water as one and in the same second Arthur heard the fish blow. It was very loud and sounded terribly close.

'Pull! He's waiting for us! Pull!'

Each time Arthur put his back into the stroke he looked into the boat-steerer's eyes to see if he could read anything there. Mr Fenby kept his gaze fixed unwaveringly over Arthur's shoulder to somewhere ahead. An inner tension had pulled the lips away from his teeth and his beard stuck out on the end of his chin like a piece of tow. Each time Arthur came forward on his oar he tried to look backwards over his shoulder, in the direction of the boat-steerer's gaze, but he couldn't see anything.

Mr Dryden must have noticed him. 'Eyes in the boat!' he ordered.

Arthur tried to curb his impatience by telling himself that they would probably approach the fish on a circuitous course. He would have a better chance of seeing it just before they turned for the attack.

The eyes of a whale are no larger than those of a horse, and a horse's eyes of the same relative size wouldn't be any larger than nail heads. In addition, the most enormous head in creation is placed between these tiny eyes which makes it impossible for both eyes to see the same object at the same time. The size of the head makes it natural that few individual items are ever seen with more than one eye. When they are, the interval between the two sightings probably makes the whale think it has seen two similar but distinct objects. It is likely that many a whale approached by two or three boats believed itself to be attacked by half a dozen.

Whatever the defects of the whale's vision might be, experience had shown that it soon observed any approach from the side. It was always advisable to attack from a blind spot, of which there were two: directly ahead and behind.

One of the oldest principles of the fishery was that a boat should never *go on the eye of a fish* or attack from a position ahead. Green-men often thought this was to avoid the terrors of the fish's mouth. It was a measurable fact that the mouth of an adult fish could easily accommodate a six-oared boat with all its crew and gear, but the terror lay in the contemplation of a theoretical possibility rather than in any likelihood. The Greenland fish were without teeth but an attack from the front, even if safe, was certainly as futile as an attack on a stone wall. A needle and thread flung against a pane of glass were more likely to find a lodging than a harpoon and line thrown at a fish's head. Hercules couldn't have made the sharpest iron penetrate that resilient skin.

It was a practice as old as the Dutch supremacy, probably as old as the Biscayan pioneers, that a fish should always be attacked from the rear. This tactic had a double advantage: not only was the boat invisible to the fish, but the target was extensive enough to allow for a fair amount of inaccuracy in the throw. Unfortunately, the approach from the rear was far and away more dangerous than from any other quarter.

The rear was the domain of the lordly and imperial tail. With an upward flip of this tremendous weapon even a small fish could send a boat so high into the air that it turned over several times and shed all its contents before it started to come down again; and even more alarming was the downward stroke, which with a casual smack could reduce a boat to splinters and its crew to bruised meat.

And now as Arthur leaned back into the stroke he could tell from the direction of Mr Fenby's stare that they were circling the fish. The boat-steerer's eyes were round and shining and there was spittle on his tuft of beard. His face showed disappointment. Or was it anger? As Arthur came forward he looked over his shoulder and saw the fish for the first time.

He expected it to be big. People had always exaggerated the size of them, and a fish that had taken two sets of lines and a boat down so far had to be big. But there wasn't anything to see apart from a bluish ridge and a dorsal fin.

'Razorback!' whispered Mr Fenby and spat on the floor. 'That bloody man Beaufort would harpoon his own grandmother if he thought she'd yield enough oil to buy him a pinch of snuff. Best to let it be, and Nellie's boat an' all.'

The man behind Arthur, catching something of this, turned his head.

'Eyes in the boat and stop talking!' ordered Mr Dryden severely. Then, in a gentler voice: 'Pull! Good lads.'

After what seemed like a quarter of an hour but couldn't have been more than half a minute the boat turned.

'Take me up to him,' Mr Dryden said quietly, as if he were asking them to do him a favour.

The boat-steerer was again looking directly over Arthur's shoulder. An expression of unease had settled on his face, but he smiled suddenly and Arthur knew that Mr Fenby and Mr Dryden were smiling at each other. Arthur would have given almost anything to turn his head and see what was happening.

'Up oars and eyes in the boat,' said Mr Dryden in a flat, conversational kind of voice.

Arthur was surprised. Surely, he thought, surely we are still too far away. They raised their oars and sat in silence. It had grown colder and within a few seconds the air began to nip them.

The boat continued under the momentum imparted to it by their last strokes, and then by the gentle sculling of the steering oar. Some Greenlanders said that the fish were dull of hearing and didn't react to talk or even shouts, no matter how close. There was debate about that, but all experienced men agreed that even if the fish were deaf to noises in the air they were quick to notice sounds in water. The boat-steerer plied his oar softly.

Arthur heard Mr Dryden's feet scrape on the planks as he stood up in the bow.

A sudden blast made him grip his oar tightly. It was like the misfire of a musket or the sharp slap of a loose sail on a stay. This damp explosion was followed by the rasping of a hundred men blowing wet trumpets. A moment later his face and neck grew warm and moist.

Big, steaming pipes were abruptly plugged. The fish had stopped blowing. The cold air moved in again. In the new silence Arthur heard Mr Dryden's *Uh*-uh as he threw the iron.

'Wood on black skin!' Mr Fenby screamed.

'Back oars! Stern hard!' shouted Mr Dryden, falling back into his place.

Arthur leaned forward on his oar. The sea rolled and dipped beneath them. The boat tilted and slewed round. He could look sideways at the fish.

Why had the boat-steerer shouted the old alarm? And why was Mr Dryden so anxious for them to back off? The loudness of the blow had made it seem near, but the head was a long way off.

'Back! Back oars! Back! Back!'

The head was in the air. It was smooth and bluish black, without any of the white patches that had decorated the fish they'd flensed. Slowly, impossibly slowly, the head fell back into the water with a dull, echoing boom. Dark waves hit the boat and pitched it about until it turned round completely and was directly in line with the fish but pointing away from it.

'Pull! Pull it away, lads!'

'Wood on black skin!' gabbled Mr Fenby again.

Now they could all row in the normal manner and look back at the fish. The iron had lodged well forward on its back, probably not much further back than the main fins. It was a good strike, particularly as that second blow so soon after breaching was an indication that the fish knew they were there and was preparing for another dive. Mr Dryden couldn't have had any time for nice calculations.

Mr Fenby had raised the jack to signal they were fast. Arthur, looking round from the fish for a moment, saw that the two fresh boats were still some distance away. And there was a suggestion of fog on the horizon.

The head was sinking and a hump had formed behind it on the back. After the head had disappeared the hump, like a living animal being sucked through the alimentary canal of a snake, travelled towards the still invisible tail. The big black ball sank. For a few seconds there was nothing in the area except the boat.

'Pull! Give way!' shrieked the boat-steerer, and the spittle flew from his lips into Arthur's face.

What was the matter with him? The wash from the sinking head wouldn't founder them now. And the head must be over a hundred feet away. They were clear.

Then the sea round about became as smooth as oil and deepened its colour. The noise of water being sucked into a cavernous pipe made Arthur's heart bang hard and then leave an empty space in his chest. The tail came out from under the gunwale. It couldn't belong to the same fish! He cried out with fright. The distance between the tips of the flukes was equal to that of the boat from stem to stern.

Up and up it went, darkening the sky. Nothing of the fish was visible but its tail, set horizontally on its soaring stalk. Up and up it went to reveal the wrinkled rump and the mottled, grey skin where the shaft joined the body. Up and up until it was perfectly erect, and the flukes spread out like a black flag waving above a tower.

'Give way! Pull! Pull!'

No need for such exhortations now. One danger was past but every man could see the danger to come. Each one of them would have broken his back and burst his muscles if he could. The tail was stationary against the cold sky. But the boat was stationary as well, stuck in the water and unable to flee from the dark shadow. Then the tail began to come down.

The movement was uncertain at first, almost as if the fish were intent on staying that way and was merely making a balancing movement. But in a moment the direction was clear and the speed increased. Long muscles shortened and bunched underneath the black skin. The edges of the flukes started to make a whistling noise as they cut the air.

The men pulled and prayed.

A giant smacked the top of the sea with the flat of his hand. A cannon fired immediately behind the stern. Arthur's ears clicked and filled with a low buzzing that prevented him from hearing anything else. The boat jumped like a horse that was taken unawares by an awkward fence, and that didn't have time to recover itself before facing another one. Concentric rings of water overtook them, one after the other, and with the passage of each the ends of the boat took it in turn to point at the sky. They shipped water every time they pitched and the air was thick with falling spray.

The tail missed us, Arthur thought, and we're still afloat. And if we're not sinking now we're not going to sink. Life was almost unbearably sweet.

The waves subsided slowly. The sea around the boat remained white with foam and bubbles and a fine spray continued to fall from the sky. Mr Dryden threw the line round the bollard and the foam, bubbles and spray disappeared. The fish was running and taking them to fresh waters.

Each man was experiencing the tumultuous joy of being alive. Mr Fenby burst into song:

> 'I'm a young virgin just come aboard,
> And I have as envious a maidenhead
> As ever a young man took in his hand.
> Besides I have forty pounds in land.'

The boat-steerer lay back in the stern with the shaft of the long oar under his armpit and his eyes raised to the cold sky. His voice was a good baritone, and he sang with a fine vibrance and depth of feeling. The words of the song were tiny things on that great expanse of sea.

> 'This young virgin as we understand
> Took a trip to a foreign land.
> Whereas forty young lovers a roving came
> To some of their callings I long for to name.'

Arthur had never travelled so fast in his life. The carvel-built bottom was slithering over the water like a sledge on ice. The sharp bows smacked now and again into small waves and made a white haze. The sea foamed under their pointed stem, hissed around their sides below the black sheer strakes and trailed away behind them in a sparkling ribbon. The fresh boats were nowhere to be seen and the *William Scoresby Senior* was slipping towards the horizon.

Mr Fenby gave them the lead to each verse. Arthur joined in as they began to work their way through the young lovers:

> 'The first was a merchant that came in,
> He told what a traveller he had been.
> He boasted how he could handle his pen,
> He said he could write the best of all men.'

A little ball of happiness in Arthur's stomach started to grow. It swelled to a great size and burst into a kind of radiance. For the second time since he entered the boat he felt that he'd somehow ceased to exist as an individual but that he lived in a more complete way as a part of something more important. The submerged fish, the running line, the hurrying boat, the deserted sea, the endless sky, the men with their raised oars, the words of the song, everything he apprehended with any of his senses was part of another song that itself was endless.

They sang of the other young lovers, and of how the young virgin dealt with each in turn. After the merchant with his pen there was the doctor with his lance; and then the apothecary with his clyster; and then the fiddler . . .

Just as they were about to begin the verse about the sailor, who would inevitably triumph over everyone who'd gone before, Mr Fenby failed to give the lead. He was staring ahead in the direction being taken by the fish. Arthur noticed that some drops of spittle had frozen in his beard. Mr Dryden stopped singing and the other voices faded one by one, until the hiss of water under the sheer strakes was the only sound in all that expanse of sea and sky.

Arthur turned round. Mr Dryden, and all the other men behind him, had turned round to look ahead. The fish was still running horizontally and at the same speed. It was probably swimming just under the surface. The fish was now too far away for any perturbation in the water to be visible from the boat, but the fulmars could see it and a flock of them was charting its passage. Beyond the birds was a bank of fog.

Mr Dryden turned to the boat. 'If he's so keen on exercise we'd better give him a bit more work. Drop your oars, lads.'

They lowered their blades and six fountains shot up and travelled alongside the boat like attendant sprites. From time to time a man's arms and shoulders would rebel against the unvarying strain, and one of the water spouts would disappear when he had to let the blade jump out for a few seconds before he resubmerged it. Arthur felt the weight of the sea running against his oar and had an awesome intuition of a strength so mighty it was beyond imagining.

'Dive, damn you!' said Mr Fenby.

If only the fish would go down and rise again within a start, they could kill it without any need for assistance from the other boats. If it continued to run on its present course, and at anything near its present speed, things were going to be different.

Mr Fenby shook his fist. 'Dive!' he ordered. 'Why won't you dive?'

'He can't,' Mr Dryden said in his quiet way. 'He's too tired. He couldn't stand all that water on top of him again.'

'That's good news, then,' the boat-steerer said.

The fish had been down more than a mile which must have squeezed his ribs and lungs. And he's got two irons in his back,

Arthur remembered, and he's carrying all the lines from two boats. That's 1,440 fathoms of wet rope and he's adding to it all the time with the line he's running out of this boat. In addition he's dragging two boats, one under the surface and full of water and the other on the surface and full of men. He couldn't last much longer.

'When you consider it rightly,' said Mr Fenby, for all the world as though he'd just thought of it himself, 'we ought to be glad he won't sound. It means he's as good as finished.'

The fish continued to swim with unabated power. The line was wearing a groove in the bollard, but the friction didn't seem to have any braking effect whatsoever. Mr Dryden was using the piggin, and the smoke was so thick that Arthur kept thinking they'd run into the fog bank.

The fog came nearer. The men kept turning round to look at it but said nothing. The fulmars disappeared. Now the fog was rushing towards them. The *William Scoresby Senior* had shaken out her canvas and piled up but she wasn't coming any closer.

'I'm sorry lads,' Mr Dryden said.

He put the piggin on the floor and reached down to the bow cupboard. The men were silent in the bitter knowledge of defeat. Perhaps if there hadn't been any fog the nearer boat might have reached them before their lines were run out. But the fish was strong enough to take them where no boat would ever find them. They hadn't any choice.

Mr Dryden took the axe from the cupboard. 'It ought to make you feel better to know that it's a razorback. They never have much oil or bone no matter how big they are.'

'And they sink when they die,' Mr Fenby added. 'Not worth bothering with when all's said and done.'

'I wouldn't have harpooned him,' Mr Dryden said, delaying until the last moment, 'if it hadn't been for Mr Nellis's boat.'

'I know what I'd like to do with Nellie's boat,' grumbled the boat-steerer.

The fog was almost on them.

'I'm sorry, lads,' said Mr Dryden again. 'But we'll be better off without him.'

He raised the axe in his unhurried, careful way. That action seemed to trigger everything that followed.

When Arthur recalled the next seconds in future days, which he often would, it always appeared that something had happened to the passage of time. To begin with things happened slowly, and with the kind of sureness and precision that characterized everything that Mr Dryden ever did. The second line-tub made a noise. The rope snagged somewhere inside and the tub coughed it out. A bight travelled along the line, flipped the turns off the bollard and threw a loop round Mr Dryden's upraised arm. It pulled tight at his elbow.

Then everything speeded up, and for a short while things happened extra quickly to make up for the time that had been lost. Mr Dryden opened his mouth so wide that his moustaches turned upwards, but he didn't have time to speak to anyone. His long body executed a tremendous forward jump out of the boat, ploughed into the sea ahead of the stem and disappeared.

The boat was losing headway before it entered the first wisps of fog. It was stationary by the time Arthur had scrambled across the thwarts to the other end.

18

'What the hell are you trying to do?' screamed the boatman who'd been pulling the oar aft of the bow.

But Arthur had already done it. His reaction to what was happening had deadened all his senses, and yet at the same time it had catapulted him to the other end of the boat and enabled him to act very quickly. He'd snatched some coils of line from the second tub and deftly wapped a couple of them on to the bollard. The slack was run out in the flick of an eye, the line bit into the grooved wood and tightened, and the running fish yanked the boat into motion so violently that Arthur fell backwards over a thwart and almost went over the gunwale.

The boat smacked into the fog. The sound of water flapping against the bows and hissing under the sheer strakes told them that they were going forward at the same speed as before.

'You meddling fool!' The boatman threw himself on Arthur. 'You bloody imbecile.'

Arthur raised his hands to loosen the grip on his throat. 'We can't just sit here! We can't let the fish take him away!'

The grip tightened and pressed the sides of his windpipe together. The boatman was out of his mind with fury and acting like a man possessed. What had happened had put a demon in him that would only be appeased by choking Arthur to death.

'A knife!' someone was shouting. 'A knife, for Jesus' sake!'

Mr Fenby ordered the men aside as he made his way forward. The boat rocked dangerously with the redistribution of weight in the bows and the shifting balance of the fighting men. A polished blade made a silver smear in the grey air and for the second time the boat lost headway. The sound of hurrying water stopped. They were surrounded by fog and silence. The boat was stationary once again.

'Everyone in their places!' the boat-steerer ordered.

Despite Arthur's youth, he had broad shoulders and big bones, and his natural strength enabled him to hold his own with the crazed boatman. The boatman wouldn't release his hold until Mr Fenby pricked his neck with his knife. They felt their way back to their seats.

They were in another world. Clammy, grey hands stroked their eyelids, pushed cold fingers up their noses and in their ears, stuffed their mouths and wrapped them round with a damp, freezing blanket. The boat was suspended outside space, outside time.

Arthur couldn't see the boat-steerer, although he was sitting opposite to him, nor the seat on which he himself was sitting, nor the oar under his own hands, nor anything except his mittened fingers when he held them up before his nose. The sea was inaudible. Nothing moved. Nothing breathed. He himself dwindled away until he was nothing but his recent memories.

He remembered the careful hands performing the various jobs preparatory to the spanning of a harpoon; and he saw the long moustaches moving up and down as Mr Dryden explained that the harpoon hadn't changed for over two hundred years. Some things didn't change. Or perhaps they changed slowly, over a long period of time, so that you didn't notice the change and it wasn't painful. Why did change sometimes come so violently? Hidden by the fog Arthur made no attempt to hide his tears.

A hand came from behind, found his shoulder and squeezed it gently. 'There's not a man that wouldn't have tried to save the Second Mate,' the old man said. 'But the fish had him and we couldn't do anything but let the line run out. When you tightened the line it must have nearly nipped his arm off.' He shook Arthur's shoulder reassuringly. 'He'd be glad when he could tell we'd cut it.'

Arthur lowered his face into his hands. I increased your suffering. I prolonged your pain. He shook his head to dispel the idea of Mr Dryden's terrible gladness when he felt the line go slack behind him. This movement of the head shuffled his thoughts and brought a new one to the top. The full wickedness of what he'd done came home to him and entered his chest like a wound. I brought the boat here. We were still outside the fog, and what I did brought us into it.

'Listen to me, lads!' came from the stern.

The boat-steerer was now the senior man in the boat. Arthur couldn't see him although he was only a few feet away.

'Listen to me. When I say so I want you to give way with a will.' He waited for any comment. 'All right, lads. Are you ready? Pull!'

The unseen oars dipped as one.

Arthur tried to recapture the sensation that had overwhelmed him when they were in pursuit of the fish, and again when the fish was running with them in tow. He told himself that he'd ceased to exist as an individual and that he and the other boatmen had grown together in some mysterious way. We share the same muscles, he thought, we bend together like branches on the same tree. But it wasn't any use. The bruised muscles in his neck where the fingers had clutched, the coldness on his cheeks where the tears had frozen and the torment of his thoughts were his alone and couldn't be shared. The sensation of belonging to a special community had gone.

Peter Gill was a murderer. The knowledge bowed his shoulders and hung from the blade of his oar like a dead weight. Peter Gill was drunk when he came up from the hold during the making-off. I smelled the rum on his breath and he couldn't walk properly. It wasn't anything to do with falling down the hatch on

Sailing Day. He was drunk when he coiled the lines of this boat. He'd murdered Mr Dryden as surely as if he'd knifed him and pushed him overboard. Aw, Mr Dryden, I would have told you like I promised. I would have told you, Mr Dryden, but there wasn't time.

Either their direction was wrong or the fog was drifting. They had rowed hard for half an hour and were seemingly still in the same place. The fog was bitterly cold and it was beginning to penetrate their clothing.

'Pull! Listen for that ship's bell! Pull! Pull!'

Arthur blinked and strained his eyes to see Mr Fenby. But even when he leaned forward on his oar he couldn't see so much as a dim outline of the boat-steerer who was sitting opposite to him. He turned his head sideways and held it attentively in various positions to catch the sounds of the men behind him. There was nothing.

How dreadful it would be to suffer this alone. A man would go mad without the knowledge that there were other men like him. Anything was bearable, any pain, even death, when you knew that others were suffering with you. And yet all the evidence of his senses told him that he was alone. When Mr Fenby fell silent there was only memory to remind him that he wasn't alone in the boat, or that he was in a boat at all.

He allowed himself to imagine for a second that he was alone and then he tried to dismiss the thought. It wouldn't go away. A sickly but vigorous weed, drawing nourishment from some necessity to experience fear and despair, took root and sprouted in his imagination. If there's nothing, absolutely nothing, to tell me that I'm not alone, how can I possibly know that I'm not alone? I must believe despite the evidence of my senses. I must have faith.

Mr Fenby was in the stern with his arm resting on the long oar. He tried to picture him sitting there, with his towy beard and round eyes, but nothing would come of it. The fog assaulted him on all sides, destroying everything.

I am alone. I am alone in an impenetrable fog that stretches for ever across an endless sea. There's no compass and no guiding light to show me the way. These grey curtains will prevent me from seeing the sun, no matter whether it's rising, setting or at its summit. The night will come and go without my knowing, because I shall see neither moon nor stars.

He tried to remember the five other men. He could imagine their hard hands and straining backs but not their faces. He remembered other faces – the pale faces of his mother and father, trying to disguise their unhappiness as they waved good-bye on the quay; Ann Paylor with the blue ribbon in her hair and eyes of brighter blue; the woman at Lerwick moving in time with the fiddle music and the light from the whale oil lamp making the shades come and go under her cheek bones; Mr Dryden showing him how to span a harpoon and his moustache moving when he smiled. Mr Dryden, aw, Mr Dryden I would have told you.

The fog pressed upon him and even these faces lost their identity. Their outlines drifted away and dispersed like smoke. Other faces that he sometimes thought he recognized stared at him out of the fog. But just as he was about to put a name to them they ran into one another, like pen and ink sketches caught in the rain. They were nothing. He was alone.

I am alone. I am alone on a sea that hasn't any features. No crumbling headlands, no wave-worn rock will intrude to show me where I might be going, or even whether I am moving. I am alone. We are all alone. I am alone as all men are alone.

He was growing very tired. The muscles in his legs, back, arms and shoulders were pleading for release from their rhythmic torture. The fog had by now so thoroughly impregnated every stitch of his clothing that he was almost as wet as if he'd been pulled out of the sea. Despite the prevailing dampness his mouth was dry.

The fatigue and the damp and the thirst were a consolation because they reminded him that he was a man pulling an oar in a boat. But as time passed even that painful consolation was taken away. The mechanical movements, by their repetition, were turning him into a machine. His limbs lost their tiredness, his skin ceased to feel and his throat stopped craving water. His entire body grew numb. His flesh lost all feeling. He had the sensation that he'd ceased to exist. In a panic he bit his forearm. There was nothing there.

There was nothing.

There was no sea, no sky, no movement, no time, no boat, no boat-steerer, no boatmen, no oars, no nothing. They were all nothing. He was nothing. The horror of utter nothingness paralysed him. He stopped rowing.

The oar behind immediately fouled his own and the old man cursed. Everything was all right.

'All right, lads.'

Arthur was so overjoyed to hear the voice that he laughed aloud.

'All right, lads. Unship oars.'

He had no difficulty at all in picturing Mr Fenby sitting opposite to him in the stern. His arm was resting on the steering oar, his round eyes were staring ahead into the boat, and his beard was sticking out like a piece of stiff tow. Wood scraped on wood. The men pushed their oars through the grommets until they dangled from their tholes alongside. Somewhere behind a man coughed, refilled his lungs with fog, coughed more violently, refilled, coughed, and continued in this way until his breath became shallow enough to control.

Everything was all right again.

'We'll have a rest, lads,' Mr Fenby said.

Arthur allowed his shoulders to sag and luxuriated in the joy of doing nothing. Only now did he realize how cold it was. In less than half a minute his teeth were chattering and his shoulders were shaking uncontrollably. He blew into his hands and put them under his oxters. In another minute he couldn't think of anything he wanted to do more than start rowing again.

'Are you ready?' asked Mr Fenby.

Arthur reached for his oar with a sharp sense of relief.

'No!' said the old boatman behind him. 'And not likely to be.'

'You want to wait till you get your breath?' asked the boat-steerer cheerily.

'I want to wait till you get your bearings. And it'll be a hell of a long wait, I'm thinking. But I don't care how long it is, I'm not pulling my guts out again until you can convince me we're not going in circles.'

'Of course we're not going in circles.'

Another voice joined in. 'Then where are we going?'

'I set our course by the wind,' said Mr Fenby, angrily. 'It was blowing over my left shoulder while the fish was running.'

'It was veering before we hit the fog,' another voice said.

'And it's probably changed a few more points while we've been in it,' said another.

That was the fourth boatman. They'd all spoken now and they wouldn't be waiting for the opinion of an apprentice: particularly one who shouldn't have been in the boat to start with and whose actions had brought them into this adversity. Arthur was grateful to be invisible.

'And what's more,' said the old boatman, concluding the argument, 'the wind is dropping and will soon have gone completely.'

They were all silent. Arthur couldn't hear anything except the rattling of his teeth. When Mr Fenby finally spoke against this universal opposition it was in a quiet, earnest, almost a pleading voice.

'But listen to me, lads,' he said. 'You'll die of cold if you sit here.'

With a shock Arthur realized that the boat-steerer wasn't going to argue on the real issue, which was whether or not he knew where he was taking them. This made him angry, but nobody made any response. His anger faded away. The other men must have known they'd been lost for some time and they all accepted it. Arthur wondered how the boat-steerer had been keeping himself warm. Perhaps he churned away with the steering oar, trying to imagine that he was driving the boat single-handed; or perhaps he let the oar trail while he clapped his arms around his chest.

'There's no need of that so long as we keep together,' the old man said. 'So let's have you all between the thwarts in t' middle.'

The boat rocked as a couple of the men stood up. Mr Fenby didn't say anything. His authority had been destroyed. Arthur stood up and groped his way forward.

'I want you on your backs between t' thwarts.' The old man spoke with the voice of command and nobody contradicted him. 'Three men on t' bottom and three men on top of them. Quickly now. I'll keep moving you round so there'll be no cause for argument.'

Some of the men were already lying down. Arthur lay on top

of one who cursed him for being so heavy. The old man lay down on top next to him. Soon the six men were lying across the boat with their head and feet next to the gunwales. It was very uncomfortable even for the men on top, because the men underneath kept trying to change the way they were positioned.

One of the men underneath complained. 'I'd rather be pulling an oar.'

'You will be,' the old boatman said. 'But not till this fog lifts and we can see what's in the sky and the sea.'

'I'd rather be pulling it now.'

Mr Fenby added his comment. 'He wants to see if the fog goes all the way to t' North Pole or not.'

None of the men laughed and Arthur felt sorry for Mr Fenby.

Arthur wished they were still rowing. It was a much better way of keeping warm. He would have run the risk that they were rowing away from the ship.

But in a little while there was an almost imperceptible sensation under the wet clothing sticking to his back. He changed his position slightly and the man below cursed him again. Yes, there it was. An undeniable warmth was creeping up his back and along his left side. The cold in his exposed right side and in his chest was increasing. Or he thought it was. Perhaps it was the new warmth being kindled in the rest of his body that made the exposed parts feel colder by comparison. But no, that couldn't be entirely correct. The right side of his face felt as if the skin was being scraped off with a blunted blubber knife.

'Time for our first move,' the old boatman said. 'Men on top move to t' left and those underneath move to t' right. Move quickly now!'

There was plenty of heaving and groaning as each man tried to gain the benefits of his new place without exposing more of himself than he need. Arthur elbowed his way to the left until he was in the old man's place. The old man remained on his left, and the man on whom he'd been lying came up on to the top layer alongside him.

It worked even better this time because his right side warmed up until it was almost as comfortable as his left. There was something profoundly wonderful about it happening so automatically. All a man had to do was lie there. He didn't have to make any effort or even to wish anything for himself or others. Indeed it didn't matter if a man actively disliked his fellow men. Each man, however selfish or undeserving, simply had to be himself. Whether he wished it or not he made his contribution to the general welfare and received his reward.

His chest, of course, remained cold and it became even colder after the next move to the left. Moreover his left side was now exposed for the first time, and it quickly lost its warmth. The pains in his chest and left arm made him desperately envious of the old man who was now beneath him. The coldness in his chest was particularly severe owing to its uninterrupted exposure.

'Move! And don't forget to listen for the ship's bell.'

Arthur was pushed sideways on to the floor. He struggled for his rightful shelter under the man who'd displaced him but couldn't force a way in. Desperately he punched and kicked, and swore at the old boatman who didn't seem willing to make room for him. For a couple of minutes they exchanged blows. When Arthur was more than half-covered he desisted, but resumed the struggle whenever he thought he was being pushed out again.

Some warmth could now be transferred to his chest for the first time. But his left side, including the part of his chest that was exposed, became so cold that it lost most of its powers of sensation. He developed a deep, gnawing envy of the man in the next position. That was the best position of them all, with someone on each side and your top completely covered. It seemed a long time before the call came, so long in fact that Arthur wondered whether the old boatman was playing the game fairly.

But when the long-desired move came Arthur found that the weight and awkwardness of the three men on top made it difficult to breathe. He was even more surprised by the attacks of the men on each side of him, although he'd so recently behaved in an exactly similar manner. Each of these men on his right and left genuinely thought he was being left out, and each fought to achieve a place nearer the centre. Arthur couldn't give an inch to either of them without taking it from the other, and under these circumstances he found the administration of justice a highly unrewarding business. He forgot the cold while he protected himself from these independent assailants, and longed to be on the outside again.

And when he was next on the outside he struggled to return to the middle.

No man was satisfied with what he had and each man envied his neighbour. Everyone fought to keep what he ought to give up and tried to seize in advance what he expected to be given. Each man's principle and idea of what was good depended on his personal situation at any particular time. They turned and they twisted, they punched and they pulled, each man striving to extract a little more than his entitlement from the warmth at the centre.

And so that little bundle of humanity rolled over and over, held in a coherent ball by the selfishness of its constituent parts.

19

Arthur opened his eyes unwillingly. The old man had been saying something urgent.

'You mustn't fall asleep!' the old man was repeating.

He closed his eyes again. Some healing balm was being applied to his tortured limbs and aching joints. A soothing ointment was being smoothed on to his burning skin. He was sinking and it was a pleasant feeling. In another minute he would be able to forget everything.

'On your feet! There's two men asleep!' The old man shook Arthur with such violence that the bones in his neck clicked. Another boatman forced him on to his knees and dragged at his collar until he stood up. 'We'll pull the oars for a bit. That'll loosen up the muscles and get the blood moving again.'

One man hadn't tried to stand up. He lay in the bottom of the boat with his breath wheezing and sucking in his wide open mouth. A couple of the boatmen set upon him unmercifully, smacking and rubbing until he opened his eyes, and then belabouring and kicking him until he struggled to his feet.

'The cold is making us all tired,' the old boatman told them. 'But you mustn't give in to it. Any man who falls asleep in this cold, and hasn't a good friend to rouse him, isn't going to wake up any more. Just try to keep thinking of that if you fancy taking a nap.' He paused to add weight to what he'd been saying. Silence and fog oppressed each man. 'Now let's get hold of those oars.'

Sleepiness and the surrounding opacity confused them. They groped and fumbled amongst themselves, anxious not to fall into the icy water. Someone tripped over one of the empty line-tubs and threw it out. The splash made the others think there was a man overboard and they wasted some time in hailing a missing comrade and then spent even more time trying to count themselves. They were all very cold and bad-tempered.

'Ready, lads?' asked the old boatman.

Curses greeted him from men who were still unsure whether they were in the bows or the stern. Slowly, very slowly, with much holding on to each other and show of anger, the men found their places. They were all shivering so much that they couldn't keep still. Arthur reached over the side for his oar. It was encrusted with particles of ice that cut his fingers as he drew it in through the grommet.

'Ready now, lads?'

Nobody replied.

'Pull! Give way, my lads! Pull!'

Their arms and legs were as stiff as the iron rods in the ship's stores. Their muscles kept bunching up into cramped knots under the skin. Arthur heard a dog whimpering, as if it had been whipped unmercifully, and realized it was himself. They rowed until they were fouling each other's oars every few seconds and it became impossible to work together. They left their places and crawled back to the middle of the boat without a word of command being given.

'Remember what I said 'bout sleep,' the old man mumbled. 'An' listen for tha' bell. Don't forget tha' bell.'

They lay in a disorganized heap, invisible and unknown to each other, at the bottom of the boat. Nobody struggled any more. They lay where they fell.

Arthur closed his eyes and a sweet foretaste of sleep swept through him. He knew that this sleep would lead to death but it didn't worry him in the slightest. The change from sleep to death would be imperceptible. It would be one of those gradual changes that eliminated the necessity of suffering. Death had to come to every man, and who wouldn't choose a gentle end like this if he had the choice? He thought of Mr Dryden, wrenched out of the boat and dragged along under water. No, this was a much better way.

Something denied him.

His body was aching for sleep. Every nerve, every fibre, every tissue of his being was crying out for sleep like thousands of parched mouths begging for water. His brain recognized this desire and acquiesced in it.

But some part of his mind refused to surrender, and this more remote faculty seemed to despise his immediate desires. Instead of going along with what he wanted to do, it coldly assessed what he ought to do in order to be faithful to the purposes of some other self. And this other self exhorted him not to sleep.

Arthur almost wept with frustration.

How can this be? My entire body, and every part of me that I am aware of desires to sleep and escape from misery. My brain agrees that it should happen. Then what is this other, obstinate thing, that persuades me against my will to do something that I don't want to do? This other thing must be part of myself, although it contradicts every part that I know of myself.

His actual will wanted him to sleep: *slip your cable*, it said, *and drift out with the tide. It will be change without pain.* Some other thing that he hated, but which impressed itself upon him as his real will, hammered its message into his head over and over again: *when you have a choice*, it said, *life is better than death, life is better than death, life is better than death.*

Something else came to distract him.

He discovered that his chest, or that part of it covered by the man lying on top of him, wasn't growing any warmer or even retaining the heat it had before he lay down. After a short while he was certain it was growing colder. He explored with his hands. The man on top of him was cold but it was the coldness of a stone.

Arthur raised a hand to the man's face. The skin was as stiff as wood and there was a little tuft of frozen beard. He struggled with the invisible, unresisting figure, until he was able to roll out from beneath it. Mr Fenby fell with a hard sound into the place he'd vacated.

He stood up and moved one stiff leg in front of the other until he knocked his shins against the gunwale.

The fog was as impenetrable as ever and seemed to have darkened. Perhaps it was night. He couldn't guess how long they'd been lying in the bottom of the boat. The fog looked so solid that he raised his hand to it.

To his astonishment it felt solid. It was like a wall. It's my fingers, he thought. My fingers are so numb that reality can play tricks on them. But when he pushed with his hand the illusion remained. He probed with both hands and found a vertical, flat surface, so palpable that he could lean against it. I've gone mad. Instead of suffering from cold and fatigue I'm now going to suffer from imaginary things. Or perhaps I am dead. Perhaps my body is still lying in the bottom of the boat.

The fog before him thinned and yet darkened in some way at the same time. When he looked up he thought he could see an eye looking down at him. It wasn't so much the eye itself as the socket where an eye might be.

Fear made him stand back a pace. The socket moved slowly downwards until it was on the same level as his head. He stared, waiting for it to open and look at him. The socket was over six inches wide and was surrounded by a red rim. It was sagging, as if the eye were over-strained and tired, or had perhaps been plucked out. The socket slowly moved lower and he saw that there were two of them, one above the other. Both the holes squirmed and contracted simultaneously as if powerful muscles behind them were sucking at the membranes. They relaxed, became baggy, and began to fall open with their pink mouths gaping.

There was a sound like the cracking of loose staysails in a squall. He no sooner realized that he was looking into the whale's blow holes than he was deafened by the sodden trumpet blast.

He was blinded, choked and thrown across the boat. The trumpets submerged, completed their fanfare under water, and the twin streams of bubbles burst into froth under the gunwale. The boat bumped and lurched. When he tried to stand his feet slid away from beneath him. Everything he touched was slippery and the air had a cloying smell that filled his lungs and stomach. And he was warm all over. *Warm!* All his senses quickened. He was alive again.

Far away, muffled by the fog and at the very margin of hearing, a brazen sound came to him.

Arthur hurled himself at the unmoving shapes on the floor of the boat. At least one of them was dead and the rest were wrapped in the sleep that would end in death. He found the old man and concentrated his attention on him, slapping his face and kicking him in the ribs.

'Don't die now,' he begged.

It was a long time since he'd tried to speak. He discovered that the sides of his face were so stiff that he couldn't form the words properly. The old boatman made a noise. Arthur bit the lobes of his ears. He opened his eyes and looked at Arthur with mild curiosity.

'Don't die now, old man,' was what he was trying to say. 'Not now. We've got everything now.'

But the eyes closed. Arthur dropped him and crawled to the stern. The boat was rocking in the eddy caused by the sinking razorback. He seized the steering oar and waited for the sound of the bell.

'Ring again! Ring, bell, ring!'

The sides of his face were so taut that all the syllables sounded the same. The bell rang with a distant, hollow sound, and he used the long oar to bring the boat round. The bell rang again, and his heart banged against his ribs in gratitude.

The whale's blood, hot from its burst heart, had passed on to him something of its living warmth. He was anointed with it from head to foot. But now it was slowly hardening and impeding his movements. It was as if the whale, having revived him so that he could hear the bell, was now doing what it could to prevent him reaching it. The ship's bell was very faint. He would never reach it by sculling.

A whistle cut the fog like a thin, sharp knife.

The ship's boat! He tried to form his hands into a speaking trumpet, but the blood had now frozen around the joints of his elbows. With arms as rigid as if they were set in splints he tried to work the steering oar.

The ship's bell sounded again a long way off. The boat's whistle shrilled, much nearer but going past.

He dropped the oar and forced his hands up to his mouth.

The carapace of blood split and he smelled its cloying scent. He gulped at the fog and shouted.

'Ahoy!'

There were two rapid blasts on the whistle followed immediately by three rumbling cheers. He lay back in the stern with his shiny red face hidden in his shiny red arms, and his mouth would have smiled if the surrounding flesh would have let it.

None of them could talk properly until they had been returned to the ship, laid out on the half-deck, and vigorously rubbed with flannel and blankets.

'It was the lad that saved us,' the old man said. 'The strongest man in t' boat.'

Arthur knew it wasn't true. It was the razorback that had saved them with the last pulse of its cavernous heart.

Two

*As George Stephenson listens to the questions of Mr Winspear
and the other leading citizens he is aware of power. It rumbles in
the quayside and in the foundations of the Angel Inn, up his legs
and into his chest, swelling him out to an enormous size. When
he looks down on these men he sees them flinch.*

*It isn't only the power that he can sense in his own muscles and
in his own brain, but something titanic outside himself like one of
John Martin's paintings. Martin was born at the same time and
on the banks of the same river as he. Some dark spirit of change
has been moving along the waters of the Tyne. With a single
sooty breath that spirit has inspired both of them, and other men
from thereabouts, to do things that are going to amaze the world.*

*It didn't seem long ago that he was one of six children with his
parents in the cottage at Wylam. He can still feel the clay floor
under his feet and hear the horses coughing as they pull the
wagons along the wooden rails that ran past their front door.*

*He had his first regular job at the age of eight, when an elderly
widow paid him twopence a day to keep her cows off the wagonway. While other children were at school he was hoeing
turnips and doing odd jobs on neighbouring farms. Later he
became a picker at sixpence a day, sorting coal from stones as it
came out of the pit. When he was fourteen he was earning a
shilling a day as assistant fireman to his father on a pumping
engine in the pit.*

*He became a fireman himself, and then a plugman, and then
he mended a winding engine and became a brakeman on one of
Robert Hawthorn's engines at Willington Quay. He went to Killingworth where he mended a Newcomen pumping engine. And
then he became an engineman.*

*He is one of the new race of men. A Northumbrian en-
gineman.*

The Tyne is like no other place on earth. The banks of the river, like the sides of a long black boot, are tightly laced by wagonways that lead from the pits to the waiting keels. The wooden rails were being replaced by cast iron. The steam engines, that had been used only for pumping and winding in the upcast and downcast shafts of the pits, were now being fixed at the tops of inclines up which they pulled the wagons by ropes.

All these engines had obsessed the youthful Stephenson and he made models of them in clay. The engines often went wrong, and this delighted him because he could snatch the opportunity to play about with them and learn how they worked and how they might be improved. In order to understand the engines better he studied arithmetic with a local schoolteacher, and by the time he was twenty or twenty-one he could read an elementary text book in a stumbling sort of way.

The demand for coal went up every year. New pits had to be opened further away from the river. The horses that pulled the chaldrons of coal along the wagonways had to travel further, and the war with France made it more expensive to feed them. The pit owners wanted to know if they could have travelling engines.

The dark spirit of change brooded on the waters of the Tyne.

A travelling engine to the design of Trevithick, with return flue boiler and with fire door and chimney at the same end, was built in Gateshead. John George Lambton bought a locomotive engine in Newcastle and it hauled coals to his staithes on the Wear. A rack rail engine designed by John Blenkinsop, with a cogged wheel acting on teeth cast on to the track, was put to work at Gosforth. William Hedley experimented with smooth wheels on smooth rails, and built some eight-wheeled engines for the Wylan wagonway.

George Stephenson built his first locomotive at Killingworth. It had vertical cylinders partly within the boiler to conserve heat, like the Blenkinsop engine, and it had smooth wheels like the Hedley engines. He coupled the axles with a pair of chains running on sprockets. Then he went on to build his first complete railway at Hetton Colliery, with stationary engines, self-acting planes and improved locomotives.

The outside world wakened up to the rumours of curious

things that were happening in the valley of the coaly Tyne. The first call came from Darlington.

Stephenson travelled down with Nicholas Wood, the viewer of Killingworth, and friend and collaborator in the first loco-motives. They took the coach from Newcastle to Stockton, and walked the twelve miles to Darlington along the route that had been proposed for the new railway. It was April, and their heavy boots cut swathes through spring flowers. Springing in Stephenson's brain was the conviction that this was the start of something tremendous. As he paced out the ground he was sure that what he'd observed at Gosforth and Wylam, what he'd learned from Robert Hawthorn at Willington Quay and what he'd already done at Killingworth and Hetton, had all been in preparation for what he was going to do now.

They were received in Northgate by Edward Pease. He was a solemn gentleman in a broad-brimmed hat who 'thee'd' and 'thou'd' them soundly. From his pronouncement it was clear that anything showing a return of five per cent would automatically receive God's blessing. He told them that John Rennie, the most famous and most respected of the London engineers, had recommended a canal instead of a railway.

Stephenson laughed loudly at that. They built the new railway in less than four years.

Early on the morning of the official opening he climbed the east incline to the top of Brusselton ridge. From his feet the railway ran on its stone sleepers down the west incline and disappeared under the mist in the bottom of the valley. Down there the invisible rails crossed the Gaunless on the world's first iron railway bridge and then began to climb the south inclines of Etherley ridge. Cold sunlight brightened the opposite hilltop, and the iron rails crawled up out of the early morning mist and went over the ridge on their way north to the pits in south west Durham. The mist began to disperse in the crisp September air and he retraced his steps.

They used horses to bring the chaldrons from the Phoenix Pit and a stationary engine to draw them up the Etherley incline; horses again to lead the chaldrons across the little river on the iron bridge, and another stationary engine to draw them up the Brusselton incline. At Shildon the locomotive was attached, with additional wagons and a carriage.

Stephenson drove the train to Darlington and then, after some delay, to the terminus in Stockton.

There were many things to distract that part of Stephenson's mind which wasn't fully occupied by the business on hand; and the distractions grew more numerous, more colourful and more noisy as he approached the end of the journey. The turnpike from the south ran alongside the railway on his left hand, and it was packed with the stylish bays and coaches of the gentry, together with every ambling nag, spavined mare, pony, gig, chaise, hackney carriage, cabriolet and plain farmyard cart that could be pressed into service from anywhere in Teesdale, Cleveland and the dales to the south.

As the railway approached the Tees it swept to the left. It skirted the short tower and ruins of the castle where the Bishops of Durham had taken refuge from time to time, to escape the plague and other enemies.

At the terminus seven cannons on the wharf fired a triple salute. The weary band from Yarm, that had played most of the way from Darlington, summoned its last energies to play the National Anthem. People tried to shake Stephenson's hand every step of the way along Finkle Street to the Town Hall. The celebratory dinner was punctuated by congratulations, toasts and speeches.

And amidst the changing scenes, colours and noises, Stephenson kept thinking of the sun moving down the south incline on Etherley ridge. That cold yellow light, creeping downwards from the north, showed the way that everything was going to go.

Everything was going to move down from the north. Everything that made this railway possible had come down from the Tyne: the cast iron rails were from Walker, the new wrought iron rails from Bedlington, the locomotives from Forth Street in Newcastle, the Gaunless Bridge from the works next door in Orchard Street; and – more important than all else – the men with the knowledge and experience to make it all work had learned everything they knew from the wagonways.

And the move from the hustling Tyne to the sleepy Tees was only the beginning. Stephenson accepted the congratulations, joined in the toasts and pretended to listen to the speeches, and thought of future things.

20

Almost a hundred ships had gone to Davis Strait. Most of them had left home by the end of March, but were subsequently delayed by head winds and didn't reach the entrance to the strait until the end of April. Once they were there everything changed for the better. All the signs indicated that this was going to be a successful season.

A wonderfully open sea was waiting to receive the entire fleet, and the weather was kind to them as they sailed up the eastern side of Baffin Bay. They made such good progress that by June almost half the fleet had sighted the Devil's Thumb. Here they all thinned out into a long line, running north and south, to follow a narrow channel along the edge of the ice. The ice didn't cause any serious problems, although its incursions split the long line of ships into three groups.

The leaders saw the opening to Melville Bay on 10 June, a month earlier than usual. By mid-June the first ships reached Lat. 76°N, and prepared to enter North Water. By that time most of the fleet was above Lat. 74°N. All the best known ships were at the edge of the most desirable grounds in the fishery and even the stragglers were into Baffin Bay.

It was then that the signs began to change.

On 23 June the wind suddenly veered to the south-west and blew strongly. On each succeeding day it blew harder and colder, and the ice started to close. The *St Andrew* of Aberdeen was the first ship to find an opening to the westward. She wriggled her way through and was followed by another twenty-two ships standing in line before the ice closed up. The *Prince of Wales* led another group to the north west where they cut a wet dock and placed themselves side by side.

But the wind continued strong and cold, as if determined to pack Melville Bay with ice floes and leave room for nothing else.

In one day most of the leaders were lost, including the *Laetitia* and *Prince of Wales*, both of Aberdeen, and the *Resolution* of 400 tons from Peterhead; others of the leaders were badly stove, including *Commerce* and *Hope* of Peterhead, *Laurel* of Hull and *North Pole* of Leith.

Then the gale moved south a little and punished the middle body of the fleet.

The *William and Ann* of Whitby was completely wrecked but the *Eagle* of Hull was at hand to take up Captain Terry, his carpenter and twelve of his seamen. The *Eagle* herself was making water, and watches from other Hull ships, the *Ingria*, *Duncombe* and the old *Volunteer* that had been built and bought in Whitby, hastened to her assistance.

Now the wind reached further down and the ice closed upon the most southerly portion of the fleet.

The *Gilder* and *North Britain* of Hull cut a dock and sought refuge within it together; but the encroaching ice broke up their haven, crushed their hulls, and squeezed their remains up into the air for all to see. The *William* of Hull, *Three Brothers* of *Dundee* and *Alexander* of Aberdeen were destroyed; the *Phoenix* of Whitby, *Traveller* of Peterhead and *Ville de Dieppe*, a Frenchman of 400 tons, were badly stove.

In accordance with custom the ruined ships were salved and set on fire. Yellow flames and black smoke ran north to south down Baffin Bay. The battle had been lost before it had properly begun. The fires showed where the most forward spirits had tried to breach the enemy's walls and been nipped and then crushed for their foolhardiness.

July saw a defeated army, over a thousand shipless men, camping on the ice. The wind howled up from the south bringing hail and snow, and the sky unrolled a black canopy over them. Most of the men had lost contact with their officers and were free to follow their own devices. Those who were too ill to walk crawled across the ice to the nearest ships that were still under command. Others with more initiative, or more confident of their strength, went from ship to ship and sometimes walked for miles before selecting the ship they judged most likely to reach home again. Several search parties looked for the famous *Truelove* of Hull, widely believed to be the luckiest ship in the fishery.

The best part of a thousand able-bodied men remained at large on the ice. They knew that this was going to be far and away the greatest disaster the industry had ever suffered. There would be no rewards for them this season, if ever again. Their very lives were of doubtful value to anyone.

But in the meanwhile they had salvaged and brought together more rum than they thought the fleets of the whole world could have contained. The quantity was beyond calculation. A man could break an unopened cask to wash his feet without being accused of wastefulness. Foraging parties retrieved broken masts, yards and spars from the wrecked and abandoned ships, and hundreds of fires were kindled on the ice. The defeated army drank themselves into a state of stupefaction and warmed their hands until their mittens caught fire.

Here and there small groups made footballs out of sailcloth bound with best white hemp, and kicked them about with happy abandon. They shouted at each other in the greatest good humour and laughed uproariously when anyone slipped and fell. When they were tired or cold or thirsty, or a mixture of any of these three, they retired happily to the blazing fires and kicked open another of the countless casks of rum.

In August most of the fleet was still beset and all the Captains had given up any ambitions of entering North Water this season. When the wind became easterly and channels opened in the ice most ships lowered boats for towing, and warped to the westward in the hope of reaching sailing water.

Early in September the *Eagle* and *Hannibal* of Hull were approaching the west land. Later in the same month the *Rambler* of Kirkaldy, *Cumbrian* of Hull and *Bon Accord* and *Dee* of Aberdeen got free to the northward. The *Harmony* and *Andrew Marvell* of Hull were almost free. Towards the end of the month the *John* of Greenock, brilliantly commanded in earlier days by Captain Scoresby Senior, was wrecked on the west coast by mutiny and incompetence, and the survivors were taken up by the *Swan* of Hull.

During most of this time the *William Scoresby Senior* was sailing in the open waters of the Greenland Sea. The water was green, with black streaks in it that glowed at night and showed it was swarming with the tiny animals on which the whales fed. But as the weeks went by it was clear that the whales had left the Greenland Sea.

Captain Stapleton decided to cut his losses by coming across to Cape Farewell.

The easterly winds, that had helped the· survivors of the

stricken Davis Strait fleet to the west land, also aided the ships that had begun the season by going to the Greenland Sea and subsequently changed their minds. It was in August that the *William Scoresby Senior*, closely followed by the *Lady Clifford* of Hull, worked her way westward round Cape Farewell and entered the strait to the other part of the fishery.

21

They were abandoning the ship!

Arthur Storm, exhausted by working for a full watch on the saws, had fallen asleep as soon as he crawled into his bed. Now he was fully awake in an instant.

The *William Scoresby Senior* was shivering and groaning like some wretched creature being tortured on a rack. Her back was being stretched until her vertebrae popped; her ribs were being twisted off her breast bone; her bones were grinding in their joints. The ingeniously constructed skeleton was being slowly, methodically and maliciously dismembered.

Arthur sat up. Fear loosened his gut. Above his head came the sound of things being dragged across the deck.

He leaped out of bed, threw his clothes into his chest and rushed up the companionway with it. The deck was in turmoil. Men were hurling their belongings overboard on to the ice – clothes, bedding, bags, chests, food and provisions taken from the galley. One of the boats was already on the ice and another was being lowered. Everyone was shouting and the din was tremendous.

Arthur ran to the bulwark with his sea chest in his arms and looked down on the disorderly scene. A score of men were down on the ice, waving their arms and yelling up to those on deck, and personal belongings were scattered about like the hasty leavings of a retreating army. So this was the way it was going to end.

He would throw his things into the boat that was being lowered, and let himself drop on to one of the heaps of bedding lying on the ice. Then he would retrieve his chest and put all his clothes on before the cold could get at him. And then he would join one of the salvage gangs. That was the way it was going to be.

'Avast! You men! Avast!'

An enormous voice boomed above the yelling of the men and faded away across the empty expanse of ice. Captain Stapleton had appeared on the quarter deck and he came to the side so that he could look down on the churning mob below. The collar of his jacket was turned up under one ear and the wind blew his white hair around his head. Everyone stood still and everyone was silent. The ship moved and the awful sound of timbers being strained was the only sound to be heard. Two men on deck lost their nerve. They threw their bags and belongings over the side and jumped after them.

Captain Stapleton raised the speaking trumpet to his mouth again. 'This is the most disgraceful scene I have witnessed in all my years of command. I am ashamed of men who have so little faith in Yorkshire oak.' His voice rolled across the desolate white wastes and would have stopped a man two miles away. He lowered the trumpet and looked towards the waist of the ship. 'Mr Beaufort, please take those men and their belongings back on board immediately.'

Captain Stapleton made a dismissive gesture with his head, slicing his beard sideways like a blubber-spade, to show that he wanted no more to do with it. He left the side and disappeared into his cabin. Mr Beaufort, hitherto unnoticed or at any rate ignored amidships, climbed on to the main fife-rail where he balanced with his feet amongst the belaying pins.

'Fishshit!' he bawled. 'Fishshit! I could make better men out of fishshit and snot from a blow hole! Mice! You squeak louder than the ship's timbers!' His face was black with anger. The normally invisible vein in the middle of his brow wriggled up to the peak of his sealskin cap. Now that he had their attention he jumped down from the fife-rail and ran to the ship's side and glared down at the men on the ice. 'I want all those stores back on board and I want those boats back under their davits. And the Captain wants you men back an' all though I don't know why.'

Arthur sidled to the 'tween deck companion. He was glad he hadn't thrown his chest overboard and then had to climb back with it under the blistering eyes of the First Mate. He went down to his berth and dropped his belongings on the floor.

'Been up topside to get some clean air in your lungs?' asked Jim Richardson.

Jim was still in bed and he'd never even thought about him. He'd cared for nothing but himself when he imagined they were being wrecked. Overcome by shame he sat on his bed.

'It'll have done you good,' Jim added.

Arthur spoke with his head in his hands. 'I can't believe it of myself. It never crossed my mind I wasn't doing the right thing.'

'Don't think about it. You've been in a boat and you've chased a fish, but you're still a green-man. Can I give you some advice?'

Arthur nodded without taking his head out of his hands.

'Don't even think of leaving the ship until Captain Stapleton has given orders for provisioning the boats. And don't move until Mr Beaufort has given orders for lowering them on to the ice. And even then I'd wait to see if the Captain didn't tell Mr Beaufort to change his mind and have them brought back up again.'

Arthur rubbed his hands down the sides of his face and lay down. 'I'll remember what you say.'

'There's something else.'

'What's that?'

Jim leaned out of his bunk. The jet cross fell out of his shirt front and was restrained by its cord. 'You stay close to me and you'll be safe whatever happens. Nothing can happen to you.'

Arthur looked up in surprise. His eyes darted instinctively to the edge of the bunk where the blunt stub of Jim's arm was visible.

'I know what you're thinking, Arthur, but you're wrong. When Mr McCabe cut the shark's head open and brought me this,' and he displayed the cross in the palm of his remaining hand, 'I realized straight away. I wasn't wearing it. It was like my grandfayther. Do you see? If I'd been wearing it I could have put my hand in that shark's mouth and nothing would have happened.' He smiled with happiness and triumph. 'And now nothing *can* happen.'

Arthur looked away so as not to meet his eyes and was relieved when Jim withdrew his head. He turned himself over to sleep.

But his fatigue had gone and he lay awake listening to the struggle between ice and wood.

The ice tightened its grip and he imagined it spreading and thickening. How could it grow like that when it was a dead thing? It was certainly dead. It was cold and white and dead. And yet it was growing with all the abundant energy of a living creature.

The ship complained piteously. He could feel the hull rising. They were being squeezed upwards like a pip out of a clenched fruit. Stanchions and carlines, beams and planks maintained a chorus of protestation, squealing and groaning, moaning and shrieking, grieving and weeping. Occasionally there was a brief interlude when they all fell silent at the same time, but then another squeeze would bring a deep, tearing groan and the agonies would start afresh.

Up the ship went – three, four, six, perhaps eight feet – until she began to keel over. The ice overlay itself and thickened, ascending the hull and exerting a new pressure on the upper timbers. This prevented the ship from falling over but she cried out with a new anguish.

It pained Arthur inside his ribs to listen to it, as if this Helmsley oak were labouring with the sinews of his own body. Every new screech or whimper from the tormented timbers made him think that the ship was being crushed like a rotten apple in the mouth of some ravenous beast. Surely it could only be a matter of time before she was stove. A more violent shudder made the timbers howl and he started up from his bed. He remembered Jim Richardson's advice and forced himself to lie down again, his muscles as stiff as backstays, waiting for the order to abandon ship.

Shortly before the end of the watch he fell asleep. When he awoke he was so tired that he was relieved to hear the ice was too thick for sawing.

Garbled versions of what could be seen from the crow's nest reached the 'tween decks. Far away to the north-west dozens of ships were beset. The more fortunate ones had been pushed clean out of the water and lay on their sides, as whole and clean as stones sucked from cherries; others that hadn't risen had been ground into splinters. Ships that had managed to keep wet docks about them were all pointing to the south. On the near side of the crippled fleet, but still a long way to the westward, men had settled on the ice in such large numbers that they could have been mistaken for birds.

To the south east the *Lady Clifford* of Hull was closely beset, and she could be seen from the deck with an unassisted eye. She was the only thing so clear to everyone that there couldn't be any argument about it.

After some days the wind veered to the southward. Fresh breezes and a swell from the south east broke up the ice. They were able to set some sail and the *William Scoresby Senior* continued her northward drive towards the coveted waters at the top of Baffin Bay. The *Lady Clifford* followed, as if anxious to share in any success she might have. The two ships made good progress.

A long way to the westward they saw scores of ships resting on their sides, or squashed to pulp, or simply beset. All the ships that had freedom of movement were pointing to the south. It was impossible to believe they were all full, and the only conclusion was that they were quitting the fishery.

The *William Scoresby Senior* and the *Lady Clifford* continued their northward drive to the fishing grounds. Once they came within hailing distance of a small encampment on the ice, with tents inexpertly rigged from sail cloth. The men were playing football, with casks of rum balanced on top of each other for goal posts. Captain Stapleton used his speaking trumpet to address them but they ignored him. He then went to considerable pains to stress the dangers of their situation and invited them aboard. A couple of the men, exasperated beyond measure by this noisy interruption, ran across to shout drunken abuse before returning to their game.

After another day's sailing the ice closed and both ships were beset. During the night the ice brought the *Lady Clifford* up to the stern of the *William Scoresby Senior*, and in the morning her jib-boom was discovered to be pointing over her companion's taff rail. The Hull ship, still clean, looked as if she were sniffing enviously after the fish and a half stowed in the other's hold.

The Captains spoke. Then a man with a handsome, droll face came forward into the bows of the *Lady Clifford* and gave them all a song. Arthur recognized James Tickelpenny. He was the man who'd joked about Blackie in Commercial Street at Lerwick, and the following morning he'd been found on the wrong ship and thrown overboard. The song was a well-known lament about the girl a sailor leaves behind him, full of serious reflections and fine sentiments. But James, without changing a single word, used his eyes and hands to turn it into a song that made everyone laugh.

Another contraction in the ice brought the *Lady Clifford* even closer. It cracked her dolphin striker, pressing it backwards towards her gilded fiddle head, and tangled her martingales until they were pulled out of their sheaves. Then, just as more serious damage was imminent, a run in the ice turned the *Lady Clifford* round, pointed her southward, and slowly but surely bore her away. By noon she was two miles off and still pointing south. By evening she was approaching the horizon, still held fast. Before nightfall she was out of sight.

The *William Scoresby Senior* had no option but to proceed in a contrary run of ice that took her northward, with winds from the north-east blowing strongly and bringing sleet. A gale came up with heavy snow, and squalls so thick that the men couldn't see from one side of the ship to the other.

The wind moved again and light breezes brought softer weather. When the snow cleared a ship appeared on the horizon to the south. Arthur joined the group of men who were staring at her. The broad white band with false gun ports running forward almost to the hawse hole and the setting of the mizzen crojack confirmed that she was the *Lady Clifford*.

But she had changed!

At this distance it was difficult to assess absolute measurements. Nevertheless it was easy to see that compared with her height the hull had been shortened to about half its original length. She looked as if she had been placed lengthwise in the jaws of some enormous vice and compressed from stem to stern.

'Look at her,' said one of the men in an awed whisper. 'I've seen ships nipped in two across the beam, but I've never seen one squashed up like that.'

Another man seized his arm. 'Look at her now!'

The *Lady Clifford* went down by the head until her bowsprit was dipping into the sea and her spanker boom pointing at the sky. Like the fish we struck, Arthur thought. She was going to hump her back, raise her tail and wave her flukes, and then she would disappear.

'There she goes,' the boatman said. 'God have mercy on every mother's son.'

'Amen to that.'

Arthur thought of James Ticklepenny who had given them all a song in his droll way. What could he be doing now to make his shipmates laugh?

The *Lady Clifford* pushed her bowsprit into the water as far as her flying jib and turned until she was standing on her stem. The rear windows of her cabin were now in the position of a skylight. If she was a fish, Arthur thought, she would smack her tail down now. But the *Lady Clifford* continued to turn until she was completely upside down and apparently resting on her trucks.

Two or three of the men cried out in fear and one of them started to pray.

Jim Richardson nudged Arthur and smiled. 'She's over the horizon,' he said quietly, 'beyond our line of sight. For all we know she's taking her ease in sailing ice.'

Arthur was still puzzled.

'A trick of light in these parts,' Jim reassured him.

Arthur had heard about the curious effects of refraction in these latitudes, but the picture had been so extraordinarily vivid that he hadn't doubted it. As he continued to watch the illusion faded. The inverted ship lost the precision of its outline and flowed out of focus like an image in disturbed water. In less than a minute the *Lady Clifford* was indistinguishable from a drifting cloud.

The run of ice continued to take the *William Scoresby Senior* slowly northward. It was several days before they saw an opening, and Captain Stapleton snatched the first opportunity of warping his ship through a channel into clear water. The *William Scoresby Senior* turned about, crowded her canvas and started to the southward.

They thought they'd escaped but in less than an hour the ice closed.

An odd conviction of the unreality of it all began to torment

Arthur Storm. What sort of world was this? How could you be sure about anything if you could see a familiar ship shrink to half of her accustomed length? And then see that same ship, fully rigged, floating upside down? The calm reassuring voice of reason told you that despite appearances everything was well; that despite the evidence of your senses the ship sailed on, upright and in her proper form. Was the calm voice really the voice of reason? Or was it merely a noise manufactured to satisfy some hunger in the heart?

This unpredictable world, where ships could stand on end and turn upside down and then sail away unscathed, was part of the world in which he had to live. And this unpredictable world was real. The wind that scraped his face like a blunt razor was always ready to convince him of that.

There were no ships in sight and there weren't any birds now. When Mr Beaufort weighed out two and a half pounds of bread to each man for the next seven days, they knew that they were going to winter in the Arctic.

22

The nights became very long. The sky didn't lighten until mid-morning, when the sun managed to raise its sickly face for a couple of hours before it fell back, white and exhausted, into its tumbled grey blankets. The days darkened earlier and earlier in the afternoon as the blackness chewed on what was left of the light. The dead sky overlay a world that was a reflection of itself. Nothing was there except a colourless desolation that sometimes darkened into blackness or lightened into the bone-whiteness of fresh snow. Nothing moved and nothing breathed in that bleached wasteland.

There weren't any shadows. Not even living men cast shadows.

From time to time Captain Stapleton, from his vantage point at the topgallant masthead, sighted a lead or lane of water in the ice. If the lead were within a reasonable distance he gave instructions for putting the ship into it.

First they would set up the tripods on the ice and suspend the huge iron saws from them. Sixteen men worked at each handle. When a channel had been cut they went ahead with axes, chopped holes in the ice, and placed the anchors and ropes by which the ship could be warped forward. When the ship was in the lead they made haste to unfurl their canvas. It was often just at this time, when the men were exhausted by sawing and warping, that the wind died. There was then nothing for it but to drop the boats, connect them to the ship with ropes, and advance by the slow and immensely laborious process of towing.

These so called leads in the ice might have been designed to drive men mad. No sooner did they begin to make some measurable headway with the ship than the lane of water closed and stopped their further progress; or the lead would remain open but take an unexpected turn and fetch them back in the direction from which they'd just come.

The leads were a repeated hope that was constantly betrayed. Each time a lane of water appeared it presented itself with the freshness of a renewed faith, or a regained sense of purpose. The men responded willingly: they set up the tripods and mounted the saws with undiminished fervour; they went forward cheerfully and warped the ship. And always they were betrayed. It went on, and on, until they became sullen and dispirited. Even the ship's officers, after a while, showed by their voices and their manner that they no longer believed in the success of such endeavours.

It seemed to Arthur Storm that he was being forced to play a part in some ritual of despair. The repeated closings of the ice just when it was opening up, and the reversals in the water lanes just when they were leading somewhere, were reminders that in the end failure was the only possible reward. Perhaps it was necessary to make these repeated efforts and to suffer these inevitable setbacks, so that men would understand that all their aspirations were ultimately futile. It was only by manufacturing illusions and actually believing in them, only by creating artifices in the void, that it was possible to live from day to day until the final day when everything would be cancelled.

On 10 November the sun capitulated to the powers of darkness. It went below the horizon and stayed there.

It was appropriate that the deathly landscape should be robed in unchanging black. The darkness rubbed away at the sharp edges of the ice barriers, filled the hollows in the snow fields, smudged every distinguishing detail until the wilderness outside became part of the desolation that the men carried in their skulls. And the blackness that dissolved all shapes seemed to magnify sound. From an immense distance where mountains of ice chafed together there was the growling of unimaginable creatures tearing at each other.

The weather became colder.

A spare harpoon dropped accidentally from one of the boats, broke in two pieces when it hit the deck. The compass grew sluggish. Speech was painful to the jaws and tongue. The mercury in the thermometer sank and froze in the bowl. Even in the cabin it was cold: the oil in the lamps and the ink in the bottles froze, so that they had to be thawed out at the cabin stove each day to bring the log up to date; and Mr Beaufort pulled a strip of skin from his lower lip on a wine glass.

Captain Stapleton was worried about coal stocks, and he gave instructions that the half-deck stove wasn't to be lighted when the temperature was higher than 5° below zero. All the men's bunks were covered with frost.

The ship was beset most of the time and they unshipped the rudder to prevent its being destroyed by the encroaching ice. Captain Stapleton tried to protect the ship by cutting docks. They sawed the ice next to the ship into pieces which they sank beneath the surrounding ice or pulled out of the way. But the water froze almost as soon as it was exposed and their labour was wasted.

The beams started and the carlines jumped, as if the ship were a neck of mutton being chined by a giant butcher ready for carving into chops. The repeated pressures gave a diamond shape to the hatches and scuttles. Arthur Storm wasn't able to grow used to the constant nipping, and it seemed to him that his fear was increasing instead of diminishing. Many and many a time he was convinced that a particularly severe nipping would be their last.

Some of the green-men could no longer control their panic. Whenever the ship trembled and sighed more than usual they rushed up on to the deck, where neither the curses of Mr

Beaufort nor the red hairy fists of Mr Nellis, nor even the freshness of the wind could prevent them from throwing their chests and bedding on to the ice. At last Captain Stapleton gave orders for the boats to be stocked with provisions and securely sheeted. It was a relief to obey the order and to know that when the time came they would be able to abandon ship in good order. It was nevertheless dreadful to know that the Captain should take such a grave view of their plight. One of Jim Richardson's conditions had now been fulfilled, and Arthur's ears were frequently on the alert for the order to leave.

The men despatched Jim Richardson to the cabin with a plea that Captain Stapleton would conduct prayers in the 'tween decks every morning as well as on a Sunday. Mr Beaufort listened to the request with an expressionless face, and came down later to announce that the Captain would conduct prayers on a Wednesday and hold a longer service on a Sunday. The men were disappointed but grateful.

Captain Stapleton administered these duties in a curiously distant way that was typical of him. He had a fine voice and spoke with great feeling for the words he used, and yet Arthur couldn't escape the conviction that he was somehow dealing with the matter at arm's length.

On Sunday mornings Captain Stapleton always read Psalm 107 to them, and some of the most hardened Greenlanders had tears in their eyes when he came to those ancient words that smelled of seasoned oak and salt water:

> They that go down to the sea in ships:
> and occupy their business in great waters;
> These men see the works of the Lord:
> and his wonders in the deep.

Even the most irreligious of the men were strengthened by these words and thanked God for his mercy.

On 23 November the moon came into the sky and stayed there. It was a dead eye looking on a dead world.

The funereal landscape changed its mourning weeds for a winding sheet. Falling snow became visible, shining in the wan light of the moon like the spirits of all the dead. Hummocks of ice, untended graves in an unending churchyard, took on a gleam of phosphorescence. The ghostly light revealed a landscape more terrible than they remembered it.

It became even colder.

Mr Beaufort had some of the men erect a canvas awning over the quarter deck. Captain Stapleton worried about the way they were exhausting their coals and ordered that the fire in the 'tween decks be discontinued no matter what the temperature. The men's bedding promptly grew so stiff that they had to prise it open with marlinspikes before they could lie down to sleep, and the ice on the dead-lights was an inch thick. Captain Stapleton also ordered that the fire in the galley was to be put out every night at eight o'clock; and he gave instructions for the whale's fins and tail to be brought out of the hold for burning under the coppers. At the same time he decided that the provisions in the sheeted boats were being stolen with such frequency that they weren't to be replaced.

Arthur Storm discovered a small island of inexpressible joy. Every day it arose in the middle of this unending sea of misery.

It was the happiness of sitting on his hunkers with his back to the fire while the cook was making soup, until he could feel the heat softening the brittle marrow in his bones; and of squatting there until he could smell the cloth of his jacket singeing, while three feet in front of his nose the water for the next lot of soup was frozen solid in the bucket. It was the bliss of turning slowly and luxuriously round, and stroking the hot copper with the wide-stretched palms of his hands until he could once more waggle his fingers one at a time; and of watching pieces of fin and tail grow brown and crisp as they burned underneath; and of snatching choice bits out of the flames and knowing that they were blistering his lips and fingers as he chewed them.

To remember each day's ecstasy and to be sure of it happening again tomorrow was to have one foot in Heaven already.

Every couple of days a few men were sent out to cut ice. It was a tedious operation, and the cold was dangerous when the wind was blowing. The work was intensely disliked and feared, but it was necessary to maintain supplies of fresh water.

Arthur had just returned from one of these outings. He was cold and hungry, and was hurrying after the rest of the gang to remove his mittens and change his stockings. Then the small ice party could go along and have some freshly made soup. The double prospect of the cook's fire and hot soup was almost unbearably pleasurable after going out of the ship to cut ice.

He stopped as he was passing the companion down to the galley. What was it?

Arthur gave a number of short sniffs, the way a man does when he is puzzled by a smell and wants to take a number of samples that he can compare quickly with each other. The sniffs became longer, so that he could savour them, and he blew the air out sharply so that he could sniff again. The sniffs grew even more protracted. He pulled the aroma as deep into his lungs as it would go, and his exhalations changed into sighs. His ice-rimed mittens and frozen stockings were forgotten.

He ducked into the companion and descended one, two, three steps very slowly and stopped. This must be a dream! But it couldn't be. The actuality of this smell was more powerful than anything a mere dream could produce. Perhaps it was the previous weeks that had been a dream?

The sharpness of the sensation was little short of painful. Nerves in his nose and mouth were jumping. His stomach was opening and closing like a drunken mouth singing hymns. Saliva leaped inside his lips and coated his teeth and gums.

He laughed. 'Hey there!' he called.

His legs moved again of their own accord. He went down four, five, six steps. The muscles in his throat were contracting, screwing themselves up tight and then relaxing almost into water. Seven, eight, nine steps. His lungs were inflating and collapsing like the blacksmith's bellows when he was beating horseshoe nails into bars for the best harpoons. Ten, eleven, twelve. Reawakened juices moistened his gullet. And as he neared the bottom steps he was remembering.

He saw his mam bending over the black-leaded oven in Ellerby Lane.

In her hand there was a dry rag that she used to lift the brass handle of the heavy door. She withdrew a tin with steep, burnished sides that had been burned to a dark brown. Aw, the smell of it! The surface of the leg had been deeply scored and well salted to ensure that the crackling would be crisp enough to snap between your teeth. She basted it in its own juice with a rhythmic, practised hand. The gravy spluttered and spat and he could hear the repeated knocking of the wooden spoon against the side of the tin. She slid it back into the oven, closed the heavy iron door and lowered the brass handle.

He reached the bottom of the companionway, stepped on to the floor and entered the galley.

It was roast pork!

'Hey there! Hey there!' He was laughing again.

The copper containing the soup for the ice gang was in its place. The flames beneath it had died down for lack of attention, and there wasn't any smell from the pot.

The cook had wrapped himself up in a blanket and was sitting comfortably in the only chair. His head was thrown well back to reveal a scrawny throat in which the Adam's apple bobbed about like the glass marble in the neck of a bottle. His mouth was open and from it there issued a deep gurgling that altered its character with each change in the direction of his breath: when air was being drawn in the noise was that of water escaping through the scuppers; when air was being driven out it sounded as if the cook were doing his level best to expel some obstruction that was almost but not quite choking him. The thought was irresistible that the obstruction was caused by his Adam's apple, and with each blow Arthur half-expected to see it fly out of his mouth like a ball from a musket.

And now Arthur's nose detected another smell. It hadn't ascended the steps to the deck, but down here it lay all around him as insistently as a fog. It was a smell he'd learned to recognize. It was rum.

Sitting on the floor, propped sideways against the chair, was the figure of Mr Beaufort's line-manager. Peter Gill's shoulders were hunched and his head was drawn down between them. The black hair on his crown and nape, and the angle of his head, made him resemble a tern looking for fish. His chin rested on his chest and his head rose and fell in time with high-pitched snores that whistled antiphonally to the rumblings of the cook. The pink-rimmed eyes were invisible but it was possible to imagine that he was staring at his feet.

His feet, or what was left of them, were resting on the hot embers under the copper pot. The shoes had burned away, and it was no longer easy to distinguish between the ashes of his stockings and the bubbles of his flesh.

Arthur dragged Peter Gill away from the fire. When the rest of the ice party came along to the galley they lost their yearning for freshly made soup. One of them ran off for the Surgeon and the rest carried the stupefied line-manager to his berth.

It was the first bad case. Mr McCabe came in with a long, new-looking bag; Mr Beaufort followed, struggling with a cask. The Surgeon rolled up the smouldering bottoms of Peter Gill's trousers. The two officers conferred and Mr McCabe nodded.

'Everyone out!' Mr Beaufort ordered.

Arthur was the last to reach the door.

'You! Stay behind and sit on his chest.'

They gave him as much rum as he wanted. Arthur, sitting on the man's chest, knew that he would never forget the childlike disbelief in Peter Gill's eyes as Mr Beaufort kept dipping a tankard into the cask for him. Peter Gill drank until the rum was almost oozing out round his eyeballs, but he still protested at the top of his voice when Mr McCabe sawed his feet off.

Later the same day Captain Stapleton took the unprecedented step of reversing one of his decisions. Once again the stove in the half-deck had to be re-lighted whenever the temperature fell more than 5° below zero.

Peter Gill's legs turned black and developed a smell which was new to most of the men. The air in the half-deck became that of an opened grave even while he was still alive.

23

The moon, a cataracted eye, stared down from the sunless heaven. Beneath its blank gaze Mr Beaufort descended the ladder. His sealskin cap was pulled well down over his ears, and he moved his boots and gloved hands with care. It was almost noon.

'What's this?' he demanded, feigning astonishment. 'Not finished yet! You stopped for a prattle, I suppose?' Then he lost his temper the way he sometimes did. 'Get your backs into it! Get your backs into it, I say, unless you want to end up in the same hole!'

The men bent to their task.

Whurrr –

The jagged teeth of the saw bit into the stillness of the day as the men put their weight behind the long handle. Their sucking breaths mingled with the softer sound the saw made each time it was drawn back for another stroke.

Arthur Storm's fingers were beginning to feel as if they were permanently crooked around the wooden shaft, and would remain clenched to its shape even when the job was done. The physical effort kept wrenching every trace of breath out of his lungs, and pumping them full again to the depths of their remotest tissues. The incoming air caused the fire in his chest to burn with a brighter and more painful flame.

'Get on with it!' shouted Mr Beaufort. 'I'm damned if I'm going to stand here and watch you play games with that saw. Get on with it, for God's sake! Or at least get on with it for my sake! I don't want to die yet.'

Arthur Storm closed his eyes and willed his muscles to assist the motions of the saw. His fingers were so numb that they didn't belong to him, and had as little to do with his body as the wooden shaft. He opened his eyes to look at Jim Richardson and saw that he had his eyes closed. We are asleep, he thought. Every single one of us is asleep. We are all dreaming the same endless nightmare. It will go on for always. We shall never wake up.

Whurrr –

After the final stroke they stood back and put their numbed hands under their armpits. Their breath groaned and whistled.

'Well done, lads! Out with it!' Mr Beaufort, more cheerful now, took a few steps back to the foot of the iron ladder. 'Wake up! Lower away!'

Arthur drove a hand-spike into the saw cut and used it to lever up the piece of freshly cut ice. Mr Beaufort returned from the foot of the ladder and soon became impatient again, stamping his feet and cursing when the ice slipped back into the hole. Arthur levered up the piece for the third time and managed to hold it until Jim Richardson could attach the tackle.

'Don't take it away,' Mr Beaufort said. 'Just lay it down nice and handy.'

Arthur stood back. A movement caught the tail of his eye, and he turned to regard the bundle that was being lowered down to them. In the uncertain light it could have been a gigantic chrysalis. At any moment the jointed frame might begin to twitch, and an enormous grey caterpillar would drag itself out on to the ice.

The descent stopped when the parcel was at waist height. He'd never seen anything so still and silent. And it looked so stiff. Aw, so stiff!

He received a blow in the ribs.

'Stop dreaming!' Mr Beaufort said. 'Take the other end.'

Arthur advanced to the package. It was wrapped in sail cloth, roughly stitched along the edges, but as unyielding to his touch as cast iron. He supported his end of the burden under one arm while he removed the rope sling. Mr Beaufort took the other end and led the way to the hole.

'Feet first,' he ordered. 'Your end.'

Arthur knew there weren't any feet. But he carefully lowered his end.

Why do I treat him so gently? Why am I so respectful? I should drop these legs as if they were no more than a couple of sticks, fit for nothing better than a casual fire. Yet I lower them towards this icy water as if my care could ease his pain. His pain is over. I should be regretting that I can't do anything that would make these dead limbs suffer some additional torment to serve as a further punishment.

'Are you going to say a few words, Mr Beaufort?' asked Jim Richardson.

'No, I'm not.'

'I think we'd all feel better if you said a few words, Mr Beaufort.'

Yes, that was it, Arthur thought, as he placed the end – the end where the feet used to be – at the edge of the hole. In the presence of the mystery you had to say something. It would be unbearable otherwise.

'You think what you like,' Mr Beaufort said, roughly steering the end into the hole as if he were pushing a wheelbarrow.

'In that case I'll say a few words mesen, Mr Beaufort.'

'There's no time! And there's no merit in the case.'

Jim Richardson, made brave by his faith in the justice of his cause, ignored the implied order. With head bowed, and his mittened fist holding the stump of his other arm, he spoke from memory. The hurried words rimed his beard with frost.

'Man that is born of woman hath but a short time to live, and is full of misery. He cometh up and is cut down like a flower. He fleeth as it were a shadow and never continueth in one stay.'

Arthur was glad to hear the words. A feeling of relief, even of gratitude, flowed through him. Why should this be? He ought to hate the dead man.

Mr Beaufort had managed to insert the end in the hole and he pushed the body into a vertical position. It sank up to about the knees. Jim Richardson continued to recite. Mr Beaufort leaned heavily and the body descended by as much again to a level below the waist.

'Damnation! The hole isn't big enough. If you hadn't been so quick with your prayers you'd have spent longer with the saw.'

Arthur felt a quick resentment at this injustice. 'Excuse me for saying so, Mr Beaufort, sir, but we didn't know they were going to lap him up like this.'

Mr Beaufort redirected his anger at the men beyond the iron ladder. 'Why did you want to lap him up like a new China teapot? He's got more canvas on him than an East Indiaman on a wind.' He returned his attention to Arthur. 'Give me a hand with him.'

Arthur groped among the iron folds of sail cloth and found the vague outline of the shoulders. He exerted a mild pressure: nothing happened. He pressed more heavily: there was still no movement. Mr Beaufort placed his hands on the shoulders from the other side and they both leaned forwards. Arthur looked into the face now brought so close to his own, and saw a blue vein jump into prominence on the forehead and run up to the sealskin cap.

'We therefore commit his body into the deep, to be turned into corruption, looking for resurrection of the body when t' sea shall give up her dead . . .'

They pressed downwards together as hard as they could. Abruptly the obstruction gave way. The body had gone in so quickly that Arthur found he was embracing Mr Beaufort cheek to cheek. The hole contained nothing but a ball whose outline was obscured by the crumpled irregularities of the sail cloth.

'... our Lord Jesus Christ. Who at his coming shall change our vile body, that it may be like his glorious body, according to t' mighty working, whereby he is able to subdue all things to hissen.'

Mr Beaufort placed his foot on the bobbing ball and deftly kicked it under the adjacent ice.

'The lid,' he said.

Arthur again applied the hand-spike and levered the piece of ice back into the hole from which it had come. Mr Beaufort stamped it firmly into place.

'Now there's no need for anyone to have bad dreams,' he said.

'Amen,' said Jim Richardson.

Mr Beaufort turned on his heel and led the way back to the iron ladder and the rest followed.

Arthur lingered a moment to look down at the grave. Already it was difficult to tell where the hole had been.

He knew he'd have bad dreams. He would see the white face with its stiff black hair and round eyes looking up through the icy lid of its coffin. Should I ask forgiveness for not pitying him more? Then he saw that other face, with its mouth open to shout the accusation even at the point of death, and a sense of guilt crushed his heart and made him catch his breath. No, I have pitied this man too much already.

The moon, like a milky eye, gazed down from the black face of heaven. Beneath its unregarding stare Arthur turned towards the ladder. It was a little after noon.

24

The first break in the weather gave some preliminary indications of how much the *William Scoresby Senior* had suffered. The longer the milder weather continued, the more evident did her injuries become.

The ship's timbers had been sprung by the repeated nipping, her seams had been opened up by the frost and the oakum was hanging out like the stuffing from a scarecrow of the previous summer. The scuttles and hatches tried to return to their original square and rectangular shapes; but like decrepit old men who reappear in the clothes of their youth their coamings no longer fitted them. The heads of the second and third tiers of casks had burst, and when the ballast water melted the hold and half-deck were filled with a stench that reminded everybody of Peter Gill's last days.

It wasn't until the ice relaxed its grip sufficiently for the *William Scoresby Senior* to settle fully back into the water that they discovered the full extent of the damage. Water came in so fast that there were soon over three feet in the hold. They worked both pumps day and night, without daring to pause for a second, amidst the reek of the melted ballast water. Shortly after the level in the hold reached five feet the ice returned and pushed them up.

The carpenter worked without sleep and with all the assistance he could command. When the weather broke again the *William Scoresby Senior* floated as soundly as she ever had.

Hunger began to trouble them more than cold. Captain Stapleton had cut the weekly allowance of bread to two pounds for each man in November, and after another stock-taking he cut it to one and a half pounds. Twice a week beef or pork was served out of the pickle. The potatoes were almost finished and the men were disappointed to learn that the remainder was to be kept for the use of the cabin.

Seals swam around the ship, as graceful and silver as fish in the moonlight. Some of the men lowered a boat and caught one. They dragged it to the nearest shelf of ice where they skinned it, but where it nevertheless continued to struggle with as much life as it had before. They returned to the ship and with some difficulty hung the carcase over the stern to purge. Some of the other men had been made so desperate by hunger, and were so inflamed by the sight of the raw flesh, that they wanted to eat it immediately. A struggle for possession developed during which the flayed creature managed to wriggle from the rope. The icy water numbed its nude body for a few seconds and then the bright red shape swam away and lost itself amongst its silvery mates of less than an hour before.

During the long periods when they were beset the officers shot whatever they could.

A flock of rotches whirred around the ship, and cheered the men because the presence of these small birds was supposed to indicate that open water wasn't very far away. Mr Beaufort shot at least half a dozen before they dispersed. He sent six men on to the ice to retrieve the birds for the cabin table. Unfortunately the wind freshened and one man lost the whole of his thumb and half a finger.

Mr Nellis shot a bear that they skinned, cut up and put into pickle. The men pulled the insides out and tasted their first fresh meat for months. The kidneys and heart were best but those who ate the liver regretted it: the most excruciating pains pierced their heads, their faces burned, their eyes swelled until they almost burst and their skin peeled off like paper.

Best of all was the fox that Mr Beaufort shot. He made sure that it was properly purged and cooked, and Captain Stapleton sent a handsome portion down to the 'tween decks. The men who were lucky enough to taste a piece swore on oath that it was better than any chicken they could remember.

Their coals were almost finished. When Captain Stapleton saw the remains of a wreck from the masthead he called for volunteers to go for fuel, as well as any provisions that might have been left aboard. Seven men launched a boat across the ice. The moon-lit landscape tricked them into thinking the wreck was much nearer than it was, and it was painful work travelling over the uneven ice. They returned empty handed after two days and more fingers and toes were lost.

Hunger, cold and fatigue began to have their effects on all the half-deck men. Mr McCabe came down to leech them every morning, and these days he always brought a block of wood, his saw and a knife. When the wind was fresh a man could suffer frostbite merely by going up to the main deck for a few moments during a cold spell. A few of the men started to experience soreness in the mouth, and their legs swelled and grew discoloured. They tried to swallow the blood that dribbled from their gums so that the others wouldn't know that scurvy had arrived.

On 23 January the sun returned to the sky. Its sallow face looked down for a few minutes on the endless waxy fields, at the frozen ship and at the bleached faces of the men who returned its unfamiliar gaze.

As if to confirm this pale promise of better things the ice thinned sufficiently for the *William Scoresby Senior* to proceed by mill-dolling. A boat loaded with men was suspended from the jibboom, and lowered to the surface. The men moved from side to side in unison which caused the boat to rock and break up the ice. The ship went ahead into the passage created for it. The boat and its men were carried forward under the jibboom and extended the passage as they went.

By working in relays and showing great perseverance they reached sailing ice. They shipped the boat and sailed several miles to the south-east before the ice closed in and thickened.

The ice thickened rapidly. Captain Stapleton feared that his ship couldn't withstand another severe squeeze and called for a dock. The men brought out the tripods and slung the big saws, but the ice was too strong for them. The weary Helmsley oak, its tough fibres nurtured by years on the sunny slopes of Bilsdale, cried loudly for release from the relentless embrace. But the ice was implacable in its cold lust. The *William Scoresby Senior* had to submit.

At the end of January the temperature was down to minus twenty degrees. The coals had long been finished, and as soon as they ran out of whalebone the men began to use any surplus wood they could find. They started on the top tier of casks, and Mr Beaufort managed to stop them only with the most dire threats and the assistance of Mr Nellis's hairy fists. When the temperature dropped another five degrees the men were so desperate that they removed some of the hatches and burned them in the 'tween decks.

Fresh breezes from the south-east brought snow and blew it down the open hatchways. Snow covered patches of the 'tween decks and neighbouring beds to a depth of six inches.

Early in February a strong wind blew up from the south which caused a heavy swell that broke up the ice. The ice was very thick, and drifting chunks of it struck the ship with great force.

Having failed to destroy them by squeezing, the enemy was now intent on bludgeoning them to pieces.

The concussions reverberated in the 'tween decks like thunder. But the thermometer was rising rapidly, and went to twenty-five degrees above zero. Arthur Storm and the more able-bodied men were glad of the opportunity to go up on to the main deck.

Arthur would have relished the novelty of not having to protect himself against the cold if it hadn't been for the drifting ice. Loose floes kept charging the ship, and he braced himself each time against the coming shock. All the while he was selecting the most convenient piece of ice, rejecting it and choosing again every time a larger piece came along, with the intention of escaping to it if the ship were stove. This was how the *Aimwell* had been destroyed six seasons ago. A piece of floating ice knocked a hole in her larboard bow, and she promptly filled and sank. He wondered if Mr Paylor had tried to scramble on to one of the floes. It would be a short life. Perhaps only an hour or two.

And then he thought of Ann Paylor's blue eyes and fair, curling hair, and of her smooth white legs when he first saw her by the rock. He desperately wanted to survive.

The floes became smaller and less numerous, and the blows to the hull were less violent and more infrequent. He hardly dared to believe it at first. After some hours the sea became reasonably open and it was clear that the *William Scoresby Senior* had survived her buffeting. One by one the men gave up their vigil on deck and returned below.

The rise in temperature meant that the thermometer had changed fifty degrees in the course of the day. When Arthur had left his bunk it was several inches thick with frost and snow that had drifted through the open hatch. Now his bedding was as wet as if it had been fished out of the sea and it dripped continuously into a large pool of water that lay beneath it.

The alternation of mild and cold spells became a recurring feature of the weather. This new variety in their living conditions, far from making their existence more bearable, actually made it worse because the effects of each extreme were made more intolerable by what had preceded them. There wasn't any satisfactory way of adapting to the irregular seesaw of change.

When the men returned from sawing, warping, mill-dolling,

shipping and unshipping the rudder, letting out and taking in canvas, or from any of their duties that took them outside, they inevitably came down with snow on their shoes. During the milder weather they soon trampled the snow into a slush, and the 'tween decks became as filthy as the area next to the Tolbooth on a market day.

Then during the cold spells the frost penetrated the ship's sides and main deck, and the wind blew snow down the companionways. The walls of the 'tween decks were coated with hoar frost and the beds were stiff with ice. The slush on the floor hardened into a corrugated surface that was difficult to walk on. When Arthur Storm lay on his crackling bed, and pulled the white-rimed blanket up to his chin, he thought anything would be preferable to this frost. But when the mild intermission came, and his bed dripped all day and all night, he wanted the frost to return.

It was at this time that whales became plentiful for a period. Arthur lay on his wet bed and listened to them blowing alongside the ship, seemingly only a few feet from his head. There wasn't so much as a hint from the cabin that they should lower a boat, and nobody paid the fish the slightest attention.

Captain Stapleton, coming down to conduct prayers after a couple of days of the milder weather, was appalled by the wetness of everything. He gave orders for a fire to be lighted and for it to be fed with casks from the hold until the sleeping quarters were dry. From then onwards he permitted a fire one day a week in the half-deck, even during mild weather, in order to dry it out.

The Captain also tried to revive morale by an improvement in messes, and under his instructions the remains of the barley were used to make one and a half gills of soup for each man. Mr Beaufort began the practice of weighing out extra flour and oatmeal for the men to mix together with a little water and roll in their hands until they had satisfying gobbets of paste; the more finical and patient of them used splinters of whalebone to cook their morsels into something resembling biscuits over the galley fire. Peelings from the cabin potatoes were boiled for the 'tween decks, and when all the potatoes had gone Captain Stapleton gave strict instructions that bread dust was to be collected daily for making soup.

Mr Beaufort encouraged the junior officers to enforce regular duties upon the men. This wasn't simply to keep things clean, but also to appeal to the men's pride and improve hygiene. The First Mate personally gave orders for the spinning of ropeyarn and the making of sennit. But both officers and men found all their tasks meaningless.

Fresh breezes from the north-west brought softer weather. They hove the ship's head to the southward and set topsails, and then top gallants, and then they ran stunsails out beyond the leeches of the mainsails so as to take every advantage they could while the fair wind lasted. The wind became stronger, carrying snow and sleet, and they had to shorten sail. Then the wind got easterly, and when the ice closed they had to unship the rudder.

Then it blew a gale, causing a heavy swell that broke up the ice. Again the ship was battered by moving floes. Again she was beset and squeezed. Whenever they could they shipped the rudder, set canvas, and made a little more progress to the south. The ice kept slacking, but the slacks were repeatedly filled up with bay ice that made it impossible for them to do anything.

By the middle of February there weren't sufficient able-bodied men to do all the work that needed to be done. Mr Beaufort made it his practice to secure the helm when the evening set in so that he could rest during the hours of darkness. At night the *William Scoresby Senior* drifted north or south at the will of the waves. When she was beset the ice carried her along like a fly in an amber pebble. The men stayed in their berths, where the stench of ballast water and blubber and kreng from the burst casks in the hold mingled with the smells of gangrene and their dead ship-mates.

Only a few months ago, when a man returned from duty suffering from exposure, the men had stretched him out on their sea chests and cut off his frozen clothes; and then they had rubbed him with pieces of flannel and blanket until his flesh glowed again. But more recently anyone who returned in that condition crawled to his bed where he became delirious and died. In the earlier days they sewed a dead man in sailcloth, cut a hole in the ice and launched him decently as they had done for Peter Gill. But now the dead men stayed in their bunks.

The living hadn't the strength to look after themselves. It wasn't surprising that they neglected the dead.

Captain Stapleton called all hands on deck with the intention of asking if they were willing to go on to a shorter allowance of bread. Nobody even tried to crawl up the companionway. The Captain, the First Mate and the Specksioneer went aloft themselves, put the ship under close-reefed topsails and left it that way.

25

The most serious result of the absence of enterprise amongst the men was the scarcity of fresh water. The men in the 'tween decks thought of little else and they cried out to the ship's Surgeon when he made his morning visit.

'Water! Water, Mr McCabe! Water for the love of Jesus, Mr McCabe!'

The Surgeon continued to move from bed to bed with his bag of leeches, his block of wood and his blood-stained knife. He had changed so much in the last few weeks that Arthur Storm had difficulty in remembering what he used to look like. The young student from Edinburgh, eager for adventure and new experiences, was turning into an old man. The eyes behind the spectacles were still timid but they'd lost their youthful curiosity about everything they saw.

'Water! Water, Mr McCabe! For love of Jesus, Mr McCabe!'

The constant begging, the clutching of weak hands, the parroting of his name and the harping religious invocation were driving him out of his mind.

'There'll be no more water today,' he said, and his voice was high and strained. 'And there'll be none at all in a few days if you can't organize an ice gang.'

Ignoring their further cries he positioned the block of wood on a man's bed and made sure it was stable. He took the man's hand, put it squarely on the block and sawed away at one of the fingers with his knife. Arthur watched without being aware of it. Such things had become commonplace.

Mr McCabe moved on to the bed next to Arthur, where Rasmie Hughson, the big Shetlander, was lying. He put his hand on the sick man's forehead, looked at his bleeding mouth, and settled a pair of leeches on his arm. Rasmie tried to speak but couldn't manage anything better than a whisper. He tried again. Mr McCabe either didn't notice or decided to ignore him. He scooped his leeches back into their bag and was about to move on when Rasmie raised a once brawny arm to detain him.

'What is it?'

Seeing the repeated effort to speak, Mr McCabe bent down and placed his ear next to the Shetlander's moving mouth.

'Go on!' he said, impatiently.

He listened to the rustling lips. His worried face, prematurely lined, gathered extra wrinkles as he screwed his eyes up tightly. He stood up.

'No!'

Rasmie Hughson made an urgent noise in his throat.

'No! You must be crazy to ask such a thing!'

The Shetlander's big, bony arm straightened and he gripped Mr McCabe's slender wrist. He twisted the Surgeon's arm in its shoulder socket and then forced it up behind his back. Mr McCabe had to bend forwards. His spectacles slipped half-way down his nose and his face was almost touching the filthy bedding. Again Rasmie tried to speak.

'No!' gasped the Surgeon. 'No! I won't be guilty of – '

With an unconscious gesture of his free hand he pushed his spectacles back to the bridge of his nose. The lenses magnified his eyes to a grotesque size as his arm was twisted through the degrees which turned mere pain to agony. His free hand now went impetuously to his pocket and withdrew his knife.

Arthur, weak although he was, raised himself up from his bed. 'Don't! Don't, Mr McCabe! Watch out, Rasmie!'

His warning was too late or not acted upon. Mr McCabe slid his blood-stained knife neatly into the arm that was torturing him. The knife, either by bad luck or design, pierced a thick, blue vein that stood up like a knotted cord inside the straining arm. Rasmie released his hold. Mr McCabe pocketed the knife, snatched up his board and bag and ran to the companionway.

'You made me do it!' he shouted over his shoulder as he

climbed the stairs. 'You animal! You made me! Don't forget!'

Rasmie Hughson keeled over with one arm dangling under his bunk. Arthur rolled to the side of his own bunk, sat up and hastily selected one of the cleaner pieces of bedding that could be used to stanch the wound. Rasmie leaned further over and looked as if he were about to fall out.

'Take it easy,' Arthur said, putting his feet to the floor and springing across with the sheet in his hand. 'Let me see that arm.'

But Rasmie recovered his balance and sat up. His face, instead of being stamped by shock or anger at the attack, was curiously softened by an expression of contentment. He waved Arthur away with a shoe that he'd picked up from under the bed.

'You're not going to try to walk?' Arthur asked. 'You're not going after him?'

The Shetlander seemed to think this was a good joke. He put the shoe on his lap and stretched his wounded arm over it. His eyes shone as he watched the blood flow. He couldn't wait for the shoe to fill and after only half a minute he lifted it, tilted it, and gulped from the heel. When his mouth sucked on dryness he put out his bright red tongue to its greatest extent and licked at the inside of the worn leather.

'Na, I'm no thinking of gaeing after him,' he said, rejoicing in his regained ability to speak. 'I'll thank the chiel taemorrow when he comes doon tae see us. That is if I'm still hereaboots. If I'm no here thoo cuid dee it for me.'

It was now Arthur who had difficulty in speaking. 'Rasmie! What are you doing to yourself?'

'Hae thoo ever wondered why those damned leeches look sae fat and bonny?' Rasmie had a cunning look in his eye and his red mouth slipped sideways in a knowing grin. 'It's because they're sucking all the goodness oot of us.'

He returned the stained shoe to his lap and stretched his arm over it. The blood didn't flow so readily this time, and he worked his arm up and down like a pump handle until it pulsed out in crimson spasms. Arthur, watching in silence, became aware of the smell. It was warm and cloying.

Rasmie drank again with gusto, working the tip of his stiff tongue into the seams like some ravening reptile searching for insects.

When he held his arm over the shoe for the third time he discovered that the blood was beginning to congeal around the wound. He placed a finger and thumb on each end of the cut and pressed until it popped open. This didn't have much effect so he inserted his little finger in the hole and waggled it about, just as he did when he was cleaning his ear with it. At the same time he bounced up and down on the bed as energetically as he could to make his heart work harder.

The combination of these methods was so efficient that he was able to fill the shoe almost to the brim. His hands were less steady now as he raised it to his mouth. He took a couple of sips and offered the shoe to Arthur.

'Taste that, laddie.' His throat sounded as if it were full of treacle. 'I've just opened a new barrel for thoo.'

'No. No, Rasmie.'

Now that the shoe was directly under his nose the smell was overpowering. It filled his nose, his throat, his stomach, his lungs. The air was alive with its cloying essence. He remembered the smell perfectly. The air was alive with it when the razorback turned on its side and pumped its living blood into his face before it rolled over.

'Drink it!' Rasmie begged. 'It'll make a man of thoo.'

Arthur reached under his pillow and pulled out the last of his flour and oatmeal. He unscrewed the paper and poured its contents into his cupped left hand. Without hesitation he took the shoe and trickled the liquor into the dry powder.

'Thank you,' he said.

He placed his right hand on top of his left. Carefully, so as not to let anything run to waste, he kneaded the wet mixture until he had a dark brown paste that could be rolled into balls.

'Thank you,' he said, again.

Rasmie Hughson smiled and lay down.

26

Arthur Storm chewed the brown spheres slowly, one at a time, and the soggy flour gradually filled his stomach and made it feel good. The seed of the earth and the juice of the man had amalgamated into a mixture that glowed inside him like a sun: not the flat, white disc that sliced through the sky to look down on their present wretchedness; but the great, golden globe that warmed speckled backs in the trout pools of the Esk and its Cleveland becks. It heated his blood and irradiated the nerves along his limbs down to his fingertips and the ends of his toes.

A memory of what it was like to be active and strong passed through his body and became present truth. He stood up.

Jim Richardson was lying in the top bunk. Reluctant blood and the cold had turned his mouth blue, and his lips were puckered and cracked. His tongue was raw and swollen from licking the frost that rimed his bedding and the adjacent bulkhead. His remaining hand was inside his shirt, pulling convulsively at the jet cross and making red marks around his neck where the cord bit into the unfeeling flesh. The eyes were sinking into his head, as if whatever it was that had pressed behind and kept them in their places was melting away.

The rough tongue rubbed against the back of his teeth and the eyes looked up from their craters. Arthur guessed that the rubbing noise was a plea for water. The message in the eyes was even easier to interpret. It was fear. Not merely the fear of dying. It was a more awful fear than that.

The expression in the eyes was unendurable. Arthur had to look away from the hand clutching the black cross. A feeling near to anger swelled inside him.

He put on another shirt, pulled on the big gansey that his grandma had knitted and then his pea jacket. He put on his second pair of trousers, woollen mittens and gloves, and his lined boots. With a wooden bucket in one hand and an axe in the other he went up on deck. There was a wind, so he would have to be careful and quick.

The *William Scoresby Senior* was tightly beset with an accumulation of ice on the windward side. It would have been madness to work there, and he used the iron ladder that was in position to leeward, just forward of the mizzen chains. By the time he was on the ice the wind had rasped his cheeks until he could almost believe the bones were exposed. Yes, he would have to be quick.

He started on the nearest knoll and cut off some useful chunks. Proceeding methodically and swiftly he chopped the slabs into smaller pieces that would fit into the bucket. He'd almost filled the bucket when a sensation like fire entered the fingers of his right hand. Hastily he examined the glove, and discovered by stretching it that the fingers were slightly threadbare. That must be due to all the work he'd done on the saws. I'll have to be particularly careful with that, he thought. I'll remember to carry the axe in my right hand, with my fingers safely round the wooden handle, so that they can't possibly touch the iron head.

He used his left hand to put some small pieces of ice into the bucket. Then with the bucket in his left hand and the wooden handle of the axe securely in his right, he turned to face the ship. It wasn't until he started to walk that he discovered he'd lost almost all sensation in his feet. I'll have to be really quick, but I must try not to hurry too much in case I do something careless.

The absence of sensation in his feet made it difficult to climb the ladder. He kept having to look down and ensure that his feet were squarely placed on the rungs. It was like being suspended in space, and just before he reached the top he began to lose his balance. I must be careful, he reminded himself. He threw the axe forward over the gunwale into the ship, so as to put the iron head out of harm's way, and seized the top rung of the ladder with his free hand. It was like being struck by lightning!

The longer he waited the worse it would be. He wrenched. There wasn't any extra pain. He climbed to the top of the ladder, trampling on the discarded flesh with his heavy boots.

The axe could stay where it was. He went directly to the forward hatch. When he was half-way down the companionway there was a clatter of feet on the steps above him. It was Mr Nellis and he was in a hurry.

'Come by!' he ordered as he pushed past.

Nobody had seen the Specksioneer for weeks. Apart from Captain Stapleton's brief appearances on Wednesdays and Sundays to lead the prayers, and Mr McCabe's daily round, they didn't see anybody from the cabin these days. This visit was so extraordinary that those who were strong enough sat up in their beds.

'East Water, lads!' Mr Nellis announced. 'There's a patch of water sky as blue as a polar bear's arse, and Captain Stapleton has sighted lanes opening up all the way to the eastward.'

Arthur reached the bottom of the steps and stood behind Mr Nellis with the bucket in his hand. Several of the men pulled themselves to the sides of their beds. Some of them tried to stand and had to sit down again. Smiles twisted their faces. Many of them gave thanks to God and a few did their best to raise a cheer.

'And rain on the horizon,' added Mr Nellis. 'Captain Stapleton can see it from the masthead.'

He turned to reascend the companionway and Arthur took a step backwards. The Specksioneer noticed the bucket full of ice and looked up in surprise.

'You've been a busy fool, boy,' he said. 'We'll have enough rain water to bath in before that's melted.'

Mr Nellis climbed the steps and Arthur walked between the berths until he came to Rasmie Hughson. The big Shetlander seemed to have grown smaller during the short time he'd been away. His skin was wrinkled like a balloon that had been blown up too far and was shrinking as the air leaked out of it. The wound in his arm gaped with the white lips of a fish on a slab, while his mouth, previously so pale, was as red as the wound had been when it was fresh.

The news had come too late for him.

Arthur used his teeth to pull the glove and mitten from his left hand and picked a small piece of ice out of the bucket. He held it tightly and it burned in his palm like a hot coal.

Another clatter of feet descended from the companion. Mr Beaufort arrived, looking mightily pleased with everything including himself. The wound on his lower lip, where the wine glass had pulled the skin off, had healed without a scar.

'Water sky,' he confirmed. 'Starting tomorrow there'll be four pounds of bread for each man and five soup days a week. Mess pots every day. That means there'll be two and a half pieces of beef five days and four and a half of pork on the other two. All this to be regular if the lanes stay open, which seems more than likely.'

Before he'd finished speaking most of the men had eaten everything that remained of their week's allowance. The only ones that restrained themselves were those who were too weak to eat. One man's stomach revolted at the unaccustomed load and he vomited on to his bedding.

'We're not home yet but I can promise you there'll be no more nipping when we come out of this and no more buffeting. So when the weather breaks, which will be any minute now, I want all available hands on deck to stow the boats.' He grinned at them, saving the most welcome instruction until the end. 'And to put water tanks out.'

Mr Beaufort reascended the stairs and Arthur turned to Jim Richardson. The sunken eyes were shining and he tried to speak.

'Wait!' Arthur said.

He raised his hand and trickled the melted ice on to the dry cracks in his lips and through the puckered opening on to the rough tongue. Now the words could come and interpret the new light that was shining in his eyes.

'I knew it.' Jim's hand gripped the black cross. 'I knew we'd be saved.'

Arthur lay on his bunk. The feeling hadn't returned to his toes and the pain hadn't yet come to his right hand. He would have to wait for Mr McCabe's next visit.

The *William Scoresby Senior* was in Latitude 53° 52′N.

The rain came that evening and Arthur discovered that he couldn't get up the companionway to help with the water tanks. During the night the ice broke up and in the morning the *William Scoresby Senior* found herself in a clear lane going eastward. A fresh breeze from north north-west kept her going at seven knots. The flocks of birds returned.

Later in the morning Mr McCabe came down with his little bag and his board and his knife. He was smiling and his face had recovered something of its youth. Through the hatch above his head came the sound of cheering.

'You know what that cheering means,' said Mr McCabe to the men who hadn't been able to leave their beds. 'It means we've left the ice.'

Arthur waited for him in his bed.

Three

George Stephenson could see that the move from the hustling Tyne to the sleepy Tees was only the beginning.

He was the man who was going to make it happen and everyone would know it. He would make sure everyone knew it, even if he had to spend the rest of his life proving it to them. There wouldn't be any repetition of the safety lamp treachery. He'd learned his lesson then and he would never need to learn it again.

How the London gentlemen had laughed! An uneducated Northumbrian pitman, who couldn't even talk English properly, invent the miners' safety lamp! Wasn't there any limit to the impudence of the ignorant? Sir Humphrey Davy, the greatest scientist of the day, had invented the safety lamp. Sir Humphrey Davy himself said he'd invented it, the Royal Society said Sir Humphrey had invented it, polite society agreed with them and the London newspapers confirmed that they were right.

Despite his determination not to be put down again he'd been forced to suffer an even more painful defeat at the hands of southerners. When the Bill for the Liverpool and Manchester Railway was in the committee stage he'd been summoned down to London to give evidence.

How the London gentlemen had laughed again! They treated him as a foreigner and a fool. In their eyes the former disability was synonymous with the latter. When he said 'coo' instead of 'cow' the lawyers thought it was the funniest thing they'd heard for years. But it was they who were the buffoons, with their Latin tags and their total unawareness of anything that was happening outside their cockney parish. The banks of the Tyne, with their iron wagonways and steam engines, could have been on another planet as far as they were concerned. They didn't understand and they didn't want to understand. It wasn't so much that they didn't know, but that they didn't know they didn't know.

When the London Committee issued its report Stephenson was dismissed from his post as Engineer with the Liverpool and Manchester Railway. They had kicked his feet from under him. To ensure that he didn't stand up again, they administered a couple of sharp kicks to the head by replacing him with London engineers, the Rennie brothers. These Rennies were the sons of the John Rennie who'd recommended the canal to Stockton and Darlington.

The new railway was soon in serious trouble. The contractors were finding it impossible to build across the swamps of Chat Moss. The directors brought Stephenson back.

Stephenson did what he'd already done at Myers Flat, north of Darlington. He gave instructions for material to be dropped continuously into the marsh. Everything they dropped in disappeared, hour after hour, day after day, week after week. He repeated his instructions, closing his mind to the possibility of failure, and refusing to believe that his will could be thwarted. And the day arrived when the material didn't sink and the marsh became firm enough to build upon.

The directors went on to organize a competition to decide upon the design of locomotive that should be used on their new railway. Five competitors were selected from the entrants.

The London steam carriage was the clear favourite both with the scientists and gentlemen who'd travelled up from the south to see the trials, and also with the huge, ill-educated mob of local observers. The London technical press had expounded the superiority of the steam carriage over all other entrants at great length, and popular news sheets had taken up the cry. Besides all this the London steam carriage was a shiny and elegant contraption. It was the kind of thing in which gentlemen of the first quality could take an interest, and so they crowded around and nodded their heads wisely as if it were a thoroughbred horse.

On the day of the trials Stephenson's locomotive crushed all the opposition, including the London steam carriage, without leaving the faintest possibility of any debate.

At the official opening of the Liverpool and Manchester Railway, Stephenson drove a locomotive similar to the one that had won the trials. His passengers included the Duke of Wellington, Sir Robert Peel, Prince Paul Esterhazy, earls, viscounts, lords, *lesser nobility, civic dignitaries without number and a handful of London engineers. Very few of them, not excluding the last, understood what was happening.*

And all this time his son, Robert, was introducing new ideas into the locomotives they were building at Forth Street in Newcastle. The Rocket *had been the first with a multi-tubular boiler. It had taken a long time to discover how to fix those tubes, but they'd managed it in time for the trials. Since then they'd produced engines that Robert thought any man should be pleased to look at. There was the* Planet, *the first to have the cylinders under the smokebox; and the latest was the* Patentee, *with extended sandwich frames and another pair of wheels.*

They were ready for the drive down to the south.

On the day when he saw the cold, September sunlight on the incline at Etherley, Stephenson had realized that he was moving everything down from the Tyne to the Tees. But it wasn't going to stop there. The railways would go further south again, from Tyne to Tees to Thames.

They would drive a line southward through rural counties that had never even heard of steam engines. He would shake them all up: the politicians who wanted the lower orders to stay in their places, the landowners who didn't want their foxes to be frightened away, the squires who didn't like anything that might affect their horses or their rents, the parsons who couldn't abide strangers within their parish boundaries, the canal companies and the coach proprietors who would face ruin side by side. They would all band together and bellow like one of Timothy Hackworth's engines with the safety valve tied down.

But the dark spirit of change was on the side of the engineers and nothing could stop them. They would drive the line southward until it arrived in London, at the very citadel of ignorance. Perhaps they would commemorate its arrival there with a triumphal arch, so that people in future times would remember the battles that had been fought and won.

The engineers were the most important men who had ever lived: more important not only than any who had gone before, but any who would come after no matter what they might do.

For century after century man hadn't been able to travel faster than the horse. Every journey, every adventure, every war, every development in trade, everything men had ever done since the beginning of recorded time had been limited by the speed and strength of horses or other animals. Now everything had changed. The Northumbrian enginemen had made it possible for any man to travel faster and move heavier loads than the swiftest and strongest horse.

That simple fact meant that the rules of existence had suddenly changed. Nothing could ever be the same again. The old ways of doing things, settled communities, rituals, the skills passed down from father to son until they seemed to be inherited, customs, traditions, the long-established festivals that gave a pattern to the recurring seasons and the circling years – all these would be thrown open to change and mutability.

Men would invent machines that could take them faster and move heavier loads as the years went by. Somebody would invent a machine powerful enough to take men to the stars. It would be spectacular but it wouldn't be absolutely new. It would be another step along the road they were building now. The absolutely new was now. It was the Northumbrian enginemen who'd broken the ancient barrier and made everything possible.

'Excuse me, Mr Stephenson.'

He returns his attention to the leading citizens in the Angel Inn. They are full of doubts and questions about their little railway.

'Excuse me, Mr Stephenson,' says Mr Winspear. 'Here's a gentleman from out of town who would like to meet you.'

27

Jim Richardson was very attentive. Or at least, he was as attentive as his duties permitted, because the depleted crew found great difficulty in working the ship, and even a man with one hand was an asset that couldn't be dispensed with. Between his spells of duty, Jim was constantly at Arthur's side. According to Jim the ship was making wonderful progress.

'We'll soon be in Lerwick,' he kept saying.

But after some days of fast sailing a gale came up from the south-east and the *William Scoresby Senior* had to run before it under double-reefed topsails. In the early hours of the morning there was a tremendous impact that threw Arthur out of his bunk. The ship pitched about in a cross sea that rolled him to and fro on the floor. He banged his head against a stanchion and it seemed a long time before Jim came down and helped him back on to his bed.

'It's nothing being thrown out of bed,' Jim said. 'Think of Mr Caspol. Thrown clean out of the foretop into t' sea.' He groped inside his shirt. 'God rest his soul.'

'What happened?'

'We ran our stem into a berg.'

Arthur used his good hand to push himself into a sitting position. 'Has it foundered us?'

'No, no, lad. You lie down and forget about it.' Jim waved off the imaginary flies which habitually plagued him. 'We've burst the gammoning tackle and pushed one of the catheads back into its hole. Our iron plates are dented a bit and we're shipping water through split timbers in the stem. But the Captain has had a topsail brought from the line room and they're putting it over the hole. There's nought to worry about.'

How strange it is, Arthur thought. I couldn't think of anything but the pains in my feet and my hand. The pains entirely disappeared when we struck. And now that I know we're safe they are coming back again.

'The berg was bigger than the ship and the current was taking it to windward. That's why we hit so hard.' Jim Richardson's face lit up with something that was very near to joy. 'Like a floating hill it was, with icy cliffs and caves that were full of noises. Half-way up the side there were ledges, one ower the other, each one with icicles growing down to the one below. It looked as if the side was built up with galleries fitted with rows and rows of pillars to stop folk falling out. On top of the hill, all shiny in the starlight, were towers and arches, spires and pinnacles, some of them blue and some of them green. I tell you, man, although we were in such a plight, it was so grand I thought it might have been a fairy palace glittering up there.'

Arthur had seen a number of icebergs but they had been a long way off. Some of them had reminded him of St Hilda's ruins on the east cliff.

'After we hit the berg it seemed to carry on to windward as if we weren't there.' Jim's eyes were withdrawn, gazing at the image which remained in his mind. 'But then I saw that it was starting to cant ower. Watter rushed out of the caverns and galleries. The side nearest to us was spurting with cascades and waterfalls, and all the colours of the rainbow were jumping about on it. By, ya bugger, you should have seen it! Then I saw that the whole mass was slowly turning and gathering speed as it went. The towers and pinnacles and spires broke away like glass and clattered down into the sea. Then the near side went under with a great roar, and t' other side came up and up until what had been hidden underneath, and only guessed at, was on top and in the sight of men for the first time. It was like a fish turning on its back after the flurry.'

Jim's face became more thoughtful, but it still gave the impression of being lit up.

'I was thrown half over the windlass drum and I hung on to it. But I couldn't take my eyes off that berg. No man would have said it was the same one. This new thing was made up with great square blocks of ice, and it was covered with rocks and stones like giddy big pimples. It was smeared with yellow clag and brown stuff was oozing out of it like it had a dose of the shits.'

Arthur looked at the radiance on the man's face and waited. He could tell there was still something else he wanted to say.

'I never knew till then,' said Jim, finally, 'how beautiful an iceberg really is.'

Jim left him for a while. The topsail sucked into the split timbers of the stem. It would serve its purpose until they reached Lerwick, unless they encountered heavy seas. Favourable winds returned. The ailing and overworked crew set stunsails and the *William Scoresby Senior* continued her drive to the southward.

The pains flowed and ebbed through the cauterized wounds in Arthur's hand and feet, and flowed again and then finally began to ebb away. But no sooner had the pains dulled sufficiently for him to put them out of his mind than the fever began.

He lost track of time. Often when he opened his eyes he didn't know where he was. Sometimes when he looked at the berth above his head and the flat roof of the 'tween deck he thought he was back in St Mary's, kneeling next to his father and mother after the loss of the *Aimwell*; and sometimes a pale shaft of sunlight wandered through the open hatch and he thought he was a small boy again, playing on the beach and searching the high tide-mark for things that took his fancy: he found pieces of wood that the sea had bleached as white as bone, and which were so smooth that he could hardly bring himself to stop stroking them.

One day, or perhaps it was one night, Arthur awoke and discovered that he was shivering. He wondered whether he'd been shivering very long. Yes, he must have been, but he couldn't decide whether it had been going on for hours, days, weeks or even months. No, I can't have been shaking like this, not as violently as this, not for very long. The chattering of his teeth echoed in his head like hail-stones on a sky-light.

Dozing by fits and starts in a bed that seemed to be swinging like a hammock, he sensed that the *William Scoresby Senior* had lost headway and was slowly coming about. The open hatchway brought him the sound of Mr Beaufort's voice, and this was followed by the rattle of anchor chains in the hawse-holes. Steps sounded on the foredeck above his head and rattled on the stairs.

'Lerwick!'

He opened his eyes. Jim Richardson was standing beside his bed, and looking down at him with a triumphant smile.

'Lerwick!' Jim repeated. "We're in Bressay Sound. You've nothing to worry about now.'

Arthur opened his mouth, but his tongue stuck to the roof of his mouth. Jim dipped a cup into a water cask that stood beside his bed and gave him a drink. It was curious that no matter how much he drank he always seemed to be thirsty.

'I must be away again but I thought I'd come down and give you the news. I'll be back for you as soon as I can.' Jim dropped his hand to Arthur's shoulder and shook it. 'A good long sleep in a warm bed is all you need.'

Jim's feet scurried back up the companionway.

Alternatively burned by fever and frozen by cold, Arthur lay under the wet sheets and listened to the footsteps and voices overhead. *Lerwick*, he thought. I know that name.

Lerwick! The mere word seemed to increase his fever. *Lerwick!* What did it mean? He remembered uneven flagstones and drunken Greenlanders dancing round a Market Cross. *Lerwick!* It was the name of a forbidden city at the edge of the world, almost beyond the reach of his secret thoughts, with narrow alleyways where you could find pleasures more fierce than the sea and darker than the northern sky. It was the name of a place he'd been to when he was a boy serving an apprenticeship, long, long ago.

Lerwick! The name was repeated endlessly in his mind until it lost any meaning it had and floated away to attach itself to other things, dim and obscure things that bobbed about in his memory and didn't seem to have any connection with the word: a temple with a pagoda roof on a painted box, the tower of a ruined abbey, a deserted island with a mountain pointing at an empty sky, a pair of wide-set blue eyes, the tail of a fish just before it sounded, long black hair that waved in the air as a woman danced to the wild wailing of a violin.

Angry voices came down to him through the open hatch. Some of them sounded from a distance beyond the ship and they presumably belonged to the islanders in their small boats. Other voices sounded on the deck above his head. And that was Mr Beaufort again. But it sounded as if the First Mate were begging, almost as if he were pleading with the islanders.

Arthur's fevered brain could make little of it. And in any case, he wasn't very interested. His swollen eyelids rolled down over his hot eyes.

28

Jim Richardson supervised the lowering of what had been Mr Dryden's boat on the ship's leeward side.

How different their arrival had been a year ago! The islanders in their small boats had made the bay clamorous – holding up their chickens, eggs, vegetables, fruit, fresh fish. The sight of such things now would have driven the men on deck almost mad. The lodberries had been piled high with sea chests and trunks and bags and bedding; the men from the islands were fighting each other to sign on at the Custom House; Mr Beaufort had been received like an imperial prince.

And now, thought Jim, as he settled himself in the stern and took hold of the long steering oar, now we are sneaking back like thieves.

The oars moved in their grommets and squeaked against the tholes. They began to thrust the slender boat through the water with swift, silent strokes, not talking at all, just as if they were coming up behind a fish.

Arthur, lying between the thwarts, raised his leaden eyelids and looked uncomprehendingly at the sky.

Jim reassured him in a voice that was little more than a whisper.

'You're all right, Arthur. Nothing to worry about.'

The whaleboat came clear of the ship's lee and entered the view of the first of the Shetland boats. Immediately an angry shout went up from the islanders. A couple of Shetland boats at a greater distance took up the cry.

The Greenlanders were enfeebled by their long imprisonment in the ice, and the consequent starvation, scurvy, frost bite and other ills. But pulling an oar when the body's muscles and nerves were crying for relief was almost as natural to them as breathing. They had often whipped themselves along in the hope of striking a fish, and whaling boats were built for speed. Besides all this there was something more important: they shared the experience of being joined together so that each man found he could draw upon the reserve strength of some larger power that took possession of them. So they bent their wasted arms to the accustomed task, the stem lifted in the water and the boat raced towards the south end of the harbour.

Arthur searched for some spittle with the tip of his tongue and used it to salve the cracks in his lips. He tried desperately to speak.

'Only the islanders,' Jim said, as he leaned forward on the steering car. 'Only the islanders up to their usual tricks.'

He read a question in Arthur's bloodshot eyes and working mouth, and was ashamed of himself for giving such an inadequate response. But it wouldn't do any good to say more now.

The whale boat was moving well and the pursuing boats were far behind. But another Shetland boat moved out of the shadows by the lodberries and placed itself between them and the quay. Jim Richardson in the stern plied the long steering oar to take them around this obstacle, but the other boat moved to intercept them. A confrontation, if not an actual collision, became more likely with every stroke.

Jim unshipped his oar and moved forward into the bows. 'Make way! Make way! We have a sick man aboard!'

Shouts and curses greeted him.

'Let us take our sick man to the hospital.' Jim waved his arms at them. 'At least let us put him ashore. He's so badly he'll likely die.'

An angry voice replied. 'And if we're fuil eneuch tae let ye bring him ashore we're all like tae die.'

A Shetlander in a bright, knitted jersey, came into the bow of the opposing boat. His face was swelling with rage and he was clearly determined upon having a fight.

'No, no, no,' Jim was still saying as the boats struck each other.

The Shetlander quickly recovered his balance and hit Jim across the head with the shaft of a boat hook. The line-manager fell to the bottom of the boat and lay still. A bald patch had just appeared on top of his head. It was beautifully shiny and white, with hair sticking up around it, but then it filled with blood. Jim's hand started to rummage about as if it didn't belong to him.

'Does anybody else want tae fecht?' demanded the man in the bright jersey.

One of the Greenlanders shortened an oar and struck him against the legs. 'Naw,' he said. 'If we catch anything your size we throw it back.'

'All recht!' he roared, flailing the boat hook round his head. 'If that's the way ye southerners want tae play we'll start by coming aboard tae teach ye some northern manners.'

Jim Richardson had pulled himself to the starboard locker in the bow. His probing hand found what it was looking for and he rose to his feet in time to receive the islander's charge.

The mouth of Mr Dryden's spare harpoon bit the man's belly. For a full two seconds nothing happened. The man stood with a foot in each boat, like some forked device for holding the gunwales together. His left arm was raised to maintain his balance and his right arm was drawn back to deliver another blow with the boat hook. Dangling from the lower half of his body, swinging slowly and ponderously with the contrary motion of the boats, was the iron shank of the harpoon. The Shetlander looked like Orion. He stared at the Greenlanders and they stared up at him.

The boat hook dropped from his raised hand and fell into the water between the bows. The splash released him from his trance. He bellowed with belated surprise, although not yet with pain, and seized the iron shank with both hands.

Everyone else began to move again. One of the Greenlanders gave the other boat a sharp push and the harpooned man fell back amongst his fellows. The rest shoved the other boat away with their oars until the gap between them was wide enough to recommence rowing, and then they gave way with a will.

Jim Richardson crawled back to his place in the stern. He wiped the blood from his eyes and resumed his grip on the long steering oar.

The islander meanwhile was pushing hard with both hands at the shank of the harpoon. One of the barbs was free already, and perhaps hadn't penetrated below the surface skin when it struck. But the other barb was securely lodged and he pushed harder. The shock of the blow was fading and the islander's face showed that the pain was getting through to him. The harder he pushed the more agonized his expression became.

'Help me!' he shouted, between great, shuddering intakes of breath. 'Help me, lads! Help me!'

The first time he shouted the two words it sounded like an order. The second time it was an urgent plea, and the third time his words went over the water in a cry of despair.

Jim looked back over his shoulder as he worked the long oar. The wounded islander was on his back in the other boat, but two of his mates obscured whatever was happening. How far had the iron penetrated? If it were well and truly lodged then the only way to extract it with the minimum damage would be to pull it until the reverse barb burst out through the flesh, saw the barb off, and then withdraw the rest of the mouth by sliding it sideways. But the Shetlanders were in too much of a hurry for such niceties of procedure.

They were pushing and pulling and bobbing about so much that they were in danger of capsizing. The other Shetland boats were holding off, and the reason was obvious. Captain Stapleton, who must have observed the affray from the *William Scoresby Senior*, had lowered another boat. Mr Nellis was in the bows, looking very fierce and gesturing with a brace of pistols. Some of the boatmen with him had been armed with muskets from the cabin.

The men in the nearest boat were too intent upon their leader's need of them to have noticed this development. For a time they didn't seem to be having any success, but one of them straightened up abruptly and almost went overboard. A second later the wounded man was on his feet again. The bright pattern of his knitted jersey had been variegated with crimson embellishments, and in his right hand he brandished the gory harpoon.

'Noo we'll see hoo ye like the taste of yeur ain murthering weapons,' he yelled.

He threw the iron inexpertly but with great force, and a red streamer trailed behind it. It was clear that he was aiming at Jim Richardson, the man whom he had most cause to hate and who was the nearest target. Brute strength went some way towards remedying the lack of skill. The harpoon fell short but it reached the tapered stern of the whale boat and one of its withers caught just inside the gunwale. The red streamer lay on top of the water.

Jim was using his hand to fan the steering oar, and holding a piece of shirt to his bleeding head with the stump of his other arm. He remained unaware of his escape.

'Stop!' shouted the islander.

Presumably he was furious at the escape of his enemies.

'Stop! Stop! *Stop!*'

He shouted again and again in a mounting crescendo. Could he really hate them so much? The man's anguish seemed disproportionate somehow to their mere escape.

'Pull!' said Jim, quietly, grinding his teeth with pain and wiping the dripping blood from his forehead with the piece of cloth. 'Pull, my lads! Pull! ... Pull!'

'Stop!' screamed the Shetlander, and there was something so

unexpected in his voice that it wasn't possible to say what it was. 'Stop! For God's sake stop! Stop! Stop! Stop!'

'Pull, lads, pull!' murmured Jim, fanning the long oar and glancing down at Arthur. 'Nothing to worry about now. Soon be over.'

'Stop! Stop! Stop if ye're men!'

'Pull! Pull! That's the way.'

'Stop, my lads! Good lads, stop! Stop! Stop for pity's sake! Stop! Stop and look at me! Stop!'

One of the Greenlanders raised his head, opened his eyes wide and faltered. The oars fouled and the whaleboat lost headway.

'The harpoon must have hooked his gut,' said the Greenlander in a wondering voice. 'We're stringing his insides across the bay like a line of washing.'

But Jim Richardson whipped them forward again. 'Pull!' he yelled at them. 'Pull! What's the matter with you? Pull ... pull ... pull ...'

The oars resumed their long, deliberate, harmonious stroke. The pointed stem of the whaleboat lifted and the water hissed under its black sheer strakes. Something snagged in the Shetlander's belly and he was pulled out of his boat with a heavy, floundering splash.

Jim talked quietly to his men. 'Pull ... pull ...'

A bump, and the whaleboat wobbled as Jim stepped out on to the quayside. The rough-hewed houses stood with their backs to the water. Their hard stones looked as if they had crystallized out of the grey air, and their empty windows looked down blankly at the Greenlanders.

29

Jim Richardson leaned down to grasp Arthur's shoulders and a boatman took his legs. They swung him between the stony sky and the dark water, and then lowered him on to the quay.

While the boatman wrapped Arthur in a strip of sailcloth Jim looked out at Bressay Sound. The Shetlander was trying to swim in a jerky, convulsive kind of way. The water all around him was streaked with red. His friends in the boat overhauled him and hands reached down to pull him out. The second boat from the *William Scoresby Senior*, with Mr Nellis at the front waving his pistols, would soon catch up with them.

Jim put out his hand to prevent the other men from climbing out of the whaleboat. 'It only needs one man to come with me until we find a place for Arthur. The rest of you stay here with the boat.'

'Somebody has got to buy food,' one of the men objected.

'We'll see to that as soon as we have the lad settled. You look after the boat.'

The man wanted to argue. 'She'll take no harm if we tie her up.'

'With the mood the islanders are in she'll not be floating when you get back.'

One of the men still in the boat pushed Jim's arm aside and came up on to the quay. 'If that happens we'll take one of theirs. And besides, if the islanders are going to be as rough as you say, there'll be need for more than two of you walking the streets. What with you and your head broken, trying to carry the boy an' all.'

Jim looked again at the waters of Bressay Sound. There wasn't a sign of the wounded Shetlander. He must have been pulled out by his companions who, instead of chasing them to their mooring place, were rowing for another quarter of the harbour. The second boat from the *William Scoresby Senior*, with its armed men, had altered its course to follow them. The other Shetlander boats were keeping their distance for the time being. Their occupants were shouting and seemed to want a fight. But they were intimidated by the pistols and muskets, and were unsure what to do.

'All right,' Jim said caustically. 'I'll leave you to explain the position to Mr Nellis. Don't forget to tell him you propose to exchange a Brodrick whaleboat for a leaky little skiff that you wouldn't trust for catching shrimps in slack water. I'll be interested to hear what Mr Nellis said when I get back.'

The man tried to make a joke of it. 'Nellie wouldn't mind. He gave a whaleboat away with no return at all.'

Some of the boatmen laughed, but Jim had won the argument. Jim wiped his forehead and looked at the back of his hand.

The blood was drying. He nodded at the first of the boatmen and they lifted Arthur with an easy movement. They moved off into one of the narrow alleyways between the houses. The rest of the men watched them leave in silence and then turned away to watch the encounter between the second whaleboat and the islanders.

The two men with their burden issued from a side alley into Commercial Street. As they proceeded a group of islanders assembled at the other end. When they were within hailing distance Jim called to them in a friendly way, asking for directions to the hospital and offering to buy food. The islanders didn't reply.

'Good English money,' called the man at Arthur's feet. 'And a good price for fresh vegetables and fresh meat.'

When they came nearer they could see that apart from a couple of old men the islanders were all old women. The group closed up more tightly as if to ensure that no newcomer could penetrate their ranks.

Jim spoke again when they were only a few yards away. 'Have pity on men only just come back from Davis Strait. The way to the hospital for this lad and fresh food for fair prices.'

One of the old women stood forward and pointed at Arthur with a crooked finger. The wind blew her filthy white hair around her ears, and her tattered black clothes waved like streamers from her skinny limbs.

'Tell us what is the matter wae him,' she demanded. 'Tell us what ails him afore ye come any nearer.'

The Greenlanders came to a halt. The woman stood as an obstacle between the two parties.

'The boy is badly,' Jim explained, 'with frost and fever. I think you have a hospital that can take care of him, but if you can tell me of some good lodging I'll be grateful to you. But at least sell us some fresh food for ourselves and our mates and we'll be grateful to you on that account.'

The old woman advanced a couple of paces to confront them squarely. The yellow skin was drawn so tightly across her face that the cheek bones stuck out in two shiny nobs. This economy had resulted in a surplus of skin beneath her chin from which it hung down in two wrinkled dewlaps.

'Show us what is the matter wae him,' she insisted. 'Show

us his hands and feet afore ye try tae do anything else. I can see somebody hae found good reason tae open yeur head already.'

Jim put his hand to the cut in his head. 'What's the matter with you, woman?' He could feel his patience slipping away. 'We've had a bad season in t' fishery with all the evils attendant on it. I can't say more than that.'

She snatched at the strip of sailcloth that covered Arthur's legs. Before they could move she gave it another, more violent tug, and the material came away sufficiently to show Arthur's feet. Jim moved to restrain her, and in doing so revealed the stump of his arm.

'Ah – ah – ah!' she cried, and her breath came out in a sigh of horror that was somehow mingled with a deep satisfaction. 'Away! Away!'

The other women set up a wailing noise, and waved their hands about over their heads as if to ward off some unspeakable evil that hovered in the air. They pulled their rags more tightly round their wasted forms, and with cries of woe shuffled away into the next side street.

The two Greenlanders, without any need for consultation, swiftly lowered Arthur to the ground and set off in pursuit. The other man caught up with one of the old men and clutched him by the arm.

'We don't want to rob you,' he shouted. 'All we want is food and drink."

The old man was confused. He shook his shrunken head and muttered in Gaelic.

Jim came up with one of the women. When he put his hand on her arm he discovered she was trembling. Poor soul, he thought. But we must get some sense out of these people, and the quicker the better so that we can make sure Arthur is in good hands. And we can't go back to the boat without food. He spoke soothingly to the old woman, as if to a child. She screeched and spat and cursed. He let her go.

The other Greenlander was threatening the old man. 'What we can't get by paying for we'll take by force. Do you understand that? You may as well deal with us fair and open while you've still got a chance.'

Jim came back and shook his head to show that it was no use. 'We'll get nothing out of them.'

The Greenlander raised his fist to the old man.

'Give over,' Jim said. 'I think I know what's the matter with them.'

The old woman with the streaming hair, who was obviously accepted as the leader of the group, turned round at the end of the sidestreet. The others assembled behind her. The old man, as soon as he was released, trundled towards her in the conviction that she could protect him against these violent men. The leader raised her thin arms, as if to gather her ragged flock together, and then she pointed at the Greenlanders with a crooked, arthritic finger. Her bulging eyes were trying to burst out of the stretched skin of her face.

'Get away with your filthy English diseases! Get away hame tae yeur wives and yeur women and gie them yeur stinking flesh! And if yeur women escape I hope ye see yeur bairns with their hands and feet dropping off.'

The boatman was frightened. 'What in hell's name is she talking about?'

'I thought that was it,' Jim said. 'Let's back to the boy.'

Arthur was lying exactly as he had been when they left him. It gave Jim a shock to see him lying so still, and he quickly bent down and listened for his breathing.

He straightened up and humped his back. 'Give me a lift.'

'You'll not carry him on your own.'

'I've got to.' Jim raised his stump. 'You'll never find anyone to talk to you, let alone sell you any food, as long as you're with him and me.'

The man was irresolute. But Jim Richardson was still a line-manager and a junior officer.

'Go back to t' quay. Mr Nellis will be there by now. Tell them the people have got another plague scare on them.'

'A plague scare?'

'They must have had shiploads of dead and dying men coming back every week since the end of the season. God alone knows what sort of a time they must have had with them all. But tell Mr Nellis it's another plague scare. He'll know what that means. Only men with all their fingers and proper lobes on their ears are going to be able to trade with the islanders. A plague scare. Have you got that?'

The man nodded.

'Give me a lift, then. Up now!'

They lifted together. Jim stooped and they balanced Arthur across his shoulders.

'All the best, Jim.'

'Thank you. Don't forget. Find Mr Nellis and give him that message before you do anything else.'

Jim Richardson walked steadily away with his burden. The street was empty. At the end he turned left into another street. It also was empty. The houses themselves appeared to be empty, as if the inhabitants had with one accord closed all their windows and locked all their doors, before leaving on some unexplained journey.

Another corner led into another street even narrower than any that had gone before. What if the streets become narrower and narrower? What if I have to turn sideways to make any headway at all? What if the stones graze the skin from my chest and my back? What if the way forward closes up entirely? It's my wound, he thought. It's this cut in my head that makes me think these crazy things. I must think about nothing but what I have to do.

The next street was wider and a cold breeze was blowing along it. Perhaps those narrow streets didn't exist at all. Perhaps they were inside my head.

A door banged some distance away and he realized how quiet everything was. The door banged again. Was that someone trying to show him that he wasn't wanted? The breeze freshened and the door banged another couple of times. No, it was only the wind. The intermittent slamming of the door deepened the surrounding quiet until he was drowning in silence.

These streets were the forgotten thoroughfares of some city of the dead. He sniffed the cold wind and told himself that it came from the hills that encircled this town of shadows. Somewhere out there grass and wild flowers were growing.

Another corner and the wind blew more sharply, gusting and sighing up and down the deserted street, rattling the windows of vacant rooms, snuffling under bolted doors. It seemed to be seeking for some movement outside its boisterous self that might indicate the existence of life. His feet moved more slowly and clumsily, and the weight across his shoulders increased with each dragging step.

Then Jim's head started to throb and hot needles entered his skull at irregular intervals. He felt a tickling on his forehead and raised his hand to scratch at it. His hand came away wet with fresh blood.

It's the exertion that's reopened the wound, he thought. Like a fit of weeping over a remembered grief. His head was banging like a pump that was intent on emptying his body of every drop of blood through the hole in his head. He swayed, and was prevented from falling only by the intervention of Arthur's legs between himself and the wall of a house. With an effort he regained his balance and stumbled another couple of steps. But the blood dripped from his brow in a stream.

Jim bowed low to acknowledge the inevitable. He lowered Arthur to the ground as gently as he could, and propped him up in a sitting position against the side of the neighbouring house.

'I'm sorry, Arthur,' he said, and leaned against the wall himself. 'I can't do any more.'

Arthur's thickened eyelids fluttered and closed again. His lips rustled together like autumn leaves but no words came out. The only men Jim had seen who looked like this had soon been dead.

Jim wiped the accumulation of blood from his brow and face. 'I'm going to leave you for a bit, Arthur, but it's in your own interest and I'll soon be back. Don't try to speak, just listen to what I say.'

The eyelids fluttered again. Jim bent down to look into Arthur's face while he spoke.

'If I'm on my own it'll be easier to find people and talk to them. It'll be easier to persuade someone to take you in if you're not ... if I'm on my own.' Jim instinctively hid his stump inside his jacket. 'I might have to go back to the boats and fetch help. But I'll be as quick as I can. Do you understand? Just nod your head if you understand.'

Arthur nodded without opening his eyes.

'Don't try to move from where you are. I'll be back as quick as I can.'

Jim stooped and clasped Arthur's hand. The hand was hot, terribly hot.

Perhaps it seemed so hot only because the air was so cold. Jim rearranged the sailcloth, tucking in the corners to exclude the wind. He might have been reefing canvas to a yard arm for all the response that Arthur made. And it was certainly cold. The wind had developed an edge like a knife.

When he was satisfied that Arthur was sealed in from the air, with the exception of his nose and the surrounding patch of his face, Jim walked unsteadily away down the deserted street. From time to time he stopped and hammered on a door and called up to a window. But always he walked on again, moving one foot slowly in front of the other. At the end of the street he turned, looked backwards for some moments at the sailcloth bundle, and then turned the corner.

30

Arthur slipped sideways against the wall. He put out a hand to stop himself falling, but his body had become unbelievably heavy and the ground was sucking at it with an irresistible force. It was good to give up the struggle, to relax all his muscles and to slip down into oblivion. Aw, that was better!

He was flat on the cobbled pavement alongside the wall.

They must have entered these long, narrow streets many years ago. What had they been looking for? It was something important, or at least they thought it was important at the time. But it didn't matter now, whatever it was.

What happiness it was not to follow those desolate, winding ways; and those alleys that pursued their random courses and fooled the traveller into thinking that if he would persevere a little longer, if he would only go to the next corner, if only he would be patient he would find the right road. What a relief it was not to wonder whether to go this way or that way, or whether to go straight on or even to double back, in the hope of finding ... what was it? But it didn't matter what it was.

It was good simply to lie here with the cobblestones under

his back and the wall against his side, and listen to the wind.

If he kept his eyes closed he could believe he was lying on his palliasse at home in Ellerby Lane, under the warm quilt that came from his grandma's house in Bay Town. His father was downstairs scraping at his clay pipe and his mam was drawing wool from the painted workbox. On the side of the quay Ann Paylor was bending her head so that he could see the big, blue bow in her hair. There were so many things he wanted to think about before he fell asleep.

Everything would be perfect if only he weren't so hot.

He was lying on the moors with the scent of bracken prickling his nose. Large white banks of cloud were drifting over and going up to the Cleveland Hills. After each huge shadow had passed, the burning sun beat directly on his face. The sweat was oozing out of every pore in his body, running in steaming rivulets behind his ears, under his arms and between his legs. His clothes were sticking to his flesh like paint. It was air that he wanted, cool air, and this damned sailcloth was stopping any air reaching him at all.

After twisting and struggling he found the edges of the cloth, pulled them apart and threw the material aside. He wrenched open his jacket. Then he unbuttoned his shirt, tugged it out of his trousers and bared his chest to the air. His flesh was glistening with sweat and there must have been a spoonful of it in his navel.

The sharpness of the wind on his skin was delicious. And then something else happened to make his bliss perfect.

A handful of indeterminate white shapes floated down from the sky. They alighted on his chest, twinkled for a few seconds like evanescent butterflies, then became transparent and disappeared. His skin was so sensitive that he could feel their powdery softness as they clung to him, and he gasped at the wonder of it.

Another handful of bright shapes followed the first, and then another and another. Each tiny creature yielded up its cold life and then expired. But soon they were settling in greater numbers than they were disappearing.

Like birds on a fish's belly at the flensing, he thought, as his dazzled eyes closed.

The awakening was painful. Each quavering intake of breath

filled his chest with a fierce gas that burned every wrinkled crevice in his lungs. Each wing-broken flutter of his eyelids stripped his eyeballs naked to sharp pin-pricks in the air. Each movement of his limbs dispatched the rudely awakened blood to hammer on every artery in his body. Something had him by the shoulder and was shaking him to pieces.

Arthur looked down at his chest. It was no longer bare but covered with a melting layer of snow from which steam was rising as steadily as from a boiling kettle.

The snow was falling sparsely but it had accumulated inside the creases of his shirt and the stiff folds of the sailcloth. The cobblestones of the pavement had completely disappeared under a smooth layer a couple of inches deep. Only one event had supervened to interrupt the smooth prospect, and that was a series of footprints that terminated at his shoulder under a pair of heavy boots.

The boots were very large and very old. When new they must have been expensive and handsome but now the leather had cracked around the toes, and the bursting of the stitches gave to the soles a partially fulfilled promise of their future independence. From their gaping tops sprouted a pair of strong legs. Only the lower parts were visible, and although these were covered with fine, dark hairs, there was something about the shape of the legs that made it clear their feet were much too small for the boots. Just above the swellings of the calves was the bedraggled hem of a hessian skirt, wet and grimy with snow.

Arthur bent his neck in stages, as if it were a mechanical device incapable of fine adjustment. He looked at the red-raw fingers clutching his shoulder, then at the frayed and threadbare sleeve, then at the patched and faded naval officer's jacket, and so upwards until he looked into the face.

The face was round and darker than he remembered it, with black hair blowing around the wide forehead. The eyes were big, round and as black as balls rolled out of pitch for stopping seams, and yet they shone as brightly as polished silver. The mouth was wide and used to laughter.

'Fair guid day tae ye,' she said. 'I'm sae glad ye've waked up because I was wanting tae ask ye something. Or would ye like tae lie doon for a wee bit longer?'

He was angry with her. Why had she awakened him? Was it her idea of a joke? He remembered the humorous lines around her mouth, although they were invisible now.

'Did ye catch many fish?'

The lines that he remembered came into her cheeks as she smiled and he saw her teeth. They were as white and clean as the insides of sea shells. The laughter shone behind her jet eyes. Why couldn't she have left him alone? Now that he was fully awake he felt very ill again.

'No, I didna think ye'd caught many.' She put the tips of her fingers on the splayed cracks in his lips. 'But I can see that ye've made up for it by catching something else instead.'

She searched under the sailcloth for his hands, picked them up in turn and then let them fall back. He tried to tell her to go away and leave him alone, but his tongue wouldn't come out from behind his teeth.

'Gan back tae sleep. Pay no attention tae me.'

When she released his shoulder he slowly subsided into his previous position alongside the wall. She wound the sailcloth round him again with great thoroughness until little more than his nose was exposed to the air. After that she pulled him into a sitting posture, bent her knees and put one arm under his shoulders and the other under his thighs. Her strong legs straightened and Arthur was amazed to find himself suspended in her arms.

'Let's be away,' she gasped.

It was a hopeless task. Illness and starvation had made Arthur thin, but his broad shoulders and big bones made him a heavy load for all that. After only a few steps her raw fingers began to slip on the wet sailcloth. She struggled another couple of steps and let him down with a bump. She stood with her hands on her wide hips and her feet immobile in the big boots. Her breasts rose and fell as she pumped the air in and out, and they gave a transient outline to the shapeless jacket.

'Ye're growing into a big boy,' she said, as soon as she had sufficient breath.

She folded the sailcloth down from his shoulders, slipped her hands under his armpits and pulled him backwards.

After about a hundred yards she stopped and he could hear her panting breath somewhere behind his head. Again she thrust her hands under his armpits and dragged him off backwards. He looked at the twin trails his heels had made in the snow. They hadn't come very far. She lugged him round a corner into another narrow street.

This change of direction reminded him of Jim Richardson. He tried to remember what Jim had said. It was something about not moving from where he was, because Jim would be coming back for him. Jim would return and he wouldn't be there!

He tried to call to the woman but found he couldn't. He twisted suddenly in her hands so that she was obliged to drop him.

She bent down to him. 'What's the matter?'

He did his best to tell her but it wasn't any use.

Perhaps Jim wouldn't realize he'd moved, but would think that he himself had become confused by these narrow streets, disguised and anonymous under their covering of snow. He would think Arthur was still lying where he'd left him and that it was his own fault he couldn't find him. This idea made Arthur feel physically sick. But no, he thought, Jim would be certain that he'd come back to the right place. The encounter with the old women couldn't have been more than a couple of streets away from Commercial Street. And how far had Jim carried him after that? His head was hot and he found it difficult to guess at the answer. Besides, he was sure he'd been unconscious for part of the time. Perhaps Jim had carried him for miles.

He groaned. The cracked boots came to stand by his head. He looked sideways. The black hairs were wet and lying flat against her dark legs. He looked up. The snow was settling on her uncovered head where it melted and glistened. It reminded him of a spider's web he'd come across in the angle of their scullery window. The early morning dew had made it sparkle and he gently touched one of the strands with a hesitant finger. He snatched his hand away when a big, black spider rushed out into the centre.

'Ye're not going tae like it.' She was still gasping for breath but she laughed at the same time. 'But ye've nae choice so ye can't argue.'

She put her hands under his arms, but instead of lifting his shoulders and pulling him backwards as before, she turned him round so that he was facing in the opposite direction. He watched her movements in an impersonal way, just as though he were regarding the scene from a window in the neighbouring house.

The crazy woman tugged at the frozen folds of sailcloth until she uncovered the feet. Then she rolled the prostrate figure about until she had pulled the stiff cloth up under its back and one of the corners was between its head and the pavement. Bending and blowing she wrestled with the rest of the cloth until she had the other three corners under the arms and between the legs.

He lay on his back and stared at the grey sky with its burden of snow. With other eyes a phantom self in a nearby window watched the woman stand with her hands on her wide hips, resting and contemplating her handiwork. He waited and listened.

Where was she? He couldn't hear anything, not even her breathing. A totally unexpected panic seized him. She'd gone away! She'd left him alone in this long empty street in this silent empty town. He wanted her to come back desperately. He opened his mouth to call her.

A sudden movement made him bite his swollen tongue. He was travelling on his back with his legs in the air. She had hold of his ankles and was backing away between the shafts of his legs like a Fell pony. It was surprisingly comfortable: she'd folded the sailcloth in a double layer under his back and shoulders so that he was protected against the uneven cobblestones; and the snow was compact enough for him to slide over it quite smoothly.

Unfortunately the covering of snow had also become more treacherous to walk upon. From time to time a sudden jerk at his ankles told him that she had almost slipped. She began to pull more slowly, and then more quickly for a short while, and he knew that she was becoming exhausted. The piece of sailcloth beneath his head worked its way sideways until it was under his shoulder. He lifted his head to avoid the irregular cobblestones, but his neck quickly became tired and he had to let his head fall back again.

She didn't notice his distress. Her chin was tucked between the frayed lapels of the naval officer's jacket, and she seemed to be lost in contemplation of the big, cracked boots which her feet carried to and fro with short, uncertain strides. A thick, black mat of hair, tangled and wet with sweat and melted snow, obscured her entire face.

The bumps in the pavement made him try to keep his head up. Not a Fell pony, he thought. A Shetland pony.

She stopped again, either out of weariness or because she sensed that something was wrong. With a toss of her head she shook the hair out of her eyes, and then pushed it back from her forehead.

Her hands were shaking with fatigue and clumsy with cold as she dragged a corner of the sailcloth from underneath his shoulders, and readjusted it under his head. As she bent over him he looked up into her face and he could feel her warm breath. Snow flakes were fluttering into her tangled hair where they melted and joined the streams of sweat that glossed her brow and ran down the sides of her nose. She was absorbed by what she was trying to do and quite unaware of his scrutiny.

Now that they were stationary he could tell that all the cloth between him and the ground was wet completely through, and its icy dampness burned against his back and neck. The canvas was of no more comfort to him than a large wet dishcloth, that had been prevented from freezing only by the friction of his passage.

When she had made as good a job as she could of rearranging his flimsy sledge, she once more took hold of his feet. Her nerveless fingers slipped and she lost her grip. Again she took hold but at the first step the oversized boot slithered forward and she almost overbalanced in the other direction and pitched forward on top of him.

She laughed. My God, how she laughed!

Perhaps she was laughing because she was amused by the implications of lying on top of him. But there was more to it than that. He knew that she was laughing at him. There wasn't anything particularly hurtful about it, because as he listened to her he realized that she was laughing at other things as well: at herself and her hopeless task, at the naval officer's jacket that sloped off her shoulders, at the split and leaking boots, at the deserted street, at the vacant houses, at the whirling snow and at the indifferent grey sky. But she was very, very tired, and slowly her laughter subsided.

'I'm sorry,' she said.

Sorry for falling on top of him? Sorry for laughing? Or sorry because she couldn't do any more?

'I'll just rest a wee while,' she said.

After a few minutes the warmth of her body penetrated the damp sailcloth, and he could feel the glow of her from the soles of his feet to the crown of his head. The memory came back to him of the way they'd kept each other alive after Mr Dryden was snatched out of the boat. She lay on top of him without moving. That made him think of Mr Fenby with the beard like a piece of tow, and how still and stiff he had become. He was frightened. What if she grew stiff like that? What if she died?

But that was impossible. She was too warm, too strong, too joyful, too full of life to die in this mean street.

31

A loud slap resounded in the narrow street. It could have been a fresh plaice hitting a fishmonger's slab.

'The nicest and roundest bum between Deptford and Stromness,' declared a happy, drunken voice.

Blackie turned on her side, partly to avoid a second assault, partly to confirm the identity of her assailant. Identification was no problem. That loud raucous voice could belong only to the Specksioneer of the *William Scoresby Senior*, and she looked up without surprise to see Mr Nellis grinning and sniffing the palm of his huge right hand. He had a brace of pistols stuck in his belt.

She retorted without a trace of ill will. 'The only man with sufficient knowledge tae make sich a general statement.'

Mr Nellis continued to snuffle at the hand that had smacked her bottom. 'I recognized it,' he told her, implying that it was as much to his credit as hers, ' 'spite of its being under two inches of snow. A shape all of its own.' He gave a valedictory sniff to his palm. 'A smell all of its own, an' all. I'll tell you this, Blackie, I don't know what I'd have done in Davis Strait if I hadn't had the smell of thy arse to think about at night and drive away the stink of fish's insides.'

The muscles around her stomach hardened and slackened. She tried not to laugh out loud.

'I want to know something,' he continued, putting on an immensely stern expression but swaying a bit. 'But before I tell you what I *want* to know I'll tell you what I *do* know.' He raised his left hand in front of his face with his fingers sticking rigidly outwards like the levers of a capstan. 'First, I know you must have been missing me.' He pulled the first finger down with his other hand, as if to give the capstan a turn. 'Second, I know you must have been wondering whether I'd died in t' ice.' He pulled the second finger down and seized the third finger in a preparatory way. 'Loneliness and grief can do queer things to folk, particularly if they're women.' He wasn't sure whether this was another point or not, and in the moment of hesitation he lost count. Her stomach contracted and loosened as Mr Nellis pulled uncertainly at his middle finger and continued. 'Particularly a woman like you. You feed on men the way a whale feeds on those little things like shrimps, swallowing them down faster than anybody could count them.'

This further point loomed so large in Mr Nellis's consideration that he knocked down the two remaining fingers at a blow. He walked up and down on the pavement, sending up a swirl of snow each time he turned on his heel. At the end of one such perambulation he suddenly stopped, bent forward at the waist and shouted into her face.

'Now I'll tell you what I *want* to know! Why couldn't you have waited? Can't you control yourself at all?' He raised his voice until it reverberated at the other end of the empty street. 'Have you no shame? Must you do it in t'road? With your hump in the air, blowing and ready for sounding like a struck fish?'

Mr Nellis was standing with his feet firmly planted and well apart just like he did when, after putting on his iron spurs, he descended on to the belly to direct the flensing. He was bellowing away as though the mallemauk boats were late in coming alongside the carcase, and the harpooners were being kept waiting for knives and spades. Quite drunk, Blackie realized, and capable of doing almost anything. She would have to play him skilfully, even if it meant spending some extra time.

She lay on her side and squinted up at him. 'I've said it before and I'm going tae say it again. Captain Stapleton's got a fine Specksioneer. But arghh! It's been a doleful loss tae the pulpit.'

Mr Nellis pretended to ignore her words, but was in fact provoked by them into a final gesture of almost episcopalian grandeur. He raised his arm and pointed a thick, fleshy finger at Arthur's sail-clothed shape.

'You do it in t' street,' he thundered, 'and with nout but a ship's apprentice.'

The cold air was being warmed with the sweet smell of ship's rum. It was still working its way through Mr Nellis's bloodstream, and was making it easier for him to work himself into a passion almost hot enough to vaporize the snow under his feet. The expression on his face was changing in a rather alarming way. From mere indignation there were signs that he was about to be carried away by fury and violence.

Blackie read the omens and pushed herself to her feet. The short rest and the necessity of coping with Mr Nellis in his present state went a long way towards restoring her full vigour. The sparks were rekindled in her dark eyes.

'Nellie, ye don't need me tae tell ye that Lerwick without ye has no more guid meat in it than a jellyfish. And like the loving man ye are, ye've come at the very time I was needing ye most.

His bad temper melted and blew away like a vapour. 'Aw, I've missed you, Blackie. When we were beset in Davis Strait I used to think about you all the time. I used to think that if you were there you could melt the ice just by turning up the wicks in those gig lamps you use instead of eyes. It's good, sweet oil that feeds those lamps, Blackie, and when I see them light up I always know I'm home again.'

'A Specksioneer and a pulpit orator!' Her admiration made her eyes sparkle even more brightly. 'And noo a poet as well!'

'Aye,' he acknowledged with some complacence. 'Aim at me and you get not only the best harpooner in t' fishery, but John Knox and Robbie Burns, all with one throw of your iron.'

He swayed towards her. She retreated a couple of steps.

'And there's other things ye cuid do,' she said.

He nodded impatiently, as if to imply that she didn't appreciate the full truth of what she was saying. 'Blackie,' he said, very seriously, 'when you're with me, I feel as if I can do anything.'

She pouted at him with her big mouth. 'Would ye do anything I wanted, Nellie?'

'Absolutely anything.'

She smiled. 'I know I cuid depend on ye for guid man. Here's what I want ye to do. Look at this – '

'Absolutely anything,' he repeated. 'You've only to name it. You can depend on me for anything at any time, and I mean things with a bit more body to them than poetry.'

'This is more important than poetry. I want ye tae – '

'I'll tell you about something that's more important than poetry. When we were beset in Davis Strait I used to lie in my bunk and look at the frost on t' bulkhead just a few inches in front of the end of my nose. Sometimes I'd go for a warm in t' cabin and sometimes I'd go into t' galley to stand by the cook's fire. But most times I'd just lie in my bunk and tell myself that if you were there with me we'd have had that frost melted and water running down t' bulkhead faster than if the ship had bust all her seams. Aye, I'd have been warm, right enough.' He stepped forward quickly and seized her tightly by the arm. 'And I'd have kept you warm an' all, even if we'd been shut up twice as long.'

She laughed and spun round quickly. The movement took him by surprise and she was free. But he lurched forward again and took her by the shoulders. She wriggled and twisted, but his big hands held her in a vice from which she couldn't escape.

'Nay,' he said. 'I've tickled this plump trout and I'm holding on to it.'

He bent down to kiss her, but she kept turning her face to right and left so that his lips were repeatedly brushed aside by her cheeks. The inaccessibility of her mouth exasperated him.

'Listen tae me, Nellie. I've been aching for ye as well, but I don't want tae show ye how much until ye've done a wee job for me.'

'Just tell me what it is, lass. It's as good as done. I've told you that before.'

She turned and pointed. 'There's a shipmate of yeurs that needs help.'

Arthur Storm hadn't moved since the arrival of the Specksioneer. The snow was light but it had continued to fall, and a fresh layer had made the canvas shape inconspicuous alongside the wall. Mr Nellis had temporarily forgotten about him, and looked at the object with genuine puzzlement. Comprehension slowly returned, accompanied by some of his earlier bad temper.

'Aye, aye,' he said, and his tone was a good deal more sober than it had been. 'One of our boatmen came back with a message about him. I sent a couple of men off to find him while I came over to pay you a visit. Not knowing, of course,' he added bitterly, 'that in t' meantime you'd made off with him yourself.'

'Ye're in luck,' she said. 'Ye can kill two birds with one stone.'

'There's only one bird that I'm interested in. And I'm trying to make up me mind whether I'd rather wring its neck or stuff it.'

She looked him steadily in the eye and the sides of her wide mouth twitched into a smile. He came forward again and this time she didn't turn her head to right or left. He gave her a long, hard kiss full on her mouth, and groaned and mumbled with the pleasure of it. She didn't hurry him, and waited until he moved his face away.

'We must get him tae my room as quickly as we can,' she said.

'What! What do you want him taken there for?'

'He's ill. He's in a fever.'

'I thought you had a hospital for the likes of him?'

'We have,' she replied. 'Ye can take him there if ye like. There's naebody tae stop ye. But when ye get there ye'll find ye can't take him in.'

'Who'll stop me?'

'Everybody. Why do ye think the toon is sae empty? Where do ye think everybody is? They're up at the hospital tae make sure there's namore Greenlanders taken in this season.'

Mr Nellis snorted. 'Ignorant peasants, that don't know the difference between frostbite and cholera or leprosy or whatever they think it is.'

'That may be. But there's nae arguing with them at present and ye can't fecht the whole toon.'

'I've already chased some of them at the lodberries.'

'What's happened there noo?' she asked.

'Don't fash yourself, woman. It'll blow over. It always does.'

To show that this incident could be forgotten and that they should think of other things, he moved towards her again. But this time she was ready for him. She knocked his hands away and her face was unsmiling.

'The sooner that boy is in my room the safer he'll be,' she said.

The memory of the long, hard kiss, and of what it might presage, came back to Mr Nellis and turned his knees to water. He lowered his big head.

'There's nothing for ye until that boy is in my room.'

'Why should I carry him?'

'*Why?*' Her fat lips thinned into a straight line and her eyes opened so wide that the entire periphery of each iris was visible. '*Why?* Do ye dare tae ask me *why?* Out of common humanity, that's *why*.' Involuntary spit flew from her lips. 'Tae say nothing of him being a shipmate. And if ye can't be couthie tae a shipmate, we may as well stop thinking about humanity.'

Her contempt was withering. Mr Nellis shuffled his feet, and smiled a little foolishly.

'Aw, you know me, Blackie, of course I'll carry him. I'd do it even if he was a complete stranger.' A thought struck him. 'In fact I'd rather do it for a complete stranger because ... well, because ...'

Blackie kept her eyes on him and waited. Mr Nellis walked away two paces and came back again.

'Because of what happened when we stopped over on the way up to t' fishery. You seemed to have taken a liking to him. More than a liking.' He looked sideways at the shape alongside the wall, and hunched his back as though something very cold were running down between his massive shoulders. 'I'll never forget the way you kept looking at him. As if you couldn't wait to find out what his mam had used to line his breeches with.'

Her hands had been clasped behind her back. The right hand, as if released by a powerful spring, swung into sight and smacked into Mr Nellis's cheek. He turned as red as his beard so that flesh and hair seemed to burn with the same flame. Then he went pale, with cheeks as white as a barnacle goose, and his beard was almost black against his waxy skin.

'Stop yattering, and pick him up! Ye great lump of hairy blubber!'

Mr Nellis crossed to where Arthur was and sank to his knees. The Specksioneer was so deathly pale that his heart might have stopped, and his uplifted gaze remained on the woman's face as if his bloodless form was drawing all its life from the light in her eyes. Without so much as looking down he thrust his arms under the prostrate form and straightened his legs. He stood still, apparently unconscious of his burden, with his eyes still on her face.

'Are you going to be kind to me when we get to your room?' he asked in a small voice.

'What do ye mean by that? I'm always kind to people.'

He winced. 'You know what I mean, Blackie. I mean like you were when we were on t' way up.'

'Come on!' she ordered, and set off at a smart pace.

He caught up with her, carrying Arthur as easily and casually as a rag doll. They hurried along side by side, Mr Nellis sometimes asking a question and Blackie pressing ahead as if she hadn't heard him. She turned aside under a low, rounded archway and entered a dark tunnel.

'Where are you going?' he called after her.

She responded for the first time since they'd set off. 'Mind how you carry him.'

Mr Nellis stopped to reposition Arthur over his right shoulder like a roll of carpet, so that his head and legs hung down before and after. Then he plunged into the narrow tunnel after her. It was dark and dry, but snow and wind returned when they issued into a small court. He followed her from there into a square, surrounded by stone houses with sleet-blinded windows, through an unpaved alleyway and into a cul-de-sac.

'Now do you know where ye are?'

'I ought to do. I come here every time we go to the Greenland Sea and put in to take men up or put them down. And if you added together all my dreams of climbing those steps you'd have a ratline stretching from my bed to the Pole Star.'

She mounted the well-worn steps to the door. The snow had obliterated most of the details on the cast iron knocker, but the tips of the flukes showed the elevation of the tail. Here and there the wind had blown a letter clean in the encircling motto: *A Dead Fish or a Stove Boat*. She turned on the top step to look at the Specksioneer. He stood still at the foot of the steps, unaware of the load on his shoulder, to look up at her.

'Blackie,' he said, 'it's been a bad season for the *William Scoresby Senior*. One and a half fish and we'd have been better off if we could have come back clean at the proper time.'

'Why are ye telling me this noo?'

'I wasn't going to tell you till later. But the fact is I've no money and no credit in t' town. I can't even promise to make it up to you at the start of my next season because the fish have gone from the Greenland Sea, and if we go direct to Davis Strait we'll put in at Stromness, and so I . . .'

He stopped protesting when he saw that she was laughing.

'Get him up here,' she said, pushing open the door, 'and ye'll be in credit with me for the next time as well.'

32

Plain wooden stairs trailed away beneath him, followed by a bare landing smelling of damp stone and rotting wood. The floor swung round him and his head knocked against a flaking wall that had been white many years ago.

'Be careful with him!'

Another flight of stairs, complaining under each ponderous footfall, dwindled away beneath his incurious eyes. Another landing with a broken balustrade and somewhere the steady dripping of melted snow on to sodden wood. An ill-fitting door sighed open on teetering hinges and sucked them into darkness.

'Put him on the bed.'

A deep voice rumbled an objection.

'On the bed,' she repeated.

Big hands tossed him sideways and he twisted his shoulder as he landed. The mattress crackled and pricked his back. Smaller hands, light and quick, pulled a rough cover up to his chin and tucked it around his neck.

'Can't ye wait?' demanded the woman's voice.

The rough voice grumbled. Something bumped against the side of the bed and the floor boards creaked. A shutter clapped against the wall and a dim light filtered into the room through a pane of dull glass. The floor boards creaked again. There was a quick padding of feet and a rustling noise. And then a scuffle.

The woman laughed. 'Greedy as the gannets of Herma Ness.'

He was back in the narrow streets. They gave him the illusion that he was making some kind of progress. But where was he going? Despair seized him. I am not going anywhere. These winding alleyways are nothing more than the wandering thoroughfares of my fevered brain. I am trapped here for ever. I am locked inside my own head. There is no way out.

A groan, long and deep, came from the intertwined shapes on the floor. The groans shortened, became more urgent and died.

What did dying men think about? He saw the black skeleton on the east cliff with St Hilda's finger pointing at the sky. Did that dark shape intrude upon their thoughts? He was certain it did. Over the centuries that huge tower must have thrust its way upwards through the last thoughts of countless men like a whale rising under frozen water, straining and breaking the ice for a mile around. Those ancient stones and derelict walls, those forsaken windows and that pointing tower, still testified to the faith of the first saints who lived between the sea and the sky.

But there was something else he wanted to think about. He remembered a pair of light blue eyes. Ann Paylor looked levelly into his own eyes before she bowed her head and he saw the big, blue ribbon. He'd never climbed so high before. Even Mr Nellis hadn't gone any higher than the main royal. Even Mr Nellis . . . Mr Nellis . . .

There was a double sigh, exhalation and inhalation, as the ill-fitting door opened and closed on its uncertain hinges; a bolt squeaked in the too-tight embrace of rusty staples as it was shot into the socket; and then silence everywhere except for the low moaning of the wind that suddenly blew in a frenzy, and there was a sound like a handful of carlings being thrown against the single window. It had grown so dark that the outline of the window was no longer visible. The wind wailed once more and died.

The other side of the room jumped into tremulous life. Naked walls quivered like reflections seen in water and leaned inwards. The opposite corner of the cracked ceiling tilted and swayed. In the flickering uncertainty nothing was real. The room and everything in it might disappear at any moment.

She took the lamp from a small table, brought it across the room and set it on the floor next to the bed. Now it was the turn of the wall on this side, and of the ceiling above his head, to tremble with a precarious vitality. The light steadied. Things became solid and cast motionless shadows. The rough surfaces of the room grew smooth and warm. At the same time the smell of the oil crawled down his windpipe and curled up in his stomach like a snake. It was the odour of standing water from a well in which some animal had drowned a long time ago; and it was the stench of tainted meat crawling with the larvae of blowflies; and it was the stink of an incurable wound in a still-living body. It was the smell of change and corruption.

She was standing next to the lamp. It shed its soft light on her bare, calloused feet, and made the whorls of black hair on her shins glitter like fine wires. The yellow flame licked the insides of her thighs and turned them to burnished copper. Everything above was in darkness.

Suddenly she leaned forward and dawned upon him with a sun-bright face. Her black eyes glowed in their pools of shadow above her cheek bones. She was wearing a tattered chemise that looked as if she'd just found it screwed up in a ball.

'Try tae drink.'

Her arm, bathed in yellow light, came out of the darkness and supported his shoulders. It wasn't until he heard the glass rattling against his teeth that he realized he was shivering. He must have been shaking for so long that he'd forgotten about it.

'Unclench yeur teeth.'

The mossy smell of whisky that had been distilled over a peat fire subdued the smell of kreng for a few seconds. The memory of it made his stomach rebel. He shook his head.

'Can ye eat anything?'

Again he shook his head.

The rough blanket was thrown back. The soft warmth of the woman pressed against him and the mattress pricked his back with an added sharpness. She pulled the blanket back over them both.

'Ye need tae sweat,' she said, and the laughter gurgled in her throat.

Very soon he stopped shivering and the smell of corruption faded away.

Four

The select group of citizens at the Angel Inn stand back to make way for their new visitor. George Stephenson judges him to be about twenty years younger than himself. In other words in his middle thirties.

He is of average height, but with broad shoulders and a deep, massive chest that he thrusts forward as if to show that he is prepared to use it as a battering ram. His head is as round as a ball, and rests directly on his body without the intermission of a neck, like the head of a snow man. The wide areas of unused muscle in his frame are beginning to sag, and give notice that rich living will make him larger and more ponderous. He is ungainly enough already, and his movements are clumsy as he comes forward to shake hands.

'George Hudson,' he says, in the broad accent of the Wolds.

He was the son of a farmer, and he is still a farmer's boy despite his tailored suit and silk neck cloth. Stephenson can see it in his lumpy fingers and his shrewd eyes.

'Aa've heard of ye,' Stephenson says, accepting the large, soft hand; and the leading citizens remove themselves to a more respectful distance.

Not many years ago, while Stephenson was building the Liverpool and Manchester Railway, Hudson was running a draper's shop in York. There wasn't any reason why he shouldn't continue as an obscure shopkeeper to the end of his days, known only to those who used his shop and forgotten almost as soon as he was dead. But then, by the kind of chance that happens in real life but which wouldn't be acceptable in a novel, a great-uncle left him an unexpected legacy of £30,000.

The legacy had made Hudson one of the richest men in York, and he started his new business career by speculating in foreign grain during the period of Wellington's sliding scale on import duties. Then a year ago he'd promoted a joint-stock bank in York and this had led almost inevitably to an interest in the new railways. By the end of the year he'd excited local interest in the building of a railway from York to Leeds, and set up a railway committee with himself as Treasurer to consider the project.

Stephenson asks him who is doing the survey for the new line.

'Ah got the Rennies,' Hudson says.

Unaware of the effect this revelation has on Stephenson, he goes on to explain how he'd accompanied the surveyors everywhere they went. He'd made it his job to meet the landowners, listen to their fears, withstand their abuse, and finally smooth away their objections with soft words and hard cash. It had pleased him to discover such talents within himself. It made him a happy man.

'And the Rennies' report?' asks Stephenson, to whom the antics of landowners had long ceased to be of more than passing interest.

'Ah got it earlier this year.'

'What about it?' Stephenson demands, very irritable not to be arriving at the point more directly. 'What d'ye think to it?'

'It's a bit disappointing.'

He almost shouts at him. 'Why? Can't ye say why?'

'It's the recommendation.' Hudson shifts his heavy weight from one foot to the other. 'They recommend horses. The kind that eat hay.'

Stephenson's laughter is as sudden as a thunderclap in a blue sky, and takes Hudson and the hovering citizens by surprise. The sound is that of genuine, almost boyish hilarity. But there is a fine edge of contempt to it.

'London engineers!' he shouts gleefully. 'London engineers! By their works ye shall knaa them. They're coming on, though. Their father recommended a canal to the folk at Stockton and Darlington.'

Stephenson roars with laughter again. Hudson is alarmed that he should have started off so badly, and hastens to point out that it is only a preliminary survey. The route is still tentative, he says, everything has still to be confirmed.

But he needn't worry. Stephenson becomes jovial. His laughter has made him relax, and the mood of the conversation changes in an unexpected way.

In this warmer and more intimate atmosphere Hudson finds himself confessing that he regards the railway from York to Leeds as only a beginning. It is merely the seed from which a huge tree will grow, sending out branches to every corner of the country. As he talks he becomes excited by the prospect in his mind. His flabby body stiffens with nervous energy and he waves his large hands about in his impatience to be getting on with it.

For the first time in his life Stephenson is listening to a man who shares his own passionate faith. The travelling engines from the wagonways on the banks of the Tyne are going to conquer Britain and then the world. He confides to Hudson his own ambition to build an east coast route from London to Newcastle. Hudson is enthusiastic until he discovers that the proposed route would go through Leeds.

'Mek all t' railways cum t' York,' he begs. 'Mek your east coast route cum t' York instead of Leeds and ah'll kick t' Rennies out.'

Hudson had given a lot of thought to the new and complex problems of railway management, and he has a number of strongly held opinions about how the job should be done. When he has the power he will be like a giant spider which sometimes spins its web in a void, and sometimes extends its territory by absorbing the labours of its predecessors. He will make a junction here and a connection there, filling in the gaps but eliminating what isn't needed, until a complete network glitters in every niche and cranny.

He is bursting with ideas about how it can be done – not only by building new lines but by purchases of existing lines, take-overs, leases, amalgamations, exchange of shares, using influence and commercial pressure to obtain running rights on other people's tracks – his ideas run ahead of his ability to express them. Snatching at the wrong words, breaking off in the middle of an idea to formulate another one, sometimes coming to a choking halt, he waves his arms about in a painful attempt to make himself understood.

Hudson had grasped the unacceptable truth that laissez-faire *and competition between rival lines can never achieve an efficient railway system. There must be a monopoly and he has countless ideas about how he can achieve it.*

This ex-draper from York is an administrator of an entirely new kind. Stephenson hates administration and listens to him with something not far short of respect. This meeting, in its own way, is as important as the one he had with Edward Pease over ten years ago, when they planned the first railway. He tells Hudson that they can do some useful work together.

'Aa'll be a tool in t' hands of genius,' says Hudson.

They shake hands again with great warmth. Secure in their mutual liking and regard they go on to talk of more personal matters.

Stephenson says he is on a visit to the town in order to answer questions about a proposed railway to Pickering. Hudson says he is here to look over some property that had come to him as part of his great-uncle's legacy. He is glad of the excuse because he considers it to be a pleasant place. And he likes the people – there's something different about them. Stephenson agrees. He tells Hudson of the time he drove the Arrow *with Captain Scoresby beside him on the footplate.*

'Scoresby?'

'William Scoresby Junior,' *Stephenson says.* 'Famous son of a famous father. They were both whaling captains from this town.'

William Scoresby Senior had been a man of little formal education who never learned to spell. Yet he'd forced his way to the top by natural aptitude, hard work and ruthlessness. Like me, Stephenson thinks. The father had given the son a better start by sending him to university at Edinburgh. Yes, exactly like me and Robert. The son had been completely under the father's thumb for years and then he'd rebelled. Yes . . .

'Aa remember him very well,' *Stephenson continues.* 'It was when we opened the Liverpool and Manchester Railway. That was the same yeor we built the forst extension to the Stockton and Darlington Railway so that they could ship coal from the sooth bank of the Tees.'

It was impossible not to be impressed by William Scoresby Junior. He was then about forty years old, retired whaling captain and arctic explorer, an internationally respected scientist and a hard-working vicar. Stephenson was intrigued by his accounts of experiences in London. The first was when the Admiralty summoned him to discuss the possibility of discovering a North West Passage: the officials let it be known that a mere whaling captain would naturally have to serve under one of their own naval officers, and so they lost the man who was better qualified than anyone alive or dead to lead such an expedition. The next experience was when the Board of Trade invited him to visit them in order to discuss the possible search for new whaling grounds. They kept him waiting for several days, dismissed his ideas and got rid of him without ceremony. On neither occasion was he rewarded with so much as his travelling expenses.

Scoresby's meetings with members of the London establishment reminded Stephenson of the way he'd been treated over the safety lamp and the railway. But whereas he had been outraged by the injustice, Scoresby showed only the cold scorn of a natural philosopher tempered by a Christian spirit. And yet Scoresby hadn't lost his amazement that ignorant men in London, without the ability or even the desire to make any contribution to the knowledge or happiness of mankind, should nevertheless have the authority to stunt projects that could promote one or sometimes both.

Northern whalers and Northumbrian enginemen. The old and the new. Stephenson was much more like the father but he was conscious of a special bond with the son.

'Aa remember him very well indeed,' he repeats. 'It was the yeor of the forst extension to the forst public railway. And he told me it was the yeor that would ruin the whaling industry.'

But Hudson is excited by another project. He is so fond of this town that he'd like to develop it into a holiday resort. He can build hotels on the bare west cliff but they'll have to advertise the attractions of the place. Most people don't know it is here. The town is so inaccessible, with the moors all round it except on the side where it faces the sea. It is a community shut away from the rest of the world. He waves his clumsy hands about to emphasize the point. Nothing he can do will be worth anything without a railway.

Stephenson smiles. 'It'll have to be with horses, mind,' he says. 'The only way oot is beside the river, and it's neither straight nor flat.'

'Ah accept that.' Hudson nods his round head in agreement. 'It's not like t' Rennies' route from York to Leeds.'

They both burst into laughter and clap each other on the

shoulder. Mr Winspear and the leading citizens, sensing that some kind of resolution has been made, close in again. There are still a number of questions they want to ask about their railway.

33

Nothing moved on Bressay Sound except the reflections of passing clouds. Fort Charlotte and the surrounding hills looked out at vacancy.

A solitary whaler was moored alongside the quay. She was a barque of about 250 tons, and the peeling gilt letters on her head boards proclaimed that she was the *Lord Neville* of Newcastle. Her missing spars, deficient rig and unchanged canvas told something of her recent history. A man was coiling a length of rope on the quayside. He was wearing a much mended pea jacket and his hair had grown in a tuft behind his head like the crest of a red-breasted merganser. The sound of footsteps made him look up and then he relaxed.

'Did you leave your ship, hinney?'

Arthur regarded the pale but good-humoured face. 'I wouldn't put it that way. I'd say she left me.'

'If she wor the new ship named in honour of old Scoresby aa can tell you she wor heor a week.'

'A week!'

'Not waiting for you, mind. They wor plugging a split in her stem. You were lucky to find a berth ashore at the present time.'

'A week?'

The man nodded his crested head. 'Nice and warm, was it?'

A week! Arthur couldn't believe it. He hadn't been in that narrow bed in that tiny room for a week! He thought of the cracked walls and the low ceiling with its dark patches from the whale oil lamp; of the rickety table with its jug of raw whisky and stained cups; of the blanket stiff with dried sweat and the prickle of the mattress in his back. And then, last of all, he thought of the woman with her jet eyes, her dark whale lips and the matted hair under her arms. He had been with her for a week!

'We can tek you as far as the Tyne,' said the man, 'and you'll

239

not gat nearer hyem than that at one go. Once you're theor you can tek a ship anywheor in the world. Howway with us, you can dee no better.'

'I suppose you're right.'

'You'd best come and see the Mate. He's been leukin for Shetlanders to help us work the ship, but they're aal afraid we've gat the plague or summat, and there's been a bit of fighting.'

'What about?'

'They say somebody poked a harpoon into a feller's belly and then unravelled his insides like a ball of wool. When his marrers took him oot of the watter he still knaad what time of day it was. But he was like a clock with nout inside te make it tick.'

The story made Arthur feel sick.

'So there'll by nay trouble with the Mate. He'll tek you be the hond and say *Thank you kindly, pleased te make your acquaintance, won't you come aboard.*'

He conducted Arthur to the cabin. On the way he said his own name was Eccles and he was the carpenter.

'An honourable profession,' he added, 'and of noble lineage.'

There was a kindness in his manner, and yet at the same time a sparkle in his eye which seemed to be saying that after all everything was no more than a joke. He had predicted the Mate's reaction correctly, although he didn't actually go so far as to shake Arthur's hand. The Mate said that outside the cabin there were only ten men able to stand on deck and only three of them capable of going aloft. He signed Arthur on for the homeward trip without more ado.

Shortly afterwards a small shore party returned to the ship. They'd failed in their quest for beef or pork but by some means or other they were in possession of modest supplies of potatoes and turnips and a little flour. The Captain decided that he couldn't spend any more time looking for either men or provisions and gave the order to weigh anchor.

Arthur pushed at his lever and with each revolution of the capstan he looked back at the deserted quayside. He saw the stone houses huddling together with their backs to the water and the dark hills rising beyond.

Everything was silent. The guns of Fort Charlotte, like toys in a model castle, pointed across the empty waste of Bressay Sound.

When he left this harbour behind a year ago he'd taken away the memory of eyes as dark as tarred rope and the wild melody of a violin. Now he had a host of pictures that he could add to that earlier memory. Another week of memories. A week no longer seemed incredible. A week was necessary to contain all the new things.

For the first two or three days he thought the palliasse was filled with straw because of the uncomfortable way it prickled him. He longed for the comfort of the horse-hair stuffing in his mattress at home. It was worse to begin with, while he was still very weak, because Blackie lay on top of him. Her energy made her seem heavier than she really was, and she kept pressing him down on to the spiky pallet until he felt as if he were being impaled on a bed of nails.

It must have been on the second or third day that her violence finally burst the mattress, and he discovered that it wasn't filled with straw but with fibrous substance. He recognized bristles which had been scraped from the plates of baleen that hung inside the mouths of Greenland whales. It hadn't been boiled to soften and clean it. The sharpness and the smell were there to remind him of how it had been used by a black fish to suck its food out of the sea, while the woman seemed intent on squeezing all the nutriment out of him.

Eccles came over while the anchors were being fished. 'Did you hev a caald winter?'

Arthur told him something about their stay in Davis Strait. Then he asked what sort of a season the *Lord Neville* had experienced, although it was clear that it must have been a bad one.

The *Lord Neville* had left with the rest of the Tyne fleet, Eccles said, and made a good passage to Baffin Bay in the company of the *Grenville Bay, Cove* and *Lady Jane.* She killed a fish with bone over twelve feet before the end of April, and everyone thought this was the start of a good season.

Then the south-west gales brought the ice across to her as she was about to enter Melville Bay, and she spent the rest of the season and most of the winter closely beset. It was months later, before she finally bored her way out to the southward.

Like most of the ships that had gone directly to the Davis Strait fishery, the *Lord Neville* had completed her crew in

Orkney and she would therefore have returned by Stromness had she been able. But with her depleted crew she had a hard time of it beating down from Baffin Bay, and they found themselves running across to Shetland. The Captain was glad to anchor safely in Lerwick where he landed his surviving Orkney boatmen.

And now they were making what sail they could for the Tyne.

The 'tween deck was like a morgue, but no worse than that of the *William Scoresby Senior*. Besides, Arthur had worked hard and he slept gratefully. When he returned to the main deck they were below Berwick. A sharp wind was blowing from the northeast and the Mate was at the helm.

Ahead and to starboard was an island about two miles from the shore. On it were the ruins of a monastery and beyond that a derelict fort. They came near enough for Arthur to see that the stones of the church were red and that a single arch remained standing over it like a rainbow.

'Holy Island,' Eccles said.

The memory punched him in the stomach. Jim Richardson had been standing beside him. He had two hands, then, and his voice was stronger:

> And now the vessel skirts the strand
> Of mountainous Northumberland.
> Towns, towers and halls . . .

He couldn't remember any more of the verse, but he recalled how Marmion had wooed Constance de Beverley, and how she had been punished for following him. He saw the girl in her page's doublet, blindfolded, being walled up in the tomb. The horror of it quickened his heart. Ann Paylor's face came to him with a timid smile on her pale lips, and she lowered her eyelids and bowed her head. The ribbon was a deeper blue than her eyes. And Marmion betrayed her for Clare.

Blackie leaped into his mind and scattered every other thought. 'I'm going tae make ye sweat some more,' she said, and she turned over like an iceberg. No. Like a fish. She rolled over like a fish with her belly in the air. 'Have ye got yeur spurs on?' she said.

'Aa wish we wor standing oot beyond Longstone,' said Eccles.

'The Mate's gannin te hev te tek us through Staple Sound.'

Further ahead on the starboard side an enormous castle was growing out of the black coastline. It continued to grow as they drew nearer, as though its keep, towers and walls were sucking extra life from roots embedded in its solitary rock. Its dark shape swelled until it menaced everything on land and sea.

A handful of small islands broke the surface of the sea opposite the castle, as black and forbidding as the mighty cliff on which the castle sat. At first there appeared to be no more than half a dozen of them. But from time to time the sea withdrew sufficiently to uncover some more black and shiny heads before it swept back again.

'Aa hope the Mate keeps a steady hond,' Eccles said. 'Aall he's got te dee is keep the Ox Scars on one side and the Crumstone on the other. But it would be easier for the lad if the Crumstone would lift its heed now and again.'

Arthur looked at the backs of the waves as they shouldered their way towards the shore. Now that he'd seen the white streamers which waved above hidden rocks he could see rocks everywhere. There must be another twenty or thirty islets all together. And the Crumstone was known to every sailor on the north-east coast.

'Aa come through this neck of the sea twice a year,' Eccles said, and there was a change in the tone of his voice. 'Each time aa'm convinced that there's something important heor that aa can't quite understand. It's a triangle, you see, with Holy Island back theor, and the castle on the shore heor, and the other islands in front of us. Aa feel as if aa'm lapped up in the middle, and the three corners are being screwed up, tighter and tighter, squeezing me to mek me understand.'

The sea was high. Heavy waves trundled past with a ponderous stride, and the spume from their breaking heads curdled along their backs in an expanding lattice of foam. The black water shattered itself into white sparks against the rocks of Holy Island, boomed under the fissured pedestal of the castle and boiled over the hidden rocks ahead.

'Aa've tried te understand by talking te folk that hev had an education. And aa've studied owld beuks so that aa could see whether what they'd told me was true. The vicar from the seamen's church at Shadwell in London told me it wor a chep from Canterbury who torned us aall into Christians. But aa knaa he was wrong. If we are a Christian country then it's because of St Aidan and the monks of Holy Island ower theor, and that goes for the sooth of the country as well as the north. And although King George lives in a little hoose in Windsor, aa knaa that the kings of England used to abide in this big castle heor. But it's not things like that aa'm thinking of. It's something more than that.'

Eccles was silent and his face was inscrutable. Some birds flew past in a long, single line. They were keeping close to the sea, and their upper parts were a startling white against the dark water. Arthur noticed their curious, wedge-shaped heads and his eyes followed them to the outer islands.

'St Cuthbert's ducks,' Eccles said.

Arthur was glad of the diversion and took him up on it. 'Why do you call them that?'

'It's the owd name for Eider ducks.' He suddenly pointed forward and to starboard. 'Do you see that island?'

'Of course I do.'

Eccles was indicating the largest of the islands, which was also the one nearest the mainland. The waves rolled and roared against its steep black cliffs. All its surfaces were as bare and looked as hard as iron, without a blade of grass or a grain of soil anywhere.

'St Cuthbert lived on that rock with the sea and the wind hoyin themselves at him for nine years. He collected stones and driftwood te build himself a hut. He made a roof of poles and straw so that there'd be nout te distract him. Not even the stars. When he lay doon on the caald stone there was only the sound of the sea and the birds.'

Sea birds by the thousand sat on the chiselled ledges of the islands, and their white breasts shone like lamps against the black stone. Hundreds of them kept leaving their angular perches to circle over the shiny rocks. Their cries mingled with the flying spray and became indistinguishable from the lamentations of the wind.

'St Cuthbert slept on the bare rock,' Eccles said. 'But we rob his ducks so that we can stuff eider-down into our quilts and pillows and mek ourselves comfortable. It's a kind of joke.'

Arthur had tried to make himself comfortable but the whale-bone bristles scratched and clawed his back every time he moved. It was a relief when she pulled him on top of her. 'Wood on black skin!' she shouted. She laughed at the joke. 'Wood on black skin! Stern hard!'

The *Lord Neville* was into Staple Sound. The north-east wind whistled against her empty top yards and sighed around her double-reefed topsails. It blew the froth off the crests of the waves, shaking it into a white mist that settled back on to the surface in a creamy net, and the waves swelled until the mesh stretched and burst. The waves laboured onwards to the shore, wrestling their way over the dark rocks and crashing round the crags, with the foam trailing like sweat along their straining backs.

'Sweat!' she said. 'Ye've got tae sweat!' Although she was now underneath she went up and down like a mad thing.

'Listen te it,' said Eccles. 'It's a constant roar, never changing, always the same. It just gans on and on. The sound of countless millions of drops of watter tumbling together. St Cuthbert listened te it for nine years. What did he think aboot? Aa wonder if he thought those millions of drops of watter are like the lives of aall who wor ever born and who ever will be. Each drop is such a tiny part of the whool that you can't possibly tell when it's no longer theor. And if any one of those drops was ten times, a hundred times, or even a hundred thousand times bigger than any other, you still wouldn't notice. There aren't any Napoleons or Dukes of Wellington in that lot. There's nothing but the noise of aall those short lives coming and going. It meks a kind of music.'

The black island of St Cuthbert slipped away to starboard. The *Lord Neville* was coming out of Staple Sound.

'On each passage,' Eccles concluded, 'aa always think aa'm nearer te understanding that music.'

The rocky coastline was replaced by small bays. Further southward a rugged headland ran out into the sea and the black cliffs returned. They arose sheer from the water to form the ramparts of another colossal fortress. Waves hurled themselves against its base, roared in the monstrous caverns, and were thrown so high that they descended as spray on to its highest turrets.

Again the black rocks disappeared. The shore turned into yellow sand, interrupted occasionally by the remains of an isolated tower. The sands continued, mile after mile, washed by assiduous tides until they were so clean they were almost white. There was some strange power in the landscape to absorb other things into itself. No matter how harshly the gales blew from the north-east, they couldn't do anything more than create dunes and gentle hills as rounded and smooth as a young woman's breasts. The sands, bays, cliffs, towers and castles were all deserted. It seemed to be a land that giants had left behind, and nobody had rediscovered it.

An island came up on the starboard bow, guarding the entrance to a river that almost encircled a castle with tall, grey towers. As the *Lord Neville* continued to the south the shore changed, slowly and almost imperceptibly. The sands darkened, and the charred ruin of a sombre mansion glared down at a darker sea.

The sands and sea turned black. Another rocky headland affronted the waves with another ruined castle on its windy top. These castles and towers were like some sturdy kind of flower. They took root wherever the ground was so hard and inhospitable that nothing else could flourish.

The *Lord Neville* rounded the point and entered the estuary of the Tyne. The priory on the headland, burial place of kings and St Hilda's martyrs, watched the whaler join the waiting fleet.

34

It was an astonishing sight. The estuary was crowded with more ships than Arthur could have imagined might be brought together in one place. Almost all of them were colliers and they were waiting to negotiate the Black Middens and the harbour bar. They were packed so closely that their blunt stems were nosing each other's blackened flanks. Beneath the dark forest of masts, spars and rigging, the work-worn hulls were a pack of ravening dogs, pressing around a closed door where they were used to being fed at a particular time. It seemed impossible that the entire world would furnish sufficient victuals to stop all those gaping mouths.

On the other side of the bar, coming down to meet them, was an even more numerous fleet. This was a flotilla of small, dumpy boats that were travelling down with the tide. The shouts, laughter and singing of their crews reached the waiting ships.

'The keelmen,' Eccles said. 'Let's gan doon and get some rest while we wait for the tide.'

Arthur was glad of the opportunity. He'd recovered most of his health and strength but he was tired.

It seemed to him that he'd scarcely closed his eyes before he was roused by a tremor in the ship. As he came awake he thought the ice was closing in on them and he couldn't fully dismiss the fear until he was back on deck.

The *Lord Neville* had slithered through a narrow channel in the bar and was entering a wide harbour about two miles long.

Eccles pointed with his merganser head. 'The busiest scene in the world,' he said with pride. 'We send oot silver, lead, iron, earthenware, butter, beer, flour, hams, copperas, grindstones, flagstones, firestones, paper, leather, tar, sugar, glass . . .'

He stopped for lack of breath rather than for want of other goods he could have added. And yet he hadn't mentioned the single item that was many times more important than all the rest put together: the Black Gold from the pits.

Scores of ships from the collier fleet had already anchored in mid-stream. Hundreds of keels had come down from Blaydon, Derwenthaugh, Dunston and Team Gut, where the coals from west and north-west Durham had followed the old wagonways to the south bank of the river; hundreds of other keels had loaded on the north bank at Scotswood, Benwell, Elswick, and at dozens of more recent staiths to which chaldrons from the North-umberland pits could now travel on the new, iron rails.

The keels clustered round each collier like black piglets thrusting themselves upon a fat, black sow, but in this case the mother was draining her dependents. Thousands of men in blue jackets and blue stockings were balancing on the limited deck space of the keels, and working hard to catch the end of the incoming tide. The heart-shaped blades of their shovels glinted silver despite the dirty air. As soon as a keel had emptied its oblong hold another keel pushed forward to take its place.

'Not a good fishing river,' Arthur said.

Eccles was prepared to argue. 'A few years ago you couldn't put yor hond in the watter without a fish swimming into it.' But then he conceded. 'The only salmon that come up now are the ones that hev been blinded by the clarts.'

The water looked as if it might be difficult to stir, a kind of black treacle, and there were green and purple streaks in it that didn't belong there. Along the waterside cheap coal and the demands of trade had caused iron works, furnaces, foundries and factories of all sorts to sprout like fungi. The intervening spaces were filled by straggling houses, dingy sheds and cavernous warehouses.

Some of the buildings contained engines with rocking beams, with half of each beam protruding outside the enclosing walls. Many of these engines were thrusting rods up and down in the shafts of pits; others, similar but smaller, were driving pulley wheels. The exposed parts of these oscillating beams resembled the legs of gigantic insects, which had been impaled and bricked in so that the energies generated by their death throes could be harnessed.

And everywhere the chimneys smoked, sucking up poisons from the man-riddled earth and vomiting them upwards. Horses stumbled across the dismal plain, dragging chaldrons of coal along the new rails; and even newer were the travelling engines, which appeared occasionally and added their mote to the pall of fume and filth that was spread out under the sky. Further away, near the first bend in the river, some forlorn windmills stood. Their sails were grimy and ragged: moth wings that had been singed by these modern fires.

'So this is Newcastle,' Arthur said in awed tones.

Eccles laughed. 'We're not gannin theor! It's another ten miles up the river. Besides, there's men to be put ashore as soon as we can dee it.'

It must have been clear to anyone who looked at her that the *Lord Neville* was in a bad way and wanted a berth quickly. The disorder of her braces and clew lines were sufficient indication of her plight. Colliers and keels made room for her and she bumped her way to a mooring on the south side of the harbour.

'Follow me,' Eccles said, and pushed his way through the anxious crowd that had assembled on the quay.

He led the way into a large market place that was dominated by a dark, square building, decorated with arcades and columns and topped by a blackened dome. They crossed this open space to the other side where an old, soot-stained church had been dedicated to St Hilda, and entered a greasy, cobbled street with a terrace of squalid cottages. They turned a corner and saw an iron arm outlined against the hanging sky. It wheezed downwards with a painful sigh, and slowly raised itself again with a retching expulsion of breath.

'St Hilda Colliery,' Eccles told him. 'Opened twenty years ago.'

Arthur pushed the hair back from his eyes to look at it. He discovered small pieces of hot cinder on his head, and when he lowered his hand it was covered with black dust. Perhaps St Hilda's spirit haunted this strip of coast, lost in wonder at the changed surroundings of her shrines.

They came to a wood-framed house with a low doorway. Eccles pushed open the door with some difficulty because of the pressure of people inside. The rough beams beneath the ceiling sagged under the weight of the rooms above, and were so low that Arthur bumped his head on one. Tobacco fumes lay under the ceiling like gas under the roof of a mine. Everybody was shouting. Arthur ducked to avoid the next beam and stumbled over a man who was spewing blackened gobbets on to the floor.

Eccles looked about and went over to a corner where a man was sitting by himself, oblivious to everything around him. He was partially barricaded by an upended cask, on which stood a triple battlement of empty bottles. To this man Eccles spoke for several minutes, bending down close to his ear and nodding his tufted head with great earnestness.

Eccles turned, beckoned Arthur and introduced him. The surrounding noise was so great that Arthur had difficulty in catching the name: Captain Pounder of the *Black Boy*.

'So you wintered in the Arctic,' shouted the Captain.

'Yes, sir.'

'You'll feel at home on this river, then. Nothing casts a shadow here either.'

Eccles nodded at them both and slipped away. The crowd closed up behind him and then Arthur saw his crested head bob under the low doorway. He hadn't given Arthur time to say good-bye, let alone a single word of thanks.

'It's lucky for you that you caught me.'

The voice demanded attention. The Captain's face was as bluff and battered as the bows of any brig riding in the harbour. The eyes were dark in the shadow of his frowning brows and there were sardonic lines at the sides of his mouth.

'You're lucky,' he explained, 'because I'm taking a load of coals to your place. They use it at the alum factories.'

Arthur felt that he must say something to this difficult man. 'They use it for boiling, sir. They boil the liquor in the leaden pans to concentrate it.'

Captain Pounder located his glass amongst the fortifications and emptied the remains of a bottle into it. 'I know. Then they put piss in it to make the crystals grow.' He raised the glass, finished it at a draught and belched. 'They put piss in this an' all, but you've got to keep drinking it to stop the dust blocking your pipes.' He handed some money over. 'Get me another and one for yourself. It'll clag the oakum in your seams.'

Arthur made his way to the bar. He had to shoulder an entry for himself, and a sailor turned on him angrily. The man was drunk, but he grabbed at Arthur in a friendly way when he saw his clothes.

'You a Greenlander?'

Arthur told him.

'Aa got back six months ago. One of the lucky ones. And aa've hord bad news every week since. Worst yeor ever in the fishery.'

Arthur made some further progress towards the bar, conscious of the need to avoid displeasing the Captain of the *Black Boy*. But the other man hung on to him, demanding the name of his ship and any other ships he'd seen. Without waiting for the information he gave Arthur his own account.

'Peterhead has lost the *Resolution* and *Hope*, Aberdeen has lost the *Alexander*, *Laetitia*, *Middleton* and *Princess of Wales*, Dundee has lost the *Achilles* and *Three Brothers*, Leith has lost the *Rattler* and the *Baffin* that was specially designed by Captain Scoresby. The top Hull ship only caught nine fish and they've lost six ships . . .'

The man held up his hand and was counting off the names of the Hull ships on his fingers. Arthur didn't hear them because he'd managed to buy a couple of bottles and, with a muttered excuse, he hastened back to the embattled Captain of the *Black Boy*.

Captain Pounder took the bottle, poured himself a glass and drank half of it. 'It makes a change.'

Arthur, thinking he'd bought the wrong drink, compared his own bottle with the clutter of empties on the top of the cask.

'It makes a change,' shouted the Captain, 'from taking coals to London. Most of the time I just go up and down between here and London. Thousands and thousands of us, just going up and down, with that wind from the sea trying to blow us on the rocks all the way along the coast.'

Arthur didn't understand his bitterness. 'It's trade, isn't it, sir?'

'Trade!' he bawled. 'Mud from the Thames to keep us in ballast and coal from the Tyne to warm the fat arses of politicians and London merchants! Mud for coal! Do you call that trade?'

Arthur didn't know what to say. In addition he'd forgotten to bring a glass for himself and he stood awkwardly with the bottle in his hand.

Captain Pounder drank, refilled his glass and dropped the empty bottle on the floor. 'London is a great whirlpool. It sucks everything in and nothing comes out.'

Arthur sneaked a look at the Captain's face as he raised his glass again to drink. It was marked by a bad-tempered use of authority, and Arthur was thankful that his spirit of bitterness was directed not so much at him but at some other part of the world.

'If there's one thing I can't stand,' said Captain Pounder, 'it's a lad who plays about with his ale.'

He reached across and took the new bottle out of Arthur's hand, refilled his glass, drank it off, refilled it again and dropped the bottle. Drinking in this confined atmosphere had made the Captain sweat, and his forehead was striped with coal dust where he kept wiping the perspiration away with the back of his hand.

'Owway,' he said, after he'd regained his wind. 'Let's be off.'

He stood up behind his bastion and accidentally knocked two or three empty bottles clinking from the parapet. For some reason this enraged him and he took a hefty kick at the barrel. It tilted sideways and deposited most of the remaining bottles on the floor before it regained its upright posture. The prevailing racket was so great that only the nearest bystanders so much as turned their heads. Captain Pounder sloped towards the low doorway and Arthur followed.

It was raining and black puddles winked amongst the greasy cobble-stones. The raindrops were as cold as ice and they made Arthur's eyelids smart. When he licked his lips he discovered a bitter taste.

In the middle of the market square the Captain came to a halt. 'I was wrong when I said nothing ever came out of London.' He was shouting as if he was still in the public house, and his voice echoed across the square. 'The hills round this town are made of London clay. They grow bigger all the time. Soon they'll be mountains. When you come up this river in a year or two you'll think you're in Switzerland.'

Captain Pounder thought this was such a good joke that he laughed all the way to the quayside. Arthur walked beside him, blinking his eyes in the poisonous rain, and absorbing shoulder charges caused by his companion's erratic progress.

The *Black Boy* was over a hundred years old and younger than she looked. She rolled horribly as soon as she was beyond the Black Middens. The crew's quarters made the 'tween decks of a whaler resemble senior officers' cabins on an East Indiaman, and no man could have stood the life for more than the three or four days it took for a collier to reach the Thames.

As Arthur went about his duties he kept telling himself that Captain Cook had served his apprenticeship on vessels like this; and he reminded himself that the ships Cook had taken on his three voyages to the South Seas – *Endeavour*, *Resolution*, *Adventure* and *Discovery* – had all been built in Whitby as northeast colliers.

Captain Pounder stumbled out of his poky cabin as they came abeam a headland that sheltered an old harbour. Cobles with pointed sterns had been drawn up on to the sand beneath ancient, crumbling walls; inside the walls little cottages crowded together on a slope; and the slope ran up to a church with a stout, battlemented tower.

'St Hilda's Church,' the Captain said. 'That's where I was baptized. I yelled then, and I've hated water ever since.'

He paced the begrimed deck, kicking stray pieces of coal as he went. At the brigsail boom he turned round and came back. Arthur was helping to lash down a split tarpaulin over the forescuttle.

'The rain is keeping the sea down,' Captain Pounder said, grudging the compliment. 'But when it goes you'll see a change.'

Arthur looked up expectantly.

'A big change,' the Captain continued. 'You'll have high seas and a snow storm. Plenty of snow. You just see if you don't.'

He indulged himself in a final scowl at the rain and stamped back to his cabin. A bottle tinkled on the rim of a glass and then the door was closed by a kick from inside.

Arthur secured the tarpaulin and straightened up. They were coming abreast of a village where fishermen's houses showed their pale faces through the slanting rain. This was the stretch of coast down which the Lady Hilda had sailed with a king's daughter. She cropped up all along this shore, withstanding sea and wind and time like the black rocks on which the castles and her churches stood.

A three-man coble was coming out, thrusting its deep bows and high shoulders at the waves. To seaward a Staithes yacker was riding to nets. The first terns had arrived and they were fishing, too, pointing their red beaks and black crowns and then dropping like stones.

The coble turned to shoot its lines and Arthur noticed that instead of a pointed stern it had a flat transom. His breath shortened as if he'd run a long way. The long shadow of St Hilda, the triangular sail of the yacker and the pointing heads of the terns, were all pulled into a pattern formed by the wake of that flat transom. His heart beat painfully. These were home waters.

The *Black Boy* reached the wide, sandy estuary of the River Tees. It was difficult to think of it as a river on the same coast as the black waters of the Tyne and the Wear.

Hundreds of seals were basking on the deserted beaches, as unconcerned as if they had only each other to fear in the whole world. Grebes and gannets were swimming and diving for fish in the undisturbed channels. Ducks dabbled in the marshy pools, wading birds poked about in the mud flats and gulls floated in the rain-sharp air. It could have been a river in an unknown continent. Those placid waters looked as though they were still waiting to be discovered. The scene held no evidence that men had been created.

But what was that? Beyond a bend in the river the dirty courses and topsails of a brig came into sight, slowly rounding a corner as the ship felt her way among the sand banks that almost clogged the estuary. By the time the *Black Boy* was going past the other vessel came about into the central channel and pointed her bluff bows at the open sea.

A collier!

An enormous flock of dunlin, several thousand of them, lifted from a neighbouring sand bank and swarmed like midges on a summer evening before they settled on the next small islet. A collier! The schools of seals ignored the interloper, treating it with the tolerance due to another creature that had come to share their unfrequented waterway.

At Loftus the alum factories began and continued in an unbroken chain to Sandsend. But the long line of chimneys, and the smouldering pyramids of the roasting clamps, were less oppressive to anyone who had seen the blighted banks of the Tyne.

And then, hauling down the coast, the *Black Boy* reached the harbour with the ruined Abbey on the east cliff.

A church on that cliff had looked down on the kings and queens of the old kingdom, on the saints of the sea and the sky and on the martyrs to that first faith, and on the Viking ships; and the stones of St Hilda's Abbey, blackened by salt winds and time, had watched the pirates and the smugglers, the alum boats and the whalers, and now they watched the *Black Boy* with an equal regard.

Arthur looked up at the Abbey and his heart lurched against his side. It beat frantically on his ribs like a bird in a cage and then it was still. A sickening emptiness filled his chest. A terrible fear gripped him, of the kind he knew when the razorback's tail came out from under the boat and its flukes waved like extended banners above his head.

What is it? he wondered. What can it be? Then he saw that St Hilda's tower had disappeared.

35

The *Black Boy*'s arrival in the outer harbour attracted little notice. She moored just beyond the short pier near the fish market.

Arthur Storm stepped on to the quay and his legs turned to rubber. He was trembling. He had the absurd sensation of being lost. Was it only a year ago that he'd last walked on these boards? Nobody came to greet him. He might have been a stranger.

Then he noticed some brown nets hanging outside a doorway to dry. A girl with smiling eyes walked by with a shrimp basket on her head. Hessian sacks of alum crystals were piled up outside one of the ghauts. Further along old men were mending fishing lines and women were preparing mussels for bait. The clang of caulking hammers and the smell of pitch reached him from the yards on both sides of the river. He breathed deeply, drawing the hundred mingled smells of the harbour into his lungs.

Nothing had changed. This was home. Absolutely nothing had changed except the tower. And himself.

He started along Sandgate and wished that the next few minutes could be compressed into a second of time so that he could jump over them. It wasn't so much that he was desperate to see his parents, but that he couldn't bear the thought of them living with their doubt for a moment longer than they need.

The pictures flickered through his mind. He saw them climbing the Church Stairs each Sunday and he knew their prayers. He saw their worry deepening into anguish with every week that passed; their relief when they heard from ports further up the coast that the *William Scoresby Senior* was making her way southwards; their joy when the news came that she was off Kettle Ness; the return of sorrow when they saw her condition and their despair when they discovered he wasn't aboard. Then a new seed of expectation must have been planted when they discovered that he'd been left alive in Lerwick. Now his return would bring that seed to a sudden blossom and put an end to the painful budding, flowering and cankering of their hopes.

He reached the market place and the Tolbooth. The pictures tormented him and he quickened his step.

The east and west piers curved their arms to take in the stricken whaler, and the houses on Staithside leaned over the water to welcome her. The six bells of St Mary's started to clamour. Men, women and children ran down the long, narrow stairs to the quays.

The *William Scoresby Senior* must have come slowly in, creaking in every joint like an old, arthritic woman. The clappers in the bells would have wagged slowly at first. They were reprimanding fingers. Where have you been? What made you so late? Why have you made us wait so long? The ship's bell replied with a single note of acknowledgement and thanksgiving.

And then the six bells on the cliff pealed more quickly, and the clappers dashed themselves against their brass shells in a frenzy of joy. Nobody cares where you've been. Nobody minds what you've done or failed to do or why you are so late! All that matters is that you are home! And the ship's bell replied with its single, hollow note, to warn that joy shouldn't be unconstrained because there was still cause for sorrow.

The town was empty and the community on the quays was silent. The bells of St Mary's continued to ring above the town, tumbling their happiness on to the red pantiles, chiming in the narrow ghauts and small courtyards, echoing across the harbour against the empty west cliff. The ship's bell tolled. The people waited.

Arthur was running before he reached Ellerby Lane. How had they stood it? What had they done?

The house was still standing there exactly as if he'd never been away and somehow that was extraordinary. The scrubbed step, the crack in the lintel over the door, the small window in its clean white frame were exactly as he remembered them. Perhaps the plain muslin curtains had been drawn closer together, as if to show that although life continued behind them it had withdrawn more into itself.

He opened the door and looked in. The room was deserted and for a moment he didn't know what to do. Then he heard a noise. He shouted, hoping his voice would lessen the shock.

His mam came through from the tiny scullery with flour up to her elbows. He laughed and went to her. With her mouth and eyes wide open she sprang forward and threw her dusty arms round him. He stood still, looking foolishly over the top of her head. She was crying, and she kept alternately holding him as tightly as she could and pushing him away so that she could look at him.

'Let me see thee,' she sobbed, and she fumbled with the buttons on his coat.

Arthur helped her. She seemed unwilling to trust the evidence of her own eyes until she could see him with his coat off. Then she unfastened his jacket, put the palm of her hand on his lean stomach, and hugged him and cried afresh.

Arthur, staring about helplessly, saw the door open and his father come in.

'Snow,' his father said as he closed the door. 'I said it would snow, missus, didn't I?'

Then he stared.

'Food!' Mrs Storm said, stopping crying and speaking up clearly for the first time. 'Food! It's food he wants!' She turned on her husband as if she'd been trying to get this idea into his head for the past ten minutes. 'He must be starving but all tho can do is stand there and go on about weather.'

She darted into the scullery and was back with a saucepan before Arthur or his father had moved. The big, iron pot was standing on its hob in the fireplace, just where it had been when he last saw it. She ladled stock from the pot into the pan, pushed it into the heart of the fire and fled back to the scullery.

His father closed the gap between them and stretched his hand out. 'How is tho, son?'

'I'm fine, dad. Fine, just fine.'

His father hadn't looked down at his hand, but he took it and kneaded it gently. He was smiling widely and showing all his teeth, and making a laughing noise as though he'd just thought of something funny. As he tightened his grip the lips pressed tightly together and his eyes grew bright.

'I'm all right, dad, honestly I am. Don't think about it, dad.'

It had been only for a moment. His father's lips relaxed and his eyes cleared. There was a final, almost painful pressure from his father's hand.

'And toes, son?'

'Only three, dad. Only three completely gone. I never miss them, honestly, dad.'

His mam bustled in with freshly cut bread piled high on a plate in one hand and a deep bowl in the other. She put these things on the table, brought the saucepan from the fire and filled the bowl to the brim. Mr Storm went out to the scullery.

'Get that down thee,' she said, 'and tho'll come to no more harm.'

Arthur sat down at the table and leaned over the bowl. The aromatic steam warmed his face. It smelled better than even the thickest soup, and the first whiff of it coated his gums and the insides of his cheeks with saliva.

'Warm the cockles of tha heart,' his mam added, waiting to see him start eating.

His father reappeared with another plate of bread and a thick slab of butter. Mrs Storm took the butter from him and pushed the plate away.

'A change from salt pork, eh?' he asked over his wife's shoulder.

Arthur made an indistinct noise. The first spoonful had burned the roof of his mouth. His mam started to butter some pieces of bread for him.

'And not much of that towards the end, eh?' asked Mr Storm over her other shoulder.

Arthur nodded and dunked a lump of bread.

'Let him be,' his mam said, 'there'll be time enough for that sort of talk. Best thing tho can do is go to t' butcher while I sort out some taters and carrots. Tell him our lad's home and see what he can do.'

His father, who hadn't found time to take his coat off, returned to the door.

'Just tell him our lad's home,' she repeated, 'and leave it to him.'

He turned the handle. The door flew back out of his hand and hit the wall. A spray of fine snow blew into the room. He went out quickly and with an effort closed the door behind him.

'Tho got back just in t' nick,' she said, replenishing the saucepan and settling it in the fire. 'It's a real back-ender and no mistake.'

Arthur smiled. Back-enders would never be the same again. 'Well, our mam, what news have tho got?'

She sat in her chair beside the fire and sighed happily. The prospect of trying to recall a year's happenings that she'd feared they would never share together was a blissful one.

'For a start,' she said, 'Jim Richardson is still badly, although he comes to see us now and again. He's never forgiven himself for leaving thee in Lerwick. But a gang of islanders brayed him until he was unconscious. He was picked up by a party from the ship and he didn't rightly know where he was until he was back at sea.'

Arthur blew on his spoon. He'd have to go and see Jim Richardson. But he was glad that Jim hadn't wasted time tramping the streets and trying to find him.

'And then the tower collapsed at the Abbey. I don't suppose tho noticed.'

'I noticed straight away.' The deep sense of unease returned. He wanted to think about something else. 'Any news from our Edward?'

Mrs Storm uttered a loud cry and jumped up from her chair. She was amazed at herself for not mentioning it first.

'A long letter,' she said, and rummaged amongst the boxes, empty tins and bits of crockery jumbled together on the mantelpiece. She extracted a folded paper from behind a tallow candle set in a scallop shell. By the look of it, the letter had been unfolded and folded many times. 'Tho get on with the meal and I'll tell thee what he says.'

Edward's letter began with a description of America that made it sound like an earthly paradise. For some reason that part of the world had been singled out by a special providence. Everything was bigger and better there. The ground produced grain and fruit of its own accord, and all that men had to do was gather it in. The soil was so black and rich and thick that you could push a walking stick into it almost anywhere and the stick would go straight in right up to the handle.

Of course, Edward said, there wasn't any soil like that in New York and he hadn't yet seen many of these marvellous things for himself.

The whaling ports were further north, to the south of Cape Cod, and he'd managed to work his way to New Bedford. It was a strange place. Some of the men were from a neighbouring island called Martha's Vineyard – 'Isn't that a lovely name?' asked Mrs Storm – but the rest came from all over. He'd managed to find a place in the *Acushnet* sailing from Nantucket.

'Of course,' Mrs Storm said, 'when they found out where he was from they'd give him a place straight away.'

They went about it in a different way over there, Edward said. The Mate, instead of throwing the harpoon himself, sat in the stern and shouted orders to a harpooneer – 'harpooneer is what he says,' said Mrs Storm – who pulled the bow oar. After the fish was struck the two men changed places and the Mate went into the bow with a lance. It sounded crazy, but they did everything differently over there. They boiled the oil out at sea. They had plenty of time because they were away for four years. Yankees could afford to take their time because there was so much of everything.

Arthur was wiping his bowl with a piece of bread. His mam jumped up and he couldn't prevent her filling it again from the saucepan.

And the fish were different, said Edward. They hadn't any lip or tongue to speak of and only one spout. But there were thousands of them. That was how everything was out there. There was so much of everything. People said there would soon be more whalers sailing out of Nantucket alone than there were in the whole of the northern fishery.

'That can't be right,' Mrs Storm said. 'That's a silly thing to say.'

There were thousands and thousands of whales, Edward continued, probably millions of them that had never been hunted, all swimming about in the warm seas to the south. The *Acushnet* was going to sail round Cape Horn to chase whales in the Pacific. And when you saw a fish there wasn't any panic about striking and killing it before it got away in the ice. The Yankees rowed after them in their vests and drawers.

'Now that isn't decent,' Mrs Storm said. 'I hope our Edward puts a clean shirt on and a proper pair of trousers like he always did.'

Arthur nodded several times. His eyelids were heavy and his stomach was full. The letter was becoming difficult to follow. Chasing whales in sunshine! ... he must have imagined it ... but that was where Cook saw them ... it must be easy ... like a holiday ... He nodded another once or twice and his eyelids closed.

36

The howling of the gale and the more distant rumbling of the sea awakened Arthur Storm.

He raised his chin from his chest and blinked his eyes. Despair and loneliness made him want to close them again and escape back to the oblivion of sleep. He didn't want to see the wrinkled bag in the next bunk, nor the stump waving from the one above him, nor those other stiff faces with the hoar frost in their beards. He opened his eyes wider.

His father had returned from the butcher's and was sitting in his rocking chair to the left of the fireplace. He was scraping at the bowl of his pipe, using his knife with as much delicate precision as if he were picking the last shred of meat out of a crab's elbow. His mam had settled herself in her tall chair with the interwoven whalebone back on the other side of the fire, and was drawing wool from her work box that stood on its wobbly, three-legged stool. On the sides of the box the graceful caravel sailed towards an island in a placid sea, and beyond that to a strange temple with a narrow door and black windows, and then it sailed on again.

Arthur looked at them with a kind of disbelief.

His father took some tobacco from a jar on the crowded mantelpiece, and his angled finger wadded it into the clay bowl of his pipe. He lit it with a length of twisted paper and sank back on to his chair. The sound of his lips on the clay stem, like small trout taking flies in Cleveland becks, mingled with the clicking of the knitting needles.

It seemed to Arthur that this moment had lasted for ever. Or perhaps he had somehow travelled backwards in time and was seeing it again. Or perhaps nothing ever changed: like the caravel and the island and the temple, everything was always the same. Everything stayed where it was, like the narwhal walking stick near the door that one of his forebears had carved in the days of the Spitzbergen fishery, and that was far too heavy to use. Everything stayed where it was and everything was always the same if you allowed it to be. If he didn't move or speak this would go on for ever.

His mam drew some more wool and looked over at him. 'Feeling better?'

'Never felt so good.' He sat up in his chair.

And now the sense of permanence wavered and went out of focus, like pebbles seen on the floor of a pool before a breeze springs up and combs the surface. The whales themselves had gone from Spitzbergen to the Greenland Sea before he was born, and now they were moving again to Davis Strait. Of course things changed. He remembered Mr Dryden's astonished face, and heard the shark's teeth meet in Jim Richardson's arm, and smelled Rasmie Hughson's blood, and saw a small white hand without a middle finger clutching at a shawl. And there were his own fingers and toes. Everything was changing.

The room was dark. He looked at the small window. Its corners were choked with snow and outside the wind was driving the flakes in great, white billows.

'God have mercy on those poor souls,' his mam said.

His father nodded and spoke round his pipe. 'Amen.'

'What poor souls?'

His father took his pipe out of his mouth to tell what he knew, but his wife was too quick for him.

'Tha fayther heard some news while he was at the butcher's,' she said, while her needles continued to flash. 'There's a ship being blown past the harbour down to North Cheek.'

'What is she?'

His father was beaten again despite his complete readiness this time.

'The snow is too thick to see,' his mam said. 'But they can tell by her rig that she's not one of ours.'

'She's not barque-rigged,' said his father, determined to add the only fact remaining to him. Then he plugged the pipe back in his mouth to show that all his other news had been expropriated.

Arthur pushed his chair back from the table and stood up. 'I think I'll just take a short walk and see if there's any more news.'

'A walk!' She couldn't have been more astounded if he'd said he was going for a swim. 'A walk!' She put her knitting down, and this unwonted interruption to her labours gave the action an extraordinary emphasis. 'A walk! We want to be sure the fever is sweated out of thee.'

'We want tae make sure the fever is sweated out of ye,' she said, lying on her side. 'Cant me over again,' she said. She went like a mad thing. Like a whale in its flurry.

He bent to kiss her on the forehead. 'Just a *little* walk.'

'And how far will that take thee? To Brewster Lane?'

She disdained to name the two public houses which faced each other in that popular street, but her husband hastened to quieten her fears.

'Nay,' he told them, 'there's a meeting in t' Tolbooth. There's no need to go further than t' market square to find out what the news is.'

Mrs Storm remained dubious, with her needles at rest on her lap.

'Let the lad go,' he continued. 'There's plenty of folk that'll be pleased to see him about who are thinking they might never see him again.' He turned to Arthur. 'Tho'll do them a kindness. There was somebody asking only t' other day if we had any more news.'

Arthur tried to make the question casual. 'Who was it?'

His father cast about for a bit and came up with a name that was no more than an empty word. But a lot of other people had kept inquiring about him, he added.

'Who else, for instance?'

Arthur was miserably aware that these questions were blatantly out of character. He wouldn't normally have been at all interested in other people's concern. His mam showed by a clash of her needles and a warning cough at her husband that she was aware of the real drift of this curiosity. Mr Storm, alerted by these signs but unable to interpret them, cautiously released a few more meaningless names.

'You haven't received any inquiry from Mrs Paylor?' asked Arthur, flushing crimson.

'Mrs Paylor?'

Mrs Storm interrupted her knitting. 'The mother of Ann Paylor,' she said, in a deliberately patient voice. 'The girl with the blonde hair that lost her finger when she was crabbing, and that looked the other way the last time I saw her in t' street.'

The needles flashed again to show that she could provide no more aid. Her husband, now that he appreciated the situation, looked unhappy.

'Ah, yes,' he said, trying to sound brisk. 'We see Mrs Paylor now and again. Husband was lost in the *Aimwell*. Hit by a floe, she was. Terrible business.'

Mr Storm seemed about to recapitulate all he knew of the loss of the *Aimwell*. His wife's needles clicked with sharp menace while he paused. Better sense prevailed.

'You've been away a long time,' he said, suddenly more serious, 'so long that some folks didn't expect to see you again. Just like I told you. So long that you couldn't expect some folk to wait, as you might say.'

'Particularly anyone who's a mite impetuous,' Mrs Storm said, unable to withold her contribution.

Mr Storm stood up, wavered towards the narwhal walking stick as if in need of such heavy support, but braced himself and returned to his chair.

'Mrs Paylor's daughter,' he said, 'Ann, is that what she's called, Ann?' He appeared to believe that being vague about her name made whatever she was doing less important. 'Ann Paylor is courting a lad who works in Henry and George Barrick's yard on t' east side. Very serious about it, too, they say.'

Arthur was unaware of his bearings for a moment. It was like being back in the whale boat, lost in the fog. He clenched his hands in an attempt to make the numbness go away.

'But there's plenty of folk that'll be glad to see thee,' his father said.

His mam didn't take her eyes from her knitting. 'Go on, then. Just like tha fayther. Can't sit still for five minutes at a time.'

He crossed the room in three strides and took his coat from a peg on the wall.

'Tho'll want more than that,' she said. 'Get properly lapped up.'

He pulled a pair of worn mittens from his pockets and moved towards the door.

His mam dropped her knitting and pounced over to intercept him. She undid the only two buttons on his coat that he'd bothered to fasten, pulled downwards at his jacket and buttoned it, refastened the coat, turned up the collar and tugged at the sleeves. His father gave him a secret smile. For someone who'd managed to survive winter in the Arctic he wasn't being given much credit for his ability to dress himself for the street.

'Don't be long,' she said. 'Tha fayther came back with a nice shoulder of lamb that's in t' oven now, and I'm putting the taters and carrots on in half an hour.'

He opened the door and further instructions became impossible. The wind flailed into the room, throwing sparks out of the fire and rustling the papers on the mantelpiece. She clung to his arm and he kissed her again quickly.

37

The snow was already thick enough to make walking difficult and the violence of the gale surprised him. The door steps and shop windows in Sandgate were stuffed with snow, and buffets of wind hurled clouds of it under the pointed gables of the houses. On his left the waters of the Esk, turgid from the Cleveland becks, had raced down from Westerdale, through the trout pools and the minnow reaches, and turned the harbour yellow.

He would have been tempted to go as far as Brewster Lane, and see what news there was in the Seven Stars or in the Jolly Butchers on the other side. But when he reached the market square he saw people going into the Tolbooth, and in view of what his father had said he turned aside to attend the meeting.

Harry Hodgson, who always smelled of blubber no matter what the state of trade or time of the year, shook him warmly by the hand as he stepped between the pillars. There was some sort of public meeting in the upper room, Harry confirmed. Arthur followed the others up the spiral staircase. Men whom he scarcely knew lingered to shake him by the hand or put an arm round his shoulders: a man who worked with his father at the sail loft, a remote cousin of his mother, and others whom he knew only by sight.

At the top of the stairs there was a rumour that more news had come in about the ship being blown down to North Cheek. Those round about wanted to know what this news was. Those further away turned round and called for silence. Everyone slowly became aware that the meeting was being called to order.

At the other end of the room a man drew attention to himself by standing on a chair. Most people recognized Mr Beaufort, the First Mate of the *William Scoresby Senior*. It was the first time Arthur had seen him without his sealskin cap, and his dark curls came down to his white, silk collar.

'Can I have your attention, gentlemen? Or perhaps I should say –' and Mr Beaufort smirked around the assembly – 'aw yes, *ladies* and gentlemen.'

There were a few cries of 'oh' and a few facetious remarks, and rather more groans and shouts of 'Get on with it'. Mr Beaufort seized the opportunity of extracting the walrus ivory box from a pocket in his velveteen waistcoat and taking a little snuff. Then he hooked his thumbs in the armholes and stuck out his chest the better to display the frills and imitation pearl buttons on his shirt front.

'He looks more like a burgomaster parading on a fish's belly,' said Harry Hodgson, 'than a man who'd learned to cut blubber.'

The men within earshot laughed appreciatively.

'Ladies and gentlemen,' Mr Beaufort resumed, 'earlier today some of you saw a ship going southward towards North Cheek. She's most probably another whaler that's managed to get out of Davis Strait. All I can add to what you know is that a messenger from Bay Town got through to us before the snow came down off the moor and closed the road by the river. He told us that she'd broken her back and gone on to the reef.' There was a long 'ah' from the audience and much shaking of heads before Mr Beaufort continued. 'There'll be no more news now because the road is closed. But you all know that the men of Bay Town haven't anything you would call a lifeboat.'

Mr Beaufort showed his white teeth in an even smile. He seemed to regard this as a marvellous opportunity for showing himself off. He stood down and was promptly forgotten in the hubbub of noise as each man talked to his neighbour.

This harsh line of the coast had been pulverized by the North Sea since the beginning of time, and its worn cliffs confronted wind and water with the dumb defiance of centuries. It was an ancient and non-denominational graveyard. The sea killed them and the shifting sands, like a tireless sexton, buried them layer upon layer. Pink sandstone and black basalt were the tombstones. Northumbrian kings and Celtic saints, Saxon princes and Viking pirates, nuns and shrimp girls were folded into the same anonymous grave by the smooth, careful sands.

And yet each time a ship was in distress the town always reacted as if it were a unique event.

An elderly man put a foot on the chair. Mr Beaufort took his ebony cane, helped him up with a deferential smile and continued to steady him after he had ascended. The new speaker's face was soft and would have been smooth had it not been for the hard lines around his mouth. His clothes were severe but of the finest quality. Arthur, and probably the entire assembly, recognized Mr Winspear who owned the largest of the sail lofts.

When he spoke he gave the curious impression of talking to himself. 'I don't know why this meeting has been called, because I don't know what there is to talk about. The rot started seven seasons ago when we lost the *Aimwell* at Greenland. Then two seasons later we lost the *Lively* and the *Esk*. Nobody can ever forget that.'

Nobody would forget. The news came from Hull that the *Lively* had been lost in the West Ice with all hands; and the *Esk* ran aground near Redcar and broke in two within sight of home, with only four live men being washed ashore. William Scoresby

Junior – or the Reverend William Scoresby as they ought to call him these days – had been very moved by the loss of his old ship and took the service in St Mary's.

'And this last season was another tragedy,' Mr Winspear resumed. 'Everybody lost money and it nearly ruined some of us. Only the *Phoenix* is going out this year and that speaks for itself.' He made as if to descend and Mr Beaufort raised his arm respectfully, but he thought of something else and stayed where he was. 'When the *William Scoresby Senior* came home, after we'd counted her in as a dead loss, it put a bit of confidence back into t' business. And I've no doubt that if this other ship managed to get home it would increase business confidence in Hull or wherever she's bound. I'm as grieved as any man, believe me, to think of a whaler not getting home, even if she's clean, and even if she's from a rival port. But there's nothing we can do about it. Absolutely nothing.'

Now he had finished. Mr Beaufort raised his arm again, and smiled at Mr Winspear as he helped him to the floor and returned his cane.

Scarcely was the chair vacated before a young man jumped on to it. He had the russet cheeks of a coble fisherman, and a much mended gansey hung down almost to his knees. He shook a rough, red fist at his listeners.

'We all know this ship isn't going to get home,' he shouted. 'We're not here to talk about that. But what about the men who are on her? We're not worrying about blubber and length of bone but the flesh and bone of living men. We've got a lifeboat, haven't we? If somebody's waiting for volunteers they can put me down and let's get on with it. While we stand here there's men on a ship that's coming to bits under their feet.'

He jumped down and immediately there was a confused din of argument. Some of the younger men were for launching the boat without more ado and they moved towards the door. Others of more experience restrained them, and angry words were exchanged. The crowd parted to make way for a man who stooped with the weight of years and toil on his back. He waved Mr Beaufort aside and climbed on to the chair only with difficulty. A respectful silence fell.

'Who's that?' whispered Arthur.

Harry Hodgson spoke out of the corner of his mouth. 'Mr Clarkson. Hasn't been seen since last Sailing Day.'

Arthur looked at the scrawny arms that had first pulled an oar in a whale boat the best part of a century ago. His mere name brought back memories of the old *Henrietta* and the Scoresbys. This public appearance had something of the marvellous about it.

'Let no man doubt our willingness,' Mr Clarkson began, in a surprisingly strong voice, 'to go to the assistance of anybody who's in trouble in these waters. The only question is whether it's possible. You've all walked here through t' wind and snow, and you know it's blowing as hard a gale as most men have seen. We've heard how it's blocked the way out alongside the river and you can't see out beyond the piers. But you've only got to look at t' watter running under the bridge into t' harbour and listen to t' noise to know there's a tremendous sea out there.'

The old man looked at their upturned faces. His faded blue eyes watered and the muscles stiffened under the loose skin of his neck. Everyone was waiting for him. His judgement would be accepted by them all.

'There can be two opinions about our ability to launch a boat. My own opinion is that we can.' A shout of approval smacked the ceiling. The younger men made a move towards the door, but something in the old man's unchanging face stopped them. 'I think we could get the boat out of the harbour and into t' sea,' he went on. 'But there can't be two opinions about what would happen next. What I say is a simple fact.' His watery eyes surveyed them all. 'It's impossible to take a boat round to Bay. If she hadn't already foundered she'd be thrown on to rocks long before she reached North Cheek.'

Mr Clarkson waved Mr Beaufort out of the way. He descended awkwardly and heavily, and the crowd opened to reabsorb him. His feet scraped along the floor and he was lost again. There was silence.

It was the kind of silence that must exist on a dead world where there is no eye to observe its deadness. People stared at each other without speaking. Nobody knew what to do next and nobody moved. The silence was unbearable. Something had to happen. Something. Anything. Anything that would release them.

And now another figure came forward. They were all grateful to him. It was possible to breathe freely again, to cough and shuffle feet. Captain Stapleton ascended the chair and leaned forward just as he did from the top of the quarter deck steps. He spoke very quietly, and in the silence this gave every word an additional weight.

'All of us act like members of a herd for at least part of the time, and many of us never behave in any other way. We see other people only as parts of the herd, with no more distinctness than drops of water in a breaking wave or flakes of snow in this storm. We don't see other people as individuals like ourselves. Often this is because we can't even see ourselves as individuals. We don't use our intelligence and we don't know how to feel. We think and feel only those things that can be understood and felt by the herd. And every man who is part of the herd is living less than his full life.'

People sought each other's eyes, nodded and shook their heads. What was the matter with him? What was he talking about? Some of them grinned and others were embarrassed.

'Always was an odd one,' muttered Harry Hodgson.

Most of those at the front fell back so that a gap appeared round the speaker's chair. Only the respect that was always due to a whaling Captain held the audience together.

'Even those of us who are aware of ourselves as individuals, still see other individuals as part of the herd. We still see other people as vague things, without a clear outline, and they become real to us only when we think we can exploit them. So we use our intelligence and our feelings to win an advantage or to gain pleasure at the expense of the herd.'

There was more shuffling and louder murmurings of discontent. Some people looked about for friends and went across to talk to them. Others simply laughed and made their way to the door. A group of coble fishermen had gathered around the man in the long gansey, who'd spoken in favour of launching the life boat without further argument. Another group had come together round Mr Winspear, including Mr Agar who had one of the banks in Church Street, Mr Milburn who owned the rope walk beyond Town End, and Mr Foster, the Quaker shipowner, who had lost more money than anybody in the last few years. Mr

Winspear spoke to the coble fisherman and the fisherman nodded in vehement agreement. The two groups, despite their obvious differences, grew closer together.

'But men who've been to the northern fishery have discovered that there's a different way to live. Men who've been in a whale boat discover the difference between living in a community and being members of a herd. A new kind of community is born in a fast boat that has nothing to do with private triumphs or personal gain. Perhaps it's only for a few seconds, but those six or seven men become fully alive to themselves as individuals and at the same time they're all possessed by a single spirit.'

Arthur shivered. It was true. He'd known it and felt it. He could testify. He scarcely breathed. He had an overwhelming conviction that something completely unexpected and very important was about to happen. So many people had fallen back that he was by now the nearest person to the chair. Even so, the noise had increased so much that it was difficult to hear clearly.

'The spirit of community that exists in a whale boat can sometimes possess an entire ship's company. I believe that if we will it to happen the same spirit could possess this town and all the people in it. I am sure this is the best hope for all mankind. Perhaps we can take that spirit of community that flickers in t' whale boat and blow on it until it burns through the whole ship, the whole town, the whole country, the whole world, and the whole of creation as far as the faintest star we can see through a telescope.'

Captain Stapleton lowered his large, square-shaped head, with the grey hair fluffed out over his ears like gulls' wings. His white beard, rounded in the form of a blubber spade, rested on his chest. Then he raised his head and his clear blue eyes, puckered as if looking to windward, gazed at some distant horizon invisible to all but him.

'This is what we must strive to do,' he said. 'We must recreate the spirit that comes to life in a whale boat. We must become individuals living in a community instead of members of a herd. All things change. But the possibility of creating a true community stays with us for ever.'

Captain Stapleton stood down.

Everyone was dumb. Slowly they overcame their surprise and

talked more loudly than before. Captain Stapleton must be ill. A winter in the Arctic had turned his brain. It would be impossible to give him another command. He had always been an odd one.

'I always knew that,' Harry Hodgson said. 'An odd one.'

Arthur stared at the vacated chair and knew exactly what he had to do. He ran to the chair and mounted it. Nobody noticed him.

'We'll take it overland!' he shouted.

Those nearest to the chair stopped talking and looked at him. More people turned round and gazed at him curiously. The area of silence grew. A silent multitude of faces, so many indistinguishable white blobs, tilted up at him.

'We'll take the boat over the moor!' he called to them. 'We'll launch it on t' other side!'

The faces took on their individual shapes. He saw excitement grow in their eyes and resolution reshape their mouths. The talking began again: it started as a tiny trickle of wonder and quickly swelled into a huge, roaring river of approval. The crowd came together, laughing and shouting. They surged out through the door in a continuous, living body, down the spiral stairs and out into the snow.

Mr Foster, wearing his broad-brimmed hat, led the way to Burgess Pier. Arthur was among the hundreds of men behind him. Their tramping feet and loud voices travelled along Brewster Lane. The doors of the Seven Stars and the Jolly Butchers opened, and the occupants didn't even wait to finish their drinks. Scores of men and women hurried away to find ropes, picks, spades, grapnels, anchors, and any tackle or equipment that might conceivably be of use. Others ran home to fetch relations and friends.

Marching feet compacted the snow and the freezing wind gave it a surface as smooth as glass. The boat slid away from its lodging as lightly as a sledge, and casual nudges from a handful of men were sufficient to keep it moving until they were crossing Church Street. Here the north-east wind, funnelled and directed by its passage along Henrietta Street, snatched at the bows and turned them aside. Extra hands straightened the boat and kept her moving, but it was only a mild foretaste of what was to come.

'Arthur! Arthur!'

He let loose of the boat and checked his stride, but the flow of the crowd was irresistible. Like a trout in a moorland beck he turned and faced upstream.

'Arthur! Arthur! Here!'

A small figure waved and ran out of Henrietta Street, only to be caught up in the mass of people and borne away. He plunged towards the place where he'd seen her, advancing with difficulty across the streaming crowd. She waved again and tried to stand still, but was being jostled this way and that like a pebble that keeps finding a resting place on a sloping beach, but is rolled to and fro by the tide. She continued to wave and he continued to struggle, so that they were both out of breath by the time he caught up with her.

'Arthur! Our mam heard you were home.'

He looked down into a face that was as pale as the fresh snow. She had wound a thick shawl about her head and neck and hurriedly pushed the ends inside her tightly buttoned coat. Snow had thickened on her shoulders.

'Someone told her who'd heard in t' butcher's.'

Her face was suddenly very pink and her eyes were shining as though some captured snow flakes had just been melted in them.

'And you're going away again already?'

'Only for a few hours.'

Her sparkling eyes overflowed. 'I thought you were dead. I would have waited. A few more hours would have been nothing.'

Ann Paylor lowered her head. He looked down at a strand of fair hair that had blown free from the shawl. In some ways he felt that he now knew her better than she knew herself. It made her more dear to him. He reached for her left hand with his right one and squeezed the shortened middle finger with the ends of his own.

Her head jerked upwards in surprise.

He kissed her startled mouth and hurried away.

38

The leaders halted at the foot of the Donkey Road and the entire company came to a stand behind them. Arthur had lost his place alongside the boat and was well back. He wanted to move up and see what was happening at the front, but the people ahead were wedged so tightly together that he couldn't make much progress. He guessed that the delay was caused by men at the front attaching ropes to the boat.

The people ahead of him moved on and he moved with them. The leaders must have gone ahead with the ropes. He strained his eyes against the falling snow but couldn't see beyond the backs of the men immediately ahead of him.

By the time Arthur was on the slope of the Donkey Road hundreds of pairs of feet had climbed it and polished the surface to the smoothness of glass. After only a few yards someone alongside him slipped and fell, and brought another man down. They both rolled about and brought down half a dozen more. Arthur dropped to his hands and knees and managed to cling there even when a falling body crashed against him. He smelled Harry Hodgson before he identified him by sight.

'As slippy as a fish's belly,' Harry said. 'You need spurs for this job.' Harry stood up tentatively, but lost his footing again and rolled away out of view.

Conditions would be better at the front. But there were hundreds of men behind who would find this slope impossible to climb. Voices overhead showed that some had decided to use the Church Stairs that led up to St Mary's. The steps would probably offer more secure footholds, but even the flattened resting places for coffin bearers would be soon obliterated.

Shouts from ahead came down on the wind. Something new was happening at the front. Arthur wondered whether the boat had somehow slipped its ropes; or whether so many of those hauling it had fallen that the boat was coming back. If it came back the boat would take hundreds of men down with it to Church Street.

The shouting came nearer and was mixed with the jingling of

bells. The men ahead divided and two shapes emerged out of the blanket of snow. The first was a bedraggled Dales pony with panniers on its back, and obviously frightened at meeting so many people. The second shape was a man clinging tenaciously to a piece of rope fastened round the pony's neck, and slithering down the slope behind it. He looked as if he'd just been dug out of a snow drift, with snow in his eyes and down his collar, and he was shouting at the top of his voice.

'Mad! Mad! All mad! Mad!'

He slipped and became entangled amongst the pony's legs. He found his feet and stood up, but the pony promptly pulled him down again.

'Mad!' he continued to shout from between his animal's legs. 'Mad! If my pony can't get up there nothing can! Mad! Mad! All mad! Mad!'

The pannier man continued willy nilly on his downward course. Whenever he managed to stand up the pony pulled him off his feet again. He refused to leave hold of the rope and was soon out of sight. The shouts and the tinkling of pack-horse bells faded away below.

Somewhere ahead, invisible in the swirling snow, was the Abbey Gatehouse. Its nearness made Arthur think of Lord Mulgrave, and the stories of how he used to drive his coach and four up this road when he was courting one of the Cholmley girls in the Abbey Gatehouse. They said that when he came back down he always hitched two of the horses behind to stop the coach running away with him.

There was another and more serious fall of men ahead. So many were knocked off their feet that everything came to a halt. Arthur pushed forward and tripped over something hard. His exploring fingers told him that he was spread-eagled on the wind-worn steps of the blackened Abbey Cross that marked the site of the ancient cemetery. The muscles along the fronts of his thighs and his hamstrings were aching painfully as he resumed his way. His fatigue made him realize how hard the men at the front with the ropes must be working.

Beyond the Gatehouse, hidden by the falling snow, was St Hilda's Abbey. He thought of the central tower rising up like the ageless mountain above the clouds on Jan Mayen Island, or the tail of a big fish high in the air just before it started to come down. Then he remembered that St Hilda's tower wasn't there any more and his heart seemed to stop beating and the sickening feeling of emptiness came back into his chest. It must still be there, he thought. It's simply hidden by the snow. It must still be there and pointing at the sky.

The gale blew harder and whipped hail into his face. The wind grabbed his coat with increasing violence. He knew that he must be nearing the top. Some of the leaders had fallen behind and they were staggering as he passed them.

One man was crawling. His face was invisible and the red hair was powdered with snow, but those massive shoulders could belong only to the Specksioneer. Mr Nellis was sobbing and swearing to himself as he dragged a twisted leg behind him up the slope. So preoccupied was he that he didn't look up as Arthur stepped over him.

A few more steps and the wind hit Arthur with such fury that he went down on to his knees. A couple of grappling irons scuttled past like frightened crabs. A moment later something lashed him across the neck. He cried out with surprise and pain and threw his hands up to protect himself. He caught hold of a piece of rope and hung on. Something at the other end gave a mighty heave that wrenched his arms in their sockets and dragged him along with his face in the snow.

He maintained his hold on the rope, struggled to his feet and tried to dig his heels into the churned snow. The invisible thing at the other end would have none of it and hauled him away. It's like a fish, he thought, as he moved hand over hand along the rope. But he knew that it must be the boat, and with the wind inside it was being blown away across the moor.

Before he reached anywhere near the end of the rope Arthur discovered that he was only one of more than a dozen men who were hanging on to it. He glimpsed the boat for the first time since Ann Paylor had called to him. There was something re-assuring in the sight, almost as if he had doubted whether it were still there. Unseen men shouted orders and they had the boat moving forward again.

Arthur and the men on his rope, together with gangs behind

and in front of them, kept to windward between the boat and the edge of the cliff. It was their job not to pull the boat, but to prevent it being blown over the moor.

The force of the wind on the bare hill was almost unbelievable. It raced in from the North Sea, was stopped by the vertical wall of the cliff and came over the top screaming like a thousand devils. Sometimes all the devils drew breath at the same time and the straining men could stand upright. Then the wind would blow again with unpredictable suddenness, and the men clenched the ropes in their bleeding hands and leaned backwards into the blast. If the wind had changed direction for a couple of seconds, the men and the boat would have gone straight over the cliff into the sea that was roaring at its base.

The men on the leading ropes entered a village. On each side of the street the windows were blocked with snow and the houses were like blind men standing unawares at a procession. The snow muffled their steps, so that men and boat travelled in silence.

But someone spied them. The doors opened one after the other. Wives and daughters, with their shawls wrapped tightly round their heads and shoulders, came out with food in both hands. Fathers, husbands and sons left their homes and joined the dwindling number of men with the boat. Even after the men on the trailing ropes had passed through the street and were leaving the village behind, the women were still running after them with jugs of steaming tea.

With the houses behind them the men marched once more into the full fury of the gale. The wind swept over the moor with increased force, blinding them with sleet, tearing at their hair and clothes, snatching the ropes from their raw hands, turning the boat this way and that and throwing it upside down.

The leaders quickened their pace and this renewed vigour ran back through the leading ropes to the boat, and out again through the side ropes and the trailing ropes. Arthur felt the tug on the line: it was alive with the nerves and muscles of scores of unseen men; the ropes had become conductors of energy, so that each man was strengthened by the spirit of all the other men around the boat. It is happening again, Arthur thought. It is exactly like it was in the whale boat. I have stopped being myself and yet I am more truly myself than I ever was. I have become part of something else.

A shape loomed beside the route. Its hard, square outlines had been rounded and softened by the snow, but Arthur recognized the church. It was this that had put fresh heart into the leaders, like weary travellers who identify the last milestone on their journey. Once when he'd stayed with his grandpa and grandma they came to a service here. He had noticed the white gloves with ribbons and paper flowers hanging from the roof, although the older pieces were yellow and blackened by decay. His grandpa told him how they came to be there. 'What are virgins?' he asked. 'Unmarried girls,' his grandma said.

The road began to descend alongside the churchyard wall. 'There are more Storms lying down in there,' his grandpa said, 'than ever sprang up at sea.' 'And they caused more trouble,' his grandma said, with that bright flash in her eyes that made it possible to imagine what she was like when she was young. The sea sent its first whisper up the long, winding hill towards Bank Top, inviting them to hurry down.

The incline became steeper and the boat moved more easily. Soon the boat was sliding down Bay Bank of its own accord, and the leaders had to move out of the way and fall back to restrain it. When the boat reached the more precipitous part of the bank it looked as if it were in danger of disappearing over the edge. By imperceptible degrees the whisper of the sea had become a deep rumbling under their feet.

The road narrowed and twisted. In the more confined space the sea perhaps sounded even louder than it really was. On the right an archway opened into the narrow alley of The Bolts, where an old woman was hanging on to her husband's arm to prevent him joining the crowd round the boat. 'Leave it to the young men, William,' she begged. Arthur kept well down on the other side so that his grandparents wouldn't see him.

They pushed the boat over the bridge that spanned the pelting beck, guided it round a corner to the left and entered upon the right-hand bend that led down to Wayfoot.

The houses of Bay Town were huddled together under the cliff, as if they were trying to keep each other warm in the northeast wind that lashed their whitened faces. Doors opened one after the other, all the way down the bank. Again the shawled women came out with food and hot tea. Again the men came out to join the exhausted gangs at the ropes and next to the boat. The rumbling under their feet turned into a growling that filled the spaces between the houses, and then into a roaring on every side and in the air above the roofs.

At Wayfoot they came to a halt and confronted the final enemy.

The sea was lying in the bay like an impatient wrestler, flexing and bunching the muscles in its broad, black back. Its uncontrollable energy was throwing up dark mounds of water, sweeping them towards the shore and expanding them as they went. The mounds grew into hills, and the hills swelled until they split open and crashed on to the beach with a sound that was lost in the tremendous noise that filled the entire bay. The maddened waters seemed to be possessed by some tormented form of life. The broken waves advanced to hurl themselves against the walls, and then ran on into Wayfoot where they hissed at the shoes of the men who were standing there.

A spasm in the gale blew a clear patch in the air and briefly revealed the ship. She was still afloat and stuck on the reef in the south side of the bay. With each sea she rose and fell and couldn't last for long.

Many men had been lost on the trek over the moor or were too fatigued to be of use. A group of the most senior men remaining had assembled at the bows and they chose a coxswain without delay. The new coxswain immediately began to select his crew. Arthur forced his way to the front where he couldn't be overlooked.

The coxswain was strutting amongst the men with his chest stuck out like a pigeon. His uncurled hair was plastered on his forehead and his cheeks had sunken into his face with exhaustion. The frills on his shirt front hung down in grimy streamers and the pearly buttons were the colour of raisins.

'Mr Beaufort! Mr Beaufort, sir!'

The First Mate looked round sharply. 'Who's that?'

'A volunteer for t' boat, sir.'

'I've got hundreds of volunteers. Can you pull an oar?'

'I've pulled one in a whale boat. For *William Scoresby Senior.*'

Mr Beaufort came closer and studied him for a second. His strained face relaxed. 'Our young apprentice again. Glad to see you.'

'Thank you, sir.'

Mr Beaufort was holding out his hand but Arthur pretended not to see it.

'Can I have a place in t' boat.'

'Give me your hand, lad.'

Arthur offered his left hand. Mr Beaufort knocked it aside with a flare of temper and snatched his right hand. He clasped it firmly, and then held it up to look at the stumps revealed by the mitten.

'Please,' Arthur said. 'I pulled an oar in Mr Dryden's boat.'

Mr Beaufort lowered the hand and stood with his head down. His eyes were hidden by the long wet hair hanging over his brow. He appeared to be counting the fingers and having great difficulty in the matter. But perhaps he was thinking about something else completely.

'You need more than fingers to pull an oar,' Arthur said.

Mr Beaufort's head came up. 'Stop wasting time and get into t' boat!'

They launched the boat three times. Twice it was thrown back on to the beach and broken oars and men with fractured arms had to be replaced. Each time they came back they heard the people singing in Wayfoot. Arthur knew his grandpa and grandma would be singing with them, and he was glad they didn't know he was in the boat.

After half an hour in the waters of the bay they had a clearer view of the ship. The foremast had been unstepped and it had gone by the board. The ship would soon be waterlogged, and her angle on the reef showed that she would go over on to her broadside at any moment.

'Pull, my lads!' called Mr Beaufort from the stern. 'It's a size fish you're pulling for. Quick, now, before he sounds. Think of his length of bone, my lads! Think of tiny waists inside those whalebone corsets! Think of fine ladies inside whalebone petticoats, my lads, and the good things they hide beneath 'em! But pull! Pull! Pull!'

The sweat ran down Arthur's forehead and into his eyes. The

aches and pains of the long haul across the moors had gone. His muscles were singing. The men in the boat, the men on the wreck, the sea, the sky, the men and women singing on the shore, they were all part of the same song.

Mr Beaufort leaned forward and shouted above the noise of the gale and the sea. 'It's something bigger than a fish, my lads! It's something bigger than the biggest fish you ever heard of. It's life you're pulling for. It's life, it's sweet life itself you're pulling for.'

They were much nearer to the ship. There was something familiar about her mizzen crojack, and the next sea went down far enough to reveal the broad white band with false gun ports running forward almost to her hawse hole. There was no need to look for the name of the *Lady Clifford* on her head boards. Arthur remembered James Tickelpenny with the droll, handsome face, who'd run off with a gentleman's daughter from Louth, but who went to the fishery every year for the sake of a day in Lerwick, and who had made them all laugh with the song about the girl he'd left behind him.

A tremendous sea rose up to hide the ship and the wind hurled a curtain of sleet across the bay. When the air cleared the sea was sweeping clear across the deck and a second later she went over. They saw a figure take an axe to the weather lanyards. The mainmast broke off not many feet above the deck and the ship righted herself sufficiently to show her larboard quarter above the water. Men were clinging to the exposed part of the hull and to the mizzen chains like limpets to a rock.

'Let them know we're here,' Mr Beaufort bawled, and stood up to wave. 'After me, now.'

Their three cheers crossed the black water. When the next sea went down they could see the white faces on the raised quarter of the *Lady Clifford*, staring in surprise through the spray and the sleet.

And before the next sea arrived their three cheers were returned.

Five

The fishbelly rails run north from Pickering, and nobody from that old market town has ever seen so much iron. The rails chew their way northward on stone sleepers and slip into Newton Dale where they wriggle along the floor. The silence is as glacial as that which prevailed aeons ago when the melted ice first cut its way through the steep-sided gorge. The rails drag their heavy length over the heather moor to the summit, where they cross the reclaimed bogland and sneak over the top to start their descent.

By the time the rails have snaked all the way down to the main valley the air has changed. The north-east wind is blowing directly up the dale and it brings the briny sharpness of the North Sea. Nearer the coast the salted air is laced with the scents of fresh fish, seaweed and tarred rope. As the rails slide closer there is the mixed aroma of wet hemp, seasoned Helmsley timber and pitch.

And when the new iron rails slither down to the ancient harbour the north-east wind brings the sound of the old iron clappers hammering inside the bells of St Mary's. Those bells, that had for so long welcomed the weary whalers from Spitzbergen and the Greenland Sea and Davis Strait, are ringing with a brazen triumph that vibrates the stones in their squat tower.

The quayside, where John Hugill had tried to give his pamphlets away, is deserted. But outside the Angel Inn, where two years ago George Stephenson and George Hudson first met and became friends, are more people than had ever assembled on Sailing Day. And the solemn exultation of the six bells in the grey tower is abruptly interrupted by the blare of trumpets and trombones and the banging of drums. The brass band, decked in gilded braid and preceded by flags, comes forward and leads the procession towards the terminus.

The lines approach the terminus of Mr Stephenson's latest

railway across derelict land, where an inquiring eye can easily identify the remains of the yard from which Fishburn and Brodrick had launched their last ship for the northern fishery. That was the area where, before their partnership, Mr Fishburn had built the ships that Captain Cook took to the South Seas under the names of Endeavour, Adventure *and* Resolution, *and where Mr Brodrick had introduced the first whale boats with straight-grained, steam-formed timbers. Before that it was the workshop which trained the carpenters who gave to St Mary's a new roof, flat enough to avoid the full rigours of the north-east winds. And long before that it was the place where Jarvis Coates had built the old ships.*

The carriages waiting on the iron rails are more gaily decorated than the whaling ships had ever been. Their elegant construction draws gasps of wonder from the admiring crowds. Each carriage bears a name and has steps to the top deck with a driver sitting at the front. The carriages are all very splendid but the bright yellow one called 'Lady Hilda' is the favourite.

The horses are brought up, stepping proudly, and are attached to the carriages. At a word of command the gorgeous spectacle is put in motion. The band plays with even more exuberance, the spectators wave their flags, and some of the more energetic run alongside the track to shout to the drivers and guards. The beaming passengers wave in acknowledgement.

The railway follows first one side of the valley and then the other, only to return or depart again whenever the opposite bank offers a more secure foundation. Crossing and recrossing the river on a series of wooden bridges, the line finally traverses the Esk for the last time at Growmond. Here it enters a dark tunnel of which the stone façade is pierced by slit windows and crowned by battlements. This romantic prelude is soon forgotten by the passengers to whom the circle of light ahead seems very small and very distant. But there isn't any cause for alarm. The horses bring them safely out into a second valley where the waiting crowd greets them with rapturous cheers.

The carriages follow this second valley to the point where the Murk Esk divides into the two contributory streams that hasten down to give it birth. Here at Beck Holes the horses are detached, and the passengers have leisure to descend and contemplate the next stage of their journey. The sight causes them even more uneasiness than the entrance to the tunnel had done.

The railway, like the river, has divided and the two tracks run side by side up an incline. The incline is very steep and the twin tracks climb in parallel for almost a mile through an avenue freshly cut into a thick wood. A hemp rope runs down from the top of the incline and the passengers watch nervously while the end is hooked to the first carriage.

A rough man, in a shaggy jacket with large, gaping pockets, tries to explain what is happening to the waiting passengers. The rumour goes round that he is an 'Engineer': the word is pronounced as tentatively and with as much quiet awe as if he were a Magician. He tells them that the other end of the rope goes round a revolving drum at the top of the incline and is attached to a counter-balance. But his accent is so thick as to be almost unintelligible and the passengers are not reassured.

Mr Winspear, who still owns the sail loft but has bought shares in a stone quarry at Goadland near the railway, judges that it would be appropriate for him to say a few words. He waves his ebony cane to command attention, and clears his throat with a good deal more noise than the act itself requires.

'Gentlemen,' he says, 'I'm sorry to see that some of you seem to have lost your enthusiasm for this new railway of ours. Instead of enjoying the privilege of riding in our new carriages, some of you seem to be looking round for volunteers to take your places.'

There are unconvincing noises of protest.

'You!' Mr Winspear says, pointing his stick at an old Greenlander. 'You! Speak up!'

Jim Richardson knows that he is indeed privileged to be riding in one of the carriages. The directors have given him a ticket because they want an old boatman to appear amongst the gentlemen, and thus show that the benefits of the railway can be extended to all classes of men. Jim knows that he should feel a deep obligation to Mr Winspear and his friends.

'Speak up! Speak up!' orders Mr Winspear, who knows his man and hasn't made any random selection from the uncertain passengers.

'I don't like that piece of rope, sir,' Jim says. 'It looks dangerous.'

'Dangerous? What are you talking about? Have you forgotten everything you knew?'

Jim Richardson hasn't been to the fishery for six years. He has tried in different seasons to find a place on the Sovereign, and then the Phoenix, and then the Camden. But nobody wants a man with only one hand, and now the trade is as good as dead. Every year for six years he has seen things that he hadn't seen since he was a small boy: fresh corn growing along the Cleveland Bottoms; spring flowers sprouting out of the cliff face and the banks of the river; warblers churring in the reeds that border the becks running down from the moors; and the martins that return every year to the eaves of Scoresby's old house in Bagdale.

But all these things remain the novelties of childhood. He would rather, much rather, have seen the ice again. And he hasn't forgotten anything.

'You've forgotten everything you know,' Mr Winspear tells him, and points with his cane at the rope which is now secured to the first carriage. 'How thick would you say that is?'

Jim eyes it suspiciously. 'Getting on for six inches, sir.'

'That's right! More than twice as thick as a whale-line! You haven't forgotten that already? And if you could hold a seventy-ton fish with the one, don't you think we can pull a few carriages with the other?'

Mr Winspear doesn't wait for a reply but resumes his seat with the dignitaries in the first carriage. The other passengers, including Jim Richardson, return to their own vehicles and climb aboard.

The hemp tightens and three fully laden carriages, their axles freshly lubricated with best whale oil, inch slowly up the incline. The spectators sigh with admiration. The carriages gather speed and glide smoothly up the avenue between the trees. The spectators break into applause.

The alternating sunlight in the glade and the shadows of the trees flicker across Jim's unseeing eyes. The contributory streams hasten down on left and right to embrace in the pool below, but Jim doesn't hear them. He sits stiffly, with his hand in his shirt clutching the jet cross. Then a four-ton water tank comes into sight. This is the counter-weight, descending on the other track with the rope pulled taut behind it. Jim watches with growing interest and when it draws abreast his face is transformed. He withdraws his hand from his shirt and leaps to his feet.

'A fast fish!' he shouts and points after it. 'A fast fish!'

The passenger sitting opposite tells him to sit down. The passenger sitting next to him sniggers and one of the others asks for the joke to be explained. But Jim's salutation has been heard by the onlookers, who receive it with delight and pass it up and down the incline. The observation runs through the crowd like a fire and spreads back to the carriages, where some of the local big-wigs see the point and cannot hide their amusement.

This general flight from decorum annoys Mr Winspear intensely, although he couldn't have said exactly why. He stares at the people lining the track and hates their happy faces. But a thought pierces him, as sudden and unexpected as the unmerited gift of grace. His displeasure vanishes. He whips out a silk handkerchief, ties it to the end of his ebony cane and holds it aloft.

'Look at my mizzen-peak!' he shouts. 'A fall! A fall!'

The railway directors in the first carriage stare at him in surprise. The people at the side of the rails clap and shout. 'Good old Mr Winspear!' they call. 'He's a good one, is Mr Winspear.'

'I can testify that to any man,' Mr Storm confirms to those about him. 'You can depend on Mr Winspear.'

Arthur Storm and his mother look at him quickly, catch each other's glance and look away again. They wonder whether they can depend on Mr Winspear for much longer.

The waters of the Eller Beck sound on the left hand, sometimes humming like a distant sea and sometimes splashing almost under the track. On the right hand little streams ripple over pebbles on their way to the West Beck. Up and up the carriages go, apparently drawn by some invisible source or even a magical device. Cheering and the firing of guns greet them at the top of the incline. Fresh horses are attached and they continue on their way down the gorge. A crowd of thousands, competing bands and a battery of cannon are waiting for them at Pickering.

The only flaw in the entire pageant is the 'Lady Hilda'. This

There's more extreme Space Marine action in Lee Lightner's new Space Wolf novel, *Wolf's Honour* coming soon from the Black Library

WHITE SUNLIGHT FLOODED the Great Wolf's council chamber. The armoured shutters had been drawn back from the tall windows that dominated the east side of the large room, providing a panoramic view of the cloud-wrapped Asaheim range and the distant, iron-grey sea. Fenris was swinging close to the Wolf's Eye once more, banishing the harsh winter and heralding the even harsher Time of Fire.

The rising temperatures had banished the heavy overcast and the clinging mist that enfolded the Fang for much of the year, and for a short time Ragnar knew that the seas would be mild and relatively free from storms. The kraken would rise from the deeps, and the people of Fenris would take to the sea in their long ships to hunt and to fight. The Iron Season, Ragnar recalled, a time of feasting and of battle, of betrothals and births: a time for offering sacrifices to the gods who watch from the clouds.

Logan Grimnar was standing before one of those tall windows as Ragnar entered the room, his wide hands clasped behind his back as he brooded upon the unsuspecting world below. The Great Wolf was in his armour, his shoulders wrapped in a cloak of sea-dragon scales. Runic charms and wolves' teeth were woven into the thick braids of his iron-grey hair, and parchment ribbons from hundreds of major campaigns fluttered like raven's feathers from his scarred grey and yellow pauldrons.

Old and fierce, as indomitable as the Fang itself, some said that Logan Grimnar was the greatest living warrior in the Imperium, and Ragnar could not help but feel awed by his presence. Nearly a dozen other Space Wolves stood around the council table, mighty priests or members of Logan's Wolf Guard, each one a towering figure in his own right.

At once, Ragnar caught a familiar scent among the fearsome Wolves and searched among the crowded warriors for its source. Lady Gabriella, Master Navigator of House Bellisarius, sat in a high-backed wooden chair at the far side of the table, studying the assembly over slim, steepled fingers. She wore the dark dress uniform of her House, ornamented with epaulettes and polished gold buttons fashioned with the wolf-and-eye symbol of Bellisarius.

Medals and ceremonial braid covered the front of her thick, woollen jacket, proclaiming her personal achievements and the great deeds of her household, and a small pistol and a gracefully curved sabre hung from a broad leather belt around her narrow waist. Her long, black hair had been bound up in a score of glossy braids that hung about her narrow shoulders *particular carriage, after being the bright yellow jewel in every eye, comes off the rails and has to be abandoned. But that is forgotten long before the first toast at the banquet in the Black Swan.*